You
Before
Me

Julieann Wallace is an author of books for adults, young adults, and children's books. Her best-selling new adult novel, *The Colour of Broken* (Amelia Grace) was longlisted twice to be made into a movie. Julieann is also an artist and secondary arts teacher, empowering students to be change-makers, to create a better world for themselves and for future generations. When she's not writing or teaching, Julieann tries not to scare her cat, Claude Monet, with her terrible cello playing.

You Before Me

JULIEANN WALLACE

Have courage, dear heart.
The Bloom of Spring
and Melody of Summer are coming.

Mama said we were all *earth stories*.
A beginning. And an end.
And the in-between where your stories shape you
into whom you were born to be.

A BEGINNING

My dream story was unfinished. The ending stolen on that fateful night where the fireflies danced to the hum of the living earth. On that night where the colours of nature glowed under the magnificent full moon.

Luminous.

Divine.

Sacred.

My dream story was obliterated on that night full of promise, when Mama's hand rested on her tummy as big as a watermelon, with Papa's hand upon hers. Mama said my tiny baby hand reached up and touched hers through the stretched, scarred skin of her belly. And our life energies connected; exploding in a pure unconditional love that drenched her being as my dream story was woven to the melody of an angelic orchestra, echoing throughout the heavens. Mama closed her eyes and saw the bright, mesmerising light, and sparkles of gold thrown into the universe by my soul print, created by our Maker. Wonderfully and fearfully made. Mama said it was so powerful she could hardly breathe.

Then, Mama said, her breath impossibly hitched. They were

not alone in the oratory of the hidden ancient castle, circled by a dense forest of gnarly manchineel trees, accurately known as the little apple of death, where the sap fell like raindrops, burning people and animals, causing the skin to blister.

Arrows dipped in the sap were lethal.

It wasn't the metallic creak of the rusty door hinges that captured Mama's attention.

Nor the disappearance of the fireflies that shepherded in a foreboding darkening.

It was the quiet sigh of a lawless one.

Planned.

Calculated.

Executed.

Mama said my hand fell away as the poison of fear surged through her blood. She said the light of my dream story vanished, and shimmers of gold fell from the heavens and crashed into the earth like shooting stars. Our soul dance returned to the castle room, unfinished, as Mama stood, trembling, in the midst of the chaos and the panic.

The unknown.

The dread.

And possibly the end of their life as they knew it. The end of that time in history that was part of *The Unfolding*. The beginning of the gentle ushering in of souls who were being planted in the midst.

Silent.

Waiting for the appointed time.

Mama breathed in, then breathed out. The sound sacred. Scarce. Despised by the lawless ones.

Papa's quick footsteps shuffled on the cold stone floor as he scrambled to stand in front of Mama.

Protecting her.

Protecting us.

Mama said the lawless ones' footsteps were delicate, like they had no feeling in their feet, calculating their balance on every movement; their eyes scanning the floor, the walls, the ceiling. They were searching for the blood of pure humans. Searching for the ones who were not of their ilk. Searching for the ones who were of the ancients. Their eyes fixed on Papa and they stilled.

Silent.

Piercing.

Threatening.

Mama said she would never forget that night. That terrible, terrifying night of darkness in their hidden kingdom. That night, when my father's face twisted in pain and sorrow, his last words whispered to Mama like they were about to be stolen from him, 'Take care of my son.' He slipped his hand under his garment and removed a key; golden and heavy. He held it behind his back, giving it to Mama.

She shook her head as tears pooled and a quiet sob escaped her. She knew what the key meant; and she didn't want to take it. This moment couldn't be here.

Their parting.

Not now.

Not when their son was due any day.

Mama said Papa pushed the key against her belly; against me.

'I love you,' Mama whispered with the quietest breath. Then Mama took the key for the hidden floor between, their skin touching, possibly for the last time, as Papa was seized by the lawless ones.

Mama moved with stealth to safety to protect me, slipping between the heavy curtains, as red as blood, and then the wall within the wall, where she stopped, her heart thumping. She put her hand on the wall, placed her forehead on her hand, and heard the sound of vases breaking, wood cracking, and Papa, yelling, before the sound of a pop, and then a groan of pain.

Silence.

And fear.

Mama said she scrambled up the twenty-one steps to the invisible floor above. The floor no one knew about and could ever find.

The room of safety.

The room of the hidden.

The room of secrets.

The night my papa disappeared.

The night my mama's heart broke.

The night she searched the hidden room for the lachrymatory bottles, and grabbed one to catch her tears filled with sorrow.

And despair.

The night my mama rocked to and fro, endless tears falling, while she created my earth song. To be sung before, during and after my birth, and each time I lay my head to sleep.

Mama said she placed her warm hand on her belly and said, 'Sweet, sweet babe, growing inside me, you are loved and cherished, forever and a day.' Her voice broke. 'Half of me … and half of your dearest papa … created in *human love* … unconditional love—love that depends on nothing.'

Mama said she looked upward at the ceiling, as blue as the summer sky, painted with floating fluffy white clouds that reminded her of the carefree, happy days of her youth.

Before *The Changing*.

Before *The Boxing*.

Before no one could distinguish between truth.

And lies.

4

She inhaled deeply, closed her eyes and imagined the wondrous heavens she had gazed at so often with Papa on their nights of solitude, where they held hands and vowed to outlive the lawless ones. Together.

Mama said she traced her belly with her finger, like a tickle of love to connect to me, outlining my bottom and legs, lodged under her rib cage, along my back and down to my head, engaged for birth.

To calm me.

'Courage and Strength. Kindness. Creativity. Imagination. Wisdom. Faithfulness and Truth. *Human Love*. Light. Hope. Breath. These are your gifts. May they be written onto your heart, to guide and protect,' Mama whispered.

Mama said she opened her eyes and gently caressed her large belly with both of her hands, and said, 'May your presence be pure and beautiful like flowers of love. May you be brave and courageous like the stars in the heavens, and may you have wisdom as deep as the oceans. And … may your kindness be breathtaking, like the living earth on its day of creation. And I pray … that you that you fully comprehend your breath, and the knowledge of it that surpasses all understanding.'

Mama said she sobbed then, catching her tears, allowing herself to feel the heaviness of her aloneness, without Papa. Mama said she couldn't possibly bear the thought of me never meeting my papa, so she avoided that thought. Mama said she wiped her tear stained face, placed both hands on her baby belly and said, 'My child, stand for what is right. Remember whose you are. Always.'

Mama said she waited in the hidden floor between for two nights and two days. She said she tried to find the courage to return to their kingdom, to face the devastation and the carnage that the lawless ones undoubtedly left.

Mama said she feared finding my papa.

And death.

Together.

Mama said she squeezed her eyes shut. The unbearable pain of loss had begun. Mama wrapped her arms around herself and opened her mouth. A horrifying, soul shattering wail of brokenness filled the room of the hidden. The room of secrets. And etched the notes of grief onto the pillar of wordless soul songs.

Mama said she had only one word for what she felt then. Numb.

CHAPTER 1

'**D**EAD.'
The word sears my ear while a hand presses hard over my mouth and nose, stopping me from breathing. With wide eyes, I desperately try to suck in some air, aware of how firmly I am being held against the person behind me; the assailant's other arm locking my arms against my body.

My heart thumps. Loud and strong. Screaming for mercy as my blood floods with the poison of panic like an instant wash of acid, depleting my body of existence.

I am suffocating.

Life.

And death.

Like day.

And night.

Welcome to the Field of Flowers. The memory of Mama's voice, flashing through my mind in a nanosecond in *The Quietus*, the forbidden place I should never have been. The knowledge that had been kept from me.

Mama's voice. My beautiful Mama's voice.

Tinged with sadness.

Gentle.

And comforting.

Delicate.

And melodic.

My body screams for oxygen, little lights floating in my vision like shooting stars, the pressure in my head immense.

Then came the narrowing. Of my vision.

And sheer terror. Death was coming.

For me.

And then Mama's voice came in my violent internal panic, 'And I pray … that you that you fully comprehend your breath, and the knowledge of it that surpasses all understanding.'

My final chapter on earth.

My first chapter in eternity.

Endings.

And beginnings.

Death.

And life.

Darkness.

And light.

CHAPTER 2

New words burn their shape and sound and accents inside me. Light in the darkness of lifelessness. Of near death. 'Remember how to use your breath, like you were taught. It's not safe here for girls. Go home. It's an order!'

Mama always said it would have been better if I was born a boy. I would be stronger then, and not become an object or a person to dominate to submission.

I fall forward to the ground. Released. Weak. Gasping for breath.

My head swims. Foggy. Headachy. I swallow. Hard. How fragile human life is.

Gasping, I turn to see who had restrained me. No one is there. But one particular word he said is familiar.

Dead.

Was it Elias?

If it was, what is he doing here in this place that appears to be in chaos, crying for help, not unheard, but ignored. Anger brews inside me like a storm. Mama never told me about what existed in *The Beyond*. She only said it is forbidden and I must never go there because it is a landscape of nothing, where people go, and never return.

She lied.

Mama always said lies result in broken trust. Destroying relationships. She said even little white lies cause trouble, the seemingly small acts of dishonesty snowballing into significant lies. And then you can't remember the lie you had started with, and tell more lies to cover the original lie. Mama said lies wreak havoc on your life, taking a serious toll on health.

Mentally.

Physically.

I pull my hood over my head and move through the shadows of the buildings in the forbidden land of nothing that was most certainly a something, and head home, concentrating on deep diaphragm breathing so I did not appear to breathe, trying to not lose consciousness.

Was an omission of truth about *The Beyond* like a lie?

Words never revealed, truth hidden?

Premeditated.

Schemed with intent to deceive.

Mama said the truth always sets you free.

Black.

And white.

Deception.

And honesty.

Destruction.

And freedom.

Why had Mama lied to me?

Betrayal.

And confusion.

The words of my unfinished dream story flow through me as I rush through the damp underground tunnel, the air still.

Heavy.

Hanging.

The odour musty and earthy.

And cold. Even though it is summer.

I cover my mouth and nose with my black bandana and make my way through the maze and find an entrance to the thousand year old castle, stunned to find that this tunnel opens up into my bedroom floor.

Surprises.

And the unknown.

Even after eighteen years of exploring the king's castle that was claimed by my family.

Is this by chance, or does Mama know and had planned the position of my bedroom from the beginning?

Upon entering my bedroom, astounded by the floor door in the corner I had never noticed, I swiftly remove my dark, masculine clothes, fold them and shove them into a box. I wrap my muddy boots in cloth and put them into the same box and lock it, then push it deep under my bed. I put on my bed clothes that double as "escape clothes"—flowing dark grey cotton pants, black undershirt, and long-sleeved grey cotton shirt.

But not my mandatory thick soled boots.

Mama said we always had to be prepared to move quickly. But she never told me what we were moving quickly from.

Or to.

I sit on the window seat at my double sash windows and open the internal shutter. The night is clear.

And bright.

I count seven stars that sit still in the heavens. Not moving. They are there every night, but sometimes I can only count three.

Sirius, Canopus and Alpha Centauri.

They try to outshine the moving stars that track across the night sky.

Mama said there were probably one hundred thousand of

them. I have seen them all my life and thought it was the normal night sky of the sacred earth.

But now I know the sky is broken.

Mama had lied to me about *The Beyond*. Has she lied to me about the moving stars as well and what their purpose is?

Is my entire life a lie?

Am I protected like Eli said to me once?

If my life is sanitized and orchestrated, where does that leave me?

Who am I being protected from?

Why do I need to be protected?

My chest rises as I inhale a deep breath to quell the nausea of anxiety. A normal deep breath. Not the deep diaphragm breathing I learned when I was fourteen. Compulsory for children of the kingdom.

Anxiety ripples along my skin. The closeness of death has unsettled me.

The heavy wooden door creaks. Not a loud creak. A quiet creak. Like the sound of the highest violin note. It will be silenced tomorrow. Our self-declared kingdom is silent, except for hushed conversations, no louder than 30 - 40 Decibels.

For survival.

I don't need to look to see who has entered my room. Mama always comes to say goodnight. Without fail. Except when she disappears, sometimes for days, the only clue she is away being the blue forget-me-not flowers left by my window in the darkness of the morningtide she leaves.

I turn to look at Mama, her face lit by the magenta glow ball she carries. Magenta: the colour that doesn't exist because it has no wavelength; there's no place for it on the spectrum. We see it is because our brain doesn't like having green between purple and red, so it substitutes a new thing. Mama showed me how to see impossible colours when I was little.

Imaginary colours.

Colours to survive by.

Whatever she meant by that.

Candles and lights are forbidden. There was to be no light at night.

It's safer that way, Mama always says.

But safe from what?

'Ari, you look worried,' Mama says, her soothing voice calming my burning anxiety.

'Just trying to count the moving stars, Ma,' I lie, and also not telling her the truth about discovering what is in *The Beyond* that she claimed didn't exist.

A truth.

And a lie.

A cover-up.

And a complication.

She looks up into the night sky. 'The scientists warned us about the sky pollution, and light pollution, and how it would make the real heavens look dull or non-existent, taking away the awe and beauty of what we could see, the treasure of stunning lights in the sky at night, signs to mark sacred times, days and years.' Mama sighs. 'The earth tribes who used the night lights as guides for earth time are now disadvantaged. Lost. The scientists were right. They even gave it a term: noctalgia, meaning sky grief.'

'How long ago was that?'

'The sky pollution multiplied not long after you were born.'

I draw in an audible breath, felling nostalgic, feeling grief for something I will never see. 'Do you miss it … the night sky?'

'Terribly. We call it *The Boxing*. Making our world singular, and not part of the enormous universe where it belongs in the creation of everything. Boxing up the earth. Boxing up the people. Boxing up the truth. But even though we can't see the symphony of stars, their music never stops—they produce stellar soundwaves—discovered by scientists.'

I look up at Mama eager to hear about science and the stars. A tear rolls down my cheek. But not because of the stars and the moving stars. Because of the lie about *The Beyond.*

Mama's finger is warm and soft as she brushes my tear away. I shuffle over so she can sit beside me, our shoulders touching. I thread my fingers through hers, our hands the same size now.

'Oh, dear Ari. How I wish you could have known your papa. You would have been the apple of his eye.' Mama blinks, and I see a moment of time that teetered on a lifetime of hopes dreams that never came.

Her chest rises as she takes a deep breath. Silent. As I have been taught to do.

And Mama blinks again, a heavy tear falling.

She quickly pulls out her lachrymatory bottle and catches it. At least this time she doesn't start sobbing like she did sometimes, and I didn't know where to look or whether to hug her or just put an arm around her or tell her a joke to distract her sadness that poked at my heart.

Mama once said that she couldn't possibly bear the thought of me never meeting my papa, so she tries to avoid that thought. But not this time.

She turns off the night ball of magenta and gathers my long messy auburn hair in her hands, and starts to braid it. Like she does every night. Tonight though, she doesn't tell me it is the same colour as my father's. And I miss it. Little comments like that make me feel closer my father. It makes him more real.

Mama says, in her voice that is like a mesmerising melody, soft and nurturing and calming, 'Courage and Strength. Kindness. Creativity. Imagination. Wisdom. Faithfulness and Truth. *Human Love.* Light. Hope. Breath. These are your gifts. May they be written onto your heart, to guide and protect.' She runs a finger along my braid and I instantly relax. 'May your presence be pure and beautiful like flowers of love. May you be brave and courageous like the stars in the heavens, and may you have wisdom as deep as the oceans. And … may your kindness be breathtaking, like the living earth on its day of creation. And I pray … that you that you fully comprehend your breath, and the knowledge of it that surpasses all understanding.'

Mama is three persons in one to me.

Mama of love. And kindness.

Mama of organisation. And leadership.

Mama of broken heartedness. And longing.

I stare out at the night, feeling my mama's grief. I have grief too, but mine is different. Mine is a longing to know the father I have never met.

'Mama, how do you remember the night of my dream story so clearly, with so much detail?' I knew that memories fade over time, becoming less vibrant and detailed.

'You never forget things like that. Memories attached to strong emotion. And I kept a journal. In fact, I've written in a journal every day since your papa was taken. So when he returns, he can read about everything Ari, and what you have done every single day since you were born.'

'Hmmm. I'm not so sure he's going to like some of the stuff I've done, Ma. And besides, it's from your point of view! My truth will be different to your assumed, observed truth.'

'Papa will laugh, dear Ari. You are so much like him. Just look at your feet. Bare. Like his always were. What is our rule about feet?'

'Always wear shoes, even to bed.'

Mama gives me a crooked smile, finds my heavy ugly shoes and puts them onto my feet with the care of a servant. 'Courage and Strength. Truth and light, my dear Ari,' Mama says again, and kisses the top of my head. She picks up the light ball and engages it's magenta hue, the colour that doesn't exist and leaves my room, her footfall non-existent. She has perfected her unheard footsteps in shoes, better than anyone else I know.

Except me.

Once the heavy wooden door closes, I remove my shoes and climb into bed, troubled by what I had found in the forbidden *Beyond*.

I need to add a fourth person of my mother—Mama of secrets.

And deception.

I swallow hard. My heart hurts. Why would Mama lie to me about *The Beyond*?

I fist my hand and thump it on the bed to release my anger.

And betrayal. Yes. It is betrayal I feel.

I move to the small patch of moon light that rests on my bed, grab my pencil and sketch book. I open up a fresh new page, and in the centre of the page draw our home, the crumbling castle of deceit, or was it where truth prevailed? And then the tunnel leading out to *The Beyond*, to the nothingness that is something. To the place I am forbidden to go to. There, I draw the buildings where I wandered amongst, shocked. And the place where I almost met the end of me.

Death.

And thankfulness.

Questions.

And no answers.

CHAPTER 3

Mama said she dreamed of a beautiful born day for me. Her, serene and expectant, glowing with love, singing my earth song while tracing her fingers over her belly, imbuing me with love. She imagined herself gazing out the window at the magical blue sky, inhaling the pure, gentle breeze created by the fluttering of angel wings, the white voile curtains dancing, carrying the whispers of bird song and my name.

Mama said Papa would have fussed over her, as nervous as an intruder navigating the deadly manchineel trees, apologizing for being the one who was responsible for putting her through so much pain.

Mama said he would have kissed her forehead, her hands, and her belly, telling me to be kind to Mama as I entered the world.

Mama said she dreamed of a calm, joy-filled birth, me entering the world to their love song, wrapping around me as the air of the earth touched my skin for the first time, for my first breath.

The beginning of chapter one of my earth time.

Mama said Papa would have held me close after I was born, gazed into my eyes with tears in his, and kissed me.

And rocked me.

And sung to me.

Pouring out his protective love that knew no bounds.

But Mama's birthing dream was stolen on that fateful night when the fireflies danced to the hum of the living earth. On that night when the colours of nature glowed under the magnificent full moon.

Luminous.

Divine.

Sacred.

Her birth dream was obliterated on that night full of promise.

Mama said I was born amongst the ruins and debris and memories of hate left by the lawless ones. There was no blue sky, just the volatile, deep grey storm clouds spitting peels of brightly charged anger. There was no calm inhaling of clean air, nor the sound of birdsong, just the short breaths of panting and groans of pain as labour tightened its grip.

And anger. Her husband was taken, stealing this moment of pure shared joy from them.

Mama said she clambered to a corner of the room of the oratory in a daze, alone and feeling weak, like her life was draining from her.

Exhausted.

And scared.

Mama said she reached down and felt my head crowning, waxy, sticky tufts of hair exposed to the outside world. And like an answered prayer, a woman rushed in carrying a birthing suitcase.

Then Mama said she lost consciousness.

Mama said she woke to my extraordinarily loud crying, like my lungs were about to be ejected from my tiny, fragile body. She said it was like I was calling for Papa, my voice somehow searching for him in the darkness of the earth.

Mama said I couldn't stand the deep sorrow written onto the cells of my blood after Papa had been taken. She said I was born a mere hour after she had found the blood trail of Papa in the oratory, two days after spending time in the secret floor between.

Mama said she collected Papa's blood in a vial, and her tears in the lachrymatory bottle, ensuring her tears didn't mix with the blood sample. Contamination. Mama always carried vials with her. She was a collector of cells. Of DNA. A genetic scientist, until the world became dark, and they fled.

Unseen.

Undetectable.

Invisible.

Mama said after a while I nuzzled at her breast. She said she was glad for the silence. She said she was tired and weak, and so very sad. My papa, he should have been there. And she said she closed her eyes and wished she could go back in time to avert the arrival of the lawless ones.

My father, Azriel, would be here then.

And none of this traumatic scene would have happened.

Mama said she wondered it was her fault that the lawless ones had found them? Was it the supposedly undetectable technology she had used that somehow had emitted their location?

Mama said she finally gazed down at me with new eyes.

I was so perfect.

So beautiful.

Mama said her eyes stopped on the strawberry coloured heart on my forehead. An Angel's kiss. She traced over it with light fingers and frowned. Mama said she wondered if my papa had met death, and this was his kiss on my forehead.

'Ari,' she whispered, 'my son's name is Ari—strong, brave and courageous. You look just like your father.'

Mama said she looked up at the midwife with a heartbreaking

smile, her heart in deep sadness that my papa was not there.

The midwife smiled. 'Your *daughter* has the most voluminous hair I have ever seen on a newborn!'

Mama said she couldn't stop her eyes widening as she shook her head. 'A girl? No, no, no, no, nooo! We need a boy! This world needs a boy!'

Mama said the midwife pressed her lips together. 'We could—'

'Never. I will NOT take the life of my daughter.'

'It will stop her from suffering from trauma when she is captured, when she wishes she had never been born.' The midwife's eyes reddened and she stiffened. She inhaled deeply. 'If you won't do it, I can arran—'

'NO!' Mama said between gritted teeth.

Mama said she looked back at me. She said a tear trickled down her cheek and fell onto my head in a kiss of connection. Forever unbreakable. 'Ari, I love you,' Mama said, then whispered, 'courage and strength. Kindness. Creativity. Imagination. Wisdom. Faithfulness and Truth. *Human Love*. Light. Hope. Breath. These are your gifts. May they be written onto your heart, to guide and protect. And I pray, that you fully comprehend your breath, and the knowledge of it that surpasses all understanding.'

Mama said the midwife helped her to the bedroom, strangely untouched by the lawless ones. Mama said she laid on the bed and held me close to her heart, our two hearts beating together, again. Mama said she closed her eyes as sadness dripped from her being.

A girl.
Her future was unsafe.
How would she protect her?

Mama said she refused to picture the future. She decided then and there that she would enjoy every moment with me like it was our last. Mama said she opened her eyes and gazed out the window. And there it was, the moon, the ruler of the night, lighting the second sky with hope.

Luminous.
Divine.
Sacred.

Mama said every breath we took was a gift,
like our heartbeats. Like *human love.*

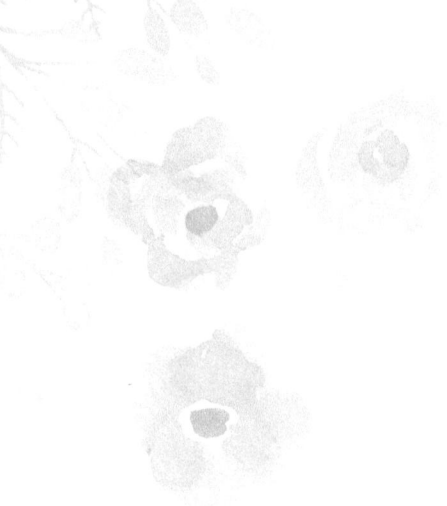

CHAPTER 4

On my windowsill sit pale pink carnations in a translucent green jar.

Hypnotic.

I fix my eyes on them, a visual delirium overcoming me, making me feel high. I want to taste the delicate pink hue. I want to run my fingers over each of the folds of soft petals. I inhale deeply to pull me down from the high I am feeling.

Mama said I have an extreme reaction to colour.

I didn't tell her that some colours make me feel happy and joyous and euphoric, and other colours make me scared and hyper-alert and suspicious, like black.

Red gives me anxiety.

As I gaze at the carnations my eyelids become heavy and close again. They are the ultimate dream weaver flower, the pale pink reminding me of low snow clouds and building a snowwoman when I was little. They are the colour of contentment, of everything right in the world.

Love *is* all around us.

The colour waves peace around my room like gentle flakes of

snow, feather soft, then cold, and makes me snuggle under the warm blanket.

Safe.

And happy.

Content.

And comfortable.

I allow myself to enjoy the moment, then leave my bed and stride toward the carnations, reach over them and pull the shutters to the windows to the side to let in the new day.

The Field of Flowers comes into view. Like it does every day.

Colourful.

And bright.

Life.

And hope.

It's Friday, and I change into my Tuesday clothes—black flowing pants and a black long-sleeved cotton shirt. Our clothes are made out of natural fibres in the kingdom. It's better for the earth. Mama says that in her youth there was something called fast fashion.

The throw-away generation.

Nearly all discarded clothing ended up in landfill, the clothing industry the fourth-most polluting industry in the world. Many clothes were made from materials that contained a high percentage of plastic. Cheap to make and cheap to sell. Devastating for the earth, taking more than two hundred years to decompose in landfill.

I shudder.

Earth is our home.

How can people be so inconsiderate of the planet that feeds us, sustains us and protects us?

I leave my room to go to the breakfast nook, forgetting to walk in silence like I have been taught.

The castle where I live is deceptive. Above ground it looks like uninhabitable ruins, yet, its outer shell disguises hidden liveable rooms.

Of love.

And laughter.

Of comfort.

And shared stories.

Of memories of yesterday.

And today.

And to be.

I sit next to Mama at the breakfast table.

I push my eggs around on the plate, gathering the courage to ask her a question.

I take a deep breath. 'What's in *The Beyond*?' The words come out in a flurry, with no eye contact. It's easier that way.

Then I look up and watch for her reaction.

She momentarily pauses as she cuts through her eggs.

It was so slight that if you blinked you would have missed it. She keeps her eyes on the eggs and shakes her head. 'Nothing. There is nothing.' No eye contact. So unlike my mother.

Lie.

'Have you ever been in *The Beyond*?' I ask.

She looks up at me with a slight smile and tilts her head to the side and considers me, like sizing me up and trying to decide how to answer my question. She lets out an audible breath.

Odd. Considering it is highly discouraged in our kingdom.

'I used to live there, until the great upheaval, *The Change*, the delusion that infiltrated the world, the loss of ourselves as our own beings, the society sedated by social media, where fighting for the truth became too hard and those of us who knew the truth scattered to remote regions in countries to save our lives, to save our intellect, to save our knowledge, to save … us. Humans.'

I still. How can I digest all of that with my breakfast?

Why is Mama giving me information now?

Mama places her knife and fork on the wooden table. Agitated. 'You must never go there, Ari. It will be your death, or worse …' Mama lifts her chin as she connects her eyes to mine, deeply, like a pleading, a begging, imploring me, with an undercurrent that she knows I will venture there.

'Worse than death?' I say. 'What could be worse than that?'

Mama shakes her head and clears her throat. 'Unspeakable things … you're old enough to know now at eighteen … physical abuse, mostly to women, forced intrusive violations of your mind, known and unknown, using you to do things that go against your will, your nature, your beliefs, the stealing of your identity.'

I stare at Mama.

How can people be so cruel to others?

My heart drops into a pit of darkness and I scramble to pull it out of there where I will over-think and over-imagine and over-panic. It's a terrible place to be.

I quickly scramble my thoughts to pull me out of rumination.

Mama said rumination was a choice, and not to choose it because it would become the blackest of black, spiralling me down into a sadness that was a waste of time, a made-up sadness not based on reality of the good that was around me.

I ask Mama another question to stop the thousand thoughts lining up to litter my mind, 'Do you think Papa is there … in *The Beyond*?'

Mama clasps her hands together in front of her mouth and closes her eyes. She opens them again, the colour of her brown eyes, normally like a winter's hot chocolate that reflects earth tones of honey when the sunset throws its golden beams into them, becoming like a muddy storm.

I hold my breath. I can't predict her answer.

'I don't know. At first, I thought he was, but—' her voice breaks and she looks down, 'sometimes I can't feel your papa here anymore.' She places her hand over her heart and a tear rolls down her face.

I swallow. Hard. Those words have never be spoken before.

I wait for her lachrymatory bottle to appear for her to catch her tears. But this time she just lets them run down her cheek.

There's an ache in my chest. She looks up at me and shakes her head, like her world is disintegrating before her.

'Is the whole world like this?' I ask, bewildered, and also distracting Mama and myself from thoughts of Papa.

'Yes,' Mama whispers, her eyes filling with tears again. 'Don't go to *The Beyond*. I couldn't bear to lose you as well. I love you, Ari. Stay safe, with me.'

I want to tell her that she isn't safe when she leaves the kingdom. She thinks I don't know what she does when she leaves the forget-me-not flowers on my window sill. She doesn't know that I followed her once, and that's how I knew to get there. To *The Beyond*.

What if she disappears, like Papa? Then what?

A shiver runs down my spine. 'I love you too, Mama,' I say, pushing the thought of being orphaned from my mind.

Nausea rolls over me. The world I thought I lived in was collapsing. Falling apart like the lost pianos that sit in the fields and rooms of our kingdom. I need to leave the table to think things through. 'Thank you for breakfast, Ma. May I leave the table?'

Mama looks at me, then at my unfinished eggs and flat bread. I follow her line of sight to my plate. *Treat each meal as though it is your last. You never know when circumstances will change. Food is energy. Energy that will help you survive.* The words of Mama. I had heard them a thousand times.

I blink, then continue to eat.

'What are you doing today?' I ask between bites of food. Change of focus in our conversation again. I like to call it distraction. Redirecting. Living in our kingdom is dominated by boredom for me. It's a struggle each day to find purpose and something to look forward to doing. It was easier when I was young to run away with my imagination, but now that I'm eighteen, I need to see that what I do has an effect, not just that my time is wasted on nothing. Each day the same as before, going nowhere.

'I have flowers to gather, some to dry, some to decorate with, some for ... medicinal purposes.'

And flowers for death? my mind asks.

Once, I had spied on my mother, after Eli challenged me while delivering a note to me while I was confined to the lighthouse in the middle of the lake, above the bodies of the dead men who sang tales of tragedy. When I escaped the lighthouse, I traversed the rooms below the castle and watched her work with a person. Dead or alive I wasn't sure, but why would you tie the hands and feet of a person?

I wonder if I should say something to Mama, and ask to join her in her work today. Would she let me?

My throat tightens, holding my words in. I pretend cough into my hand to clear the traffic jam of words. 'Do you need some help? I've been studying books in the library about medicinal plants—you know, the lessons you set for me,' I say, just to hear her reply, and, if I ask to work with her enough, she will eventually consent to my request.

'Perhaps another day, dear Ari. I already have my group of scientists organised for today.'

Expectant of this answer, I stand, my breakfast now finished. 'May I leave the table, please?'

Mama nods. 'And put shoes on at once!' she adds.

I gather my plate and take it to the castle kitchen, swipe a couple of bread rolls, and disappear to my room, my bare feet making no sound on the cold stone floor this time. I lower myself to the window seat and gaze out at the warm day. I smile as a plan for today comes to mind. I would walk to the old farm house and check on the apple cider I have been brewing. Everything about it forbidden, of course.

Rules.

And control.

Expected behaviours.

And consequences.

I gather my vintage blue school port of *everything*, add pencils, paints and paintbrushes, sketch book, a book to read, a glass bottle with a cork and a cocktail glass borrowed from the Museum of Earth Time, and the bread rolls I had collected from the kitchen. Then jump out the window with it, my bare feet landing on the pink and white cosmos flowers outside my room, squashing some like the footsteps of a giant. I walk through the multi-fruiting trees, snap off an apple, a nectarine and an orange, and set off for the hour walk to the old farm house.

The moment I arrive I sit on an upturned apple box in the barn where the cider fruit press is. My mind wanders back to *The Beyond* the night before, being restrained, and death.

After Mama's words at breakfast, I decide if it is going to be dangerous being identified as female in *The Beyond*, then I will present as male. I can disguise myself.

There is no way that I wasn't returning to *The Beyond* again. I need to know what was going on in the world. I need to know the truth. I can't stay in my bubble of safety at the kingdom anymore. I need to know more. I need to help, if our kingdom, whatever that represents, needs help.

Mama always said the truth will set you free.

I stand and stretch, go to the hard apple cider I had made sixteen weeks ago, and pour some into the glass bottle I had brought, squeeze the cork into the top, and stash it inside my vintage blue school port of *everything*, and leave on my hour long journey along the King's Forest edge, and arrive lakeside where I can sit and ponder my future.

The lake is calm today as I slide onto the bright blue deck chair under the multi-coloured beach umbrella. I'm like a sitting duck. A target. Our kingdom rule is camouflage colours only.

I wriggle my bare feet and push my pink retro sunglasses up higher on my nose and sip my apple cider out of a cocktail glass I found, frozen in time in the forbidden room at the Museum of Earth Time. If only those radios in the forbidden room worked I could listen to some music as well, like the girls in the magazines stashed in the library of Once Upon a Time.

I narrow my eyes. Were there anymore radio stations like Mama had reminisced about?

'Dead.' Eli folds his body onto the blue deck chair beside me. I don't even flinch at the sound of his voice. I have been dead three thousand, eight hundred and twenty-seven times, if my memory serves me correctly.

'Care to join me in death?' Sarcasm coils its way out of me.

Eli looks up at the loud beach umbrella.

'Before you ask, yes, I dyed it in the many colours of Joseph's amazing technicolour dreamcoat, and yes, I know it's not camouflaged like our entire lives spent invisible, like I have been instructed to do all of my life, which, apparently has been lived inside a lie.'

'What are you drinking, Ari Flora?'

'Pure, sweet apple juice, Elias Wolfe, my friend.' I take another sip.

Eli takes the cocktail glass from my hand and lifts it to his lips. 'Liar. Did you create this drink?'

'Perhaps I found the cider recipe in an old book in the ancient library of Once Upon a Time.'

'The forbidden library, of course,' he said and sighs.

'And a cider press at that old farm house sitting in the forest. And you know the rest … you were there. I saw you.'

'You saw me?' His voice rises in disbelief.

'Yep,' I say, popping the "p".

'Ari, I wasn't there. Remember your request to leave you alone?'

I clench my jaw and my stomach tenses at the realisation that Eli was not there. His words pierce their claws into me. I inhale deeply, then sigh. 'Since when do you do what I ask? And ... am I dead because your weren't there?' I giggle, louder than I intended. 'Ooops!' The alcoholic beverage is making me feel giddy and happy and sad and ... brave.

I watch as Eli runs his hand over his face then rubs his forehead. 'Seriously, Ari. I am furious with you!'

'Because I have freedom from you now?'

'Are you serious? If you're drunk, you can't protect yourself! And ... you could have died at the farm house, or worse!'

'There's worse? What could be worse than death?' Deja vu of the same question slaps me in the face.

I hiccup.

Eli clasps his hands together in front of his mouth and closes his eyes. 'I cannot verbalise it. The trauma of visualizing what they can do to you ...' He winces and shakes his head.

'They?' I look at him, tears pooling in my eyes. Nausea rises and I lean over the deck chair and vomit.

Loudly.

I feel Eli gather my hair and pull it away from my face. 'Ari Flora. What am I going to do with you?'

I sit back up. 'Tease me like you have for my entire life so far because I la-la-la-la-loooove you!' I lean over and expel my stomach contents again. Spitting the lingering bitterness.

One.

Two.

Three.

'Let's call a truce,' he says, his words dropping onto the pebbles of the lakeside like glass, and shattering.

I have never felt so bad in my life. Alcohol is a phoney unfriend, whispering fun and carefree and happy times, only to wring you out and hang you upside-down at the end. 'Neverrrrrr,' I say.

'Do you really love me?' Eli says, his eyebrows raised.

'How could I not?'

I puke and the world goes black.

Mama said the *heart* is deceitful above all things.
She said it tells us that we are entitled to have
what we want, but doesn't tell us if it is bad for us.
The *heart* shows us a
distorted view of reality,
like glasses that hide the truth,
sprinkling a delusion over the mind.

Mama said we need to question
what we want, *why* we want it,
and *how it will affect us*
if we got what we wanted.

Mama said you can't *undo* what is done.
You *always* live with the consequences.

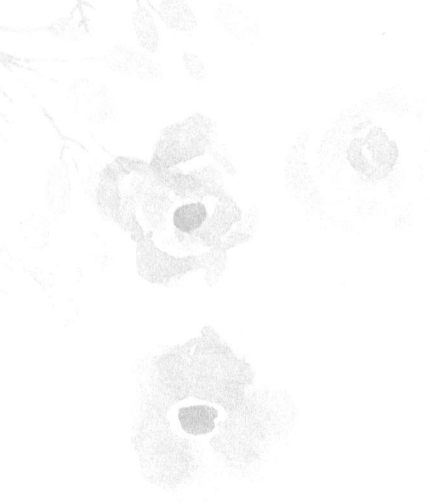

CHAPTER 5

The morningtide sun squints at me. Or do I squint at the sun peeking through my window? The window shutters are open and a vase of perky, large, yellow sunflowers stand smiling at me.

Arrogant.

Nausea rolls through me as my head throbs. I close my eyes and turn away from the cheery sunflowers left on the windowsill by Mama. The darkness is far better for the morning after intoxication. Are the sunflowers mocking me? Does Mama know that I had consumed alcohol? Too much alcohol? And without shoes?

I slide my hand under my pillow and pause. There's paper there. I pull it out and half open one eye. It's a note, and on my bedside table sits a tall jug of water, and next to it a drinking glass. I sigh. I'm in trouble.

Again.

Mama knows all about yesterday's foible and she's sure to banish me to the lighthouse on the sea of souls again. I open the note and try to focus on the writing.

Ari Flora,

1. Drink water.
Lots of it.
2. I've ordered eggs for you for breakfast.
3. Sip on the ginger tea in the kitchen for the nausea.
Your mother doesn't know what happened yesterday.
Do you remember any of the conversation we had?

E

P.S. Stay inside today. It will be safer for you in this state.
You cannot possibly think clearly.
P.P.S. I do not want to join you in death as per our conversation.

I place my hand onto my forehead and groan as nausea rolls
through me again.
Eli and I had conversations yesterday?
How did I get from the lakeside to my room?
My eyes widen. *What did I say to him?*
Wait … Eli was in my bedroom? It was forbidden.
I hoist myself up in the bed, my head pounding, the room
spinning a little. I pour water into the glass and drink it with
reluctance. After a beat, I drag myself out of bed for breakfast,
and change into my Saturday clothes—light blue denim jeans
and white long sleeved cotton button-up shirt. It is Saturday. I
absolutely am unwell.
I don't look out at the Field of Flowers as I always do, but go
and open my door, take a deep breath and add an air of happiness

to my face to counter my true morning after effect, then walk to the breakfast nook, challenged by my imbalance.

I slow my step as I notice a person with dark hair sitting at the table with Mama. I want to creep back to my room. Dealing with Mama and another person this morning is more than I can handle. I take a step backward and slowly turn.

'Ari, good morning!' Mama's cheery voice matches her sunny smile, like the cheery sunflowers on my window sill.

I wince then roll my eyes, wanting to cover my ears to stop her bright, loud voice from weaving its way inside my brain like a glow worm highlighting the bad choices of yesterday. I turn and enter the breakfast nook.

'Ari, good morning!' It was Eli. He turns toward me and grins. I want to roll my eyes at him too, but Mama would reprimand me for not being kind. Mama always said to be kind to people. You never know what they're going through.

'Good morning, Ma, Eli,' I say as I make my way to the table and sit to Mama's left and Eli's right. Between with them. Perpendicular. I run my fingers through my hair to give it some sort of decent look instead of the fuzzies I have this morning. Why didn't Mama wake me and braid my hair last night like she always did?

Mama casts a focussed gaze over me. 'And your shoes are?'

'Eli stole them,' I lie.

Mother looks at Eli.

'That I did,' he says, adding to the lie, then bites into his toast. 'Eat your eggs, Ari. They will add to your intelligence so you can find your shoes!'

Mama sighs and looks at her tea cup, giving me the chance to narrow my eyes at Eli. He raises an eyebrow at me.

'Thank you for the eggs today, Ma. I thought the hens had stopped laying?' Redirecting the conversation.

'With the sunshine lately, they're back to their normal selves. Eli collected these at morningtide. I saw him in the kitchen with them.'

I looked at Eli. 'Ah, he'll make a fine maid one day.' I smile at him with as much sarcasm as my words.

'You're looking a little seedy today, Ari. Is everything okay?' Mama says.

I pat my stomach filled with the nasty nausea. But not too hard. 'I think I drank too much water earlier.'

Eli gives a short cough.

I place a forkful of eggs into my mouth and swallow, trying hard to keep it down.

'While you are both here, and how fortunate with the timing today, I need to tell you Ari, that Elias's tenure here at the kingdom has finished.'

I pause in body, feeling like my breath has been vacuumed from me, then turn my face to Eli, my eyebrows raised in shock.

He pulls his eyebrows together. Did he not know about this?

I look back at Mama. 'Does that mean that I am free now, and not needing to be babysat like a child all the time?'

'Yes and no,' Mama says.

'Yes and no?'

'You have a new overseer watching you on your travels and … adventures, as you like to call them … but they will not be as close to you in distance as Eli was.'

A new overseer?

Eli places his knife and fork quietly and neatly onto his plate of unfinished food. He folds his hands together neatly in front of him. 'Thank you, Mrs Cohen. It has been an honour to serve your daughter. May I have permission to leave the table?' Even his words are neat.

Mama looks at Eli and her chest expands as she takes a deep, soundless breath. 'Granted.'

I watch as Eli stands, pushes his chair in, neatly, bows his head to Mama and leaves the room without even a glance at me.

'Mama?' The unfinished question about Eli leaving wobbles

from my mouth and hangs in the air.

'A changing of the guard is always a good thing. No more questions on this matter.'

'Is my new guard a man or a woman?' I need to know.

'No. More. Questions.' Mama's answer is absolute. Based on past discussions with her I know she will not even entertain anymore questions from me.

I push the food around on my plate, a wave of nausea washing over me. 'Do I get to meet the new guard, so to speak?' I press and breathe between pursed lips to try to control the nausea.

'It's best if you didn't know the name or identity. You will grow more as a person this way.'

At once I cover my mouth and run from the breakfast nook. I lift my white button-up cotton to catch my stomach contents as it leaves my body. I walk gingerly back to my room where I want to hide for the rest of my miserable life.

I don't want a new guard.

I don't need a new guard.

I can look after myself.

CHAPTER 6

Mid-afternoon seems safe. My stomach is behaving itself and my headache has evaporated like the spring fog. I climb out my window and head to my name tree. It's foliage is glorious in the summer and sets a large diameter of shade to rest under to keep cool. Mama says the earth is hotter than it used to be. I stop before the tree and look up at its branches and abundant green leaves, protecting everything beneath it like a mother does for her children.

It's eighteen years old.

Like me.

Peaceful.
And graceful.
Enduring.
And nurturing.

Unlike me.

Eighteen years of memories. Perhaps it should be called the

memory tree.

The corner of some paper protrudes through some leaves. I smile. It was my artwork I had painted onto some paper when I was eleven years old.

That day I sat outside in the courtyard painting until my heart was content. It was a picture of Mama and Papa and me. Together. A family.

I slowed my paintbrush as a shadow threw its gloom over me, swallowing my own shadow, and before I knew it, Eli had snatched my painting.

'Give it back!' I yelled. I reached out to grab it, but he held it high above his head and I jumped for it, not grabbing it. Even though Eli was the same age as me, he had a height advantage. I wanted to kick him in the shins, but thought twice about it because he would go and dob on me to my mother.

'Give it back, Elias, you dumb ox!' I said, anger colouring my words in red.

'You dumb ox? So funny, little Ari girl!' Eli opened his fingers and I watched as my painting floated off with the wind like a kite, past the vegetable gardens, the fruit trees and to the tree with my name, planted on the day I was born.

And there it stopped.

Stuck.

On the upper most branches.

I stood at the trunk of the tree after chasing the wind. Was it in on this game too?

There was no way I could reach my best painting ever. Mama would have been proud of it. She would have said that Papa would have framed it and placed it above the fireplace. And Papa would have said, *That's such a beautiful painting, like you, my girl. I love it.* I know it because I imagined that's what a father would say to a daughter with the best painting in the world. I always had pretend conversations with Papa. But now I wondered, how could Papa find the painting in the tree with my name if he ever returned?

I dropped my shoulders and sighed. Eli was incredibly mean. Up in the tree he had thrown my doll, my teddy bear, my skipping rope, my most favourite story I had ever written, and now, my painting was there, in cahoots with Eli and the wind.

I pressed my lips together and clenched my fists, then turned.

'Dead,' Eli said. 'You had no idea I was behind you!'

This time, I did kick him in the shins. I didn't care if he told on me. I ran back to my blanket, collected my paint, paint brushes and paper and returned to my room and fell onto my bed and let my tears fall, staining my pillow with the colour of sadness. My room was out of bounds to him. Maybe I should stay in here and never venture out.

I lower my head and smile at the memory. After all this time, I think I kind of like having memories stuck in the tree. I graze my fingers over the rough tree trunk, then turn and sit, leaning against it, slight nausea reminding me why I shouldn't drink alcohol.

'Dead.'

I jump.

Eli's voice sounds strained. He is on the other side of the tree trunk.

'For goodness sake, Elias Wolfe!'

'I failed you. I'm sorry,' he says, his voice cracking.

My heart falls. I always thought he would be relieved to not have to hang around me anymore.

I stand. 'I'm not dead, in case you didn't notice, so you didn't fail me!' I walk around the tree trunk with careful barefoot steps, my hand brushing the rough trunk of my tree leaving feelings of sadness ingrained in the bark.

I stop before him. His dark curly hair looks like a matted, fuzzy mess, his hands covering his face. My heart cries for him and I want to bend down and wrap my arms around him.

He pokes my big toe. 'You really should listen to your mother about wearing shoes. One day it will slow you down when you get something stuck in your foot. You have to be prepared to run at any time.'

'What if that's a story they tell me just to get me to wear shoes?'

Eli looks up at me and shakes his head. The rims of his eyes are red. 'If you knew what I knew, you would not question it.'

I lower myself next to him and lean back on the trunk of the tree that shares my name. 'Speak of what you know. You are no longer bound to protect me.'

He shakes his head and connects his heterochromia eyes to mine. One blue like the dancing ocean waves, illuminated by warmth and light, the other green, like the soul of nature, and tales of evergreen giants. I hate when he does that. I never know which eye to focus on. They are equally beautiful and soul attracting. But I can never tell him that. 'I—'

He frowns at me. 'You—' he interrupts, then shakes his head and looks away from me.

'I'm sorry if it was my fault that you have been replaced.' The jumble of words spills from my lips and rearranges themselves to make a sentence.

Eli lowers his head. 'I can only blame myself,' he whispers.

'For the record, every time you said "dead" to me, I didn't know you were there.'

'I always knew you were lying.' He looks up at me with a crooked smile.

My heart skips a beat. 'You were good at protecting me.'

'And?'

'Teasing me,' I say.

'And?'

'Wrecking my games.'

'And?' he says.

'Ruining my days.'

'And?'

'Making me cry,' I say.

'And?'

'Making me feel safe.' There. I said it. I let out a heavy breath.

His eyes wander to my lips and a warmth rushes through me. He lifts his chin then and looks up into the tree. 'After you lost consciousness yesterday, I quickly hid your technicolour lakeside chairs and umbrella in the forest, then put you over my shoulder and took you home. I didn't want anyone to see you that way.'

'Asleep?'

He looks at me with his lips in a hard line and shakes his head. 'I broke one of my rules. But I wanted to stop you being sent to the lighthouse. I know how much you hate it there.'

'Which rule? The one where you are obligated to annoy me?'

Eli smirks. 'Your bedroom is out of bounds. I had to prise open the window and shove you through it. I put shoes on your feet and placed you in your bed so your mother would think you were sleeping.'

I raise an eyebrow at him. 'Now I know what gave it away. I never wear shoes to bed. And Mama puts flowers on my window sill each morning before I wake—the jug of water—there would have been an interrogation to find the culprit.'

'My father will be furious,' he says.

'Apologise. Ask for forgiveness. Ask my mother for another chance.' My words are unbelievably fast and filled with sparkles of hope.

'It's too late. I made a bad choice.' Eli looks down and sadness drips from his face like melting wax.

'What were you meant to do? Leave me there, and then I would have been—'

'Dead,' he finishes. He runs a hand through his hair and looks into the distance. 'I should have taken you to your mother and let her deal with you. I was being too … kind … to you.' He closes his eyes for a moment.

'That's where your problem was. If you were mean to me like you always are, we wouldn't be having this conversation.'

Eli lets out a long breath. 'Yeah.' He stands and blinks rapidly, then reaches inside his shirt and pulls out a necklace, lifts the gold medallion with a king's crown on it, kisses it, and pulls the chain, breaking it, then launches it up into the tree with my name and watches as it catches on a branch.

'I never thought it would be a blue sky day when we parted,' I say while looking up into the tree branches, the gold chain swinging to and fro with a glint of golden light.

'You actually thought about when we would say goodbye?'

'Yes. Didn't you?'

'No. I've always been with you. It's always been we. When did you think it would happen if not a blue sky day?'

'Oh, I don't know,' I say, looking up at his tallness. I want to pull him back down to sit next to me so our shoulders could touch.

'Liar.'

I look at him and wonder whether to let him into my mindscape of feelings. 'On one of those days when the heavy clouds cry,' I finally say.

He narrows his eyes at me. 'Rain?'

'Yes. You know, like tears.'

'Ari Flora, I'm not sure I will miss your perplexing associations, cute as they are.'

'Cute! I was trying to tell you something.' I am trying to tell him that I will miss him without telling him I will miss him. Why are boys so daft?

'That you like to cry?'

I shake my head and roll my eyes. 'You know, this ending is the beginning of anything you want.'

Eli shoves his hands into his pockets. 'What if I already have everything I wanted?'

'No, you don't. Now you can move forward and follow your dreams.'

His eyes linger in mine, trying to steal my light. He raises one eyebrow. 'Maybe I should do that?'

I take a deep breath to stop my chin from trembling as sadness grips my heart. My eyes burn. 'Parting is such sweet sorrow that I shall say goodnight—'

'Till it be morrow,' Eli finishes. He looks down at my hand. I raise my hand to him and he touches his fingers to mine. 'Our sun has set, Ari.' He turns then, and takes the long walk into the King's Forest, punctuated by the tallest alpine trees of graduating hues of green, and the dark, lonely trunks, straight and upright like soldiers guarding secrets, dragging his heavy heart behind him. I want to pick it up and hug it close to my heart.

Healing.

And loving.

Beating as two.

And then one.

I watch him until he wasn't anymore.

Completely disappeared.

My stomach knots.

Would that be the last time I would ever see him?

What rules is he bound to when his employment ceases?

I turn around to see where my new guard is.

Nobody.

No shadows lurking behind trees or walls or boulders. Paranoia sets in.

Was I being watched?

And where from?

If they are protecting me, how can they do it from such a

distance?

And … if I am conscious of being watched by someone I don't know, would that distract from me being conscious of my surroundings in case I have to protect my own life?

Mama said it would make me grow as a person.

How can that be? Right at this moment, all I know is, that it causes me anxiety.

My skin burns. Intense energy I need to douse.

And right at this moment, all I know is, that I want Eli back.

I place my hand over the ache in my heart. I catch an unexpected sob in my throat as my world comes crashing down.

Scattering pieces of me.

And I run.

Barefoot.

In a straight line back to my room, drips of my sadness leaving their own footsteps behind me, sending silent prayers to above.

I wonder for a moment whether I should catch my tears in a lachrymatory bottle like my mama and study their shape under the microscope. But hers are tears of a broken heart. And that can't be mine.

Mine are tears of fear, aren't they?

Of the unknown? I am sure of it.

I stop before my room then climb through my window, pushing aside the vase of sunflowers.

Of happiness.

I go to my bedside drawer and grab Eli's note from beside the jug of water, reread it, and trace my fingers over his handwriting. Did he write it, or did he have someone write it for him? And what could I possibly have said yesterday by the lake that I can't remember.

'I'm sorry, Eli,' I whisper, then lay on my bed and let my tears fall, filled with memories of Eli and stories of unsaid words, glimpses of what could have been and worry for his future.

Endings.

And beginnings.
Said.

And unsaid.

Mama said everyone was born *brave*.
But for some, *fear* squashed their brave.

Mama said that everyone is *imperfect*,
and once you realise that,
it increases your *bravery*.

Mama said to make sure what you
stand up for is right,
not for what is popular,
for sometimes the popular following
leads to *destruction of mind,
body and soul*.

Mama said you will know what is
wrong and *right*.
The *truth* is written across your *heart*.
You innately know.

CHAPTER 7

Snapdragon flowers sit on my windowsill. Pastel pink and peach coloured blooms smiling on their spikes of green foliage, their sweet fruity scent permeating my bedroom. They are the colour of happy hot summers and the shade of the afternoon sun when the cool breeze runs its fingers through my hair. And when Mama once raced me to the wild snapdragon patch when I was little, where she told me dragons had sewn their stories in flower form. She would grab a flower bloom and gently squeeze it so it took on the shape of a dragon's head. She would squeeze it a little more, and it would open its mouth, like it was talking.

Mama created stories about heroes and villains and kingdoms, and dragons that were ferocious and wild on the outside, but kind and gentle and scared on the inside. Mama was her happiest in the snapdragon field, the sun sending threads of gold through her brown hair, her eyes shining with happiness that looked like a sparkle in her eyes. Her face changed, and became youthful and joyous instead of worried and burdened like it often was when she thought I wasn't watching her.

Once, Mama picked up one of the skull-like seed heads and moved it closer to my eyes. I let out a squeal of horror at the little creepy human-like skull, and Mama chased me until I fell over, and then she tickled me until my cheeks hurt from laughter.

Mama laid beside me and said that some women used to eat the skull seeds because they believed they would regain their youth and beauty again.

My eyes widened. 'So they could be little, like me, again?' I had asked.

Mama smiled. 'They would have to shrink to do that, my sweet, Ari Flora Heart Flower. It didn't work of course. It was just wishful thinking. But, the flower extract inhibits cell growth of particular cancer cells, stopping people getting very sick. Humans have been given everything they need on the earth. They just need to cultivate it to create the anti-disease, anti-sickness medicines we need.'

'What happens if we get sick, Mama?' I had asked. I had never known sickness.

'Mmmm … your body temperature rises and you feel very hot, sometimes parts of your body gets sore and ache. Sometimes you don't want to eat. Sometimes you sleep a lot as your body fights the sickness.'

I cross my arms. 'I don't want to get sick, Mama. It sounds awful.'

'You won't get sick, Ari Bear. There is no sickness in our kingdom.'

I nodded and gazed into Mama's brown eyes. I knew I wanted to be as smart as Mama when I grew up.

I peel my eyes from the snapdragons and my childhood memory, then pull my bed covers over my head as melancholy falls upon me like a heavy weight, it's shadow covering my body perfectly like a glove. I want it to be my cocoon, so I can emerge after a long deep sleep, like a new person, who isn't the cause of Eli's sadness and the loss of his job.

Elias.

He would surely hate me now.

Emotions. Where did they come from, and how did will feel them?

Head?

Heart?

Gut?

Why did they make me feel so damn bad.

Guilt.

Shame.

And regret.

Am I a bad person?

Do I just pretend I am a good person?

The loud knock on the heavy wooden door tells me to get up for breakfast. I wriggle lower under my bedcover. I want to stay here and wallow in my sadness. I know I always wished that Eli would go away, but now that he is gone, I want him back.

The knock on the door is louder this time. 'Miss Ari. Breakfast is waiting for you.' A servant's voice. Mama calls them servants, but I know they are the eyes and ears of the hidden castle. Like spies. I notice how they are positioned at particular places, and replaced by another person every three hours. If I don't respond to the door knock and request for my presence at breakfast, I know the door will open and three people will enter to see if I am still here. The aggressiveness of their body language, drawn weapons, and their scanning around the room is terrifying. I made that mistake once, and I wouldn't again.

'Coming,' I say, then haul my doom and gloom from the comfort of darkness under the bedcover, change into Wednesday clothes—olive coloured wide-leg pants and a beige long-sleeved cotton shirt. It's Sunday. I open the window shutters and look out at the Field of Flowers—pinks and dark pinks proliferated today, like my seventh birthday cupcakes with icing in shades of pink. I squeeze my feet into some shoes, even though I hate the feel of them, and drag my cumbersome shoes to the breakfast nook.

I stop at the doorway. The table has four chairs and only one breakfast plate.

I sigh. Mama is always at the table before me, unless she has left blue forget-me-not flowers to tell me she will be absent for a couple of days.

I move to the table, too aware of my shoes intended to please another. Now worn for nothing. I need to remove them. As I bend to unlace my right shoe, Mama enters the room like a whirlwind of cheer.

Aggravating.

'It's a beautiful day, Ari,' she says, her voice all sing-songy and full of happiness.

Irritating.

'Every day is beautiful, Ma, no matter the weather,' I say, knowing full well that her favourite days are the cloudless variety.

'Even the wild, westerly, windy days when you hide in corners because you can't control anything outdoors?' she says.

Truth.

Exacerbating.

Why does she always remind me of shaking my fist at the wind because I hate how it battles with me? A breeze is a different matter.

I keep my eyes on my food, and push it around with my fork. I'm not hungry. My heart aches and I want to disappear into thin air, like the magicians Mama told me about who once entertained people back before *The Unfolding* began. Their magical trickery. Their practise over and over to get the act so perfect it was seamless and believable, resulting in the gasps of believing spectators.

Treat each meal as though it is your last. You never know when circumstances will change. Food is energy. Energy that will help you survive, the words of Mama filled my mind. If I had heard them once, I had heard them a thousand times. I blink, then start to eat.

'You are defeated,' Mama says, this time her voice covered in warm pink clouds of love.

I look up at her. 'Defeated?'

'Yes. You have shoes on. You are submitting to our rules. It won't bring Elias back.'

'I lied yesterday morning about Elias hiding my shoes,' I confess, reaching out and caressing the petal of the pastel pink snapdragon on the table.

'I know you did, and Elias went along with your lie, that is one of the reasons I had to let him go—'

'It was done in humour—'

'He had one purpose, to ensure your safety. Your relationship had become too … familiar. And that could have disastrous consequences!' Mama's voice is a storm, matching her eyes that are sharply focussed on me.

I look away as my tears build. I want to run from the room. I want to hear my mother demand that I return at once. And I want to ignore her in defiance, stamping my feet. Instead, I let out a long breath, overcome, and return to eating my breakfast.

'May I help you today, Mama?' I ask, my voice deflated. Redirection.

'You are grieving, Ari. It will get better with time. Change your mindset, look at the situation as the beginning of something new.' Mama's voice is gentle now, like the falling of the first snow.

'But Mama, because of me, he is suffering, and goodness knows how his family reacted!'

'You are our number one priority, Ari. Above everyone else and—'

'What if I am not worthy of that attention, that privilege, that importance?' I lock my eyes with Mama's, making a stand against her declaration of my high position in this kingdom, if you could call it that? Can a kingdom have no physical castle that stands, complete and strong? And no king or queen?

'Ari Flora Cohen, the moment you were born I vowed to protect you for all your days until your father returns, and that is what I will do until my last breath. How I do that is up to my discretion, and if I engage others to help me, that is what will be done!'

A tear slides down my cheek. *Until my father returns …* what if that until is a never. What if my father is dead, and my mother won't accept it?

'Should I have a lachrymatory bottle to study my tears?' I ask to douse the flames of our words. Redirection.

'If you feel that it will help while you grieve,' Mama says, her words unconvincing. She's patronising me.

'May I help you today, Mama?' I ask again.

Mama closes her eyes and whispers words of thanks for her food, then takes her first bite of flatbread covered with honey and chopped nuts. She sighs. 'We had many deliveries last night. There's a lot of work to do.'

Hope blossoms in my chest like the first almond blossoms of spring, trying to cover the heartache of Eli's absence. I have no idea of what Mama means by "deliveries". I have no idea what is done with the "deliveries", whatever they are.

My mind wanders to that twenty-seventh day of solitary confinement at the lighthouse, when Eli visited for thirty minutes and said, 'You don't even know what your mother really does!' He was right.

'Eli will be redeployed in a new role, Ari,' Mama says, 'he will be well-cared for … and you can help in the Field of Flowers. They will help with the grief you are feeling.'

Hope sinks in my chest like a sack of potatoes. I don't want to be in the Field of Flowers, in the eternal field of colour and scents and happiness and of hanging floral umbrellas creating a distraction of the Field of Flowers and the patches of freshly dug dirt to obscure our activity from view by the surveillance satellites. Apparently, our kingdom doesn't exist. From the sky, all it appears to be, is a thousand year old pile of ruins that was once a castle, Mama had said.

Uninhabited.

Uninhabitable.

Lifeless.

'Thank you, Ma. May I leave the table?' I ask, my voice lowered. I want to add that I would most certainly would not be helping in the Field of Flowers today. But I don't. I wonder whether my new protector would give account of my wanderings and actions within the boundaries of the kingdom today.

My heart smiles. What if I choose not to stay within the boundaries of the kingdom? Will my new protector keep up with me? Will my new protector be forced to reveal their identity?

Mama nods and I turn on the heel of my hated shoes and leave the breakfast nook. A plan for the day has presented itself to me, and it's nothing like Mama's suggestion.

My shoes clunk clumsily against the stone flooring through the castle corridors as I return to my room, earning me looks of displeasure with silent aggressive frowns of chiding from positioned servants. I am sure Mama will send me to "walking with shoes" lessons. Again. Something my shoe walking teacher finds challenging, frustrating and most annoying as I fail to achieve the given noise limit for shoes. In her exasperation, she would dismiss me early from class each time. I didn't let her know I was adept at walking silently with shoes on. I had a reputation to uphold.

I enter my room and rip my shoes off and kick them under the bed, then pace the floor.

CHAPTER 8

The only way to be safe in *The Beyond* ... is to be a boy.

My long hair that Mama braided every night has to be hidden, or removed. Cut.

My chest that had grown from a flatness I enjoyed when I was younger, now cumbersome and difficult, making me feel self-conscious and ill at ease at times, had to be concealed.

I'm not a boy but I can act like one.

I can't cut my hair, lest my mother becomes suspicious. I will have to hide it.

I run my hands over the curve of my breasts. They need to be flattened if I am to pass as a boy. At once, I grab the snapdragon flowers from the vase, the water dripping on the floor, and leave my room, carrying them in front of me so that eyes and ears of the kingdom will think I have been working in the Field of Flowers as Mama suggested.

With silence of my bare feet, I ascend one of the many spiral staircases to the upper floor and make my way to the unused main bed chamber. I linger outside, ensuring that nobody has followed me, nor are watching me, then turn the rusty door knob and enter the dusty room.

I place the snapdragon flowers on a writing table then beeline for the old wooden wardrobe. I open the double doors, immediately assaulted by a powerful musty odour that steals my breath, then turn my head away and suck in fresh air, hold my breath, and push aside the old clothing and reveal the double doors at the back.

Once, when I had been playing in the forbidden main bed chamber when I was twelve, I discovered the room beyond, through the wardrobe. It was like stepping back in time in the history books I had read, when there were real kingdoms and kings and queens and princes and princesses, and my imagined dragons.

In here is the item that will solve my curvy chest problem. A chest plate made of iron. I would have gone to the Armourer's tower of the castle, except, it had been ransacked long ago. So this fortunate find in my bored explorations of the kingdom is perfect for now.

I walk in haste past the bows and arrows, shields, swords, daggers, flags and banners, chain mail shirts and helmets, hammers and long lances, and stop before the chest plates. There are three different sizes. I choose the smallest one, presumably made for a teen in training for combat. I remove it from its place on the wall and carry it out of the room, through the acrid wardrobe, closing each of the doors as I go, and stop in the bed chamber.

Now I have a problem. How do I conceal the fact that I have a chest plate stolen from the forbidden, hidden garderobe? I push my fingers through my hair. All problems have solutions. It just takes creativity. As my eyes settle on the snapdragon flowers, I picture them laying across the up-side down chest plate, like they are placed in an oval type of bowl. Walking through the castle like that will cement the lie that I have been working in the Field of Flowers.

It was perfect.

I place the snapdragon flowers in the breastplate then stop before the door and listen for movement. Hearing none, I open the door a fraction and spy outside. Sensing the peacefulness of the upper floor, I step outside the bed chamber and close the door behind me with minimal movement.

I am safe.

I am alone.

And I am on course with my planned activity for today.

As I move with perfectly concealed barefoot steps through the castle, I grab a flower from each vase I pass, and place it onto my growing bouquet in my new metal bowl. A rose here, a cosmos there, a cornflower here, a carnation there, a zinnia here, a sunflower there. I notice that questioning prying eyes examine my flower collection, then crinkle with a smile, approving of my flower gathering today. Mama will be pleased by reports of my day's occupation of presumed working in the Field of Flowers.

Entering my room, I place the breastplate onto my bed, jab the snapdragons back into the vase, then open my window and throw the other flowers outside.

Over my undergarments, I fit the breastplate. It is heavy and awkward, but gives the effect of a flat chest. I groan as I try to bend over to retrieve my locked box of dark masculine clothes and muddied shoes under my bed. I unlock it and dress my new boy body—dark pants and an oversized shirt with a hood. I pull back my long locks of auburn hair and push the pony tail down the back of my shirt.

I stand before the polished silver serving plate that doubles as a type of mirror, and turn side-on. I smile. I look like a boy. A teenage boy.

Do I feel like I am a boy? Absolutely not.

And I never want to be a boy, or identify as a boy, except for survival purposes. I pull the hood over my head and practise using it to conceal my face.

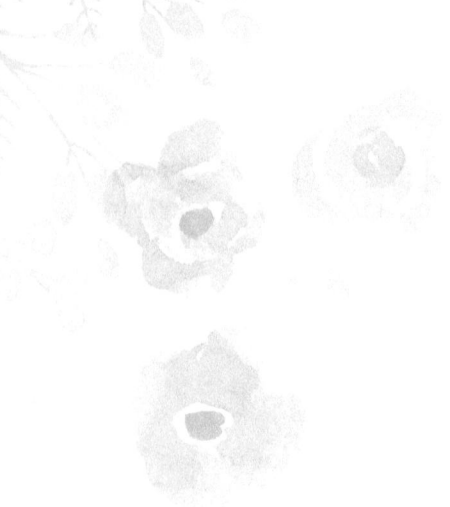

CHAPTER 9

Mama said I was born with a passionate and curious spirit. She also said it would get me into trouble, often. Was it true, or was it the self-fulfilling prophecy?

I go to the corner of my room, open the floor door and climb down on to the ladder, closing the floor door after me, then proceed to the underground tunnel and follow it for an hour until I come to the entrance of *The Forbidden Beyond*, hidden behind a mirrored wall in a room inside an unfamiliar building swarming with people hurrying about.

Quiet people.

Quiet people who walk with shoes that make no sound.

Like back in the kingdom.

I step out into the room of whiteness and tall ceilings and glass panels all around. 360 degree views. And desks with people standing at them, talking to people with dark sunglasses and pointing out directions to them.

The building architecture is breathtaking. Never have I seen glass in a building like this. After I haul in my admiration, I stand to the side and pull my hood further over my head, aware that I don't fit in with my knowledge of how this space works, and observe others to try to become one of them. To blend in.

'Have you lost your glasses?' A voice beside me.

'Y-yes,' I say, trying to sense if I'm in a hostile environment or not.

I look up at her. She eyes me warily then gives black glasses to me. 'According to our sources, danger is low in Jedburgh today. Do you have your assignment number?'

My stomach twists. I have no idea what she is talking about but I nod anyway.

'Give me your hand.'

I hold my breath and place my hand in hers, and she jumps, like she has received a bolt of energy. Like a shock. Her eyes widen then she averts her eyes from me. 'Go in peace,' she says, and dips her head.

I frown and dip my head to her then turn toward where I assume the exit of the building is. I pause out of her view and bite my lip. What an unusual reaction she had to my touch. I stop by a group of people and about turn, back to the centre of the building.

Why was there silence?

A row of people enter from the hidden doors, carrying flowers like Mama grew at the kingdom. They stand to the side and others approach them, exchanging the flowers for folded pieces of paper.

The flower carriers turn and leave through the hidden entrance behind the mirrored wall with the notes, the mirrored wall that, from this perspective, is impossible to see where it begins and where it ends. If you didn't know about the entrance, it would be like it didn't exist. In fact, if you look at it long enough, it becomes disorientating.

I look to the left, and a line of seven people arrive. They wait in one of the many spirals on the floor. Silent. From the hidden entrance appear another seven people carrying sacks of food. Our food. From the kingdom. Again, they exchange pieces of paper. Then they turn and begin walking in the same direction as the people who have taken the flowers.

I decide to follow them, and being a kingdom person, I'm aware that my footsteps must be silent on the large white floor tiles, like I have been taught and perfected in my times of solitude at the lighthouse, when I was banished as punishment for non-compliance of the kingdom rules. I join the end of their line, walking in sync.

We walk toward a large glass door that is guarded by a tall, solid man dressed in white. The person first in line stops and holds up a piece of paper. The man straightens, reads the paper, and opens a sliding glass door. They put their dark sunglasses on, so I do, remembering that game of copycat I played so often as a child.

And then we step outside.

Into *The Beyond*. Forbidden for me to enter.

Ever.

They scatter, and I am left standing. Shocked. The street is busy with people walking, not talking. Stopping at times and interacting with things that aren't there, like they are seeing things. Hallucinating.

Multilevel buildings are all about. White. Grey. In perfect keep. No greenery. There is a main street and narrower off-streets, lined by smaller buildings in different shades of grey, the roads made of pebble stone, the word "help" scratched onto the stones here and there.

After a moment of watching the direction of the travellers, I decide to follow the most common direction of people movement. North. In silence.

There is a railway line to my right and a train is pulling in, a red carpet rolled out over the pebble stones leading to a car. I turn my head away when I notice that nobody else looks at it. Is it dangerous to do so?

The place I'm in isn't a major city like I had seen in the history books in learning with my governess, with spectacularly tall buildings and shops and lights and the rushing of people. Happy people. It is compact here, and clean and tidy. But beyond the perfectly kept buildings are streets with no buildings, or perhaps, where there were once buildings, rubble, left like it has suffered some sort of catastrophic event. It feels like this location is an outlier where exchanges, important exchanges, take place perhaps. An artery to the heartbeat of a motherland, a governing body, perhaps.

But where was life in the landscape, beside people who are acting like they are happy and content but giving off the scent of scared? Where are the plants and the trees? Why is everything so grey and dull and lifeless?

I lift my eyes to the above. A dark coloured object hovers like the one I had seen when I was nine, lying in the rectangular hole dug into the earth. Except, there is not one dark coloured object, there's many. Hundreds perhaps. What are they doing?

A shiver runs down my spine and I return my eyes to front and centre.

Is my protector here?

My protector should be here.

All of a sudden I feel exposed.

And vulnerable.

Threatened.

Anxious.

And alone.

Words hit me like a slap in the face: *Remember how to use your breath, like you were taught.* I swallow. Hard. Then concentrate on deep diaphragm breathing so I do not appear to breathe, trying not to lose consciousness. At that moment, I realise wearing a breast plate was a bad idea. My body is so restricted. But then, it may be the thing that helps me. Nobody can see the rise and fall of my breath. I relax a little and look at the people. It would be better to be amongst the multitudes to stay invisible.

To fit in.

I watch them closely. Their steps. Their posture. Their actions and reactions. The way they smile. Or not. They stop and reach up to touch something, but there is nothing there. Or they stop and bend down to something and interact with it, like petting a dog, but there is nothing there.

They no longer walk with silent steps like I had been taught. Sometimes, they lift their hands and look at it, then tap the back of it, before continuing toward the low level structures in the distance, getting closer now.

Is this their destination?

To the left or right of the cobblestone path is nothing but dried out bush and the burnt trunks of trees that perhaps used to be a lush forest. There is nothing of note.

A person in white pants and shirt walks toward us and people slow down, then stop, the queue building like a length of dominoes. I step into the queue, my skin starting to burn with anxiety, and silent, and obedient like the others, oblivious to what is happening ahead, except for a beeping sound.

After a while I am second in line to the person with the power to control the flow of walkers. I watch as a device is handed to the person in front of me, and the person places it against their right hand in the flesh between the index finger and thumb.

It beeps.

They hand the device back. The person in control of the line of people steps aside and allows them to continue on their traverse.

I take a step toward the … person? And stop. It takes a step and stills, and there is a sound like a sigh, like the releasing of some air. Blood rushes through my ears and my stomach churns. Hello my unfriend, Anxiety.

I want to run.

Back to the kingdom.

The person before me isn't human. They're a close copy of one with hair and facial features, but lack humanness at their core. Their movements are smooth and automated. Cold and precise. I watch with intensity as the "person" holds the device before me with an inflexible mechanical type of action. My heart races as my gut tells me I am in danger. I look up into the eyes of the person, the colour of green with a central white ring. There is no soul connection like I feel with a human. Terror rushes through me like a stampede.

Breathe, I tell myself. But not in the human way. In the way I was taught that makes me feel like I am about to pass out.

I copy the actions of the person who preceded me, holding the black device against the flesh between my index finger and thumb, wondering on earth what the device did, and hoping they don't detect the tremor of nervousness in my hand.

I don't hear a beep like I did with all the people before me, and my heart starts to thump in my chest. In a panic, I pass the device back to the "person", terrified of what will happen next.

Is this the moment I will be "dead" like Eli always said?

'Please scan your chip again,' the "person" says, the feminine voice devoid of emotion or intonation, its articulation perfect.

A chip? I push the device onto my hand again. No beep. 'It keeps happening. I mean … it doesn't beep like it used to. I should get it checked,' I lie in a deep boyish voice that is smooth and foreign to me.

'I have noted that you need re-chipping with the government. Remove your glasses for iris scanning for order confirmation.'

At that moment, I want to sink into the ground and disappear.

Dead. Eli's word returns to me. What is going to happen when "it" discovers I am a non-resident? That I come from the castle ruins that appear to be devoid of life.

That I'm not a real boy?

Blood pounds in my ears as the poison of panic spreads through my body. Dread fills my mind. I clench my teeth together to stop a piercing scream from escaping.

I was done.

'Is there a problem? Can I help? I'd like to earn some credits.' The deep voice comes from behind me. I watch as a bearded man steps forward and takes the device from the hand of the "person".

Credits?

'I work in technology and we repair the scanners that stop working.' He turns it over in his hand and fiddles with it. He puts his hand into his pocket and pulls out a tool. 'You know technology. Sometimes it glitches, like your kind.'

Your kind?

'I must scan your iris first to confirm your identity.'

The man removes his glasses and the "person" faces her head towards him and looks at his eyes, a green light glowing in hers. The glow stops.

'Do I have permission to use your scanning device?' he says.

'Yes.'

Out of the sight of the "person", he holds the tool against my skin, then places the scanner on top of it. It beeps. He hands the device back to her. 'Fixed. Have a good day. I guess you're headed to Jedburgh, where there are about a thousand people. I'm sure the surveillance drones have communicated with you about that.'

'I do not have permission to release information,' the "person" says. Then she adds, 'Have a good day,' exactly in the sound of the man's voice.

My eyes widen. Nausea rises in my stomach. There is so much wrong going on. It feel like I am fighting for my life every moment. My body is in a hyper-aware state, energy buzzing at an uncontrollable level through me, making me want to run.

And vomit.

The man's hand clutches my upper arm, and he pulls me along quickly to the structures ahead.

'Don't speak. Don't look around. Don't run.' He tightens his grip around my arm further, and it smarts. Somehow I feel like I have been captured.

Today is a bad day.

A very bad day.

CHAPTER 10

I should never have come to *The Beyond*.

I may never get back home.

As I am pulled along to the low level structures, I see that they are a group of close knit houses and alleyways. All in disrepair. Peeling paint on single storey once-were homes and perhaps still-are homes of history of an event that has shaped them into permanent reminders. Broken windows and weeds singing sad songs of lament, closed curtains with bony hands creating a gap to nervously peek outside at the commuters.

The man leads me up the third alleyway on the right, walking in footsteps left by others before, leaving no evidence of his presence. He veers to the right to the partially rotting four steps of timber, up to a front door, the colour of dried wood with the scrapings of blue paint of yesteryear.

He pauses before he places his hand on the brass door knob, then turns it five times to the left, then eight times to the right. There's a click, and he pushes on the door to open it, and ushers me inside like we are being chased by an angry bear.

Inside the room are red sofas and a dark coloured coffee table, a dining table and blue chairs. Upon the chairs sit manikins in various poses, mimicking human life.

For a moment, my extreme visualisation and imagination, my hyper-phantasia brings the manikins to life, and they go on with life like humans, cutting up food, drinking from glasses, having conversations and laughing. One stands from the table and leaves the room ... I stop my hyper-phantasia. I have to be present in the moment.

The man gives a hand signal and the floor to the left opens, revealing a set of stairs leading underground.

'Down,' he says.

I turn to look at him, furrowing my eyebrows.

'There's something you need to learn ... when you are told to do something, you do it, if you want to live.'

A threat.

Butterflies haphazardly collide in my stomach making me feel like I am about to pass out. My breath hiccups, and knowing I have no other choice, I turn and descend the steps with caution.

I step onto the concrete floor, my legs feeling weak.

Is this the moment my mother had warned me about, when it was better to be born a boy? At least I look like one at the moment. I hope I'd done a good enough job to pull it off.

The instant the man stands beside me in the room below the floor door, now a ceiling door, a light comes on, revealing dark green walls and eight white doors around the periphery.

He presses a button on the wall and three people come to the central room. Two male, one female.

'I rescued this human on the trail, about to get scanned without a chip,' he says with a look of disgust.

'How is he still here?'

'By pure luck that I was near,' the man says.

'What training have you had, son?' asks another.

I swallow the lump in my throat. I'm not prepared for anything like this. 'None.'

My rescuer narrows his eyes at me and removes his hood. The look of horror fills his eyes. 'Damn it.' He looks away from me and runs his hand through his dark hair. 'If you're going to parade around as a teenage boy, you'd better make your voice real low, you hear.'

I clear my throat.

I clench my hand to stop it shaking.

I want to go home.

I wish I had never stepped out into *The Beyond*.

'Have you been sent by someone?' asks the female.

I shake my head.

'Then why on earth would you come here. Inexperienced. You'll end up dead. Where did you come from?' The man's anger was rising.

I have no idea how to answer his question. I come from the kingdom. Mama called it the kingdom. How can I explain that I followed a series of underground tunnels to get here? If I do explain it, is our kingdom at risk of being discovered?

Invaded?

Taken over?

My chin starts to quiver. I stop it by exhaling a slow breath. *Toughen up,* Ari. *Toughen up.* 'I'm exploring,' I say, lowering my voice.

Laughter erupts from the four.

'Exploring?' The man's face becomes flat. Emotionless. 'For goodness sake. Talk in a normal voice. We know your gender. If you were born here, you would never have used the word exploring! We want the truth.'

I want to ask if he knows where my father is, Azriel Cohen. But the words won't form. Anxiety is tripping in my body, partying in places I haven't felt it before, and using it like a punching bag.

I want Eli here.

He would make me feel safe.

He would protect me.

'Truth,' I swallow some courage. 'I wanted to see what was beyond where I grew up. To see why my mother would not let me out of our home borders.'

The man raises his chin. 'And does your mother know you are here?'

I shake my head. 'Why did you help me with that … that—'

'That device … that humanoid?'

Humanoid? I nod.

The man lets out a heavy breath. 'We are Leges, helping humans, but masquerading as belonging to the ones who govern the earth, who control everything and everyone. Vigilantes, if you like.'

Ones who govern the earth?

'We need to return you to your home. Safely.'

He turns and walks away from me and cusses under his breath, then turns to the others. 'This is a problem we don't need. Saffron, take her to give her supplies and make her blend in.'

'Come,' Saffron says, her face without emotion.

I follow her into a room. It is filled with shelves of items. She throws a charcoal grey backpack at me, dark glasses, numerous items of clothing, a breast plate. And dark shoes.

She pauses at the furthest shelf, looks back at me like she is trying to make up her mind if I am worthy, then pulls one last item off the shelf. It looks like a cloak, although when she holds it up, she disappears, or more likely, she blends into the walls around her.

Completely invisible.

She folds it and reappears again, then walks towards me, stopping in front of me. She picks up the dark glasses. 'VR replica glasses, although they aren't VR like the "owned" ones wear. Idiots addicted to the virtual world. Such a lie.' She places them in the side of the backpack.

'What's VR?'

'You seriously don't know?'

I shake my head.

'Virtual reality. When they put on the glasses, it changes everything around them. It's a simulated, interactive 3D environment that users can choose whatever they want to be surrounded by. Dry and dead plants in real life will look in good health with the VR glasses, they will see animals in front of them that are not there in reality. They could be walking in a desert, yet in their VR world, they are in a busy city. It's one of the biggest lies of technology, addictive, and covers up the truth of the world, putting people into denial about what is really happening.'

She had used so many words that are not in my vocabulary or learning back in the kingdom. I can't even imagine what people would see.

Saffron picks up the next item. 'Hoody to hide your face. Guy pants. Shoes of the only kind here. Flexible breast plate—more comfortable for us women, but still perfect for hiding our gender.' She lifts the next item of clothing. It was black, long-sleeved, long-legs, high necked and a zipper at the side. 'This is your best friend. It's too hard for an attacker to take off quickly. It has a good reputation. If an assailant sees that you have it on, they will leave you alone. But first, you don't want them to know you are female. They think we are weak and easily dominated. A plaything—' She stops and eyes me warily. She smiles. 'Women have strength beyond theirs that scares them. Cowards.'

Mama said some boys were only after one thing. Physical intimacy.

Mama said that real men were still around who treated women with respect. Those were the ones who loved you for you, and not your body, or what they could use you for.

'Have you ever been … attacked?' I say, and gulp the word down like it is a toxic weed.

'Who do you think invented the black suit? There are things I cannot speak of because of my trauma. You are part of the sisterhood, as I am.' Saffron folds the clothing piece up and puts it into my backpack. 'I thank God daily for the good men here, for their courage, for their commitment to protecting our kind, for their honesty, for their integrity, for their kindness.'

Our kind?

Saffron sits beside me and takes my hand. She looks me in the eyes, like a warning. 'Don't let anyone insert a microchip into your hand. Don't let them tattoo a barcode on you. If you have either of those, the government owns you. Don't let them scan your iris.'

Them? Who are they?

She stands and pulls two more items off a shelf. 'Take this,' she holds a small black device in her hand. 'It will give a piercing humanly inaudible sound that will bring your attacker to their knees, if they are human, but it will also affect you … insert these into your ears before you use it to protect yourself, and use the device only in the direst of situations. Keep them in your pocket.'

She indicates for me to stand. When I do, she helps me with the backpack. It feels a little heavy, but comfortable, although, it pushes my metal breast plate harder on my collar bones.

Saffron looks me over. 'Everyone here carries this backpack. You'll blend in and be less suspicious.'

Less suspicious? 'Thank you. For your kindness,' I say.

Saffron gives me a small smile and we exit the room and return to the central room where the other men are sitting, talking in hushed tones. They stop and turn their attention to us.

The man stands and approaches me. 'We're going to ensure you go home. But first—' he holds up what looks like a grain of rice, but a little bigger. 'A microchip to—'

'No,' I say, and step back from him.

'Here's a rule for you … always let a person finish their sentence so you don't jump to incorrect conclusions.' He raises his eyebrows at me, unimpressed by my interruption. 'I was going to say, a microchip to tape to your hand between your thumb and index finger on the palm side. When they scan your hand, it will pick up the chip and its data, allowing you to go.' He scans the chip, ensuring it works, then adds a sticky substance and places it on my hand. 'Now, give me your hand like I need to scan it. Wait for the beep.'

I hold out my hand. He places a reader device on the back of my hand, but it doesn't beep. He pulls the scanner back and tries again. No beep. He looks closely at the scanner and fiddles with it a little, and attempts to scan my hand again. No beep. He lifts his chin and looks down at me with a studies my face. 'We'll try another chip.'

We do the same process, with the same scanner, and when it doesn't beep, we use a different scanner. Even when I turn my hand over so that it directly scans the chip, there is no beep.

Mama said one day I would accidentally release my gift, and then I would have to work out how to use it … intentionally.

Mama said my gift would be revealed at the appointed time. I had to be patient. Other things had to take place first in my dream story, now my life story.

Was this my gift? The chip not working?

'Argh! We'll have to use the barcode,' he says to the others.

Barcode? No, no, no.

Saffron returns with a package and pulls out a piece of paper with black thin and wide lines and numbers on it. She hands it to the man with a bottle of water.

I pull my eyebrows together and look at the girl.

'This is a stick-on barcode. You can wash it off. A real barcode is when they tattoo it onto your skin with a fine needling patch punched onto your wrist. It's permanent,' she says.

Hesitating, I hold out my arm as I am told too. He wets my skin then places the tattoo barcode patch over it. After a minute he peels it off, the barcode staying. He dries it off.

'I'll put this bag of barcodes into your bag. There's 250 of them. If you ever come back, ensure you have applied the barcode. You must stay safe. Do you understand?'

I nod.

'Any questions before we go? I'm Sorrel by the way,' he says.

'How did the humanoid copy your voice and are you my protector?'

He clenches his jaws together and looks away for a moment before meeting my eyes. 'It ... recorded my voice, cloned it and spoke it back to us. It's the technology of untruth, of lies, or deceit, and ... I am not your personal protector, if that is what you are asking.'

I lower my head.

I need to cry.

Mama said it always made us feel better.

He puts a finger under my chin and lifts my eyes to his. 'Never cry here, only in secret. If you cry in front of others, they will realise you are human, and will become targeted. Survival #101—don't cry, don't consume drink or food, hide your breath. In other words, act like them.'

Act like them?

Who are they?

How do they act?

I swallow and a tear escapes. I flick it away and toughen my resolve. I understand Survival #101. But I still need to know who "they" are. I decide not to ask.

Yet.

'If you are asked why you have a barcode, and not a chip, tell them you have an allergic reaction to the chip.'

I blink.

I want to go home.

To Mama's kingdom.

Where it is safe.

Where nothing bad ever happens, well except for that time of the lightning strike when I was ten. Anxiety burns through my skin.

'Hood up. Let's go—'

'Wait,' I say, gathering my courage like gathering flowers from the Field of Flowers. 'Is there more here, like … where are the people?'

He gives me a crooked smile. 'You know, curiosity killed the cat—'

'But the human learned from failures and increased their knowledge and skill,' I say, gaining more bravery.

He looks at the others and back to me. '*If* … you return, I will personally take you to where the humans are. Once you have been there, you will never come back! Now, let's go!' He turns and walks toward the steps, places his hand on the wall, and starts ascending the steps to the floor above. When we step into the room of the replica house, he stops and turns to me. 'Don't be fooled in our travels. What you see is not what you get. Some people are not entirely human here. And some are not human at all. They will stand out. They walk amongst us. See if you can pick them out. Glasses on. Ready?'

I put my black glasses on and follow him out onto the street, and we walk the same path that had led us here.

There are more people about this time, clothed in a similar way, hoods covering heads, backpacks, not a word spoken. Dark glasses on. Some smile at times like they have seen something pleasant. And then there are those whose walking is not as smooth as ours, their steps kind of stiff and mechanical even, not the free flowing, smooth movement like we have.

All of a sudden, the man's walking slows and I feel a panic in the air. Up ahead is queue of people, hands outstretched, chips being scanned. A person in front of me turns around in haste, bumping me as he hurries past.

My helper stands in front of me, and is scanned first.

I push up my sleeve to have the barcode scanned.

'You look too young to have a barcode—that's old technology,' the "female-like person" says.

'My body kept rejecting the chip … like an allergic reaction,'

I say.

'It happens to some.' She holds the scanner close to my skin, but there is no beep. My heart races.

'Arrrrck. Not again!' my helper says. 'This happened this morning? Can I help with your device? I'd like to earn some credits.'

Credits?

I watch as he takes the device from the hand of the "person". 'I work in technology and we repair the scanners that stop working.' He turns it over in his hand and fiddles with it. He puts his hand into his pocket and pulls out a tool. 'You know—technology. It sometimes glitches, like you, at times.'

'Let me scan your iris first to confirm your identity,' the human-looking woman says.

He removes his glasses and the "person" looks into his eyes, a green light glowing in her right eye. The glow stops.

'Do I have permission to use your scanning device?'

'Yes.'

He holds the tool against my skin, then places the scanner on top of it. It beeps. He hands the device back. He pulls out a flat hand-sized device with a screen and starts tapping on it. 'I've have recorded the glitch in your device, so when you hand it in at the end of the day, it can be thoroughly checked for errors or bugs.'

'Thank you. I will add your credits.'

'Thank you. Have a good day,' he says, and as we walk onward, I can hear him mumbling with anger under his breath.

After half an hour we arrive at the building from which I came from. I turn to the man who has helped me. 'Thank you for escorting me and for my safety,' I say.

He bows his head and half turns before he faces me again. 'My advice to you … if you are safe where you live, don't come back. And, you might want to get that little shock you give people who touch you, looked at. I'm beginning to think you are not entirely human.' Then he turns and leaves.

My breath stops.

How can I not be entirely human?

Is there something wrong with me?

Is there something Mama has not told me?

My eyes burn but I can't let any tears drop.

I walk through the building with soundless footsteps, find the mirror hidden door to enter, and feeling disorientated, stumble my way through the entrance, then proceed to the underground tunnel and follow it for an hour until I come upon the tunnel offshoot that leads to my bedroom.

I climb the ladder, push the floor door away and pull myself onto the floorboards of my room, then close the entrance. I sit for a moment in stunned silence, the events unfolding in my mind at speed. My heart sinks. The world is not like in the books I have read. The world is not like our kingdom of nature and homemade and kindness and goodness and serving others.

I shake my head.

The world is like an attack, on humans, on freedom, controlled and tracked and … manipulated.

In anger, I kick my new backpack under the bed, stand and undress myself of my boy disguise, that by the way, unravelled by the sound of my voice still too high for a boy.

I put on a dress and rid my feet of my shoes then pace my room before the weight of the day becomes too heavy, then lie on my bed, curl up and cry.

Mama said there was more to our world than we could see. More to the world that we knew.

And, I decide, what was seen could not be unseen.

And, I decide, *The Beyond* was the opposite of my world, the castle ruins that was our safe haven. The castle ruins that we called a kingdom because once, a king did live here. The kingdom we live in that does not have a king or queen.

The kingdom I have grown up in.

The Beyond was like night.

Our kingdom was like day.
Like black.
And white.
Like dream.

And nightmare.

Mama said not to seek *happiness,*
because you will *never* find it.
Instead, seek to *serve,* to *help others,*
be *kind* to yourself,
and happiness will *find you.*

CHAPTER 11

The perfume of roses permeates the room. A light, delicate sweet fragrance, much like almond blossom, cucumber and lemon zest. It is the first of a new month. Mama always leaves roses at the beginning of every new month. I open my eyes. The bouquet sits on my window sill. White. Pure. Like Mama's love for Papa.

I place my hand over my heart as the ache of his absence manifests again. He is my hero. I love him even though I have never met him. If it wasn't for Papa, Mama and I would be dead.

Mama was still catching her tears for Papa, even after eighteen years, and studying the structure of her tears. When will she stop?

I gaze out the window, opened by Mama while I was still sleeping. Did she sense my sadness, knowing that I need the sky like a sea of blue wellness this morning to cast its relaxation and calmness over me.

What colour eyes does Papa have? What does Papa look like? Mama said I was part of her and part of him. How am I like him, besides our dislike of wearing shoes?

I rise from bed, my "quick escape" clothes rearranging

themselves after a night of sleep. I change into my Thursday outfit—off-white wide-leg pants and a chocolate long-sleeved cotton button-up shirt—though it's Monday. It's my way of declaring my freedom of choice and independence. I look out at the Field of Flowers and its blooms, lush in vibrant hues like they were painted with the brush and colour palette of *Vincent van Gogh*. Even the clouds seem to swirl. Then I walk to the breakfast nook, barefooted, as per every day. Rebellious. Rule breaker.

No morning ever changes here. I used to hate it, but now, after my adventure to *The Beyond* yesterday, our mornings of peacefulness and freedom are a wonderful thing. It's a funny thing what a change of perspective can give. Maybe I should wear my shoes as a sign of thankfulness?

'Good morning, my Ari Flora Bear.'

I smile. 'Good morning, Ma. Remember, I'm not eight years old anymore,' I say, referring to her use of Ari Flora Bear, and sit perpendicular to her at the breakfast table. Like we have done for what seems like a thousand years.

'I know, my beautiful, I couldn't bear to not call you that anymore.' Mama smiles at me, her face lighting up the room like sunshine.

She lowers her head and gives thanks for our food, then we start eating. It's eggs again, and flat bread with a small bowl of fruit on the side.

'Ma, I was thinking of Papa this morning when I woke. What colour eyes did he have?'

'Did? Your father's eyes *are* the same colour as yours—springtime grey, or sage green, or blue like the ocean, sometimes even violet, depending on wherever he was. They reflected earth tones and sky tones and sea tones and sunsets painted with colour reflected in them. He has kind eyes, full of love and compassion.' Mama's eyes seem to glow as she speaks, and then an impossible sadness falls over her face. She lowers her eyes. 'I'll find a photo of him later today.'

'I'd love that,' I say, a lump forming in my throat. I place my hand on her arm for a moment, my heart filling with compassion for my grieving mother.

We eat in silence, a question buzzing in my mind that I need to ask, hoping it won't make Mama reach for her lachrymatory bottle. There was a sound back in *The Beyond* that bugged me …

'Ma, when I was thinking about Papa, I also thought back to the night he was taken, except, I just can't quite remember the details about the noise in the oratory that made you both turn around.'

'The quiet sigh?'

'Yes. What did it sound like?'

Mama sighs, letting a breath out. 'Just like that,' she says.

'Like it was exasperated, or something?'

'No, like … air was escaping from it.'

'Why do you ask?'

'Just thinking, you know, like when you are awake in bed and your mind wanders,' I say, but not adding that I am curious about the sound of the human-looking female yesterday that read my microchip. That quiet sigh that triggered the memory of my dream story and the mention of a lawless ones. I had asked Mama about it once—

'A lawless one?' I had said.

Mama nodded. 'It had no human heart, so it had no law.'

I narrowed my eyes at Mama. 'What do you mean?'

'Well, dear Ari, every human mind has the moral code of life innately in its DNA—it has been proven time and time again in all cultures, and the laws are written on our hearts. We are born knowing right from wrong. Our own conscience and thoughts tell us whether we are doing right or wrong. When we don't choose the right thing, that's where guilt and shame and regret come from. The lawless ones don't have a heart or a mind, therefore they have no law to abide by, and do not know right and wrong in society. They have no emotion to feel guilt or shame.'

'Minds like to wander when you are trying to sleep,' Mama says, breaking into my memory.

'Tell me again, what happens when a dream story is not finished, like … what happened with my dream story on that night that Papa disappeared?' I hate the thought that I have an unfinished dream story. It feels dangerous, or, that I am unprotected, somehow.

'Ari, the writing of your dream story on that night was interrupted. It doesn't mean that the dream story cannot be finished. When Papa returns, we will finish your dream story.' Mama gives me a small smile.

I want to ask her what will happen to my dream story if Papa has met death. Where does that leave me? But I didn't want to hurt Mama's heart. I don't think she could bear it if Papa has died. I think that living on the tiny flicker of hope that he is still alive keeps her going each day. 'Just wondering though, what happens, say, hypothetically speaking, if a baby's dream story cannot be finished?' I ask.

'Overthinking I would call it, Ari! You have always been prone to depths of thinking and analysing and synthesising to come to conclusions. Sometimes the wrong conclusions after too much overthinking.' Mama gives me a gentle smile. She sips on her lemon tea, the citrus fragrance weaving its way around the table like it's writing a story. She places the tea cup onto the saucer, the sound of the clink echoing around the breakfast nook. Mama is looking for the right wording. I can see it in her eyes.

Mama always said that words have weight, and some words are impossibly heavy.

I'm sure she is searching for the light words to tell me so I don't carry a heavy burden.

Mama places her hands on top of each other in front of her on the table. She clears her throat. 'The dream story of a baby are the aspirations and prayers created for a child, the beginning to the end of life, filled with unconditional love. It's the hopes, happiness and wellness in life. All babies have a dream story created before they are born made by their mother or father, or both, made consciously or not. A conscious dream story, created with the joining of three souls, like ours that we started on that night, is a powerful moment for us to treasure, bonding us ... what happens when the dream story is interrupted?' Mama shakes her head. A sadness falls over her face like a cloud blocking out the sun. Is it because my dream story was not finished, or is it because of what happened on that night?

Then Mama adds, 'Everyone has a life story too, Ari, which is different to a dream story. A life story is all the bits in between the beginning and the end of the dream story. That's what you get to choose. You are responsible for your life. Sometimes you'll make good choices, sometimes not so good choices.' Mama's face brightens. 'Just remember to learn from not so good choices.'

'What happens if my dream story is unfinished and my life choices are terribly bad?' I hold my breath. My spontaneous decisions got me into trouble. A lot.

'In the reality of it all ... the dream story is our human projection for your life, and when your life story is different to the one we dreamed of, we are reminded not to be filled with disappointment, but with hope. We cannot see into the future, unless you have the gift of prophesy. We can't see exactly what is coming in your life. It's your life and your choices. The Ancient of Days gives us free will. He is so good. He knows your beginning and the end with perfect clarity.' Mama smiles. 'You'll be guided at the right time.' Mama lifts her tea cup to her lips, and closes her eyes for a moment as she drinks. 'Papa and I are your earth parents, Ari, and blessed beyond measure to have you. I have to have faith that I have taught you well, based on my knowledge and experiences.'

Rumination throws a veil over my mind. I have a hundred questions that need a hundred answers. I look down at my food and tap my barefoot on the rug.

Mama's hand covers mine then, her touch warm and soft, filled with love. 'Your life will be as it should be. Talk to the Ancient of Days. Ask and you shall receive. And Ari … don't worry about something that may or may not happen. Worry steals your happiness. Deal with things when they happen, if they happen. Finish your breakfast. I have a list of errands for you to do today.'

A list of errands? I nod, then continue to eat, the food losing its flavour with my mood. When I finish breakfast, I look at Mama, 'May I work alongside you today? I'm craving an intellectual challenge.'

Mama clasps her hands together in front of her face and lets out an audible breath. 'Let's make it tomorrow.'

I close my eyes and smile. I've been waiting for this day since I was sixteen after witnessing Mama on that day I stood in the shadows in the forbidden part of the underground castle. What I saw had confused me, and shocked me, to the point that I felt faint and was nauseous, but I couldn't risk being caught, so I ran with quiet steps to my room, released my stomach contents out the window, then laid on my bed and cried.

I open my eyes and look at Mama. 'Thank you. Tomorrow will be great. I'm really keen to enter the world of scientists!' I hope my words deter Mama from thinking that I know exactly what she does in the ventilated rooms filled with jars of flowers, of perfumes, of paint and paint brushes, with an artist busily sketching and painting beside her as she worked. The castle has eyes and ears and my known movements are reported to Mama. Perhaps she knows that I saw her that day.

'It will be lovely to have you beside me. I think it's time for my Ari Bear to step into the world of adulthood. At eighteen, you're old enough.' Mama stands and pushes in her chair. 'Under your plate is the list of errands you need to complete today. Wear your favourite flower in your hair for dinner tonight.' Mama bends over and kisses my forehead.

'Sounds like fun,' I say, my voice too bubbly. Will she believe my lie?

As she leaves the room, I push my plate to the side, revealing the note with the list of errands.

- Carry baskets of apples to the kitchen from the fruit trees.
- Freshen flowers in the vases around our home, and create an extra special one for the centrepiece at the dinner table tonight. We're having guests.
- There's a book in the upper library I have put aside with some carnations on top of it. The book needs to be delivered to Mrs Grobbler.
- Ensure you wear shoes to dinner tonight.

CHAPTER 12

I mentally calculate how long each of the unchallenging errands will take, which in reality could be carried out by the castle workers. It's my intention to return to *The Beyond* and observe and learn today. I note that I will need to take a sketchbook and pencil to keep details. I shake my head. The errands have thrown my plans into disarray. I will have to wait until the day after the morrow as going to *The Beyond* will take the entirety of a day and I would never get my errands done, disappointing Mama. The flowers and trees as my witnesses, I have already disappointed her enough in my lifetime so far.

I pick up the note and put it in my pocket, push my chair in, pick up my plate to take to the kitchen. The sooner I finish my chores for the day, the sooner I will have time to work on tasks for myself.

I prioritise the list.

1. Apples
2. Deliver the book
3. Flowers for decorating

Then head to my room to dress in camouflage outside wear for chores. A dress with equal parts floral and greens and greys. Flower house and forest colours. The cloak I was given from *The Beyond* would be perfect for in our kingdom. I would blend in perfectly. Unseen.

I jump out the window, my bare feet squashing a white cosmos flower. As I feel the bare earth beneath my feet, I sigh. I'm eighteen. Is it time for me to wear shoes as per the kingdom rule? At what point does defiant lose its flavour? Did Papa wear shoes when he was a grown up?

I wriggle my toes. Nah. It's safe in the kingdom. I'll stand by my bare feet policy. With that decided, I take off to the fruit orchard, running and jumping over logs and small boulders along the way. I turn back to see if my new protector is following me. No sign of anyone. How can he, she, or it, be protecting me?

I slow when I arrive at the orchard of fruit salad trees in the cool of the morning. It's the month of apples—red, green and yellow—on the same tree. This is the perfect time of the day to pick the fruit.

'Good morning, Ari,' voices call as I arrive.

'Good morning. It's lovely to see you today,' I say in return, following their eyes as they gaze at my bare feet with a slight smile decorated on their faces.

I watch as apples are tasted before harvesting from the tree. It is the best way to check for ripeness. They wear baskets in front of them to help with the strain on their backs. It's easier to place apples gently into the baskets after twisting them off, stopping them from bruising. I watch as they gently hold the fruit in the palm of their hands with their thumbs near the stem, then, with a simple twist and a gentle lift upward, the apple releases with the stem attached. Apparently the stem increases the apple storage life.

When I was little, I often played in amongst the fruit trees. I started calling them the fruit salad trees and it stuck. Each tree produces a different fruit each month. It's a perfect visual calendar for the passage of time. Mama said the trees had been grafted to fruit that way, here in our very own kingdom, and the leaves were used for medicinal and scientific purposes.

As the filled baskets are placed on the ground, I pick them up and, one at a time, deliver them to the castle kitchen where they will be taken to storage below ground, where the temperature is optimal so the apples last for six months.

Twelve baskets of apples are delivered. I stretch out my back as my muscles complain. When I wander through the kitchen after the last basket, green apples are on the table. Apple pie for dessert tonight. My stomach smiles.

Errand one complete.

I head to the upper library to find the book needed for delivery. But I don't take the direct route, I head to the floors below the castle first, the ones that Mama calls the heartbeat. After a glimpse inside the building in *The Beyond* yesterday, I want to see if similar people traversed through the heartbeat of our castle.

I stand out of sight behind a supporting column, making myself invisible. And there I see people carrying bundles of flowers, dressed in the same garb as I saw in *The Beyond* yesterday. My breath hitches. Is Mama in on this? Does she know what was going on?

When the coast is clear, I make haste and ascend the hidden steps to the ground floor, and then continue until I find the concealed spiral set of steps that lead to the library. I pause before I enter, looking behind me. I had yet to glimpse of my new protector.

I place my back against the door, and run my hand down the timber until I find the secret latch, which I push inward, and the door opens. I slip inside the room and close the door, delighted to be met by the smell of old library—*vellichor*—the smell of old books, alluring, woody and earthy, which makes sense considering books are made from paper that comes from trees. There's also the slight hint of smokiness. For a moment I wonder what the flavour of books would be—would it be dictated by the art on the cover, by the words kept within them, waiting to be released to enter into the mind of the reader, or by the vintage of the paper.

I decide I am a library sniffer tragic.

I walk around the room, running my index finger over the spines of the books, meticulously placed on the shelves. I climb the ladder right up to the top shelf of books, because, what are ladders for, and then mosey my way to the book that sits on a small table in the middle of the room, with a small bouquet of pink and white carnations on top.

I push the flowers off the hard book cover and look at the title, appreciating the book cover art of a kaleidoscope of flower colours and the font used: *The Psychology of Flowers*. My heart smiles. Mama has been using the psychology and language of flowers all my life by using fresh bouquets on my windowsill every morning.

I unwrap the string that has been wound around the book and finished with a tag that has the name of the person to deliver the book to. I pick up the book and sit in the wing chair and open the first page.

Then close it again.

The inside and the outside titles don't match: *The Psychology of Flowers* and *The Quest for Immortality – the experiments, the science, and the reality.*

Slowly, I open the book again, and flick through the pages.

Handmade paper.

And all handwritten words. Some by Mama, and others by multiple scientists. The contents read like a history of the search for immortality, followed by specific scientific experiments, and the progress, including the very precise scientific method of question, research, hypothesis, experiment, data analysis, conclusion, and communication, as Mama had taught me, and when I was younger, the do, does, what or will, taught to me by my governess, whom I outgrew with my knowledge.

The Quest for Immortality … Mama said not to fear death, because it was like a new beginning, like birth. If that is what she believed, then why was she contributing to a scientific and medical book about never dying? About being immortal?

I look up. Claude Monet presents himself. The brown mink Tonkinese cat with blue eyes that mysteriously seems to appear in castle rooms like he was stalking people and could materialise through walls. He jumps onto my lap and starts to purr loudly, then turns around several times before he curls up.

'I know, Claude. You are the spectator, the judge and the psychologist, wrapped up in the nine lives of Claude Monet. We should have named you Vincent van Gogh after your vertigo incident when you moved in with us as a wee little kitten. But it was your chewing of the paint brushes that sealed your name. What do you think of living forever?'

Claude meows.

'I agree. It would have to come with strings attached, like the type of life you would live. Imagine living in a terrified state, or a broken body or mind, or where you knew not of where your next meal would come from, or if you were even going to be safe. And that aging body. I wonder what Noah looked like at 950 years of age?' I stroke the soft fur of Claude, behind his ears and under his chin. 'Thanks for the conversation. It was on point as usual. Gotta errand to do though. We'll speak again, Lord Claude,' I say, then encourage him off my lap.

I close the book, wrap the string around it exactly as I had found it, pick up the flowers and leave the ancient library with its hidden secrets. The name on the tag for delivery will take me on a small journey. My shoulders slump. It will take me longer than I anticipated. Why couldn't Mama have a servant do this menial task?

CHAPTER 13

Annoyed, I decide to cut down the time of the journey by taking a short cut through the King's Forest. Forbidden, naturally. But with no protector following me like a dark, heavy cloud, there would be no one to tattle on me.

The moment my bare feet connect to the ground of the King's Forest, I can feel life.

And strangely, death.

I can feel living rocks, and connection, like an eternal storm of happiness.

And sadness.

Of stories desperate to be told from the trees, their wind whispers filled with the age of the earth, its past, present and future. Their branches reaching down to embrace me to tell me of the gift of life, whispering secrets into my ears. The glorious sun beams down on the leaves, scattering its light from the canopy to the ground, flickering on me to the same rhythm of the beat of my heart. We are all connected.

By life.

After half an hour of running, swallowed up by the wonders of the trees that give the earth life with their breath, I arrive at the lakeside and stop. Breathless.

In the middle of the lake sits the lighthouse.

Empty.

And battered.

Windswept.

And lonely.

My place of discipline of my youth.

At least once a year.

I shake my head. Mama said forced contemplation and reflection would reset my inner self-control. Except my forced contemplation and reflection was like being in prison. It was true that I lived my life on the edge, following my emotions, my imagination, ignoring that voice that said no, don't do it!

Ignoring rules.

Ignoring the honour of others.

Mama said the one thing that doesn't abide by the rule of the majority, the popular vote, that thing that you are doing that feels good at the time, but is not good, is a person's conscience.

Mama said that conscience is like one thousand eye witnesses, the reflection of our souls.

Mama said there is no accuser so formidable as conscience, which resides within us.

Mama said we know what is right and wrong, the moral law written on our hearts.

The lake looks magical today. Calm. Like it rarely is. I find my deck chair and drag it from where Eli had hidden it after my run-in with alcoholic apple cider. The incident that caused a rift and broke our connectedness.

I lower myself onto the chair, wishing I had my groovy

sunglasses, and suddenly feel the severing of my tie to my protector, Eli, like a punch to the gut travelling through my body like a wave.

The lake shimmers in one particular place, like it has a tremor. Exactly like that time Mama had banished me to the lighthouse again, like the locking up of a princess in the tower.

Control. It was all about control. Discipline Mama called it. But I beg to differ.

My mind wanders. Back to that day when I was sixteen, doing solitary confinement at the lighthouse. That day when the lake shimmered, like it had a tremor. But only in one patch of the lake that was a different hue of blue, just beyond the rocks of death. Sometimes the blue hue was there. Sometimes it was so faint that you easily miss it.

But I knew.

For all the days I had spent at the wretched lighthouse, I was an observer. I knew the lake like the back of my hand. Back on that day, that patch of water was lighter in colour. Vibrant. Like a glowing light aqua blue halo. And it was always calm. Even during the tumultuous storms that ravaged the water and made the lighthouse structure creak like the bones of an old person.

Except for that tremor. On that day.

I sucked in a deep breath, seething that Mama had forced me to stay at the lighthouse against my will like a prisoner. I was a prisoner.

'ABUSE!' I wanted to yell out to her at the top of my lungs, screaming so loudly that she would hear my voice, making it gravelly and scratchy and sore. Mama would have said I was only hurting myself, child!

The sky changed colour. Sunset. Yellows and oranges and pinks and purples rising to hues of gradating blues, brushed onto the sky canvas leaving me ache for freedom. And for my own easel and canvas to replicate what I see. I dragged myself inside and added a tally mark onto the wall where I counted my sunsets of imprisonment. Of punishment. Of confinement. Of refinement. Of disappointment. This time, twenty-seven. I had one more day to go before someone would come from the mainland to get me.

It wasn't the longest time I had been here. Nor the shortest.

I winced at the memory of my brilliantly designed brightly coloured paper planes, and how they caused me to be at the lighthouse. Again. I didn't even get to record the all results of my uplift experiment. The possibilities of my paper planes were boundless. Their height. The distance travelled ... I got caught for breaking the rule about colour.

I returned to my spot on the deck of the lighthouse. My sunset spot, where a symphony of yellow, orange and red hues painted the sky while the day dissolved into a soft, dreamy twilight. And then there were the colours of that place in the water that never changed. An aqua blue. Like a halo.

The lake, now a dark ink blue in colour, shimmered again.

And stilled.

White bubbles appeared in the centre of the water halo, popping like bubbles in the bath. One or two at first before a rush of bubbles created a rapture of violent looking water that was letting out its anger, like a volcano about to erupt.

I stilled and held my breath, my heart thumping.

Should I run to the panic room?

Should I stay to see what happens next?

Fight or flight or freeze?

A dark head popped up in the midst of bubbles. I gasped. Human or animal, I wasn't sure. It began to move away from the halo of light and the bubbles in the halo ceased. The creature barely disturbed the water in its smooth swimming action.

I hid around the corner of the lighthouse house watching it with dread.

Did it know I was here?

I slipped inside the lighthouse to the store room and grabbed the broom and a knife. Defence.

I would kill it before it killed me. Mama wouldn't survive if I died too. Like Papa.

I stepped back outside and looked over the side of the railing. The creature moved closer to the lighthouse. Seal like in shape and movement. It stopped at the end of the jetty and reached up to the ladder. Long arms and hands. It wasn't a seal. It was a person.

My heart raced. The lighthouse was our safe haven, inaccessible to the lawless ones. I chose to fight with an unexpected and surprising charge from the shadow of the lighthouse. I didn't want to be like a scared victim hiding, shaking in wait of my fate.

I blew a breath between my lips and positioned myself in the shadows. And waited. And listened.

The deck of the lighthouse could never be silent with the loose nails and bolts and uneven weather beaten wooden boards that had been severely damaged during a violent storm. It was hazardous to say the least. If you fell through the boards you would join the dead men in the rocks below.

The creaks came unevenly like an unsyncopated rhythm. The intruder was unsure of its steps. And then the creaks came at an even sound, like the beat of a metronome. My heartbeat quickened. There was no attempt to conceal the sound of footsteps. Was this intruder from our kingdom?

The footsteps stopped, and then I heard a loud sigh.

I peeked around the side of the lighthouse. There was a human form in a dark wetsuit. A man with broad shoulders. He pushed the hood from his head and a mop of dark hair fell across his eyes. He pushed it to the side and looked up at the lighthouse light that didn't work, and shook his head from side to side, then took a step toward the door.

Do I attack now, or follow him inside and attack from behind? If I attack out here I can wrangle him to the side of the jetty and push him over the edge. Inside would not offer such a victory.

I jumped out from the shadow with a loud wail, 'AAAAAAH!'

and charged at him holding the broom in front on me like a joust, ready to push him to the edge.

He moved impossibly fast as I swung the knife around, and then he was behind me and pulled me against him. He held my hand with the knife and moved it towards my neck.

Panting hard I knew this was it. I should have hid in the panic room. Mama said that baby girls often didn't live long. It was an act of compassion to prevent a traumatic future. I froze, nausea filling me.

'Dead. I thought you might have perfected your defence, Ari.' His voice was deep.

I narrowed my eyes. *Dead.* The word I could never forget from our childhood. Our play fights. 'Elias?'

'The one and only.'

He released me and I turned to face him. 'I wished you were dead … that day we were struck by lightning.'

He looked into my eyes then lowered his head and gave a crooked smile. Like he always did. That crooked smile that made me absolutely furious. It was so smug. But this time, it sent a warm glow through me. My breath hitched.

'Long story.' He presses his lips together. 'I'm here to deliver a note from your mother.' He unzipped his wetsuit a little, reached inside and pulled out a folded note and handed it to me.

Our fingers touched as he handed it to me and he raised an eyebrow.

'A note from Mama can't be good,' I whispered. I traced my index finger over the rough homemade paper and opened it.

My Dearest Ari,

Another 2 weeks.
Sorry. It's for your safety. My priority.
I love you, Ari Bear.

Mama Bear xx

I folded the note and shoved it into my pocket, anger filling me. She was treating me like a child. Again. I was sixteen!

I looked up at Eli. 'My jail time has been extended. I was hoping I would get an early release for good behaviour.'

Eli chuckled. 'I doubt that you can be good, Ari. You're always in trouble.'

I gave him a shove. 'Hey! That's because you always did something to my game and I had to retaliate. That's when I got into trouble.' I poked him in the chest. 'Because of you.'

He raised his eyebrows. 'I can't argue with that.'

He looked to the side and I followed his gaze to the aqua blue glowing halo.

'You have a lot of explaining to do. Will you stay and eat with me? It has been twenty-seven days since I have seen someone.'

He closed his eyes and shook his head.

'Please. It will take thirty minutes at the most to eat together.'

He walked over to the handrail and looked out. 'The lake can change at any moment. I need to get back.'

I looked at the water, then up at the indigo sky. I put my finger into my mouth to wet it and then held it up to feel the air. It was still, and the smell of marine heart notes wafted up from the lapping water. I turned to Eli and looked up into his eyes, one blue, one green. I shook my head. 'Thirty minutes won't change the weather today.'

He looked over the water and to where the glowing halo was.

'Please,' I whispered.

He turned back to me and narrowed his eyes at me. 'Fine. But no longer than thirty minutes.'

'Fine.' I turned on my heel and made my way inside the

lighthouse, to the kitchen, and fussed about finding the more "tasty" foods I had in storage. I paused. What if I shared my portions with him, and then I was left with no food? An extra two weeks will really stretch what I have here. I flutter blinked. I could do this. As I gathered food I said over my shoulder, 'Do you want to get out of your wetsuit? I have some dresses you could wear.' I turned to him with a smile.

He raised an eyebrow at me started to unzip his wetsuit. 'Sure.'

'Through that doorway you'll find a lovely assortment of fine couture for dining. There is a dress code. No wetsuits.' I turned away from him with a smirk.

I quickly arranged the food on a platter in the middle of the small, scarred, square wooden table and placed two plates down, then sat and waited. When I heard his footfall I looked up. He stopped walking and took a bow in his black wetsuit rolled down to his waist, wearing a cerulean tie. I raised my eyebrows at him. 'Is that it? A rolled down wetsuit and that tie?'

He looked down and ran the tie through his long fingers. 'Yep. Putting on a wet wetsuit is difficult … and if I have to move fast it will cost me precious time.'

I lifted my chin at him and gestured for him to sit opposite me. I couldn't believe he had found that tie. That tie I had made him wear when we were young.

'You know. I always hoped that we could be friends when we were younger—' he started.

'Friends don't treat people like the way you treated me.'

'But your reactions were always so good.' He chuckled.

'You were downright annoying and insufferable.'

Eli ran his hand down the tie again. 'Why do you have this here?'

'It's my proof of victory.'

'Your *one* victory,' he added.

'A very satisfying one at that.' My memories floated before me. The invitation to the treehouse. That call in the letter for him to wear the tie I had left for him in a secret location. The exact place for him to stand and the whistle rhythm he was to use to tell me he had arrived for our grand tea party, knowing perfectly well that he hated tea parties. But he always went along with my shenanigans. I had made it my lot in life to outdo him, and I would keep trying until I did. I hid in the treehouse and watched him approach from far off, looking through Papa's binoculars. The ones I was told not to touch. Nobody saw me take them.

Eli's strides were long and determined. He stopped at the cross on the ground where I had told him to in the note, then whistled the beginning of the happy birthday tune. It was then that I released a rope, and a net came up from underneath him, trapping him off the ground unable to escape. I climbed down the ladder and stood underneath him, his eyes penetrating mine with hatred. I smiled. 'Dead,' I said, using his word he always threw at me when we were in a game and I had lost.

'I hate you, Ari Flora!' he said through gritted teeth.

'The feeling is mutual, Elias Wolfe!' I crossed my arms and smirked at him, and left.

That night as I turned in for bed, the tie was neatly laid on my pillow. I'd be in trouble again. Mama always believed Eli's word over mine.

'Non-deniable,' he said, his words cutting into my memory, and looked up at me with a smile in his eyes.

'Please, eat. It's a peace offering.'

He lowered his head, then closed his eyes and sat still, before opening his eyes again and started to select foods from the platter. 'Thank you.'

'Thank you for staying for a while. That tie still looks good on you.'

He looked up at me. 'Still?'

'Yep. It looked good on you when you were walking towards the tree house. And when you were fuming with anger, it matched the colour of your right eye.'

Eli shook his head. 'Girls and their comments about my eye colours.'

'Do you feel like a freak?'

'A freak?'

'Well, your unmatching eyes are … rare.'

'Except in the story of the wolf my father always told me.'

'Is that where your middle name comes from?'

He nodded. 'Which of my eye colours do you like best?' he asked.

'Who said I liked your eye colours?'

He looked at his food, shook his head and smirked. 'Touche!'

We ate in silence then, a peace falling around me making me uncomfortable. He was always my nemesis when we were younger. Did he feel it too?

He stopped eating and gazed at me, for too long, making me feel self-conscious.

'What?' I shook my head and blinked with anxiety.

He narrowed his eyes at me again then shook his head, mimicking me. 'Nothing.'

'Liar!' I said.

His eyebrows creased. 'I kindly stay to eat with you at your request and you call me a liar?'

I closed my eyes and sighed, opened then and looked into his eyes. 'Bad choice of words.' I raised an eyebrow at him. 'Care to share your thoughts?'

He lowered his head and gave a crooked smile, then looked up at me. 'No.'

I looked down at my food and closed my eyes for a moment. 'Fine.' I looked at my clock, the second hand ticking away the movement of time. 'Fifteen minutes and you are free to go.'

'What? I'm a prisoner?'

'Obviously, I'm the prisoner. You are just the forced visitor.' I put my hand onto my forehead and closed my eyes. I wanted to stand abruptly and put my food in the trash and tell him to leave, now. I didn't like how he was making me feel. Vulnerable. Weak. But I knew I needed to eat to keep up my strength to get off this lighthouse. I was planning to escape.

'You've changed. That's all,' he said, breaking into my thoughts.

I opened my eyes and raised an eyebrow at him. I wanted to say, "Thank you, Captain Obvious," but I held my tongue. I decided to make him squirm. 'How's that?'

His Adam's apple bobbed up and down. He finished his mouthful of food then sat back on the chair. 'Well … you're taller—'

'As are you … expected of course. That's what growth hormones do.'

'Nah. It's not that. You seem … calmer—'

'Do you want to test it out like you did when we were young?'

And there was that crooked smiled again, sending a warmth along my skin. I looked at my food, then shoved the last mouthful into my mouth, my cheeks flushing, the effect of his presence giving me away.

'It's nearly time for you to leave,' I said, standing and clearing the table and moving to the kitchen. It would soon be dark and I would have no light.

Eli walked over to my wall of *everything*. My mind ponderings, my inventions, my artwork. Mama said it looked like I had lost my mind. Little did she know it was the exact opposite. It was finding my mind. Finding me.

He scanned the entire wall, tilting his head left and right as he read my genius scribing onto the wall. My wall of *everything*.

'What are you thinking … about my wall of *everything*?' He was making me nervous. Or maybe he didn't understand any of it, my intellect superior to his.

'Well. I see it is the world as you know it.' He pointed to the map I had created. 'But here,' pointing to a large boulder, 'is incorrect.'

'Incorrect?'

'Yes. When you return home, go and check it out.'

'I will … to prove you wrong, Elias Wolfe.'

He looked down with that smirk. That smug smirk like he was right and I was wrong. 'You know, this wall is nothing. You know nothing except your sheltered existence of protection in the bubble of the precious castle with your entitled life. You know nothing but your learned education from books. You know nothing about the outsi—' Assim stopped.

'Outside of what?'

He let out a sharp breath. 'I've said too much.' He shook his head. 'You don't even know what your mother really does!'

'My mother? Tell me!' My voice was quiet. Too quiet.

He shook his head. 'I'm sorry.' He winced, pulled off the tie and dropped it onto the table, fitted his wetsuit and pulled out a silver canister. 'I have to go.' He turned and left the room in haste, walking along the dilapidated jetty.

I ran after him and stopped in front of him. 'What is that?' I pointed to the canister that was now gripped between his teeth. 'And, what is that?' I pointed to the glowing halo. I had meant to ask him earlier. When he had arrived.

He ran his hand over his forehead, removed the canister and took a deep breath. 'This is my oxygen, and that,' he pointed to the glowing halo, 'is like … an underwater cave.'

'That leads to?'

'Somewhere.'

'Somewhere,' I whispered full of anger, fuming at his lack of information like I was not his equal. Why was he treating me like I was a child? 'And if I were to dive down into it—'

'You'd die. Dead. And your mother would be furious with me.'

'Now that's the understatement of the year!'

'She's protecting you. I am merely the messenger. Obey your mother.'

'My mother, who apparently I don't really know! Am I living inside a lie?'

Eli cleared his throat. 'Thank you for the food.' He raised his chin and looked down into my eyes, holding my eyes in his, like he was trying to tell me something. He walked briskly then, carefully choosing his footfall on the timber jetty that was strewn with rotting timber. I followed, trying to keep up, and stopped at the end hand rail, watched him climb down the ladder to the platform, put on long black swim fins and a black diving mask. And then he was gone.

After three minutes, the glow of the aqua blue halo went out, and the lake became pitch black, indistinguishable to the silhouetted mountains in the distance that I knew were there.

Suddenly I felt alone. Like his presence had taken some of mine with him.

I turned and walked back to the lighthouse, barely visible in the fading light, taking care to walk on the jetty boards I knew would not fail me.

Two more weeks according to Mama. Less, according to me.

I woke early the next morning before the sun kissed my face, and returned to the large basket I had woven from all the baskets of supplies my mother had sent over the years. It was my escape plan, acting as a type of boat that would allow me to get back to land. I had almost finished waterproofing it with materials removed from the numerous umbrellas stashed in the rooms of the lighthouse. One more layer and it was done.

My fingers worked nimbly, weaving and securing, connecting and smoothing, and then it was finished. A woven forbidden escape boat for one, with a ridiculously, insanely haphazardly coloured interior that would make a rainbow flip upside-down into a smile, and laugh.

I was keen to leave the lighthouse of my isolation.

And ready.

Chapter 14

I ate food from my pantry like it was my last meal, just in case my escape ended badly and I joined the tales and songs of the sea of souls, of the once upon a time, of lost and broken boats and dead bodies of ancient sailors, where their flesh once fell off their bones as fish nibbled at them. Then I grabbed my vintage blue school port of *everything*, already packed with my diaries filled with secrets, my art supplies, my dried flowers, and my coloured ribbons of remembrance, and placed it into the waterproof boat, then dragged it along the dilapidated jetty, grabbed a plank of broken jetty wood, and lowered the boat into the surprisingly calm lake.

Anxious. And worried.

I held the boat still with one foot as it gently bobbed up and down with the excitement of a child about to go on an adventure, then, holding on to an old creaky pier, placed my other bare foot into the boat, and pushed off with the plank of wood. Once I had my balance, and had checked for leaks, I started to paddle with the wood, a faux oar, hoping that I wasn't being watched.

After twenty minutes of battling the now choppy lake, the

shape of my basket boat and my aching arm muscles, I hit the shore line. Wasting no time, I alighted with my vintage blue school port of *everything*, and headed towards the stone I had sat on when I was twelve. It was a marker for the tunnel entrance that led to the kingdom. Or out of the kingdom I should say. We used it once, when we evacuated the kingdom to save our lives. All I had to do was to recall the right pathway amongst the deceptive false walkways that all led to a trap, an underground cell where you were sorted as "ours" or "theirs". Mama said that being "theirs" was a bad thing, and to make sure that I *never* went there.

My memory served me well. Mama told me to always be aware of my surroundings, and to note way markers. I found myself in a familiar thoroughfare beneath the castle. I hid in gaps and behind structural pillars to remain unseen. I was meant to be at the lighthouse, after all.

Then I walked to the place Mama told me I was never welcome to. Ever. She said it was a place that broke her heart. It was a place that made her tears cascade like waterfalls. It was a place where she never wanted Papa to do the dance of sleep with death. It was the place she wished had never existed. It was the place she wanted to protect me from, and the great heartache it caused.

As I turned the corner to that place, an earthy sweet scent, sharp like the smell of cut grass lingered, that smell, which was the grass sending out an aromatic distress signal to surrounding vegetation. As brutal as the conjured image of grass screaming for help was, my mind drifted to hot summer days and running under the sprinkler to get cool, and ice-creams melting faster than I could eat them.

Mama's voice flowed from the room in a sing-songy voice that was filled with love and sadness at the same time. In that place that broke her heart. I put down my vintage blue school port of *everything* and moved closer to the entrance, remaining hidden behind the structural post.

'Welcome to the Field of Flowers, my love,' Mama said.

I peered around the doorway, pretending I was invisible. The room was filled with light. Mama wore an apron over her shirt and pants and she stood beside a stone table next to a person who was lying on a large piece of off-white cloth, like cotton. Beside the person was a man, sketching.

Mama reached over to the metal trolley that held a number of instruments and jars and flowers and string. She picked up a cloth and dipped in into a solution. 'My love, this will sting for a little bit. I'm sorry if it hurts you.' Mama moved the person's hair behind their ear to the side, and wiped the skin with the cloth. She seemed to let out a breath of relief.

I inhaled sharply. Loudly. It was an involuntary reaction. Mama moved her head to look up, and I moved behind the doorway to keep out of sight. I used my deep diaphragm breathing so I did not appear to breathe. Silent. So I didn't arouse suspicion.

Outside the door it was hard to hear. I waited some time before I had the courage to peak around the door again. Mama grabbed some string and tied the hands together of the person, and then the feet.

My heart raced. What was she doing?

Mama reached for some oil scents, and dabbed them on the person. 'You'll love these perfumes of parsley, sage, rosemary and thyme—for Quietus, immortality, remembrance, and courage. They are to honour you with their scented kiss.'

A kiss?

'Jacob, how's the portrait?' she said.

'Almost finished,' he said.

'Wonderful. Help me prepare the cocoon once you are done.'

Cocoon?

I swallowed the lump in my throat. Too loudly. Mama moved her head to look up again, and I moved behind the doorway to keep out of sight.

Why would you put someone in a cocoon?

Emotionally charged tendrils spiralled out from me and

shock shuddered through my bones. Was this person was dead? I couldn't breathe. Mama's job was with death? Violent nausea rose and I held my hand over my mouth tightly. I turned and ran, grabbing my vintage blue school port of *everything*, that now seemed like nothing.

I ran through the castle floors below, up the hidden spiral stairs and to my bedroom, where I made it to my open window and released the contents of my stomach.

Death? Mama worked with death? Surely I had misinterpreted what I had seen in bits and pieces like a jigsaw? Surely I had misunderstood. Mama would never work with death. Or cause death … would she?

A light breeze licks my cheek and brings me back to the present, my mind emptying as I sit on the blue deck chair of swiped alcoholic apple cider memories. After the revelation of that day of witnessing Mama, possibly working with death, I found it hard to come to terms with what Mama had possibly hidden from me. It can't be real. And I consciously pretended I had never seen it. I pretended it never happened, and I did the only thing I could. I forgave Mama for her omission of truth about her job. *If* I was correct in what I saw.

Mama said that memories are changeable, and can evolve based on the recalling of the memory. Perhaps my mind was filling in the blank parts. Making it up. Perhaps Mama didn't work with death, but worked to help people with their health.

I inhale deeply then stand. I have a book to deliver. I drag the deck chair back to its place of hiding, then continue along the lakeside for a bit before I enter the King's Forest, the clearing, and over to the multi-coloured camouflage coloured doors that stand beside trees in the village, masking the steps that go below ground to quaint homes of kingdom residents.

No. 82. The sage coloured door.

I turn the door knob, open the door and enter, taking three

steps before the ground opens with a concealed staircase that leads to another door. A bright orange door. I smile.

Mrs Grobbler opens the door before I knock on it, and welcomes me with grin. 'A lovely, but expected visit, Ari. Would you like to share in a cup of tea?'

I return her smile, but not with my eyes. 'Do you have any other beverage on offer?' I ask, not a huge fan of the fabulous tea society.

'Lemonade? Freshly made this morning.'

'Absolutely, yes please!' I say with enthusiasm. Mrs Grobbler leaves to prepare the drinks, and I look about at the room filled with plants and musical instruments. An experiment she is conducting, I am sure.

'Don't touch anything, and do sit at the table, lovely Ari,' she calls, her voice echoing with tones of baroque, of curvy lines and golden leaf.

I place the book and flowers on the table and argue with myself about which is the best seat to take. I choose the one where I have a view of the entry door, as well as a view of the doorway to the kitchen.

Mrs Grobbler appears with a tray of drinks and … cake? Mrs Grobbler isn't known for her fine baking, but she is known for her rustic cake styles, no two cakes ever looking the same. She says the problem always occurs when she removes the cake from the tin.

She places the tray in the middle of the table, and proceeds to pour the lemonade into my glass and the … *was it cake?* … on plates. I inhale the delicious air, the song of the lemon in the lemonade overtaken by a chorus of the sweetness of chocolate and sugar and a little vanilla gracing our presence.

She takes off her glasses and places them on the table. I frown. Surely the glasses help her to see better?

I sip the cool, sweet lemonade. 'The best lemonade,' I say.

'Oh Ari, you're too kind.' I watch as Mrs Grobbler uses a fork to dig into the what smells like chocolate cake. Sweet and inviting.

Mama said everything had a story. Everything. Even the piano sitting out in the Field of Flowers. Did that include Mrs Grobbler's cake? I pick up my fork and slice off a piece of the spongy sweet food.

Mrs Grobbler giggles. 'I call it my earthquake cake. Whenever I make it, it splits like it has been in an earthquake. It likes to give me a different perspective of topography each time—you know, mountains and valleys, and when I ice it, the rivers are created.'

I tilt my head to the side a little, surprised I can see the topography she is talking about. I place the chocolate cake into my mouth. It is soft and delicious. 'Mmmm! A party for my tastebuds. I love your earthquake cake!' I say.

Mrs Grobbler squints as she cuts another piece of cake. I lift her glasses from the table and hand them to her.

'Thanks,' she says, 'but I like to listen without them on. 'I can hear the shape of words better without clear physical vision.'

I push my cake around on my plate. What an odd thing to do.

'You know ... like hearing truth in words, versus deceit in words,' she adds, answering my unasked question.

Is she accusing me of being one who would lie? 'Oh,' I say, my voice little. Am I that transparent? Do others think the same thing?

When I finish the earthquake cake and lemonade, which, I decide do not go together well—I should have opted for the cup of tea like Mrs Grobbler—I sit back in my chair and look about the eccentric room again.

'My living experiment,' Mrs Grobbler says, answering my unasked question again. 'I am exploring whether the resonance of music creates changes to the chemical composition of any of the plants, and then if so, what happens to them. The study is almost finished.'

'I didn't know plants had ears,' I say, knowing very well they do not.

'They don't, but they most certainly have vibration-sensing receptors, and can feel the music.' Mrs Grobbler puts her glasses on.

Is this part of the immortality research? It would make sense that I was delivering the book to her to contribute her results to.

'I love the sciences and maths. I want to step into the world of science as my chosen field.'

'We'd love to have you on board, Ari.'

'I'm just waiting on Mama to approve of my request.'

'Perhaps I can help persuade her decision.'

I give Mrs Grobbler a smile full of sunshine and yes pleases. 'Mrs Grobbler, did you know my father?'

'Everyone knew your father, Ari. He was an amazing man. What in particular would you like to know?'

'How did he make people feel? Like … were people scared of him?'

'Oh gosh, people were not scared of him. They respected him. He was held in high esteem. He had a gift of making people feel important, and valued, no matter their role in the kingdom. He would often sit and eat with the cleaners, thanking them for their service, which he told them was the most important job in every place on the earth.'

I raise my eyebrows.

Mrs Grobbler narrows her eyes at me. 'His flaw though … he hated wearing shoes, and would go bare feet throughout the kingdom, much to your mother's dislike.'

I wriggle my toes. If I had shoes on, I wouldn't be able to feel how cold the floor was sub-ground level. Nor would I be able to feel any vibrations, like I can feel now. There are footsteps coming down the stairs toward the entrance of Mrs Grobbler's house.

There's a knock at the door.

'Come in,' Mrs Grobbler calls.

I watch as the door opens, and Eli stands there. His eyes wander from Mrs Grobbler to me and back again. He walks toward Mrs Grobbler and holds out a letter to her. 'A dinner invitation … for tonight.' Eli releases the letter into her hands.

'Thank you. Care to join us for cake?' Mrs Grobbler asks.

Eli gives her a smile. 'Thank you, but not today. Another time would be nice. I've got to go,' he says, dips his head, turns and leaves the room, without even a glance at me.

'Oh, that reminds me. I have to do the floral arrangement for the dining table for tonight. I must go, Mrs Grobbler. Thank you so much for the refreshments and conversation. It was lovely,' I say, and stand.

'Of course. Go you must. I'll see you tonight, Ari.' Mrs Grobbler waves me off with her hand.

I push my chair in before I leave. Mama said good manners are vital. Always. I ascend the stairs two at a time and look about for Eli. He is headed for the castle ruins. I run and catch up to him, and punch him on the arm.

'Lame,' he says, keeping his eyes locked on the castle.

'Lame? What is lame is you not even acknowledging me at Mrs Grobbler's!'

'Yeah, well …'

Using two hands, I give him a heavy shove to release some of my anger.

He winces. 'Are you done?' He looks at me and raises an eyebrow.

'Why are you treating me like this? I don't understand?'

He stops walking and faces me. 'I am no longer your protector. There is no need for us to interact.'

'But how could we not. It has been you and me since we were born. You before me.'

'Not anymore.' He looks around then starts walking briskly again. 'By the way, your new protector will be at dinner tonight.'

'How do you know?'

'The invitations. Twelve guests.'

'You know my new protector?'

'I've always known your new protector.'

'And …'

'And that's all I can tell you.' Eli starts to jog.

But I stop walking. 'You're not even going to say goodbye!' I yell.

Mama said words have weight, and some words are impossibly heavy. But what about unspoken words? Are they more painful? I turn my head to the side and a tear falls. Eli's and my story isn't supposed to end like this. Our story is meant to be that we would be friends forever, no matter what.

I sigh. In the end, I thought, we have no control over another person's actions or feelings.

Mama said don't look back on negative occurrences. Don't ruminate. Don't dwell in the past. Mama said to choose to move forward. The past has finished. You can't change it. Just learn from it.

I inhale deeply and head east to the greenhouses of fruits and vegetables and herbs and spices, and the flower house, the grandest glass house of them all. It's filled with flowers and work tables and colours and floral scents that make you think of happiness and wonderful dreams. Perhaps a dream of Eli and I as friends could be created there.

The flower house sits in the middle of a circular configuration of eight other glasshouses. And this configuration sits in the middle of a large farming field of crops where people work from the morningtide to eventide.

I smile at people and say hello to the farmers as I walk past them, barefooted. It is something I imagined my father would say, and undoubtedly my mother. I find a path lined with flowers and smile—the path to the flower house—not planted, purely organic as seeds from flowers fell to the ground as they were carried. Wild flowers.

The moment I open the white wooden door to the flower

house, floral scents loom. I walk in and look about. Glass walls and ceilings. And colour. Everywhere. It is my favourite spot to hang out when it rains, watching the rain fall on the glass ceiling, then run down the window panes on the sides.

I grab a bucket and some floral scissors. Ordinary scissors never do as they crush the little water carrying vessels in the stems.

Even though my encounter with Eli has not been a good one, he did give me some information about the dinner tonight. Twelve guests. Including mother and me, that makes fourteen. Two floral bouquets are required.

To the bucket I add white roses, apricot peonies, spectacular pink dahlias and the palest and most delicate pink roses, as well as some green fern leaves. It is like a touch of spring elegance for the dining table.

Then I grab another bucket, this time to add blooms around the castle rooms. White hydrangeas, pink carnations and orange snapdragons.

I head back to the castle, entering through the main doors, then to flower table in the kitchen to create the floral arrangements, a cleaner following me, washing the dirt off the floor from my bare feet. 'Just like your father, Miss!'

I smile.

I place the floral arrangements in their set places, then return to my bedroom and await the door knock that would be Mama. She would oversee how I dress tonight and how I would control my curly auburn hair.

I sit at my window seat and watch the sea of coloured flowers dance to the inaudible music. If I went to the Field of Flowers, would I hear the music too? If I danced, would Eli dance with me too? Or would my new protector step out from their camouflage?

Three knocks on the door. I turn my head and watch Mama come towards me. I move to a chair. This is what Mama and I always did when we would invite others to our table for dinner.

Mama stands behind me, and creates an updo with my hair

that would be acceptable for guests. Taming my wild locks. I shake my head. 'I don't want to look like your twin with our hair,' I say, not to be mean, but I don't like being compared to her, as much as I love her.

Mama blinks when I say that. Did I hurt her feelings?

'Noted. But dear Ari, your hair is far more beautiful than mine. It is a joy to style.'

'Thank you, Ma. You know that I love you, but I want to be my own person.'

'As you always have.' Mama finishes my hair and smiles. 'Now that you're eighteen, choose your own clothing for the dinner.' Mama places her hands lightly on my shoulders. 'The floral arrangements on the dining table look stunning by the way. Thank you.' Then she leaves.

Eighteen is starting to feel good. Eighteen is starting to feel like freedom. If only I didn't have to do things in secret, like going to *The Beyond*.

CHAPTER 15

I don't join the guests for pre-dinner drinks. I hate small talk. I hate trying to find a common piece of ground that we both share and then talk about, and offer pleasantries based on physical attributes to break the ice. It is exhausting. Too many questions trying to pry out information just for a pleasant discussion. I'd prefer that mother gave me a cheat sheet about each person so I could cut to the relevant conversation. It would save time and energy.

When the bell sounds for dinner, I enter the noisy dining room, and at once the chatter stops. Eyes fall on me and then after a beat, a couple of smiles. My eyes connect with Mama's and I wait for her approval, but it doesn't come. Anxiety pools in my stomach as I am guided to my seat at the table by a servant, the fabric of my pants making a swooshing sound in the silence, not that I could've missed my seat, it's the only one left. I am placed beside women dressed in beautiful floral gowns, like Mama would have chosen for me to wear. I unbutton my father's black coat when I sit. At least Mama will be happy that I wore shoes.

I look over at Mrs Grobbler and she gives me a smile. I smile back.

'For those who have not formally met my daughter, this is Ari—intelligent, kind, curious and … sometimes full of surprises,' Mama says with a smile.

Quiet laughs sound around the room.

Did Mama mean I am challenging, non-conforming, stubborn, opinionated or difficult?

'Ari—the twelve from your right—Miss Alice Horton, Mrs Rose Franklyn, Mr Edward Franklyn, Miss Charlotte Hays, Miss Emily Lewis, Mr Alex Franks, Mr Ben Fisher, Mrs Sophie Harvey, Mr Garrett Harvey, Mrs Claudia Grobbler, Mr Nate Quinn, and Mr Asher Cooper.'

I smile at each as their names are said. Some hold up their wine glass in greeting. Why did it matter whether they are Miss or Mrs or Mr? We should be introduced as ourselves. We are not the possessions of another, even if we are married. Furthermore, why are women called Mrs when they are married, but the title of a man does not change?

'Lovely to meet you all,' I say, wondering who is my new protector?

As dinner is served I look over the guests, trying to read body language, eye glances or eye avoidance, to try to figure out who my protector is.

'Penny for your thoughts, Ari,' says Nate.

'I don't even know if my thoughts are worth a penny,' I say.

'Share and let's see,' he says with a grin.

'Well,' I look around the table, all eyes are on me, 'I was mentally calculating the required force to catapult rubbish into space—not that we have any rubbish here in the kingdom—but, hypothetically, if the world was over populated and rubbish was a major problem in climate change, how much energy would that take? And then, I was wondering why rubbish would be catapulted into space, or dumped on the moon? Surely rubbish floating around in space will end up A) plummeting back to earth or B) on another planet, that is, if it doesn't burn up on entry, assuming the planet has an atmosphere. And if it's dumped on the moon, that is just an abomination! Can you imagine looking up at a moon that looks like a rubbish tip?' I close my eyes then say, 'Gosh, keep our rubbish here on the earth, or better still, don't produce volumes of useless crap!' I press my lips together and shake my head.

Conversation breaks out around the table, and arguments. Alice, beside me, asks what the rubbish is that I am speaking of. Has she never seen the photographs of rubbish in the magazines in the Museum of Earth Time, or read the stories of climate change, or … it dawns on me then, she is a rule keeper, obedient to the rules, and never ventures where she is told not to go, unlike me.

Mama clears her throat and avoids eye contact with me. She is the only one who returns to eating dinner. Does she disapprove of me sharing my thoughts, or of my brash wording?

'Sorry, Mama. I will choose my words more carefully,' I whisper.

Mama stops eating, puts down her fork and says, 'No, Ari. I want you to be yourself.'

I tap my foot on the floor. Mama's words and her facial expression do not match. She lied.

Whilst guests are in conversations about rubbish, I watch them. I have pegged Asher as my protector. He seems braver than the others. Fearless even. I just need Eli to confirm my suspicions.

'Papa's coat looks good on you,' Mama says to me. 'He would have loved your company here at the table with us.'

I put my hand over Mama's and give it a gentle squeeze. Then I sit back in my chair and listen to conversations and watch body expressions. People are more interesting than I thought.

'Zarah,' Rose says to Mama. 'I have word of a change in Jedburgh, one that might be to our advantage, though there is no word from Lerwick.'

From the corner of my eye I see Mama's head shake side to

side quickly, with a side-eye aimed at me, and a sudden hush falls over the table.

'Jedburgh has been … feeling unwell lately,' Mama says, a lie and an attempt at a cover up. I narrow my eyes at the words of Mama's lie. There is no one called Jedburgh. It is the name of the city in *The Beyond?*

'But I saw Lerwick just the other day,' I add. This statement is entirely untrue. I'm wanting to feel the reaction in the room, and to see if any more information slithers out.

'If you see him again, tell him to visit me, Ari. He loves my earthquake cake,' Mrs Grobbler says.

I raise an eyebrow at her and give her a nod. I feel embarrassed. Caught out. She would have felt the shape of my words. My lie.

At that moment dessert is served. Apple pie as I expected after my apple basket deliveries this morning.

'The flower arrangements on the table are divine, Zarah. Who created them?' Charlotte says.

'It was Ari. Freshly collected today,' Mama says, smiling at me.

'Will you re-purpose them to *The Quietus* in a few days?'

Mama clears her throat and looks down at her dessert. 'No. These flowers are from the Flower Glass House at the farm where all varieties of flowers grow throughout the year.'

The Quietus. Is this where I witnessed Mama working with death? Supposedly? Or had she killed someone? Was the person even dead, or had my mind connected the dots of what I saw incorrectly? I looked around the table, wondering which order the guests would eventually die in. Who would be first?

'Ari, you've been quiet. What are you thinking?' asks Garrett.

Oh—such a dangerous question. My current thoughts will not go over well. I should make something up. Something cheery. I look over at Mrs Grobbler. She takes off her glasses. They are like a truth detector. I have to tell the truth.

I take a deep breath, rolling the words around in my mouth,

hoping they will come out with the least bit of sting. 'Well,' I move my dessert spoon around in my bowl, 'I was ruminating … about life, and … I thought that … one day … everyone you know, will die.' There. I said it.

'That is true or course, Ari,' says Sophie. 'It's the circle of life, unless you find the elixir of immortality.'

'But,' says Alice, 'if people lived forever on the earth, would they lose their value, their importance to you? Would moments be so flat and boring? Would there be no hope for something better?'

'Imagine watching history unfold before your eyes,' says Nate.

'We are unfolding history, Nate,' I say. 'But what if, your body was diseased, or you were poor, or homeless, or hungry all the time, would you enjoy immortality? Is immortality only for the rich who live a supposedly wonderful life?'

'Good point, Ari. The quality or quantity question,' says Mama. 'How do you know about capitalism?' Mama pulls her eyebrows together.

'From my history lessons, of course,' I say.

'Ari,' says Asher. Our eyes connect for a moment, then he looks down at a speck on the table cloth. 'Don't wade in the waters of deep thought of the unknown too often, it will pull you down.'

'Thanks for the reminder,' I say.

Mama always said to think about whatever is true, whatever is noble, whatever is lovely, whatever is admirable, whatever is excellent or worthy of praise for my mental health and happiness. I am prone to overthinking. Asher had just said the same thing in different words. Is he my protector?

Hot drinks are served after dinner, but I decline. I bid the guests goodnight, for tomorrow I am working alongside Mama. The evening has been revealing. Information spilled that was not supposed to be shared, and the possible identity of my new protector.

Silence.

And speaking.
Revelations.

And cover-ups.

Mama said to be *careful* how you
write your chapters of life,
and the *choices* you make,
for you are *accountable*.
It is expected that *mistakes*
will be made along the way.

Learn from them.

Always seek to *forgive* others to *release yourself*
from the *control* of the person who harmed you.
Always *seek forgiveness* from ones you harmed.
And *forgive yourself*.

Ask for *wisdom* in all things.

CHAPTER 16

Blue forget-me-not flowers sit in a small white vase on my window sill. The colour of the spring sky. Cute. And delicate.

And makes me cry.

Mama always leaves forget-me-not flowers on my window sill when she will be gone for a day or two. It is her goodbye without saying goodbye because she hates saying goodbye. I am never up early enough to catch her when she leaves. I had no idea when she would go, or exactly where she went, or what she did. All I knew is that she is not here. And that meant that I will not be working alongside her today.

My heart sinks and my energy evaporates like the wispy clouds blown in the winter wind. I was more than ready to adult. Why is she always the block to me helping like an adult?

The first time Mama left without saying goodbye, I was five. I woke to the sight of the blue forget-me-not flowers on my window sill. And a note. I could already read. Mama said that reading was the most important thing to learn at school, as once you could read, you could do anything.

Dear Ari Bear,

I'll be away until you wake tomorrow.
We'll have a fun breakfast together down by the river.
These flowers are called forget-me-nots. If you look at
the tiny, pointed leaves, they look like mouse ears!

But more so, I left them for you because they mean
remembrance, true and eternal love, and devotion.

I love you, Ari Bear. See you tomorrow at breakfast time,
down by the river.

XX Mama

P.S. Don't forget your shoes!

Mama always said when something happens that's not in your plan, to ask, "what's next?" and to change your plan and move on. So that's what I'll do. My heart lifts. Today is now a freedom day for eighteen-year-old me. A gift Mama did not know she was giving me. Mama is not here to go looking for me, or asking after me. I render a working mind plan for my return to *The Beyond*. Had dinner guests reinforced the name of *The Beyond* slip at dinner last night? Jedburgh? Lerwick?

I want to visit the village. Where the humans are.

I throw my blankets off and leap out of bed, invigorated with a sense of dangerous exploring, open the window shutters and look out at the Field of Flowers, looking serene and in full bloom spritzing the air with happiness.

I dress in my designated Friday clothes—clay brown wide-leg pants and a coconut hue long-sleeved button-up shirt even though it's Tuesday. And leave my bedroom and go to the kitchen and grab some bread and fruit.

'Miss Ari, are you off on an adventure today?' asks the kitchen hand.

'Yeah, nah. Just around the kingdom today to do some sketching. And … I want to lay back on the grass and watch the clouds collide,' I say, absolutely telling a yarn. Mama would call it a lie, but I like to call it creative licence.

A thousand mind witnesses pleaded with me to tell the truth. My chest tightens and guilt washes over me.

'Watch out for the storm clouds. Ya don't want them throwing lightning bolts at you!'

'That's for sure,' I say, and remember that day back when I was with Mama, when I was ten. The summer sky was a perfect blue and a cool breeze licked the beads of sweat off my face. Back before the afternoon of the terrible storm. Just one, unexpected lightning bolt. Mama should never have gone inside the castle to fetch the afternoon fruit. If she was with me, she would have stopped my argument with Eli, before the incredible blinding light and deafening crack.

I reach up to my shoulder and follow my lightning scar with my finger for as long as I can reach, over my back. It's my forever reminder of that day that can't be changed. That day I nearly died.

Did I deserve to be hit by lightning?

Was it because I was being mean to Eli?

If I had been kind to him, would I be living a different life now?

I shake my head. He deserved it. He deserved every one of my words of spite. Of words shaped with ugliness, of words Mama always said to swallow because they would hurt the heart of another. But they tasted so bitter I had to spit them out.

I gaze out the kitchen window toward the lightning tree, split in half, but growing stronger than it has ever grown. My ten year old self came into my mind vision, like watching myself in third person, and then I slipped into the person of my memory.

I had spent the entire afternoon building a house from sticks under the shade of the tree. It was magnificent. Mama called me a clever architect, my heart glowing with pride. I gathered some leaves to place on the roof of the house, and organised some more as a little blanket to have a pretend tea party.

Mama ran her finger down the side of my face, tilted her head to the side and sent a smile to me, filled with warmth and sunshine. She loved me. I could feel it. 'I'll be right back with some fruit.'

I returned her smile and she left. I looked back to my colourful leaf assortment.

A shoe appeared in front of me.

Then another shoe.

I knew who it was. Eli. In one swift movement, he swung his foot into my stick house.

'Nooooooo!' I yelled, but it was too late. The house I had spent an entire hour building came crashing down.

I clenched my fists and stood up, facing Eli. 'You always ruin my games!'

'Not.'

'Do! You wrecked the doll I made. You ripped her arm off! And when I was about to catch a butterfly, you blew on it and it flew away. And my tree swing. You raised it so high I could never get onto it again. Not to mention the mud pie I made that you pushed into my face. You ruin everything! I don't want to see you. Ever. gO aWAy! ELIAS!'

Eli took a step closer to me. 'I can't. I mean … I want … to never see you again. But I can't.'

'Go away! I HATE YOU!' Tears streamed down my face.

Eli grabbed my arm. Tightly. 'I told you. I can't.' He narrowed his eyes at me in anger and a lock of his dark hair fell over his right eye, blue, his other eye green. I wished I had blue eyes like his one, instead of the changing moody grey eyes of my father.

'And look at you. You're ten but you act like a twenty year old. I haven't even seen you smile! Flynn is waaaaay nicer than you!'

He swallowed, and his eyes filled with tears, then he released my arm.

A sharp sizzle sounded, followed by an immense cracking boom and the world exploded in white light that slowed-down time. The world became silent as I fell to the ground in slow motion, my back searing with pain. Jolting, excruciating pain. Followed by the tingling of pins and needles over my entire body, like ants walking all over me. My mother's face was over me then. She was blurry. Her mouth was moving but all I could hear were some high pitched sounds like the hiss of a snake. I turned my head to the side and saw a blurry Eli lying beside me. Motionless. Was he dead?

Then I could see no more.

I woke in the cot in the underground medical room of the kingdom. That place where injured people went for treatment. The lightning had struck the tree, and then one arm of the lightning hit both Eli and me. It's called a side flash, Mama said, and Eli and I acted as a "short circuit" for some of the energy in the lightning discharge.

Eli wasn't there in the underground medical room. He had disappeared.

'What's for dinner tonight?' I ask the kitchen hand, back in the present.

She gives me a smile with the tilt of her head. 'You are really thinking of dessert, aren't you?'

'Yes,' I say, 'I'm hoping it's apple crumble.' I place my hands in front of me like I am praying.

'Let me have a little whisper in the dessert chef's ear, Miss Ari.'

I lean forward and hug her. 'You're the best!' Then I turn and start to walk away.

'Don't be late. We don't want your mother to be suspicious of what you are planning to do today,' she calls after me.

I turn and walk backwards, giving her the thumbs up with a smile.

I enter my bedroom and close the door, then pull the charcoal grey backpack out from under my bed, unzip it and remove the clothing to wear, including the new flexible breast plate.

After I change clothes for *The Beyond*, I place my food and flask of water, my sketchbook, pencils and watercolours, and a forget-me-not flower into the backpack.

I wet my right arm with some water, then place the tattoo barcode patch over it. After a minute I peel off the paper, and the tattoo is on my skin. I add a couple of spares to my bag just in case of emergency.

I slip the small black sound device into the pocket of my dark grey hoodie in case I get attacked. Humans or animals, what else could there be that would attack?

I sling the backpack over my shoulders, go to the floor door and open it, and climb down the ladder a little, close the floor above, and descend the ladder to the tunnel below my room. I pull my hair back to look like a boy, adjust my hood over my head to conceal my face, then begin my adventure to *The Beyond*. My quest to find answers.

The tunnel ends when it becomes the entrance of *The Forbidden Beyond*, hidden behind a mirrored wall in a room inside a building with people hurrying about. Quiet people. Quiet people who walk with shoes that make no sound. Like back in the kingdom. I step out into the large area like a foyer and pull my hood further over my head, put on my black sunglasses, and leave the building into the outside of lifeless grey. I lift my eyes, but not my head, to the above. Drones are flying about like flies, monitoring. Hundreds of them. A shiver runs down my spine and I return my eyes to the front.

Is my protector here? What if I need my protector?

I use my breath like I was taught, concentrating on deep diaphragm breathing so I don't appear to breathe, trying not to lose consciousness. My new breast plate is so much more comfortable. I relax a little and look for people. Real people. It would be better to be amongst multitudes of people, to stay invisible. Safer.

They are up ahead. I walk towards the low level structures where I had been previously, copying how others walk. Again, some stop and seem to reach up to touch something, but there is nothing there. They don't walk with silent steps like I have been taught. Sometimes, they lift their hands and look at it, then tap it, before continuing toward the structures, getting closer now.

A checkpoint appears. The feminine being holds out a device and people place their right hand near it, the device scanning the flesh between the index finger and thumb on their hand. It beeps, and the person continues to walk.

The being stops before me, and there's a sound like a sigh, like the releasing of some air. I push up my sleeve on my right hand and hold out the stick-on tattoo barcode for scanning. I hope that if I don't touch the device it will still work.

I close my eyes briefly, my heart thumping in my chest. The scanner beeps and relief floods through me. I want to let out a quiet breath in relief, but it feels too dangerous.

'You look too young to have a barcode,' the being says, its voice too smooth and devoid of emotion.

'My body keeps rejecting the chip … like an allergic reaction,' I say in my practised teenage boy voice.

'It happens,' it says. 'Have a good day,' it says then, its voice now a replica of my fake voice.

My arms prickle with goosebumps.

I gaze at the face of the checkpoint being. Its facial expressions seem restricted. Frozen and limited. It seems so … empty. Soulless. And how can it copy my voice like that?

'Thanks,' I say, then walk in haste, worried that I will be found out for having a fake barcode, or worse, being found out that I am not from here. Worse still, that I am a girl.

In the distance are low level structures where people walk to. A destination. I pick up my pace, adrenaline telling me that I am not safe here, and I need to hurry.

The grey structures in the distance can be seen now, and I step into the group of close knit houses and alleyways.

I slow my pace as I look for the waymarker for the alleyway I had committed to memory before I left with my helper.

I stand outside the door of where he had taken me, and raise my hand to open the doorknob. I turn it.

It was locked.

What next? He said he would take me to where the humans are. Why did he keep saying the humans? What else is here? Aliens? Monsters? Shapeshifting creatures? Why aren't humans everywhere?

Mama said there was more to our world than we could see. Sometimes the unseen was heard, felt, or smelt, and most of the time we recognise it as a knowing within our spirit, knowing that something wasn't right. Mama also called it intuition, the gut feeling, instinct, our seventh sense.

I turn and walk back down the alleyway, keeping my hooded head lowered, and controlling my breath like I have been taught. At the end of the alleyway, I turn right and kept walking along the roadway.

A presence appears beside me. I can feel it, but I don't turn my head to look at it.

'You need a new name for your boyhood.' It's him. My helper.

'I have already chosen. Yarrow,' I say with my new voice.

'A herb.'

'Correct. I also have some in my pocket as a distractor. Do you?'

He chuckles. 'I used to keep the edible green plant, Sorrel, on me. But now I wear the scent for when I can't get my hands on the herb. People assume I'm named after my scent.'

I nod, noting the notes of lemon zest that lingered about him. 'Walking to find the humans?'

'Yes.'

'Anyone in particular?'

'Yes.'

'Who?'

'My father. Mother said that one day I will meet my papa. She said I will recognise him instantly because our souls are connected.'

There is silence. And it unnerves me. 'Do you know my father, Azriel Cohen?'

'Nay,' he says. 'When did you last see your father?'

'Never. He was taken before I was born.'

'You know … Yarrow … there is a very high possibility that your father is dead—not that I want to upset you, just don't get your hopes up.'

'But Mama said she can still feel him in her heart. She said if he was dead, she would know it.'

'I really want you to return to your home. It's not safe here.'

'I need to know what all of—' I wave my hand around over the landscape, '—this is. I need to know why it is so different from where my home is. I need to know what my mother is lying to me about.'

Sorrel inhales deeply, not concealing the noise. 'Then survival 101 is your speed lesson. Are you ready?'

'As ever.'

'This way.'

We make a right turn down a pathway that is less travelled. I make a mental note of a landscape mark so I can identify it again.

The basic landscape does not change.

'Walk in front of me. We'll look less like humans then. The others don't walk in pairs or groups. They're not social beings.'

Less like humans?

Sorrel slows while I keep the same pace. I listen for his voice from behind, not knowing whether to trust him or not. I need to see what he is doing. But what choice do I have?

'Wherever you are, observe others around you and act like them, socially and physically. Do not underestimate the power of mimicry. It will save your life.'

'Is that it? Monkey see, monkey do?'

'You need to conform and fit in as a survival tactic. You will meet some humans. If they suddenly act cold, non-reactive or don't acknowledge you, that means there is danger about. Copy them. It will save your life.'

Mama used to play a game with me when I was nine. She called it copycat. Whatever she did, I had to copy, exactly. We played the game in the castle, outside in the castle grounds, and she would dare me to copy the servants until I annoyed them and they got angry with me. That meant I had won.

'Also know that the Leges walk among you. They will step in at the eleventh hour to help you. Sometimes they are not successful.'

'What then?'

'Pray.'

'Pray?'

'For divine protection. Pray for *The Unfolding* in history to come soon so that all of this age of deceit stops, and we can reclaim what is rightfully ours again. Pray that your name is in the Book of Life.'

A shiver runs down my spine. Death. He is talking about my impending doom. My impending demise that will break my mother's heart.

There's silence now. And I start to doubt the wisdom of coming here. Would it be better for me to stay in the kingdom where it was safe? And happy? Lost in my books and art and history of the world that seems to be in denial about the reality of the here and now.

'Anything else I need to know?' I ask.

'Just … keep your wits about you, and don't stay here too long. You need to return to your mother. She will never recover if something happens to you.'

I close my eyes for a moment while I walk. He spoke the truth. But what if, what I was doing will help *The Unfolding*? I just have to make sure that nothing happens to me. Isn't that why Mama has given me a protector?

Where is he? Or she?

'Before I leave you, remember the name Cassia. She is a miracle worker in Lerwick, where you are headed to. And knowing her, she will probably find you first. Stay safe, Yarrow. Don't look back at me.'

I fault in my step. Sorrel is leaving? I want to look back and ask him to come with me, or to thank him if he won't, but he has told me not to. So instead, I pick up my pace. Lerwick is in my sight.

And then it is closer. The various shades of brown timber, the grey smoke rising into the air, van Gogh swirl style, and as I come closer, there are people. Everywhere.

I hope they are the humans I am looking for.

Soon after, I find myself on the main street of Lerwick, each foot step creating a powder puff of dirt that rises and disappears. On either side of the street are propped up roofs and annexes made of shabby material or mismatching iron, connected houses that have been hand built from left over wood, scrap plywood and corrugated metal, thick cardboard and plastics. It's like its own little bustling village.

And people are everywhere. And hidden food and water in glass bottles with a blue label, clothing, household items, exchanges made with the sleight of hand if you watched long enough. Most things are handmade.

These are the people not interested in earning credits to enter the next hierarchy in the control of their lives. These are the people who are aware of the timeline of the future of the world.

What was to come.

I stand to the side and watch people like Sorrel told me to.

Monkey see. Monkey do.

Mostly they don't talk to each other. Mostly they don't move their heads to look at each other. Mostly, but not always, their heads are covered with a hood, their faces concealed, dark glasses on. Mostly, their mannerisms and physical movements are like mine. And for some, they are not. They are different. Their balance seems centred differently, their footsteps too careful like they are thinking about where to place their next footstep, their arm movements too smooth and lacking in flexibility, and their blinking too calculated.

Odd.

And then I see a familiar face and my heart lifts like a paper plane soaring into the sky. 'Lou?' I say, and surge forward toward her. She's dressed in garb similar to mine, except her head isn't covered and I wonder why for the briefest of moments. Why is she here and how is it that she knows about *The Beyond* and I didn't? My heart swells with sunshine, and then I gasp as my breath is knocked out of me. An arm wraps around my waist and I'm pulled to the side into the dark shadows of a gap between huts.

'That's not Lou. Stay behind me and don't speak, Ari.' It's Eli.

'I'm Yarrow, and I can look after myself, Elias!' I say.

'I'm Kale, and clearly you can't. Now hush!'

I peer over Eli's shoulder. A group of three are gathered, wearing light blue shirts. I watch as others slip in shadows and disappear into dwellings.

'Breathe like we were taught,' he whispers.

I breathe without detection and listen as footsteps come

closer. I press myself against the rough metal side of the dwelling, and turn my head to the side to try to disappear completely.

Eli reaches inside his pocket, slowly, then tosses a small item up the street, the clank of it hitting the ground in the silence. Startling. I watch as the blue shirt "people" run up the street, their movements smooth, not like the up and down motion of a normal person.

'Don't move,' Eli says.

And I don't, trying not to faint from my restricted breathing. It is the panic inside me stealing my oxygen.

One by one, life returns to the street. But it is still far less populated now after the commotion I had caused.

'Follow me, Yarrow. Two metres behind. Head down.'

Eli turns this way and that, and finally into a shanty that has no windows, then into a side room, after he knocks on the door. If I have to make my way back to return home, there is no way I will be able to navigate it.

He pushes his hood off and his dark curly locks fall over half of his face, concealing the green eye, leaving his blue eye exposed. He paces the floor, stretching and fisting his hands too many times to count. Then he stops before me, pushes the hood off my head and slaps my breast plate with the back of his hand. 'Dead. I couldn't forgive myself if that happened. What are you doing here? Why are you here? I don't want you here ... Ari.'

He paces the floor again. Then stops. 'I knew who you were, even dressed to look like a boy.'

'I look exactly like a boy, Elias!'

'But I could smell you before I saw you!'

I narrow my eyes at him and shake my head.

'I've been around you since your birth, for eighteen years. You have a ... scent ... unique to you.' He reaches forward and pulls me toward him, and holds me in an embrace, almost like he cares about me. 'Please ... go home and never return. You don't belong here,' he whispers into my ear.

I allow myself to sink into his arms for a moment. My face is close to his neck, his skin warm and comforting. I turn my face to his shoulder, close my eyes and give him a quick kiss on his exposed skin. 'Thank you,' I say and step back from him.

He runs his hand through his hair, like he is disarmed. Challenged. Undone.

'Lou?' I say with an unfinished question.

'That wasn't her. It was a humanoid made in her image?'

A sinking feeling fills my stomach, and I shake my head. My throat feels tight. I have been deceived by a humanoid built to look like my friend, Lou. My day has shattered.

Eli closes his eyes. 'Look. I want to get you back home where you'll be safe. I'll talk to you there about Lerwick and humanoids and immortals and the trapped.'

'Eli, you know that I will keep returning here until I have exhausted all my questions about this place.'

He presses his lips together. 'My life's challenge. The uncontrollable king's daughter.'

'King's daughter?'

'You don't know, do you?'

'Apparently not.'

Eli reaches for my hand, his eyebrows pulled together. 'You're too pretty to be a boy,' he whispers.

'Then I shall unpretty myself,' I say.

He looks down with a crooked smile, then looks up at me. 'Let's go home,' he says. 'Follow me.'

He drops my hand and pulls his hood over his head. I follow suit and walk behind him out the room and out of the windowless dwelling and onto the laneway, staying two metres behind with my head low. After walking for about fifteen minutes, the street become busy and voices can be heard.

Eli stops walking and stands under a roof made of hessian. 'This is the market place where you want to be, and where you will possibly find your answers. But you need to visit often so that you become familiar and they accept you as one of their own. Ten minutes to observe, and then we leave.'

CHAPTER 17

Eli wanders away, walking through the market tables and sits around a fire with some others, shaking hands in that manly way that I need to learn to do. After five minutes of strolling slowly past food and water and clothing, I turn a corner to another gathering. A man sits on a small stool, whittling wood. In a basket beside him are wooden toys he has made. And beside him sits a man who paints the wooden toys. I pick up one toy that looks like a doll and run my finger over the curves and the smoothness of the wood. The whittler looks up at me.

And my breath catches.

His eyes are the same colour as mine and I feel a tug at my heart. All of a sudden I forget how to breathe and stumble backwards, then leave in haste, back to where Eli had left me.

I realise then that I still have the wooden doll in my hand.

I can't return it.

I don't have the courage to go back there. I shove it into my pocket and try to quiet my racing heart, shuffling from foot to foot while I wait for Eli.

All I want to do is to run.

'Follow me ... Yarrow,' Eli says.

'Two metres behind ... Kale,' I say, and follow him.

But instead of following the road to the checkpoints for scanning, he turns right on a lesser path and into a dense dead wooden forest, then down a concealed hole which leads to a tunnel.

We remove our dark glasses and walk for twenty minutes until we find ourselves at a crossroad of many tunnels. It's like a labyrinth. Eli points to a mark on a wall—a flower—this is our tunnel back to the kingdom. He picks up the pace then, and I follow behind in quick steps.

'Why are we walking so fast?' I whisper.

'To beat your mother. I don't want her to know that you have been to Lerwick or Jedburgh. She would be horrified and probably isolate you at the lighthouse again, this time with a guard.'

'My moth—'

'Shhhh,' Eli says. 'The less noise the better.'

We travel in silence for an hour. At the waymarker to my room, Eli stops walking and faces me. 'Remember where you had a tea party with the skeletons? I'll meet you there at 2 pm tomorrow.'

I nod, then hold out my hand, the wooden doll on it. 'I stole this doll, accidentally. Can you take it back for me. I feel terrible.'

Eli takes it from my hand and looks it over, his eyes meeting mine at times. He places it back in my hand. 'Keep it ... as a souvenir, or better still, you return it with an apology.'

I let out an audible breath. Eli is right. I should be the one to return it.

I start to walk toward my tunnel then stop, and turn to him. 'Ah ... thanks for ... today. And yeah ... I still haven't seen my protector, have you?'

Eli smiles. 'I have. It just hasn't shown itself to you yet.'

'It?'

'Them, they, he, she ...'

'I get it. See you tomorrow. 2 pm with the tea party chatterboxes. Man I kept you entertained when I was young.'

Eli gives me that crooked smile again, and this time he smiles with his eyes.

I inhale sharply as a warmth rushes through me, lifting me and making me feel high for a moment in time. I blush and hurry off.

I can't have feelings for him.

He is my childhood protector, my nemesis.

I told him I hated him too many times to count.

I find the ladder to my room and climb it, stop near the top to listen for noises, like the sound of castle servants who carry out maintenance or cleaning. It's quiet, so I open the floor door and climb up into my room, and remove my masculine clothing, keeping the wooden doll, and change into loose fitting trousers, the colour of indigo blue and a white blouse. No shoes. I slide the wooden doll into my pocket.

I push my *Beyond* backpack containing *The Beyond* gear and slide it way under my bed, then grab a new sketch book, climb out the window and go to my secret place, the dusty broken black grand piano beneath the dangerous ornate dusty staircase in an unused, forbidden part of the castle.

The dilapidated grand piano has black and white keys that are broken and uneven, and I discovered in my exploring days, that if I push one key, a secret miniature door opens beneath the piano, at the wall behind it.

I push that key now and crawl under the piano, through the door the size of a large dog, then stand in the clean, airy, semicircular room with a view to where the north wind begins. I walk to the tall window and look beyond the King's Forest, and beyond the dense jungle of gnarly manchineel trees, where the sap falls like raindrops, burning people and animals, causing the skin to blister and even death. My eyes greet the mountains on the horizon where the sky meets the earth with gentle stories of history, of writings of a new day.

Then I sit in the midnight blue wing chair, white walls surrounding me, and look at each of the plants I have brought here to make it homely, pretending that I am a grown up with my own house.

This is my place of chosen solitude, unlike the lighthouse that is forced solitude.

I remove the wooden doll from my pocket and place it on the wooden side table, and reach for a pencil that sits in a baby blue case. I open my new sketch book and start to detail everything I have seen and smelled and felt in *The Beyond*, mapping and labelling and illustrating, adding watercolours that sit ready in wait on the side table.

Mama said memories were malleable. Whenever you recalled one, it changed a little, like a grape vine of gossip. That's why she keeps daily journals, so the truth would not be distorted.

I lift the wooden doll and caress the smooth timber, rolling it, turning it, studying the carved details.

I sketch it, paint the sketch, and add a rough portrait of the doll maker.

Then I sit in silence and gaze out the windows, my memories of *The Beyond* now permanent, recorded as letters and words and sentences and paint.

When long shadows waft into my secret place, growing like they are living, breathing creatures, I close my sketch book. I pocket the wooden doll, stand and pirouette, slowly, taking in the changing light inside and outside the room, and note the daytime sky stories told to the mountains, coming to an end as their colours blend together.

I crawl through the miniature door, under the groaning grand piano and back outside, where I lie on the grass and watch the clouds collide for a moment, then to my bedroom.

I steal a moment in time to recount my day before I walk with bare footsteps that slap a beat on the cold stone floor to the dining room.

Two dinner plates sit on the table.

Mama will be joining me.

While I wait for Mama, I place the doll near the arrangement of flowers; pink forget-me-nots and small leaves with a bluish-green tinge.

Mama enters the room and sits next to me.

I smile at her. 'How was your day?'

'Busy. And good. Yours?'

'As per usual. I'm looking forward to helping you.'

While dinner is served, I watch Mama's eyes wander to the wooden doll. She reaches over and picks it up. 'Where did you get this from?'

'I found it deep in a garden where I used to play when I was little,' I lie—my conscience like a thousand witnesses burning my skin pleading with me to tell the truth.

I ignore it.

'Your father liked to work with wood, creating toys for the little ones in the kingdom.'

'Mama, do you have any photos of Papa?' A change of topic will stop the flow of interrogatory questions, pushing me deeper into the lie that I will get lost in and make more complicated, forgetting the details of the lie.

'I do.'

'May I see them?'

'Of course. After dinner.'

'Mama, what did you do today?'

'I visited a friend and we did some research together … he—'

'He? Was it Papa?'

Mama shakes her head. 'I wish.'

'Are you romantically involved with him?'

'No. There could never be another after your father. He's coming back one day, Ari. I know it.'

'But what if he doesn't?'

'He will. I can feel it here.' She places her hand over her heart.

I look down at my food, then eat in silence beside my mama. My beautiful mama, tinged with a sadness the colour of grey that follows her everywhere.

Is it grief?

Is it a longing?

Is it a yearning?

Is it a never-ending internal wail that started the night that Papa was taken?

What if she is wrong and he is long dead?

I feel so confused. I need answers.

Why is *The Beyond* like it is? Why does it feel like the people are captives? Why do I smell fear in the air and see it in their eyes, and if not fear, their eyes are dull, hope lost, like pieces are missing from them.

And what is the humanoid that Eli spoke of?

What is Mama protecting me from?

I place my knife and fork together in the middle of my plate like they are hands on a clock. 12 o'clock. The language of cutlery. Table etiquette, as Mama has taught me. Good manners. Self-control. The sign of a respectful person. I have to work on both, they don't come naturally to me. Mama said I was born with a mop of defiant hair to match my spirit, and unconventional was my favourite pastime. She also said I was born with a strawberry coloured angel's kiss in the shape of a heart on my forehead, and in the right light, she could still see it.

Mama places her knife and fork in the middle of her plate. I lean over and pick her plate up and place it on mine, then stand, and take them to the kitchen.

When I return, Mama has a photo of Papa on the dining table. I still as my heart quickens at the sight of my papa. He is real. He is not a once upon a time. I want to cry.

'Can I keep it?'

'No. But you can keep it while you draw a portrait of him.'

'Thanks, Ma … can I work with you the day after tomorrow?'

'I'll let you know. My day to day can change at the drop of a hat, as you know.'

I nod, then run my finger over my father's photograph, his auburn hair the same colour as mine, short sides and back, his hair longer on top and a wayward lock, wild like the storm clouds. His moustache and beard have streaks of golden highlights, and were groomed to perfection. His grey eyes were sparkling, like he was laughing at something, with overflowing warmth and love. I wish I could look into those eyes. I wonder if I would see a reflection of myself in them. Acceptance. Love. Would Papa love me even if Mama said I was stubborn and defiant. Am I really like Papa?

'Ma, what did you love most about Papa?'

Mama closes her eyes for a bit, like she is travelling back in time, back to Papa. Then she opens her chocolate brown eyes, lit up with threads of gold, of love. 'Oh … he was physically strong, a protector, but he was also so gentle, so thoughtful, so full of kindness and compassion for others, serving them. He was a one of a kind.'

'Tell me how you met again, Mama. It makes me laugh and gives me hope.'

Mama smiles. 'I had just bought lunch at the cafeteria at university, and was carrying my tray of food to a table to sit with my friend, when the heel of my shoe broke. I wobbled like jelly on a plate and my tray tilted and my strawberry milkshake spilled over a man who happened to be sitting in the wrong place at the wrong time. He was wearing a white cotton shirt, now splashed with pink.' Mama burst out laughing. 'I picked up my serviette and tried to clean it off, apologising profusely … and then we both laughed, and our eyes met, and that was when boy met girl and our hearts entwined. I ended up splattering strawberry milkshake on other parts of his shirt to make it look like it was a work of art.'

I laugh so hard. Imagining my very careful and particular mother being clumsy is hilarious. 'What did Papa study at university?'

'He had finished his medical degree and was an anaesthetist, and was researching a new type of anaesthesia, a state of unconsciousness but where the surgeons can communicate with the patient's internal body awareness that innately knows exactly where that place in the body is, that needs repairing or curing, removing the sometimes guesswork of doctors, and the unknowns that had not been identified. It was bordering on being able to train the mind for self-repair and rejuvenation, perhaps even being able to extend life spans. He was also investigating where body time could be suspended, where you could perhaps go into hibernation like some of the animals do ... slowing aging ... healing in sleep ... and then *The Unfolding* started, and everyone scattered. And that's how we ended up here.'

'*The Unfolding?*'

'Mmmm.' Mama looks at her watch. 'I'll tell you more another time. I have things to attend to before I come to do your hair before bed.'

'I can do my hair myself, Ma.'

'I know, my love. I just enjoy spending that quiet time with you while I can.'

I share my smile with Mama. 'Thanks for the photograph of Papa. I'll start on the portrait so you can have it back soon.' Mama gives me a gentle smile, then I leave, skipping along the stone floor to my room like a young child.

I quickly bathe and dress for bed in my escape clothing, then settle at my desk with my drawing paper and lead pencil. Under the magenta orb light, I study my father's features, and the fall of light and shadows on the photograph, then start on my representational portrait. If I have time, I will create a portrait of the three of us, together. Mama, Papa and me.

My mind wanders as I sketch. Should I create the family portrait with me as a boy, the boy my father believed I would be? The son he longed for? A tear rolls down my face. Would he be disappointed because of my birth gender?

I drop my pencil and shake my head. Mama said that inside we are all the same. Our outward appearance doesn't define us, nor make us mentally weaker or stronger. Mama said what mattered was how we treated others, and it was better to be ugly with a beautiful heart and mind than to be beautiful with an ugly heart and mind. One has true friends, the other attracts fake friends, and beauty fades, and then what do you have left if it is not kindness, nor friends?

I wipe the tear from my face, turn off my magenta orb, leave my desk and sit on the window seat and look out at eventide. The full moon floats in the heavens, it's face marred by the mining and moon wars that are taking place.

I wonder what it was like when the sky was filled with just the sun with one kind of splendour, the moon another and the stars another, like when Mama was young. I grieve for that time I had never known, and despise the human-made satellites polluting the purity of the universe.

The sky is broken.

And my heart feels heavy.

And angry.

And hurt.

The greed of people is an ugly, entitled and selfish thing.

My bedroom door squeaks. Mama walks in holding her magenta orb. Magenta: the colour that doesn't exist. She stands behind me and starts brushing my hair with gentle, rhythmic strokes. Calming. Hypnotising. Then she braids it, like she always does.

Mama sits beside me then, and puts her head on my shoulder. 'I'm so blessed to have you, Ari Bear.'

'And I, you, Ma.'

'I pray that one day you find someone who will love you, adore you, and cherish you deeply, and understand your wildly independent ways that you need to express. Otherwise you can't be you, and will suffer.'

Mama's words don't absorb into my mind like they should. I have a question I need to ask. 'Would Papa have preferred that I was a boy?' I say. I already know the answer, but I need to hear Mama say the words.

'My beautiful girl, you and Papa would have had the strongest bond, you, his princess for always. You are his, and carry his bloodline. He gave you life, and all life is sacred. What if, my darling, you had a brother and, you could outdo him in everything? Would it matter if you were a boy or a girl then? What matters is that you are you, and not a copy of anyone else. Imagine if everyone decided to copy others in looks and behaviour and thoughts. How boring and repulsive!'

'Thank you, Ma.' A tear slides down my cheek, the cheek facing the window that shows the sad outside world to me with the broken night sky. Mama can't see my tear.

Mama picks up my shoes and puts them on my feet and ties the laces.

I stand and climb into bed and Mama pulls up the blankets.

She kneels beside the bed and holds my hand. 'Courage and Strength. Kindness. Creativity. Imagination. Wisdom. Faithfulness and Truth. *Human Love.* Light. Hope. Breath. These are your gifts. May they be written onto your heart, to guide and protect. May your presence be pure and beautiful like flowers of love. May you be brave and courageous like the stars in the heavens, and may you have wisdom as deep as the oceans. And … may your kindness be breathtaking, like the living earth on its day of creation. And I pray … that you that you fully comprehend your breath, and the knowledge of it that surpasses all understanding,' Mama whispers.

'Thank you. Good night.'

'Sleep well, my love.'
Brave.
And courageous.
True.

And original.

Mama said to *never wish*
you were someone else,
and *never copy* the image
or personality of another.
It's exhausting and disappointing,
because you *will never be them*.

Mama said *comparing yourself*
to others will make you depressed.
You were chosen to be exactly *who you are*.
You are perfect for the role of you
in your own story.

CHAPTER 18

Cornflowers are my favourite, like a daydream in blue.
Luminous blue flowers, soft, frilly dual blooms with
fringed petals and elegant sage feathered leaves. They
sit on my window sill this morningtide. I've never told Mama
how much I loved them since I was five, when Mama made me
a cornflower crown. She had placed it on my head and we held
both hands and skipped around and around and around. Mama
tilted her head back and a beautiful smile lit up her face, the
golden sun creating a halo around her like she was an angel. It felt
like freedom. And hope. It felt like a celebration that Papa was
returning.

Mama's heartsong.

I climb out of bed, change into my sage cotton wide-leg
pants and off-white long-sleeved shirt, my Sunday clothes on
Wednesday. I open the window shutters and look out at the Field
of Flowers, a blush of pinks, like the cotton candy the chefs make
for my birthday. I love how Mama had sewn a great variety of
flower seeds that bloom at different times during the year. It's
a source of joy. Of something to look forward to each day and

month and year.

I unleash my auburn hair, the waves of the once braid controlling the hair artistry of wild. I pull a daydream blue cornflower from the vase and place it over my ear, hoping it would remind me to focus on things that are true, things that are honest, things that are just, things that are pure, things that are lovely, and things that are good. Glimmers. Sparkles. They would stop me from thinking on what I had seen in Lerwick, and how their narrative is different. Darker. Constrained.

I pick up the photograph of Papa and swoosh it into my trouser pocket—the best invention ever in the history of women's clothing—and leave my room for the breakfast nook. The table prepared for one.

I place Papa's photograph beside my plate, and study the direction of light, the shadows, and the highlights while I eat my eggs and toast. Then I look deeper into the photograph. The nuances. The assumptions. The emotions. The words not spoken. What knowledge is he hiding, and then, completely off-kilter, I wonder if food ever got stuck in his beard, the gnarly whiskers wrapping their tendrils around it and devouring every morsel and belching in satisfaction.

'Sorry, Papa. My mind is a storyteller, and likes to create something from nothing. Mama said never to stop it, but I should know there are times for truth and times for fiction. Your living beard is a concoction of my imagination, as pretty as it is. If you were here with us, I'm sure Mama would have decorated your beard with flowers. You know how she lives and breathes them.'

I finish my breakfast, place Papa into my pocket, stand and take my plate and cutlery to the kitchen and thank them. I grab some freshly baked bread rolls and cookies and apples and hold them in my shirt folded up to form a pouch, like those kangaroos I've seen in books. Then I set off to my bedroom, my day planned—sketching, to be finished today, and to meet Eli at 2pm at the tea party tipi tent.

I gather my vintage blue school port of *everything*, adding the photograph of Papa, pencils, paints and paintbrushes, sketch book, diary, a book to read, the food I have swiped from the kitchen, plus some water and a collection of colourful flowers. Then I jump out the window with it, my bare feet landing on the cosmos flowers outside my room as wild as ever, the spiky seeds scattering and falling in a heap.

'Sorry,' I whisper before I walk off in the direction of the rainforest garden, planted as a reminder of what they earth once had—curious ferns and palms and cycads and mosses vines and orchards, its tall, straight tree trunks and cacao plants for chocolate, it's flowers in subtle pinks and yellows and vibrant reds and splashes of orange and purple. And the abandoned upright oak coloured piano that sits amongst it, keys mishappen, the varnish peeling off the body, an ivy plant spreading its leaves along it like it was reaching to play a melody. I run my fingers over the keys lightly, wondering why Mama had never let me learn to play this instrument, considering there were seven pianos inside and outside the kingdom I had found.

Once, when I was twelve, I pushed down a key, and then was locked up in the lighthouse.

With no escape.

I deserved it. I shouldn't have made the broken and old dusty piano make a sound in the empty room in the castle. The one where the fireplace was crumbling. The one where the ceiling was covered in black smudges and dust, and ash covered the floor. I accidentally broke the door trying to get into the room. It wasn't even worth it when I took a step into the room. There was nothing exciting. Why was it even locked like it contained something precious? Mama said that was the first problem—breaking into the room. The second problem was that I played the "G" key on the grand piano. Whatever that meant. I didn't tell her that I pushed every other "key" on the "grand" piano randomly, except one, none of them working before the "G" key sounded.

As soon as the sound vibrated, three grown-ups appeared in the room like they had been released from the grubby grey walls after a hundred years, or walked through the walls like they were ghosts. One grown-up ran at the piano and put his hand on the string to stop the sound. Another, with a rifle, rushed to the window and looked out, expectant. And the other grabbed my upper arm and pulled me out of the room like I was an errant child, or like there was something chasing us and we had to evacuate, my feet dragging along the wooden floor, a sharp piece of wood splintering my foot.

I wanted to scream in pain, but didn't. He would have won then.

He sat me on a whitewashed chair in the underground castle kitchen amongst the seven table tops and pots and pans and bowls and wooden spoons and ladles, and stood in front of me with his arms folded until mother arrived. Like a guard. Not a word was spoken. But his silence spoke volumes, yelling like the wood in my foot.

Mama entered the room after I had counted to three hundred and forty-three. She pulled up a chair and sat opposite me. She sat in silence, then blinked. I swallowed.

My stomach quivered. I was in trouble. Again.

Mama placed her right hand over her mouth, then closed her eyes. Was she stopping herself from saying something bad, or was she going to cry? I had seen her sometimes, looking out the window, or looking at some white flowers. She would still for a moment, like deciding what to do next, then clasp her hand over her mouth. Her eyebrows would draw together and wrinkles would form at the corner of her eyes. Then tears would run down her face. Is Mama going to cry, because of me?

'Ari…' Mama lowered her head and closed her eyes. When she looked back at me, her brown eyes, the colour of chocolate, dripped with melancholy. Her head moved from side to side.

'No, Mama!' I cried. I knew what she was about to say.

Isolation. I hated isolation in my room.

'I have no choice after this incident. I need to take you to the lighthouse. It's for your own good.'

'No, Mama. Not the lighthouse! The dead men—'

'Are dead.'

'But Eli said—'

'He was trying to scare you.'

'But Mama, I hear things—'

'It's just the lighthouse moving with the waves crashing against the rocks.'

'But, Mam—'

'Enough! We leave before dawn tomorrow. Be prepared. You are not to leave your room. You will eat dinner there, and I will not be braiding your hair nor reading to you tonight!' Mama stood and left the room, her footfall heavy. I had never heard her footsteps before. They were always silent. She didn't even look back at me.

'Mama,' I cried in a whisper, my tears leaving splattered blobs on the stone floor. I looked down to see if they made a picture. My tears always made some sort of picture on the floor. But not this time.

'Child.' I jumped. The governess's voice was sharp. I didn't even hear her enter the kitchen. I raised my head but didn't look at her. I wanted to tell her that I had a name. I wanted to tell her that I am not a child anymore. I wanted to tell her that I am twelve! 'Come,' she said.

I rose from the chair, feeling the pain of the pierce of wood in my foot. But I didn't wince. I didn't limp. I didn't want it to look like I deserved the splinter embedded in my foot. I hoped it would not leave blood prints on the floor. I didn't feel like getting onto my hands and knees to scrub it off. The fact that I would be at the lighthouse tomorrow was bad enough. My life was nothing but endless misery. I wanted to pack my suitcase and run away.

I lifted my chin higher and followed the governess to my

room. One of my many rooms. Sometimes I slept in different room each night. It was safer that way I had been told.

But safer from what?

The governess opened the wooden door. It was silent. Like all of the room doors of the castle ruins below the ground. Hidden. Everything had been sound proofed. We had even been drilled in silence and stillness because our lives depended on it.

I walked through the doorway. This was the room with the pretty view of eventide. Sunset. It had an adjoining door to my mother's room.

It was safer that way, I had been told.

'Dinner will be delivered when the sun reaches half way down the trees. I expect you to be washed and your lighthouse bag packed before the arrival of your food. This is not a time for daydreaming, or for creating fluffy animals from the figment of your imagination.'

'Yes, Mrs Gee.' I had learned to be polite to the governess, otherwise my lessons were extended and boring. She narrowed her eyes at me, and closed the door without a sound.

I was alone but not alone. I was never alone. Outside my door was a door keeper, instructed to kill in defence.

It was safer that way I was told.

I sat on the floor and grabbed my left foot. I winced as I twisted it so I could see the splinter. It was horizontal and near the surface, superficial, Mama would have said, with a part of it exposed at the entry. Easy to remove. Good. And done while I held my breath. I was being a brave girl my mama would have said. I stood and limped over to the wooden washstand. As I poured the water from the pitcher into the wash basin, I longed for a bath. It was three days since my last one. Fat chance of a bath tonight after what I had done.

Mama said I was my own worst enemy. It appears that she was right. But the problem wasn't that I had broken into the room with the grand piano, nor that I had hit a key that made a sound; the problem was that I had been caught.

As I finished cleaning myself with a cloth, my dinner arrived. Thank goodness for the room divider. Translucent. I could be seen, but not in detail. My whereabouts was to be known at all times.

It was safer that way, Mama had said.

I put my escape clothes on for bed. There was no such thing as sleep clothes. We had to be ready to run at any time of the night. I didn't know what we were running from. Or maybe we were running to something?

I sat at the aged grey wooden desk where my dinner was placed. A wooden cup of water plus five fruits on top of a plate made of bread. I was hoping that we had some lamb tonight. Mama and her team of scientists had been creating cows and sheep in their cell experiments. She had successfully brought them to life from extinction. But they weren't ready for the kill yet. We have to be careful, she had said.

I rested my elbows on the desktop and clasped my hands together and closed my eyes, like Mama did before she ate. I wondered what she would be thinking of when she did that. I raised my left eyebrow. My mind was empty. My tummy growled and I opened my eyes and looked at my food. A white peach, nectarine, a red plum, and an apricot, all from the same fruit salad tree, cut up into bite size pieces. Plus five mulberries. Lots of vitamins and minerals and iron, Mama would have said, eat it all up for energy to grow and to be smart. And that's what I did. Not a crumb was left.

I sat at the window seat and looked out at the colours of eventide above the dark, dense forest. The King's Forest. The orange and red and pink looked angry tonight. Fiery. Like I imagined a dragon would breathe out of its mouth.

I was told to pack my bag for the lighthouse. I had plenty of time to do that being confined to my room. I would do it later. I don't know why I was told to pack it before dinner.

I gazed out at the beauty of the sky that was made to be admired. And it absolutely must be admired. By me. Ari Flora Cohen. It surely was a crime not to admire it! I cast my eyes over the delicious colours that had changed from the colour of anger before. They were molten now, melting into more peaceful hues as they slowly turned to deep blues to black. They filled my heart every time, my eyes stuck like they were trying to pull me up into the sky with them to touch the real stars, beyond the broken sky. The stars that didn't move all the time.

I stilled.

Something moved in the trees. My papa's trees. The King's Forest.

A dark shadow?

Or was I seeing things?

Mama said I had an overactive imagination.

A red light blinked. Just one red light.

Once.

My heart raced and I stiffened. Flight or fright of freeze.

I froze.

Mama said if you froze, you were dead.

I didn't want to be dead.

CHAPTER 19

As my body started to shake, a hand tightened around my upper arm and pulled me up off the chair. 'Run, Ari. Run. I love you.' Mama's voice was whispered, her words filled with tears from her heart and fear.

My wide eyes met hers, trying to pull her inside me so we were one, so I would be safe. With her. 'Where to?' I said. And there it was. I wasn't running from something; I was running to something.

'The lighthouse, my darling—' And then she was gone as I was lifted off the ground by a man. I looked over his shoulder as he carried me away, Mama getting smaller in the distance next to the castle walls. I lifted my hand in goodbye. Then dropped it as Mama disappeared completely. Not even a glance back at me.

My heart hurt and my eyes flooded.

Panic was everywhere. I could feel it. Pushing down trying to suffocate. Life was suddenly in fast forward, like running with a wild storm.

'You'll be safe,' the man said, his voice low and gentle.

But what about everyone else? What about Mama? My

bottom lip trembled, and then I remembered what Mama had said about panic and fear—to slow everything down. Use your breathing. It would help me focus on what I had to do. Survival was everything.

I looked forward instead of back. Mama said to leave the past in the past. Mama said when something bad happens, to ask what next, instead of being stuck in the present and pulled down into the darkness of that moment. Survival was everything.

The grey stone walls became a blur as the man ran. He descended steps lower than I thought the castle could go, then entered a network of tunnels I had never seen before. He slowed. Was he lost? His eyes darted between the tunnel entrances, like he was counting, then he fell into an even stepped run again and entered another tunnel, third from the left. Our world became dark, profuse with a wet, musty odour that stuck to my skin like a spider web.

We stopped. He took a careful side-ward step to the left, like stepping through a wall as though we were spirits, but in reality, he slithered between camouflaged hidden walls into another opening.

He slowed, then lowered me to the cool, dirt ground. 'We made it.' He smiled. 'I'm Oliver, by the way.'

I pulled my eyebrows together. 'You don't look like an Oliver!'

He crossed his arms over his broad chest. 'What does an Oliver look like?'

'You know … kind, sweet, friendly.' I raised my eyebrows at him.

He chuckled. 'That is the perfect compliment. Thank you, Ari!'

'What's next?' I asked. 'Mama always said to focus on what's next.'

'Wise words from your mama.' He looked up. 'Next is waiting for others. And then we exit.'

'Is Mama one of the others?'

Oliver closed his eyes and let out a deep breath.

'You're trying to be brave, aren't you?'

He lowered his head. 'Yes.'

'Just tell me. Mama is always honest with me. She said it is how we survive.'

'There's a plan for when this happens.'

'For when what happens?' My eyes burn and fill with tears.

'When there is an intrusion, or an attack.'

'From what?' My heart thumped.

'Your mama hasn't told you?'

I shook my head.

'Then I will leave it for her to tell you.'

'I need to know the plan, in case …' I began.

'In case of what?'

'Something goes … you know, wrong.' His eyes met mine and I blinked, pleading with him.

'You're right. Follow me.' Oliver walked a little way further, where some light entered the tunnel. 'Sit on that stone,' he said, pointing.

I sat. But Oliver didn't. 'Are you going to sit?'

He shook his head. 'Ari, I am your protector—one of your many protectors.'

My eyebrows squish together. *Why would I need protecting?*

'If I'm standing, there's a better chance of me taking action to protect you.'

I squeezed my eyes shut. I wanted to cry. Was I going to die like the dead men in the sea?

'The plan is … in the event of invasion, or an intruder, a protector takes you to a safe place. Your mama joins us later once she has retrieved items of importance.'

'Like the bottles filled with tears for Papa?' A tear rolled down my cheek. I didn't want to be separated from Mama. *What if …*

Oliver smiled and his eyes softened. 'Yes.'

'What else would Mama bring with her?'

Oliver placed his finger over his lips. 'Hush now. We must be silent. I need to listen for movement.'

I slumped my shoulders. 'Can you please tell me one thing … did you know my papa?'

His eyes twinkled. He placed his finger over his lips once again.

And there we waited. Oliver, who knew my father, Azriel David Cohen, and me, Ari Flora Cohen. I looked down and grinned. A grin that reached my heart and filled it with sunshine.

Two men arrived. As big as Oliver. Muscly, and serious. They didn't speak, but nodded to each other. They continued forward in the tunnel toward the light. Then another man arrived. He stopped before Oliver, his face taut, his eyes wide. He moved from side to side like he was about to run. Was he nervous? Worried? He swallowed then shook his head.

I looked at Oliver. He raised his eyebrows and pressed his lips together, and closed his eyes. When he opened them, he looked down at me and ruffled my hair. 'Follow me,' he whispered.

'Did the plan change?' I said, my chin trembling.

'Not yet.' Oliver started walking and I followed. The other man followed behind like I was the salad between two slices of flat bread. After a short while the air smelled sweet and fresh and the tunnel became a little easier to see in. We exited the tunnel onto a rocky shore and moved to the right. The men gathered there but I walked towards the shoreline.

I looked up at the end of eventide, like the closing of the book at the end of a story. The coloured clouds became darker and hovered low, masking our presence. And there was the lighthouse. Barely visible, except for one occasion, when the moon peeked through the clouds and exposed its weathered boards. I swallowed. *To the lighthouse … my darling*, Mama had said. *The dead men*, I thought. Instinctively, I looked down at my feet, scanning for the bones of dead men washed ashore.

I turned when a hand latched around my upper arm and

guided me to where the men stood.

'Sit down and be still,' Oliver whispered. 'Just like the trees.'

I sat. We had played this game many times in my twelve years with my governess. I was good at it. Perfect she said once. I wanted to tell Oliver that the trees could never be still. I wanted to tell him they danced with the breeze and dropped their leaves and grew flowers and fruit. But didn't. Mama said there were times when I shouldn't talk. This seemed like one of those times.

Where was Mama? My chest tightened. I wanted to cry. I wanted to yell out to Mama to tell her we were here. Just like when I was born and Mama said I cried extraordinarily loud, like my lungs were about to be ejected from my tiny, fragile body. She said it was like I was calling for Papa, my voice somehow searching for him in the darkness of the earth. I wanted to cry like that now, so Mama could find me. My mama, Zarah Opal Cohen.

The big, muscular, serious men nodded in unison, then stopped. Oddly. Oliver lifted his chin a little higher then closed his eyes and lowered his head like he was a servant to them. Or saying goodbye. I didn't know which. I frowned.

Oliver stepped over the rocks and stones to where the water splashed the ground. He manoeuvred a wooden stick, and a boat rose up from the shallows. As water dripped from the canvas over the top, Oliver bent down and found a rope and hauled it toward us.

He turned to me. 'Come.' He gestured with his hand.

I shook my head at a short erratic pace with my eyes wide. Where was Mama? I didn't want to go to the lighthouse with the dead men. I couldn't without Mama. Nausea bubbled in my stomach.

Oliver's expression changed. His eyes narrowed and set his lips in a hard line. He raised his hand and pointed to me, and then the boat and raised his eyebrows.

I squeezed my eyes shut and curled myself up into a ball. If I couldn't see him I didn't have to get in the boat, right?

I heard the crunching of stones underfoot, getting louder and louder, like the thumping of my heart. The sound stopped in front of me. I peeked through my scrunched up eyes, and there was Oliver's face, opposite mine.

'If you don't come to the boat, I will carry you there,' he said, his words curt.

'I'm waiting for Mama,' I whispered with a prayer that she would arrive, and not disappear like my father did before I was born.

A sob escaped from me. It was hurting my throat so I had to let it out.

I watched Oliver close his eyes. He opened them. 'Your mama … can't make it,' he said, then his eyes wrinkled at the corners in a wince, sadness dripping from them like wax melting. 'We need to go.'

'No … no … no-no … no. I can't. Not without Mama.' I tried to hold my breath to stop the sobbing.

Oliver held out his large, strong hand. He wasn't angry. He wasn't forceful. His gentleness lured me like a cupcake on the table. Resigned to what must be done, I placed my small hand in his giant one and stood, then stepped on rocks and over stones to the boat with my bare feet, the splinter wound hurting on each step.

'Stop! Oliver, stop!' Mama's voice. 'Where are your shoes, Ari? How many times have I told you to wear shoes, even to bed! And your bag? Where is it?' She shook her head.

I had disappointed her. I was a bad daughter. My bottom lip trembled and I ran at her then wrapped my arms around her and squeezed her as tightly as I could. 'I'm sorry, Mama.'

Mama ran her hand over my head and down my braid, soothing my aching heart and healing it with unconditional love that felt like rainbows after the rain and the warmth of the winter sun. 'I'm sorry too, Ari. Let's go to the lighthouse. We'll be safe there.'

Oliver offered his hand to Mama and me as we climbed inside the small, black, wooden boat and laid low. He placed the canvas over the top and then started to pull on the winch.

Slowly, pull by pull, we moved through the water, gentle, feeling like we were floating on the clouds. When the boat stopped moving, Mama pushed the cover aside, and there was the lighthouse jetty, still holding strong after hundreds of years.

Mama helped me as I climbed up the freezing metal ladder. Then followed. In the dim light, we walked along the long precarious jetty until we found another ladder, and ascended it.

Before us was the lighthouse keeper houses. Two of them. A single story and a double story. Then upward was a tall tower to the light. Though, there was no longer any light shining from it. It just stood like a tall soldier, guarding the sea, and the dead men.

I shivered.

Mama went inside the first floor of the two storey house. I followed. It was dark now. Eventide was long gone. And so had the colours of fire in the sky that I had tried to paint so often. Mama reached behind her searching for my hand and held it, and together we found the cot. Mama patted the mattress and I laid down. I didn't want her to let go of my hand. The time of darkness was the worst time with the dead men. I'm certain I could hear them singing sometimes.

Mama lay beside me and I snuggled into her. Her fingers brushed through my hair and followed my lines of hair in my braid. 'I'm sorry for being mad at you,' she said, her voice soft and comforting like the sound of lullabies.

'I'm sorry for not wearing shoes or packing my bag.'

'I know. Let's sleep for now. Birdsong awaits.'

'Yes, and with the new day, anything is possible, right, Mama?'

'Of course. Now close your eyes, my sweetness. I love you,' Mama said, then whispered, 'courage and strength. Kindness. Creativity. Imagination. Wisdom. Faithfulness and Truth. *Human*

Love. Light. Hope. Breath.'

'I love you too, Mama, more than all the flowers in the kingdom.'

'The kingdom?'

'Yes. We live in a ruined castle, and a king must have lived there once, so it's a kingdom,' I said.

'But, what if a queen lived there?' Mama said.

'Then it's a queendom … yes, we live in a queendom, and you are the queen, and I am the princess!'

Mama laughed hard, her happiness reaching inside me and painting a smile on my face making it glow with love. 'The barefoot princess!' Mama laughed again then kissed my forehead, making the world feel like it was a good place instead of the things we had to escape from. 'Good night, Princess Ari Flora!'

'Good night, my Queen. Love you forever,' I whispered back.

'I love you more, and forever and a day.' Mama's breath was warm on the top of my head. This was *human love* and breath. But why did Mama speak that every night?

I took a deep breath. A gift. For without our breath, we had no life.

Dead.

My memory fades and I continue on my journey to meet Eli at the tea party tipi, past the well-tended crops, past the colourful Field of Flowers and into the mighty King's Forest, stepping into the forbidden land, stepping over the rules that were made to protect me and into the land of psithurism—the sound of the wind whispering melodies in the trees—telling me secrets I don't want to hear. I gaze at the straight tree trunks and upward to the graduating shades of dark green to light green and to the blue day sky with the sun filtering through. I return my focus in front of me then, and find my waymarker, one of twelve I have placed around the kingdom. The rockbeings I call them, painted with a wash of white, stacked, and waiting. Just for me. I imagine them smiling at me every time I meet one, as they stand like friends greeting me with open arms, trained to be secret keepers of my presence.

I place my vintage school blue port of *everything* on the ground, and pull one luminous blue fringed petal from the cornflower, sitting triumphantly atop of my ear, then squat and place it on top of the waymarker. I smile. Colour adds charm and happiness to everything it meets. Especially this flower that was a daydream in blue.

I stand, pick up my vintage school blue port of *everything*, suddenly aware that I am alone.

An odd feeling.

Eli is always where I am. But not anymore. I look around. Where is my new protector Mama had assigned to me? Where was my new protector yesterday when Eli had intervened to help me in Lerwick?

I turn to the direction I need to go. I don't need a protector. I will be stronger if I only have myself to rely on. No moment of distraction looking for my protector. No moment of waiting for my protector to step in to help me. I will be more alert at all times. Ready. My self-defence stronger. Maybe Mama has done me a favour. Besides, we are safe in the kingdom from whatever wanted to intrude. Aren't we? I wish I knew, so I could identify the enemy.

I press my lips in a hard line. Conversations are needed with Mama. I'm eighteen now. Officially an adult. I look down at my vintage blue school port of *everything* from my childhood and my lips relax, then curl upward at the ends. Being an adult doesn't mean leaving everything behind from your younger years and youth. Let wisdom prevail.

I walk for one hundred steps then stop, turn left, and walk for another one hundred steps. But before I finish those steps, the tea party tipi comes into view. The camouflaged material the colours of the forest, the inverted cone shaped tent with a hole in the top, a flap for the opening. It was sturdy and repelled the wind and rain. A perfect hideout that had standing room as well, plus two skeletons. Real skeletons. I had collected them from the forbidden room in the science lab in the floor below the castle when I was thirteen, where there sat, literally, forty skeletons, now thirty-eight, borrowed before morningtide before the scientists began their day's work, and when the castle had a minimum number of people guarding it. I'd covered the skeletons in fabric and carried them out to the tipi on two separate mornings a week apart, positioning them in a cross legged sit, balancing on the picnic blanket facing each other.

They were friends I had decided. Smart friends who had seen a lot in the science rooms. I named them Azriel and Zarah after my parents, and sometimes I leaned them forward so their skeleton teeth met in a kiss.

They were in love.

Skeleton love.

CHAPTER 20

I stop before the teat party tipi and open the flap. I stop before the tea party tipi and open the flap. And there is Azriel and Zarah sitting in the same position waiting for me. Except, Azriel's left arm has dropped off, the humerus detached. I smile. Humour. Of course it would be the humerus bone that had fallen off.

I pull the entry flap of the tipi to the side wider, and step through the triangular entry, stooped over in my eighteen year old body. I'm inside the tea party tipi of my childhood and youth. I sit perpendicular to the skeletons. I must have visited my tipi over a hundred times in my lifetime. It's a place of imagination, and solace. With the flap closed, I can hide from the very annoying Eli, except sometimes, I invited him in under the guise that he would behave, but he proved me wrong, every single time. For a moment, I wonder if he had been here and dismantled Azriel's left arm. I wouldn't put it past him. That is exactly something he would do.

I shrug, then open my vintage blue school port of *everything*, and take out the flowers, then add them to the skeletons, between the teeth, the rib cage, eyes and fingers. Then I take out Papa's photograph, the portrait I have started, and my pencils. I need to finish the portrait to give the photograph back to Mama. The sun shines in through the open top of the tipi, providing the perfect amount of light to work by.

After an hour I have finished the portrait of Papa I had started last night. It's almost a perfect copy of him. If I could just make him 3D and bring him to life. For a moment I kind of wish that Mama hadn't shown me his picture. Now I miss him more, and it feels like it's becoming an obsession. I put the portrait between the skeletons and stretch out my hand, then retrieve another piece of paper. This is the one to create a family portrait. I hope it will please Mama. This one is less detailed than Papa's portrait. A minimalist watercolour one with creative license. We three are linked, by brush strokes, by colour, by love.

By hope.

I paint a third one, with me as a boy—the son my father believed I would be.

And then a fourth, with me and Mama.

Four portraits. Three fictional, one real—just Mama and me.

I throw all four into the centre of the picnic blanket missing the floral tea cups that have sat here for eight years. I leave the tipi and collect sticks of various sizes and shapes and colours textures, all supplied by the trees of the wonderful King's Forest.

I enter the tipi again and sit with Azriel and Zarah, and start to build a stick stack on top of the portraits in the middle of the picnic blanket, starting with the thicker, longer sticks at the bottom, and then building my way up to the smaller more fragile sticks.

'Dead,' Eli says, and I jump as I place the last stick onto the stick stack. I look up at him. Tall. Broad shoulders. His square jawline like it had be sculptured. A slight cleft chin. His wavy hair falling over his right eye, the green one, leaving the blue one exposed. I give him a slight smile after I recover from the unexpected warmth that flows through me.

'We only ever meet when I am dead,' I say.

'True,' he says, and sits opposite me. 'I like your shoes.'

I gaze down at my bare feet, brushed with dirt, then I point to Azriel's fallen arm, the humerus separated. 'Did you do this to Azriel? It looks like something you would do.'

Eli raises an eyebrow, then laughs. 'I can't take the credit for this one.' He looks closely at my stick stack, then reaches over and pokes it with his finger, and it collapses.

'Expected,' I say. 'You wouldn't be Eli without wreaking my creations.'

He gives me a crooked smile and I melt.

He pulls my artworks out from under the stick stack and looks at the lifelike pencil portrait.

'My Papa.'

Eli smiles gently. 'Did you see him?'

'No, it's a copy from Mama's photograph that she showed me for the first time last night. I'm kinda angry that she kept his identity from me for eighteen years.'

'I wonder if he looks like this now?'

'If he's still alive, which I think he is not. He would have contacted Mama by now if he was.'

'Ari,' Eli says, the letters of my name delivered in a tenderness that felt like love. He looks deeply into my eyes and I soak him in, 'Perhaps he is protecting you both if he hasn't made contact. My papa often spoke about the intensity of your parents love for each other and how it could be felt by others, their eye contract so intimate others would have to look away. If he could be sure that he was not endangering you and your mother, he would have returned.'

I shake my head. What would it have been like to feel my father's love? A tear rolls down my cheek, and Eli wipes it away, his finger leaving a trail of sparkles on my skin.

He picks up the watercolour portrait of Mama, Papa and I,

and smiles. Then he picks up the watercolour portrait of Mama, Papa and me as a boy. He grimaced. 'What is this? Do you have a brother I haven't met?'

I smirk. 'No. That's me. Papa was sure I would be a boy, so I created the boy he never had.' I cover my eyes to stop the tears from falling. I would have been such a disappointment to my father. Born a girl. One to be protected instead of being the protector. I was determined to be able to protect myself. Girls don't need protecting.

Eli stands, grabs my elbows and lifts me to my feet, then he pulls me in close and hugs me. I want him to hold me tighter to push all my broken bits together. 'My papa says that you are so much like your father, and he would have been so proud of you. It doesn't matter whether you are a boy or a girl, it's about the love and kindness that you share. Love and kindness are everything,' Eli whispers.

I relax further into his arms, drop my hands from my eyes and wrap my arms around him and allow myself to sob. A little. But not too much. 'Thank you,' I whisper, then lower my arms and stand back from him, and join Zarah and Azriel on the picnic blanket again. I suck in a deep shaky breath to calm my inner being and look at the stick stack that is in the order of chaos. A beautiful mess. I am blessed with being able to see the beauty in ugliness. It could be a work of art.

I watch as Eli reconstructs my stick stack exactly as I had constructed it. I raise my eyebrows at this strangeness. 'Have you got a photographic memory?'

'Yes.'

'Blessing or curse?'

'Neither. It's how I use it. I struggled with it when I was younger as I kept replaying bad things over in my mind. I've learned to turn that way of thinking off. However, I can access it at any time that I choose.'

He finishes the stick stack and sits up with a perfect posture.

'Done. I have reversed time.' He winks at me and I smile back. If only time could be reversed.

I hand him a bread roll. 'Please accept this bread roll as a token of my appreciation of reversing time. The king's daughter is most pleased.'

'Thank you, Princess Ari,' he says.

'Tell me why you called me the king's daughter.'

'Apparently your father's bloodline is connected to a king, and he is the last of his family tree left.'

'And hence his wish for a son to carry the family name.'

'Nope. Your father vehemently denied his bloodline is connected to a king. It's a case of mistaken identity, especially when the king he is supposedly related to, never had any offspring. The people who believe that king did have children have been deceived by lies.'

'So my father is not a king?'

'No, but he was instrumental in rescuing people and bringing them here to this protected area with an uninhabitable castle that is in ruins, as viewed from above by satellites and drones. And because of the castle, he is fondly called the king. So you are the king's daughter.' Eli raises an eyebrow at me. 'Your mother hasn't told you much about your father, has she?'

I shake my head. 'Bit and pieces spill out at times. But to me, my father feels … like a character from a book … fictional.' I look down at the stick stack as my heart lets out a heavy sigh. 'I wish I could light a fire,' I say and add another stick to the stick stack. 'I know Mama said we can't light fires in the King's Forest because it will catch on fire and burn it down, but we are in a safe place here inside the tipi, just with a little, controlled fire.'

'It's not just that,' Eli says. 'The real reason is so the satellites don't see our location by the smoke that will be cast into the air, and draw attention to the fact that people do live here.'

'But the satellites aren't here during the day.'

Eli raised his eyebrows at me. 'I see a large gap in your

education. You're not up with modern today, life outside the kingdom, are you?'

'How would I know if I'm not aware of life in *The Beyond*, except for the two times I have ventured there without permission?'

'Ah … the protected girl … everyone has knowledge of *The Beyond* as you call it, except you. Naïve. Pure in mind. Pure in heart.'

My right eye squints at him in anger.

'Ah … not pure now according to that single eye squint filled with hate.'

'Anger, not hate.'

'I beg to differ, Ari. It's the same look you would give me every time you told me that you hated me when we were growing up.'

I look down. My heart is thumping against my ribs. Everyone knows the truth, except me. I have been excluded. Laughed at. Pitied?

'Tell me about *The Beyond*, Eli. You are not indebted to my mother now as you are no longer my protector.'

He inhales deeply and lifts his chin and looks down at me, like he was assessing whether I was worthy of the truth.

'Tell me?' I say, a little louder than I intended.

He presses his lips together. 'I'm the messenger. Don't shoot the messenger.'

I put my hands on my hips, the bees of anxiety bumbling in my stomach.

'We live in a "kingdom" that is protected and inaccessible by outsiders who are not of our ilk.'

'What do you mean by our ilk?'

'Humans. Pure. Not tainted by technology.'

'Micro-chips, barcodes?'

Eli nods. 'Social media. Connected devices. Our movements not tracked. Our actions and thoughts not recorded. Your mother gave you boundaries for a reason, and there are deadly boundaries that I stopped you from going into, like the dense forest of gnarly manchineel trees, where the sap falls like acid. Arrows dipped in the sap are lethal. Our entire kingdom grounds are surrounded by them.'

Eli runs a hand through his curly dark hair. He shakes his head. 'There's so much to tell you, so many details, but I will cut to the chase, hoping your mother can fill you in on other historical events that lead to us being here.'

Eli draws a map on the dirt floor of the tipi. I watch as his finger marks the dirt map with landmarks and details like his is drawing from his photographic memory. 'We are here, and this is *The Beyond*, as you call it. This is Jedburgh, where you first entered *The Beyond*, in that building where notes and flowers and food are exchanged for notes that contain information, and here is Lerwick, where we met. The locations are not important. What is important are the people you saw there. The captured. It's happened all over the world. And this is what you saw: robots, humanoids, clones, avatars, starving humans and controlled humans. And then there are things that are unseen, happening behind closed doors and in the realm of virtual reality—the Artificial Intelligence who is a self-claimed true god, who has been lurking, desensitizing humans, and secretly controlling the narrative, shaping the history of the world, controlled by the prophesied dark entity ... deception, control. Humans deceived without their knowledge. A war of power, physical and spiritual. The lawless ones are soul seekers—to seek and destroy.'

My stomach turns and I squeeze my eyes shut. No freedom. No choices. No freewill.

'It will be short lived, Ari,' Eli says. 'Where darkness rules, the Ancient of Days will overrule. The darkness cannot hide from the Light.'

I swallow. Hard. Living in *The Beyond* must be like being a prisoner in your own body where—

'—From your studies,' Eli's voice breaks into my thoughts, 'remember the first industrial revolution with coal in 1765. Then there came—'

'The second revolution with the discovery of electricity, gas and oil in 1870. And in 1969, the third industrial revolution was where nuclear energy and electronics entered the picture.'

'And the fourth industrial revolution?'

I shake my head. There is no fourth industrial revolution.

'Internet and renewable energy in the year 2000.'

'I know what renewable energy is, we use it here with solar and wind, but the Internet?'

'Aah. You have much to learn. It's about the acceleration of digital technology. The explosion of knowledge. It's about artificial intelligence, and a virtual world that merges with the physical world. It's hard to explain. You need to see the computers and the world-wide Internet. I'll find a way to show you.'

'Eli, you are starting to scare me,' I say, my eyes reddening.

'It's better for you to know than not to know. Then you won't be shocked by what you see. Nor deceived.'

'Just … give me a moment,' I stand and go out into the King's Forest for some freedom, to stop the suffocating feeling that has enveloped me. I look upward to all the colours above, to steal a glimpse of the blue sky day and to inhale it inside of me, giving me courage to listen again.

I enter the tipi and sit opposite Eli.

His eyes wander over my face like he is assessing my emotion, and then he continues, 'And there's the fifth industrial revolution … the fourth industrial revolution was less about humans, and more about intelligent computers, but the fifth industrial revolution incorporated sustainability, human-centeredness, and concern for the environment in to the transformation while still utilising artificial intelligence, connected Internet devices and communications, and data, and creating mindfiles of people's thoughts, vision, memories, feelings and experiences. Where artificial intelligence becomes the keeper of peoples' memories. To imitate, control and manipulate. Artificial immortality.'

I look away. My brain feels like it is overloaded.

'The sixth industrial revolution—'

'Stop, Eli.' I put my hand over his mouth, his lips warm under my touch, and turn away from him. He removes my hand with his, and threads his fingers through mine, making us one. Stronger together.

'The sixth industrial revolution,' he continues, 'was where every task was controlled by human minds and performed by automated robots by covering all the planetary boundaries. It combines human intelligence, artificial intelligence, cloud computing energy, human–robot working big data, quantum computing … the seventh is mentally directed brain/machine interfaces, being implemented now, and the eighth stage, humans and artificial intelligence are one—where humans lose control of their identity, of who they are as humans. Trans-humans—Neo-humans. Making death optional. This is where mortal humans will be eradicated, where we are just an annoying rebellious thing to overcome, and dispose of, in order to hide the truth of true human spirituality and true human soul. Of *human love*. Of love of the Ancient of Days.'

I turn back to him. 'You're lying. This can't be true.'

'In the sixth revolution some people started to wake up to what was happening. Little changes were made over time to society, unnoticed and desensitizing us to the lies that became truth in the eyes of people. Good was bad and right was wrong. Humans were introduced to humanoids slowly. They were created after the image of man, but experiments showed that people didn't trust the male humanoids, so they created them as female, which seemed less aggressive and welcoming. And then there were the child humanoids, connecting that human protectiveness over them and creating an acceptance of them. It was all a precisely developed plan to lure people into a false sense of security, of trust. Most people couldn't see what was going on behind the scenes, the bigger picture, the life to come. But some people could. After a while, when the world was divided, pitted against each other and hatred became the norm, our families went off grid. Undetectable. But we also chose to help those who are caught in the world events without their consent. That's how we ended up here.'

Eli bends down and draws a map of the earth on the ground, adding dots in each of the countries. 'This is our world, as you know from your learning. These dots represent others, like us. Un-barcoded, un-microchipped, resistant to the world control that is currently happening, not bowing to the coercion, suppression, control, not deceived by the lie that humans can become immortal on the earth. This time in history that is part of *The Unfolding*. The gentle ushering in of souls who are being planted in the midst. Silent. Waiting for the appointed time to take action.'

'The Unfolding?'

He looks up at me, one eyebrow raised. 'Yes. When *The Unfolding* of layers of lies has finished, what has been hidden from people will be clearly seen. Truth. The fight for power and control. People … have been manipulated, coerced, buried in such an explosion of information and discoveries that they have become lost, oppressed. Suppressed even.'

'I need some water.' I pour water into two teacups and offer one to Eli. I drink one cup of water, then two and three. How could the world be so different to here?

'What you saw in Jedburgh and Lerwick was the tip of the iceberg of how technology has affected people. Those walking with the dark glasses have an addiction to technology and the virtual world. Even having virtual relationships with digital girlfriends and boyfriends. Digital love, not *human love*. What they see through the glasses is the same that we see, but embellished with beautiful plants and life and animals and trees and buildings that aren't really there—but they believe it is. It gives them a feeling of happiness. If they take off their glasses and see the real world, they are overcome with a deep feeling of grief and shame and can't cope with the reality. It's like their brain shuts down due to shock. They enter denial, and put their virtual reality glasses back on where they feel comfortable and not threatened and ... at home. A home that does not exist. Every movement, action and thought is tracked, recorded and the data stored as evidence to use for or against you.'

'And Lou?'

'Lou was a copy of Lou. In their world, there are four versions of everyone—those created by humans who are naturally conceived, a clone of a person—the embryo grown in a lab, a humanoid in the image of the person, and a digital version of a person in the virtual world, which can also be a hologram.'

Tears flow down my face. Untethered. Filled with the colour of dead flowers.

'The two most valuable of the four versions are the human versions, ones naturally conceived, the other created in a science lab, with flexible microchips inserted into their brains before birth. Out of these, the clone is preferred by the government because it's mind can be totally controlled. And those people have no idea they are being controlled. They are nothing but an asset to the government, one that's easily disposed of if something goes wrong—'

'How many Eli's are there?' I was angry.

'One.'

'And me?'

'One. Your mother has protected you, and this is why your mother continues to protect you.'

I take a deep breath. Mama's prayer comes to me: *And I pray ... that you that you fully comprehend your breath, and the knowledge of it that surpasses all understanding.*

I squeeze my eyes shut and shake my head. My heart feels like it is breaking. I quickly gather my paper and pencils and Papa's photograph, and portraits and one stick, and place them into my vintage blue school port of *everything*, close the lid and flip the latches closed.

I stand still and look at Eli, but don't say a word.

And then I run.

Trying to escape the polluted words that Eli has just released. Eli's words of a complicated, deceitful, sad world where humans have lost control of everything. Including themselves.

Mama said that words have colour. Some are dark and some are light, and that words have weight, and some words are impossibly heavy. Eli's words were black and threatening, and so heavy I thought they would weigh me down so I would disappear beneath the tall trees of the King's forest and be woven into the roots like a prisoner, unable to escape, then pushed up to the highest branches so I could look down on the created earth to see the ugliness that had engulfed it, this time unable to find any beauty.

As my bare feet pound the ground I wish I could fly like a bird. *I wish I could ... I wish I could ...* but Mama said not to wish for anything because it won't happen. I had to pray for it, for then my words are delivered to God who hears us and helps us. If I was little I would have prayed to be turned into a bird to fly, but now I am old enough to know that there is a difference between innocent prayers of impossible earthly things and mature prayers of those who seek to help others instead of just themselves. So instead of praying to fly like a bird, I pray for guidance to see clearly where I need to help those who are lost in *The Beyond*, to give them freedom, and hope, and happiness.

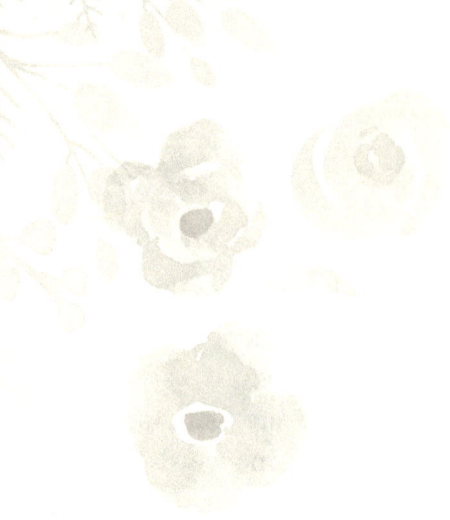

CHAPTER 21

I stop outside my bedroom window, my breathing rapid and shallow, and crush more cosmos flowers than I had this morning. I lean in my window and place my vintage blue school port of *everything* onto my window seat, and then climb in after it, this time not apologising for hurting the flowers.

My world view has changed.

It feels like a seismic shift, an earthquake of knowledge, the pulling back of the curtains revealing an ugly truth that has pierced my soul.

I walk over to my wardrobe, open the door and sit down in it, grab my stuffed childhood bear and close the door. In the darkness I pull Cardi to my chest, and sob. Deep and cathartic.

My world is now tainted. Stained. Once, I was filled with the goodness of people, but now, I wonder how that ugly canvas of lies could ever be painted over with brushstrokes of truth.

After an hour I leave the comforting darkness of my wardrobe and find a floral dress to wear to dinner, pick up my portrait of Papa and the photograph, then join Mama at the dining table.

'You're very quiet tonight, Ari. Is everything okay?'

I want to say that, shouldn't my new protector have told her about my day. But I don't. 'Just tired from the concentration doing Papa's portrait.' I move the portrait in front of Mama.

'Oh my. It looks like the original photograph.'

I hand the photograph of Papa back to her, then show her the family portraits. I watch her face.

'This representational portrait is perfect, Ari, and so is the family of us.' Mama's voice cracks and her eyes fill with tears, though they don't spill over her lashes. 'May I keep this one?'

'Of course.'

Mama looks at the third portrait. 'What's this? Your father and I and a son?'

'Yes. You said that papa said look after my son, and you have said a number of times that it would be better to be born a boy, so I created the family with a boy that Papa dreamed of.' My words are snarky.

A tear rolls down Mama's face this time. I didn't mean to make her cry.

'And besides, it takes the pressure off me, trying to be a girl who is also a boy, not able to be myself, trying to reach approval of someone I can never be. I am … me. Just me. Just Ari.'

Mama covers her mouth with her hand as her eyes release a flood of tears. When she composes herself, she says, 'I wondered when this day would come. I have been trying to protect you from sadness.'

'But Ma, true happiness can only be felt if you have experienced sadness.'

'When did you become so wise?' Mama's eyebrows furrow. 'Childbirth prepared me for the deep pain in my soul that I would suffer when you were unhappy. I just prayed that your sadness would be a long way off. There's nothing worse for a mother or father to see their child unhappy, and there's nothing they can do to help. Ari, you are beyond anything your father and I could have ever imagined, or dreamed of. We would never want you to feel that you have to act like someone else. We need you to be true to yourself, your story that was created for you.' Mama reaches over and wraps her hands around mine. 'I was never prepared for the complete joy and unconditional love you would bring me, and I hope, I give you. I love you, Ari.'

'I love you too, Ma.' My voice softens as my heart and head fill with the *human love* of my mama.

'Now, have I told you about how your father like to stick little dinosaurs to the ceiling in every room of the house?'

'No, why did he do that?' I light up with eagerness to hear a story about my father.

'To see who would notice them on the ceiling when they visited. It was his own little private joke. And when we went to visit friends, he would leave a toy dinosaur in their fridge.'

'Did he ever leave any dinosaurs for you?'

'All the time. I found them in my drawers, in my handbag, in my lunchbox, in the shower, under my pillow. I kept them all until his birthday, then I wrapped them up and gave them back to him. He should have been a paleontologist.'

'But then you would never have met!'

'Oh no ... we still would have met. Life is like that.'

'Do you think I will meet someone to fall in love with one day?'

'You will, and it will happen when you least expect it.'

'Ma, can I work with you tomorrow?'

'I'd like that,' she says.

'And, Ma. I'm ready to study at university level like you and Pa did. I'm ready to expand my knowledge and find what I want to do with my life.'

Mama stills and stares at one spot on the table. Then she looks at me. 'Let's talk about your options tomorrow when you are working with me.'

'Okay.' I stand from the table and push my chair in. 'See you in the morning. I'll do my hair, and you'll have more time for yourself.' I lean over and kiss her cheek. 'Goodnight, Mama Bear.'

'Goodnight, Ari Bear. Sleep well.'

I grab my portraits and return to my room and place them on my desk. Then I sit on my window seat and look up at the heavens. Satellites move across the sky at all angles, in a constant state of movement. Sometimes they crash into each other, falling with a light trail behind them. The sky is so broken. It feels like star wars.

I brush my hair and plait it. My bed hair. The anti-knot solution. I prepare for bed with teeth cleaning and bathing, washing the King's Forest dirt off my feet, clothe myself in my quick escape clothes, close the window shutters, then climbed into bed. No shoes.

I stare at the ceiling. I am adulting by going to bed by myself, without Mama grooming my hair or tying on my shoes. I am adulting without Mama saying my birth prayer. And strangely, I feel so alone.

Although that is not the entire truth. I roll onto my side, facing the shutters. In fact I had spent many nights without Mama, isolated at the lighthouse where Mama said I had to remain hidden. On the sea of souls, of the once upon a time, of lost and broken boats and dead bodies of ancient sailors, where their flesh once fell off their bones as fish nibbled at them. Of tormenting, turbulent, savage waves that engulfed the bay, of endless gales and rusting sea sprays. Of salty air that coated everything on the lighthouse like an artist in a psychotic episode. Mama said it was safer there, until my dream story could be finished, at least. Until it could be delivered.

But I wasn't safe there. I wasn't safe from my nightmares, from my loneliness. I wasn't safe from my frustrations. And I was definitely not safe from myself. From my curious, questioning mind and my stubborn nature.

The silence of no conversation with anyone at the lighthouse was like torture.

My mind wanders, back to the first time I was isolated at the lighthouse without Mama.

I gazed over the bay. Two bays. Mama always said there was two of everything, like the day sky and the night sky. I always thought there was three of everything. Like the day sky, the night sky, and the cloudy sky. Like the good me, the rebellious me, and the detached me, who viewed my life in third person, like watching myself as if I was a different person.

The normally chaotic, violent lake was calm today. Too calm and too blue like a perfect reflection of the sky. I looked up. The Endling sea birds were restless, silent and flying in an unusual circular path, the sound of their beating wings in a panic. There were seven of them, their whiteness juxtaposed against the purplish-black clouds gathering in the sky. That makes four of everything—the stormy sky.

Mama said there was always a calm before the storm. And the calmer it was, the bigger the storm. This time, it wasn't a blue sky storm, a wind storm, a sand storm, or a snow storm. It was the worst kind for me: a thunder storm. My right arm tingled and ached. I put my left hand on my right shoulder and ran my hand down my arm to my fingers to try to stop the "storm ache".

Mama said to watch the animals. Watch their behaviour. They are the beacons of impending weather phenomena and other events. The Endlings broke their infinite flight path and disappeared beyond the darkening horizon.

To *The Beyond* that is never spoken of.

To *The Beyond* that is forbidden.

Would they ever return?

It is said that those who go to *The Beyond*, never return. And Mama said that it why I must never go there.

My stomach knotted. I closed my eyes trying to stop the veil of sadness from covering me. I had friends who went to *The*

Beyond, and never returned. What happened to them?

The silence of my lighthouse "hide-out" unnerved me. There was not even the metallic scrapping of metal on metal of the lighthouse that was my constant companion. Anxiety skirted along my skin as the silence became deafening, menacing like a vulture circling and threatening to overpower.

Devour.

A sound crept up in the distance. Tiptoeing. Soft. I opened my eyes and looked up when a rhythmic whooshing became louder. The sea birds were returning. Tenfold.

A sharp gust of wind flicked my wild, windswept, auburn locks and pulled me from my focus. The hairs on my arm stiffened, and I ran. 116 steps to the top of the lighthouse to close just one small window. Then I slid down the helical staircase to the top floor of the two storey lighthouse house and closed eight windows, down the steps to the lower floor and closed four windows and one door. Out the other door to the outside annex and closed four windows and one door.

As I was about to close the outside door on the lighthouse decking, the Endlings landed. Squawking. High pitched and fast. They needed shelter and I was their only hope. I herded them into the annex room and closed the door, then ran back to the main house and shut the final door behind me.

I made my way to the safe room on the upper floor in haste, pulled the door shut and sat in the corner and waited, the darkness enveloping me like a cocoon.

Safety.

And there it was. The shudder, followed by a deep metallic bass vibrating through the bones of the structure. The lighthouse was restless. It wanted to be freed from its mooring to the reef below. Freed from its capture. Like me. This second time on the lighthouse I had been punished for something I didn't do. Mama said it was safer here. Again. Like that time when I was twelve.

A loud moan followed another shudder like a mythical beast

was mourning its soulmate. Once, when I heard that same loud moan when a storm came, part of the attached jetty fell into the reef below leaving a void along the wooden walk to meet the rowboat back to the mainland.

My skin burned.

Panic.

Mama said when panic started, I needed to slow time down. She said I could do that with my breathing. She said I could remove myself from the situation by separating myself from reality. I inhaled deeply, then released it slowly through my pursed lips.

Breathe in. Breathe out ... separate myself from my present ...

And while I did that, the storm rolled in and left. I emerged from the safe room as a victor, elated that I indeed had reached inside myself for strength. I released the Endlings, one of them staying behind and looking at me like saying a personal thank you. Then it too flew off. Free. And I was alone again, on the sea of souls, of the once upon a time, of lost and broken boats and dead bodies of ancient sailors ...

I roll onto my back on the bed. How could a mother leave her daughter on a lighthouse in the middle of a lake, alone? Or was I not alone all those times, just unaware of someone being with me?

My life was full of complexities, omissions and secrets. Mama always said the truth comes out.

I take a deep breath in, then out, and close my eyes and whisper, 'Courage and Strength. Kindness. Creativity. Imagination. Wisdom. Faithfulness and Truth. Human Love. Light. Hope. Breath. These are my gifts. May they be written onto my heart, to guide and protect. And I pray, that I fully comprehend my breath, and the knowledge of it that surpasses all understanding.'

What other type of love could there be?

Human love.

To have.
And to hold.
To love.

And to cherish.

Mama said that *two people*
can look at the same thing,
and *see it* differently,
and *feel it* differently.
She said it's *not what you look at* that matters,
but what you see from *your life experience,*
and *how you react to it.*

CHAPTER 22

The fresh daisies on my window sill are yellow, like the sun has a paint brush and coated the petals with a lick of sunshine. Daisies. Uncomplicated. If I stare at the flowers long enough, my mind can make the yellow hue drip onto the window sill and run down onto the floor. Mama said I had a good imagination. But I didn't tell her that I can make the trees walk away in my visual field like they have legs. I didn't tell Mama that I can make the white winged horses in the paintings in the oratory take flight off the canvas like they have come to life. I didn't tell Mama about the nightmares that came at night from the shadows. The nightmares. Usually about Papa being taken. An event I never witnessed. Or dying in the rectangular hole in the ground in the Field of Flowers I fell into, my flesh decaying so my skeleton is left. Or the worst one. Mama leaving and never returning, like Papa.

I throw my thoughts of woe to the side to stop my day being bathed in sadness. Mama said when I wake each morning to find three things to be thankful for. Mama's are always waking up to a new day, a new day to do good for others, and to gift love to others, no matter who they are, as it has been gifted to us, unconditionally. Today, I am thankful for Eli telling me about *The Beyond,* working alongside Mama today, and for seeing a photograph of Papa.

I climb out of bed and open the window shutters. The sun is bright, sprinkling it's happiness on the Field of Flowers, the zinnia's in every colour looking up at the sun.

I change out of my escape clothes and into my Monday clothes—light gray wide-leg pants and a powder blue long-sleeved cotton t-shirt—it's Thursday. I head to the breakfast nook. There on the table is my breakfast, and a note.

My joy sinks like a stone that has landed in a pond. I won't be working with Mama today.

I pick up the note, looking for stringed letters and words and sentences running into each other forming an apology.

Dear Ari,

I'm in the flower house collecting blooms for today. I'll see you in the science lab once you have finished breakfast.

Love, Mama.
P.S. Shoes are a *must.* No *shoes.* No *work.*

I sigh. The science lab. My second choice. I was hoping to work alongside Mama, and death.

Did she work with death?

Maybe on that day I saw her working with flowers and a person and tying hands and feet, I had missed too much conversation and left too early to be certain the person was dead. After all, Mama stroked the head of the person and said, 'My love, this will sting for a little bit. I'm sorry if it hurts you.' Why would she say that if the person was dead?

What if my memory is wrong, and that person was not dead?

Maybe Mama does some sort of care package for others? She did use the word "cocoon". A caterpillar makes a cocoon to transform, then emerges as a beautiful butterfly.

Maybe Mama was working some sort of psychology with people here, to improve their lives?

Maybe what I thought I saw, was wrong? Like memories that change each time you retrieve them.

Maybe I violently vomited on that day for nothing, and the sleepless nights that followed were a waste of precious sleep?

I sit down to my eggs and toast, and imagine Mama opening the white wooden door to the flower house and inhaling the glorious floral scents, walking in and looking about at the glass walls and ceilings. And colour. Everywhere. I'm keen to see which flowers she chooses for our work today, and what we'll be doing with them in the science lab.

After breakfast I return to my room and put on my heavy black shoes, grimacing the whole time as my feet protest by cramping up, then head to the floors below the castle and to the Science Lab. I push on the door gingerly and enter, firstly noting the room where I had taken two skeletons when I was thirteen, on the right. Then I see the bounty of freshly cut flowers in all colours. And Mama.

'Good morning, Ari,' Mama says, her voice cheery like the yellow daisies on my window sill.

'Morning, Ma,' I say, and stop beside her.

'Nice shoes,' she says.

That comment isn't worth acknowledgement. 'What are we doing today?'

Mama places a flower wreath on my head, but it isn't made of fancy flowers that share their perfume in the air, just a pink and white clover chain without scent. Just a clover chain. Surely I was worth more than just a clover chain? 'Pink—love and protection. White—thoughtfulness and kindness. Life, and hope of the life to come.' Then she places one onto her head. 'And a frenzy of buzzing bees that love clover. I hope you can run fast!' Mama smiles. An easy smile I rarely see.

'What are we doing here today?' I ask again. Impatient.

'We're collecting flower petals and placing them in jars. To use them today, we need them to be fresh. Others in the room with us are extracting oils and fragrances to make perfume, and also collecting petals for drying.'

'But isn't that what the flower house is for?'

'Yes. But we need more space than the area allows there. Our flowers, and flower products are in high demand right now.'

'You sell them for money like in the books I've read?'

'We … trade … them for products we need. No money exchanged. I'd like you to start with the roses. Group the petals in the jars by their colour. Don't mix colours. And don't go near the computers and other technology on the other side of the room.'

I turn and look at the computers and other technology and frown. Mama has only let me near technology a couple of times when I was little. And then no more. 'Gotcha. I sure am glad I put shoes on to work here. I'd hate to think what would happen if a rose petal fell on my foot!' I say, tongue in cheek.

'You'd probably change your mind if one of the scissors dropped onto your foot, the sharp ends embedding themselves between the tarsus bones of your foot.'

No comment. Point taken.

'Do you remember how to get the petals off a rose the easy way, like we used to do when you were little, where we would then throw the petals high in the air and watch it rain petals?'

I smile. 'Of course. The upside-down trick. How could I forget?'

I reach for a pale pink rose, hold it upside-down, grasp the rose head with my left hand, hold on to the stem where the stem and petals meet with my right hand, then carefully disconnect them. The petals separate easily. I gather them together and place them in a large jar. My work has begun, and I work in silence beside Mama. It is a minimal use of words day for me today. I'm disappointed to be working with flower petals.

After we have filled one hundred jars, Mama leaves and returns with boxes.

'Part one complete. Part two. Follow me,' Mama says.

Mama gathers the boxes and places the jars of petals inside them. She finds a four wheeled trolley and stacks the boxes onto it, then pulls the trolley out of the Science Lab, and along the thoroughfare beneath the castle. She keeps walking past the place I thought we would go to, the ground floor above, to use the petals for decorations.

She keeps walking past the kitchen where I thought the petals would be used in baking.

Then Mama keeps walking toward the place she told me I was never welcome at. Ever. That place she said broke her heart. That place that made her tears cascade like waterfalls. That place where she never wanted Papa to do the dance of sleep with death. It was the place she wished had never existed. It was the place she wanted to protect me from, and the great heartache it caused.

That place I had observed Mama in. Once.

That place that made me so sick it was embedded in my memory and marked as a do not return.

As we turn the corner to that place, a strong, bitter, sharp smell lingered and I wince.

Mama enters the room, a large space with a light coloured stone floor, walls and columns, a timber ceiling and three small open windows. She stops the trolley in front of a tall shelf, but instead of books, it holds jars and cloth. 'Ari, place the jars on the shelves.'

As I place each jar onto the shelf, I make a mind note of what else sits on the shelf: cotton material, twine, sage, rosemary and thyme, paper, pencils, and empty jars.

I look over at Mama, who stands next to a metal, waist high trolley on wheels. She arranges some surgical instruments: scalpels, scissors and rat toothed forceps and seven empty jars. She walks over to me. 'When you finish adding the jars, please go out and harvest some flowers—yellow, pink, red, purple, white— keep the stems on them. Take two buckets and fill them. We are welcoming seven people today.'

I dip my head. *Welcoming?*

There must be a gathering for a celebration happening.

After finishing the jars, I grab the buckets and navigate under the castle, through to outside and to the flower house. I fill the buckets with the requested colours, then return to the welcoming room.

The man I saw sketching when I was sixteen is in the room too.

Mama paces the floor with her eyes closed, whispering to herself. She opens her eyes and gives me a small smile. 'First we begin with laying the cotton fabric over the slab, Ari.'

Like setting the table, I think.

Mama puts on an apron, and hands one to me.

We stand back from the table, and then it began, the activity, flowing through the room like it has been done a thousand times, each person knowing the order of the process, working together with perfect synchronicity.

'Jacob, would you let Levi know that we are ready to begin.'

'Sure,' Jacob says, and leaves the room. A few moments later he returns with three others. They carry a person on a stretcher. My eyes widen. This is not like the welcoming I know when people attend to eat with us at the kingdom's gracious dining hall with the ridiculously long dining table that could fit fifty people.

The person is placed on the table on the cotton fabric. It's a woman, older than Mama. She has a wild tangle of dark brown hair, her skin pale. One eye open. Mouth open. Hands flat beside body, palms down. Is she unwell? Is Mama going to help her to heal?

And then I realise … she's dead.

A chill runs down my spine and makes me shudder. My head swims and I feel faint.

Breathe, Ari, breathe …

This table is most definitely not for a banquet of food for a grand celebration. I shove my hands into the pockets of my apron to hide their trembling. Surely Mama is a good person.

'Thank you, gentlemen,' Mama says, and they leave, except for Jacob, who gathers a pencil and two sheets of paper. I keep my eyes on Jacob to distract myself from the body.

'Jacob, this is my daughter, Ari. She will be assisting us today. She is a gifted artist, her portraits exceptional.'

Jacob raises his eyebrows then smiles at me. 'Pleased to meet you, Ari.'

'Likewise,' I say, trying to keep my voice at a normal tone, not the soprano panicking voice that wants to come out instead.

Jacob starts sketching the person's face, one piece of art paper on top of the other. I wonder what the purpose of it is.

Mama touches the person's shoulder. 'Welcome to the Field of Flowers, my love.'

My heartbeat spikes and my skins burns with anxiety.

Mama reaches over to the metal trolley that holds a number of instruments and jars and flowers and string and cloth strips. She picks up a small square piece of cloth with tweezers and dips it into a solution.

'This is ethanol, Ari. I use it behind the ear to determine if the person is human.'

I take a step backwards, feeling faint and nauseous. This person absolutely looks human. But how could Mama question it? What happened to all life is sacred?

Mama leans over the person. 'My love, this will sting for a little bit. I'm sorry if it hurts you.' Mama moves the person's hair behind their ear to the side, and wipes the skin with the cloth. She lets out of breath of relief.

I'm confused. *Is the woman dead or alive?*

Mama reaches for the person's right hand, and feels the flesh between the thumb and first finger. She turns and picks up a black device like the one used in *The Beyond,* and holds it over that place of flesh. The black box beeps, just like the scanners in Lerwick and Jedburgh.

'Human, not a humanoid clone,' she says, and looks at a screen on the device. 'Jacob, Ari, this is Delilah Jones. She is forty-two years of age, has three children, worked as a nurse and was red flagged for opposing the removal of babies from their mothers, and hence why she is here with us today.'

Mama places her gloved hand over the face of the person. One eye is open. 'Close your eyes now, it's time to rest. You have finished your journey well.' Mama pushes the eyelid closed, but it opens again, although not as much. Then Mama holds the hand of the person, and feels the flesh between the thumb and index finger again. 'You don't need this anymore, Delilah. You are freed. You'll feel a little sting.' I watch as Mama reaches for the scalpel and cuts the person's hand, and pulls out something just a little bigger than a grain of rice, washes it, and drops it into a jar, the ting echoing throughout the room.

'What is that?' I'm pretty sure it's a microchip but I want it to be confirmed by Mama. Besides, she might give me more information.

'It's a microchip. It's digital, which I will explain to you later. Around the world, you can't buy or sell anything without a microchip. It stores all of your information … birth, family, education, employment, health records, bank details. Not everyone has one though. There are people who refuse to get one, or a barcode, or the ring. Those are the people we help with food and water and clothing and medical supplies. As well as those who do have the microchip or barcode, but do not have enough credits to survive. There used to be ways to use physical money on the black market, but the government removed money from circulation, promising to double the amount of the cash you surrendered them, putting it into your digital bank account. When people are starving, it feels like a great deal to double your money and be guaranteed food. It was incomprehensible that people were manipulated like that.'

Mama reaches for the scissors, and snips off some hair and places string around it, and puts it in a jar. She runs her hands down her apron. 'There's so much I haven't told you, Ari. I had hoped goodness and freedom would return to society. And I wanted you to live a happy life. When the world started to became a compulsory cashless society, it was just the beginning of sorrows. People have been deceived. They were fed a delusion, drip by drip, desensitised and manipulated. And we are perhaps, *The Lastlings*. Ari, if you are ever taken, don't let them microchip you. If you get the chip, or barcode, you lose your identity, you lose your freedom. Your free will. You are owned, controlled, manipulated.' There is panic in Mama's voice I have never heard before. 'Baby's born are now taken from the mother under the guise of a medical check, they do that, but then insert a flexible microchip and guide it into the baby's brain. Thoughts can be read. Knowledge can be downloaded. Behaviour can be controlled. All without parental consent. It's dehumanising—the blending of artificial intelligence and humans. Some people have woken up to the world plan being forced upon civilisation, and go with their baby to ensure that they are safe. There have been heavily protected alternative maternity hospitals set up that are not associated with the government to protect the human race. Promise me, Ari, that you will never receive the microchip, or barcode.'

I want to say yes Mama, but I can't form the words with my mouth. I'm scared. Sad. Bewildered. Numb. So I just nod instead.

Mama leans back and takes a deep breath, then leans forward again, and straightens the clothes on Delilah. 'I'm going to wash you now. It will make you feel good,' Mama says, and uses a wet cloth and wipes over the exposed limbs, humming a pretty tune. Then she dries her limbs.

'How's your portrait going, Jacob?'

'Well. The first is finished.' I watch as he puts the portrait to the side, then proceeds to draw on the second piece, tracing the lines imprinted from the first portrait. Clever, I think. It will save him time with the portrait. Then he uses colours to add dimension and life to the representational portrait.

I look back at Delilah. 'Ma, she looks like she is still alive. Are you sure she's …' It is the first time I have seen a dead person. She looks like she is sleeping. So peaceful.

'Yes. Let me show you something, Ari.' Mama pulls back Delilah's eyelid. 'Look at her eye. There is a distinct change in the cornea, the clear, dome-shaped outer layer of the eye that covers the iris and pupil, which is normally transparent. A hazy film covers the eyeball, giving the eyes a blue or grey-like appearance due to the opacity of the cornea. The pupil is enlarged, as the body has relaxed and lost oxygen. The pupil is now fixed and will not be reactive to light. Before her body came here, our people checked for a pulse, listened to her chest for sounds of breath and heartbeat, and looked at her pupils. Then they delivered her here. *The Quietus* Room. The release from life; death.' Mama closes Delilah's eyelid, lightly pressing down on the eyelid for around 30 seconds. This time it stays closed. 'These beautiful souls lost their lives in *The Beyond*. Their bodies, if found by the establishment, are just thrown into a deep pit and burned like they are nothing but an inconvenience. We try to retrieve the bodies before they are found, then bring them here to acknowledge their life and honour them with a beautiful burial.'

'Was she murdered?'

'Most are, but not all. Some die due to natural causes. The

information on Delilah's microchip tells us she certainly was a target. Ari, please choose a flower of each colour and bring them here.'

Mama picks up a pink carnation and holds it near Delilah's face and says to her, 'I'm just matching a colour flower to your skin. The pastel pink tone looks lovely.' Mama picks seven pink flowers of different varieties and places them in Delilah's hair and around her face. She lifts the hands of the person and places them on the stomach, pushing a small flower posy between the hands, then Mama grabs a strip of cloth and ties the hands together at the wrist, and then the feet.

Mama reaches for some oil scents that were in bottles on the trolley, and dabs them on the person. 'You'll love these perfumes of parsley, sage, rosemary and thyme—for Quietus, immortality, remembrance, and courage. They are to honour you with their scented kiss.'

I watch as Mama dabs the scented oils on the person with a gentleness that speaks of love.

'Jacob, how's the second portrait?'

'Just finished.'

'Wonderful. Help me prepare the cocoon?'

Cocoon? I take a big step backward to get out of the way. Jacob stands and rolls the portrait up and adds it to the jar where Mama had dropped the microchip into, and the hair cutting, then he stands on the opposite side of Mama.

They reach down to the fabric, and lift and roll Delilah, wrapping and tucking the fabric, and watch as her body settles.

'This wrapping is like the final earthly hug.' Mama strokes the head of the cocooned Delilah. 'You're ready to join your friends in the Field of Flowers. Your resting place has been prepared. I'll see you later, my love, when we'll say goodbye under the safety of the night.'

Jacob and Mama stand in silence for a moment, their heads bowed. Then Jacob leaves and returns with the three men who had delivered Delilah. They carefully place her body onto a stretcher and leave. Once they are gone, Mama becomes busy, labelling the jar with the microchip, the hair clipping, and the portrait, then places it on an empty shelf.

'Ari, sit beside me as I write notes.'

I sit beside Mama at a desk. On a previously prepared piece of paper, she records the details of Delilah, including the time that she came in, the number on her microchip, age, sex, employment, education, offspring, partner, and draws on a map where her body will be laid to rest in the Field of Flowers.

Then she removes a large leather bound book from the shelf. She opens it to a page marked with a lavender coloured ribbon, and adds Delilah's name using a pen with a nib and ink onto the homemade paper. 'This is the Book of Life, Ari. Some would label it as death records, but I prefer to honour the dead by calling it the Book of Life, to acknowledge their history, their presence of being a soul who once walked on our beautiful earth, and their spirit, returned to heaven.'

Mama blows on the ink on the page before she marks the page with the lavender coloured ribbon. Then she places it back on the shelf. It is one of many.

'How many people have you honoured in death?'

'Delilah is number 303, just in that book.'

CHAPTER 23

My eyes widen as I start to see stars, and I gasp. I sway. Mama stands at once and puts her hands on my shoulders and guides me to her seat and I sit, leaning forward with my hand on my forehead. Mama disappears for a moment, then returns with a glass of water. I take a sip, and start to feel better.

'How long have you been doing this?' I ask.

Mama looks up, like looking back into memories, painful ones. Her eyes redden. 'After you were born. It started with a request to bring the dead here so I could find your father, and honour him with a burial filled with the love he gave to others. And to have a place to go to visit his memory. And at first it was just male bodies, because I was looking for your father, but then, it became men, women and children. Some people are found close to death, Ari. We bring them here to the medical rooms and try to save them. Successfully at times.'

'Are you still waiting for … Papa's … body to come in?'

'If Papa is deceased, I pray that his body returns to us, but since it has been so long I think he is still alive. And I can feel it in my spirit. And that is hope.'

'Imagine if Papa walked back into the castle one day,' I say with a smile of my face. There could be no better thing.

'My answered prayer,' says Mama, and gives me a hug.

She stands then, fetches a cloth and dips it in liquid and wipes over the stone slab. The room is filled with that strong, bitter, sharp smell again. I wince.

'This is a disinfectant, Ari. It will kill any bacteria leaked from the previous body. Gloves are a must.' Mama dries the stone slab with a towel and drops it into a container. She walks over to the shelf and collects a cotton sheet, and returns to the slab. She looks at me and I go to her and help her drape the sheet over the slab.

Jacob and the three men enter with a stretcher, and place a body onto the cotton sheet.

I watched as Mama gazes over it and her eyebrows pull together. 'There's no pooling of blood or discolouration. I'm pretty sure this one is not human.' She opens the eyelid and shakes her head. Then she reaches for the ethanol, pushes the person's hair at their temple to the side, and wipes the skin with the cloth. Under the skin is a metallic colour.

'Humanoid. Have a look, Ari. Touch it. You need to know how it is different to the feel of a human. Then would you please scan the microchip so we can get details of who the humanoid is a copy of.'

'A humanoid?' I say, and reach out to touch the humanoid body, the skin a little rubbery, the body cold to touch. I collect the scanner from the trolley.

'It's a type of robot design to resemble and interact with humans. This one has human form with artificial skin and eyes, but they are not made of flesh or bones and organs and brains, and have no blood. They have been embedded with neural networks and artificial intelligence to recognize human faces and understand gestures and emotions, and can interact with people and respond appropriately, in a human-like way. They can talk like humans, walk like humans, and mimic the emotions of humans, and can even identify smell and taste, though they cannot taste or smell anything—it's simply its program that finds the markers and labels the taste and smell. They make eye contact, remember conversations, can have a programmed personality, mood, and emotions, and some are more likely to be a realistic twin of someone, without their consent.'

'And record voices and play them back?' I ask.

'Yes.' I watch as Mama feels behind the humanoid's head. 'GPS Jammer has been placed in position prior to coming here. Safe to commence.'

Jacob steps forward and starts to remove the outer skin mask off the face, then removes the robotic eyes and places them into a box. The humanoid is now faceless, its aluminium, rubber, hard plastics and wires exposed, circuit boards and foam and little motors. It is nothing. Destroying it wouldn't even hurt it.

'This one is an older humanoid version made mainly from metal, the new ones are made from polyacrylates with 3D printing. Find the chip in the hand and scan it please, Ari.'

I raise my eyebrows at Mama's request for me to find the chip, and step forward to it. I touch the hand of the robot, find where the chip is on the right hand, then bring the scanner close to the skin. But it does not beep. I place it directly on top of the position of the chip, and it still does not beep. I'm not surprised after the trouble I have with the scanners in *The Beyond*. 'Mama?'

Mama takes the device from my hand and tries it. It doesn't beep. She looks at me then puts the device to the side and uses a different one. It beeps. She gives the device to me so I can copy what she has done. It doesn't beep. I pass the device back to Mama.

She turns it this way and that. 'Did you hold it correctly?'

'Yes.'

'Did you press too hard on it somewhere?'

'No.'

She rubs her forehead. 'Matteo, please find a spare chip with information on it, and two scanners that are in working order.'

Matteo returns after a moment. 'Scan the chip Matteo, please.'

He does and it beeps. Matteo reads the information on the scanner. He gives the chip and scanner to Mama. She places the microchip onto her hand then passes the scanner to me. 'Trying scanning, Ari.'

I hold the scanner over the microchip. It doesn't beep. The light on the scanner has gone out like the other two.

'Matteo, scan the chip with the other scanner.'

It beeps.

'Ari, take the microchip from me and hold it between your thumb and index finger, then give it back to me.'

I do as Mama has instructed me.

'Matteo, scan the chip, please.'

Matteo brings the scanner close, almost touching the chip. It beeps.

'Read the information on the chip please.'

'There's nothing.'

Mama looks at me with one eyebrow raised. 'Hmmm.'

'Is there something wrong with me?' I say, my hands beginning to shake again.

'No. Just don't handle any technology.'

I frown and look around the room. The four men stare at me as if I am a freak.

'Jacob, is the mask and microchip in the box and labelled?'

'Done.'

'Can you remove the microchip as well.'

'Certainly.'

'Gentlemen, you may take the humanoid to the technology lab once Jacob is done. Thank you.'

I watch as Jacob cuts into the humanoid's hand and locates the chip and removes it and places it into the box, then the men gather around and lift the humanoid and leave the room with it.

'Mama?'

'Which topic—you or the humanoid?'

'Both.'

'Let's leave that to tonight at dinner. I'll need to catch you up on history, and what's to come—the 8th Industrial Revolution. We still have people to welcome before nightfall for the farewell ceremonies. Please take the box with the mask into the adjoining room. Once you are in there, you'll know what to do.'

I collect the box and take it into the adjoining room. As soon as I enter, a light comes on, revealing walls of jars containing portraits, hair and microchips to the left, and humanoid face masks and microchips and eyeballs to the right. The face masks are all kinds of skin colours and ethnicities. It's like being in a room with a hundred faces all looking at you. Judging you.

I find a vacant position on the wall and display the new mask with its accessories there. Just like the others. Creepy.

I return to Mama just as a new body is delivered.

'Thank you, gentlemen,' Mama says, and they leave, except for Jacob, who gathers a pencil and two sheets of paper. Like he's in automatic mode.

Mama glances over the person, then touches the shoulder. She knows they are human. Instinct, or experience? 'Welcome to the Field of Flowers, my love.' Her voice is gentle. Mama reaches over to the metal trolley that holds a number of instruments and jars and flowers and string and cloth strips. She picks up a small square piece of cloth with tweezers and dips it into a solution.

Mama leans over the person. 'My love, this will sting for a little bit. I'm sorry if it hurts you.' Mama moves the person's hair behind the ear to the side, and wipes the skin with the cloth.

Mama reaches for the person's right hand, and feels the flesh between the thumb and first finger. She turns and picks up a black scanning device, and holds it over that place of flesh. The black box beeps.

'Human,' she says. 'Jacob, Ari, this is Jaimee Stevens. She is twenty-nine years of age, has two children, worked in technology and was red flagged for speaking up about artificial intelligence, and hence why she is here with us today.'

Mama places her gloved hand over the face of the Jaimee. 'Keep your eyes closed, it's time to rest. You have finished your journey well.' Mama holds the hand of the person and feels the flesh between the thumb and index finger again. 'You don't need this anymore, Jaimee. You are freed. You'll feel a little sting.' I watch as Mama reaches for the scalpel and cuts the person's hand, and pulls out the microchip, washes it, and drops it into a jar, the ting echoing throughout the room.

Mama reaches for the scissors, and snips off some hair and places string around it, and puts it in the jar. She runs her hands down her apron, takes a deep breath, then leans forward and straightens the clothes on Jaimee. 'I'm going to wash you, now. It will make you feel good,' Mama says, and uses a wet cloth and wipes over the exposed limbs, humming a pretty tune. She dries the limbs.

'How's your portrait going, Jacob?'

'Well. The first is finished.' I watch as he puts the portrait to the side, then proceeds to draw on the second piece, tracing the lines imprinted from the first portrait Then he uses the colours to add dimension and life to the representational portrait. I'm flabbergasted at how quick he is with portraits. But I guess, the more you draw portraits, the easier it gets with the technique, and knowing what to look for.

'Ari, please choose a flower of each colour and bring it here.'

Mama picks up a white daisy and holds it near Jaimee's face. 'I'm just matching a colour flower to your skin. The white daisy looks lovely.' Mama picks seven white flowers of different varieties and places them in Jaimee's hair and around her face. She lifts the hands of the person and places them on the stomach, pushing a small flower posy between the hands, then Mama grabs a strip of cloth and ties the hands together at the wrist, and then the feet.

Mama reaches for some oil scents that were in bottles on the trolley, and dabs them on the person. 'You'll love these perfumes of parsley, sage, rosemary and thyme—for Quietus, immortality, remembrance, and courage. They are to honour you with their scented kiss.'

I watch as Mama dabs the scented oils on Jaimee with a gentleness that spoke of love.

'Jacob, how's the second portrait?'

'Just finished.'

'Wonderful. Help me prepare the cocoon with the cotton shroud?'

I take a big step backward again to get out of the way. Jacob stands and rolls the portrait and adds it to the jar where Mama has dropped the micro-chip and hair cutting, then he moves to the opposite side of Mama.

They reach down to the fabric, and lift and roll Jaimee, wrapping and tucking the fabric, and watch as she settles.

Mama strokes the head of the cocooned Jaimee. 'You're ready to join your friends in the Field of Flowers. Your resting place has been prepared. I'll see you later, my love, when we'll say goodbye under the safety of the night.'

Jacob and Mama stand in silence for a moment, their heads bowed. I join them. Then Jacob leaves and returns with the three others who had delivered Jaimee. They carefully place her body onto a stretcher and leave. Once they are gone, Mama becomes busy, labelling the jar with the microchip, the hair clipping, and the portrait, then places it on the empty shelf next to the first jar.

I sit beside Mama at the desk. On a previously prepared piece of paper, she records the details of Jaimee, including the time that she came in, the number on her microchip, age, sex, employment, education, offspring, partner, and draws on the map where her body will be laid to rest.

Then she removes the large leather bound book from the shelf. She opens it up to a page that is marked with a lavender coloured ribbon. 'Ari, would you please add Jaimee's name to the

Book of Life.' I pick up the calligraphy pen, dip it into the blue ink and add Jaimee's name, then blow of the page and check that the ink is dry before I replace the book on the shelf.

When I finish, Mama is drying the stone slab after disinfecting it. So I walked over and grab the cotton shroud to help put in place for the next person.

'That corpse was quite fresh. Our aim is to retrieve bodies within an eight hour window to protect ourselves from any dangerous decomposing bacteria that will be present.'

A new body arrives then and was placed onto the stone slab.

'Welcome to the King's Forest,' Mama said.

I gasp at the realisation that my tea party tipi is in the King's Forest, and is most probably sitting on top of a dead body. I close my eyes and vow to retrieve the tipi and skeletons from the forest tomorrow.

I watch Mama perform the process of de-microchipping, washing, drying, tying, adding herbs and spices to the man, and decorating him with flowers, detached from the room. He, Edward, has a beard like Papa's, and contrastingly, a bald head.

When Mama calls me to write his name in the Book of Life, I do, my head in a swirl of emotion and questions and in, I think, a state of shock. I feel numb.

Edward.

Edward is dead.

The final body is delivered to *The Quietus*. A girl. My age. Jacob and the three men look away from her body as they carry her in, two of them with faces streaked with tears. She has been beaten, or worse, and is covered in blood, her clothing torn. Her eyes are open, filled with fear. Mama cries as she washes her body. I can't watch. I crouch on the floor in the foetal position and sob, my body trembling at the realisation of the violence and horror that has been inflicted on her. How can a human be so cruel? Was it a human who attacked her? Or humanoid or robot?

'Monsters!' Mama shouts, her voice shaky. 'A real man would

never hurt a woman!' I have never heard Mama so angry before.

My skin burns. Panic. Mama said when panic starts, I need to slow time down. She said I could do that with my breathing. She said I could remove myself from the situation by separating myself from reality. I inhale deeply, then release it slowly through my pursed lips. *Breathe in. Breathe out* ... separate myself from my present ... *Breathe in. Breathe out* ... *Breathe in. Breathe out.*

'Ari, Phoebe is prepared now. Look how beautiful she is.'

I am back in the present. I stand and look at her, and Mama puts her arm around my shoulder in a warmth that feels like lying amongst the daisies in the summer sunshine without a care in the world. It's solace and calmness in the chaos and the shock. A comforting embrace for my soul. Phoebe has flowers of all colours in her hair and in her hands, her new white dress as white a snow. There is no sign of blood and her eyes are closed like she is in a peaceful sleep.

Mama and Jacob shroud her and her body is taken from the room. Mama sits and records her details while I write her name in The Book of Life, never to be forgotten.

How has Mama kept the sorrows and horrors of *The Quietus* secret from me all of my life?

CHAPTER 24

Mama leads me to the room where the shrouded bodies wait for burial. Bodies and death.

I shiver.

The room is cold and dimly lit.

Mama stays in one place while I walk around the bodies. Each of the shrouds decorated with flowers and small branches. And for a moment in time, I wonder when my time will come, and would I be ready, or would my life be taken without warning. I realise then that focusing on life is a great gift. Focusing on the present. Not worrying about what is to come that may not come. I decide then and there to not think about the day I die.

It happens to everyone. No one escapes it.

Well, except Enoch and Elijah, as recorded in earth history.

I walk back to Mama and she pulls me into her arms and holds me while I cry. Then Mama holds my hand as we walk back through the castle underground at a slow pace, then up to the ground floor, where our hands part and I go outside.

And I run.

Flicking my shoes off my feet.

I need to feel the ground under my bare feet.
I need to feel the sun on my face.
I need to breathe the fresh air.
I need to feel life around me.
I need to talk to Eli.
But he isn't here.

❀

The afternoon, followed by dinner, goes by in a blur of existential crisis that leaves me stuck in a feeling of unease, dragging my heavy heart behind me. I can't even scrape up the energy or courage to ask Mama about what happened today.

I'm not ready to process anything.

I'm not ready to process … death.

The irony of Eli saying dead to me all my life isn't lost on me. In fact, it has taken power away from the word and it's finality.

I imagine the last inhale and final exhale. The end of breath, the sacred gift. The end of a beating heart, that came before our first earthly breath. The end of circulating blood that completes the trinity of life. The end of identity. The end of earthly human love.

The end of the essence, of *us*.

Dead had just become a word without meaning.

Without emotion. Until today, when I was with death.

I dress in black as requested by Mama so that we are not visible from above.

Surveillance. Control.

I wander to the innocent Field of Flowers of my youth that is filled with the beauty of colour, of petals, of little miracles that stand proudly facing the sun.

Flowers of love.

And of romance.

And of songs and of eternal memories of happiness, of he loves me, he loves me not …

The Field of Flowers now the Field of Death,

of dead people, of bones.

And of decomposition.

And lost dreams.

Of rest.

Of quietus.

Of flowers of remembrance.

Mama said death is not the ending, but a new beginning, the last chapter of earth time, the first chapter of eternity. Perhaps the flowers were symbolic of life, new beginnings, of the loved and loving, of remembrance that we are planted on the earth to grow towards the light, to embrace life and all the goodness it has to offer, all the seasons to journey through, sharing our colour and beauty with others, then return home.

I look up into the heavens to see the majesty of creation.

Of love. And light.

But between the numerous floral umbrellas hung above us tonight, to shield the grave and hide our movements, the proliferation of satellites stops us from seeing the awe of the universe, and sends arrows of mourning onto my shoulders, heavy and filled with a dark sadness the colour of charcoal gray, the bitter taste, vile and repugnant.

The sky is broken.

Like my heart.

What right does humankind have to blemish the beauty of above?

Is it to stop us from seeing the wonderment and the fact that there is more to life than just our existence on earth?

What could be so important that they need to monitor and

control everything?

People—were we really that dangerous to them?

Dangerous to their mission? Dangerous to their objectives?

Did they, whoever they are, hate humankind that much?

The earth is broken.

Humans are broken.

I stand beside Mama, a cloud of sadness lingering around me like a fog.

Mama gives me a gentle smile, filled with the colour and perfume of a multitude of flowers throwing sparkles of hope. I slide my fingers between hers.

Love entwined.

I look down into the grave. It is deeper than the one I fell into when I followed the sun when I was nine. East to west. Like the sunflowers. Except, there were no sunflowers. Just me and my map and my vintage blue school port of *everything*, on the vast grounds of the ugly grey castle ruins that I was sure was becoming a pile of rubble. I opened my hand drawn map and checked my waymarkers, forbidden places and safe havens, and ... the Field of Flowers. That's where I wanted to follow the sun today, disturbing the bees and dead flowers and petals that had lost their hold on the receptacle, with a spiral of joyous air flowing with freedom through my auburn long wild locks, and after me. I imagined a murmuration of colourful Hildebrandt's starlings birds gliding behind me, with a melody of trills and happiness that would make the yellow sunshine sparkle with golden flecks that would kiss my head and weave its magical gold dust through my hair.

Except, there were no starlings. Just mockingbirds that copied sounds. Mama said they were bred and trained here for a purpose. But she didn't tell me anything else. I just nodded, my nine year old mind in a whirl that a bird could copy sounds.

I had left my bedroom at the sound of the rooster at

morningtide, throwing off my bedcover, already dressed in my pastel pink tulle dress so I could twirl around and around and around in the sun and the flowers, and watch my skirt lift high around me. I climbed out the window with my vintage blue school port of *everything*, my bare feet hitting the soft grass with a squelch.

And I ran.

I followed my map to the east to the start of the Field of Flowers, and turned and faced the sun with my homemade sundial made of cardboard.

Each time the sun's shadow moved to the next mark on my sundial, I picked up my vintage blue port of *everything* and took a step backwards. I placed my port down and sat amongst the Field of Flowers, and created flower art on the ground, picking flowers that tickled my fancy. Then I would open by port of *everything*, pull out my sketch book and sketch what I had created, and paint it with watercolours, using my spit as water.

At noontide, I picked up my vintage blue school port of *everything*, looked up and took one very big step backwards as a celebration of the disappearing of shadows. The time of invisibility. The time of one of me.

And screamed.

I had fallen. Into a hole. A very dirty rectangular hole. I let out a cry at the pain in my back, then sat up, gingerly. My pink tulle dress was dirty! Mama was going to be cranky with me. Again. If I could just climb out of the hole I could run back to my room, get changed, and wash my favourite dress. Mama would never know.

I stood and looked up. The hole was deeper than I thought. I lifted my arms and couldn't even reach the top of the hole. I looked around. Perhaps I could dig footholds in the walls, in the corner, alternating footholds on either wall to climb up. I started. But stopped. My feet kept slipping. So I centred myself in the middle of the rectangular below ground room, sat down, and looked up and squinted at the sun. Now I was living in a sundial.

Someone would find me soon. And it would most probably be that very annoying Eli. Why did it always have to be him? He was the most annoying human I knew.

After a while I laid back. The sky was bright blue. I watched the clouds. Changing. Inventing and reinventing themselves as animals and trees and faces. Evaporating. It was like I had my own rectangular window to the heavens.

A bird flew over. Then a dark coloured object hovered. I frowned. Mama had never told me about the things in the first sky. The day sky.

A type of net shot up at the object, and down they both went. I wonder what had just happened and what it means.

I sat up and opened my blue school port of *everything*, and found my pencil to sketch what I saw. I pulled out the blanket then, and tea cups, the only doll that Eli hadn't broken, and my best teddy bear, bald in patches, and sat them around our blanket for our own private tea party. I shared my broken biscuits I had smuggled from the kitchen and the bottle of water, pouring it into the teacups. As the shadows in the rectangular hideaway became longer, I pulled out my art journal and worked in it to pass the time.

As the fleeting eventide colours of purple, pink, orange and light blue blossomed, then faded in the sky, I packed away my friends and wrapped the blanket around me. Perhaps I wasn't going to be rescued. I wondered, if I was here long enough, if I would die here, and I wondered what it would be like to die.

I would call out in my biggest voice to Mama. But it was forbidden. So I sat as still as a statue, pretending to be dead. Like that word that Eli always said to me. Like that game we always played with the governess.

I changed my dead position. This time lying on my side and staring at the dirt wall. Mama said I was good at pretending to be dead, like she had taught me. She said it might save my life one day. And that didn't make sense. How could being dead allow you to live?

I rolled onto my back and crossed my arms over my chest and stared up at the night sky. The second sky. Three still stars blinked at me. Sirius, Canopus and Alpha Centauri Mama had told me. And there were hundreds of stars that moved across the sky.

Mama said that the still stars were the real ones in the universe, the moving stars, thousands of them, were like spies.

What were they spying on?

I sighed and closed my eyes but opened them again. Wide. What if it started raining? Would I drown as the rectangular hole filled with water? Then I would be dead. Would Eli be pleased?

I pulled the blanket over me and closed my eyes. I fell into my imagination like Mama had taught me to do. To disconnect from real time and events, and the fear that was starting to bubble inside me.

'What have you done?' It was Mama's voice. My eyes snapped open. She was angry. 'You have one job to do! ONE! To keep her safe. And today, you have failed!'

'I'm sorry. I will find her an—'

'You'll be more sorry if something has happened to her! Now get out of my sight!'

I scurried to the corner of the rectangular hole and put the blanket over the top of me. If Mama was that angry with him, she would be even more furious with me. She can't know I am stuck down here. It will be the lighthouse punishment. One hundred percent.

'I'll be waiting in the oratory. Bring her to me there when you find her!'

'Yes, Ma'am.'

The sound of the squishing of plants faded into the distance, and then the same sound came closer. 'PSsst.'

I looked up. It was dark, but there was a person there. I could just make out the silhouette.

'It's me.' It was Eli's voice.

'You knew I was here?'

'Yes.' He threw a ladder down the side of the hole in the ground, turned on a magenta light, then jumped down next to me. I wanted the hole to swallow me up. I didn't want it to be Eli who was here to rescue me.

'Why didn't you tell my mother I was here?'

'She ... doesn't like you playing in the Field of Flowers.'

'Why? It's beautiful.'

'It's ... dangerous. That's all.'

'Why is this hole here?'

'It's for—'

'Growing more flowers?'

'Yes. Yes it is.' But Eli's face fell. Was he lying? 'Your mama has planted lots of flowers. You know how much she loves flowers.'

I smiled, and there was a silence between us.

'Why did Mama say you have a job to keep me safe?'

Eli scratched his chin. 'Everyone has the job to keep you safe. Your mama worries about you, that's all.'

'Because I am a girl?'

He nodded. 'And especially because you are her daughter.'

Silence sat between us again, but the weight of being a girl was starting to feel heavy. What was wrong with being a girl? I liked being a girl.

'Can we go now so I can get into trouble and get it over with?' I said.

'No. Let's wait here a little longer. I'm in trouble too.'

'What happens when you get into trouble?'

He took a deep breath, 'I have to—'

'I'm sorry that you'll be in trouble because of me.'

He shook his head. 'My fault. I know you well enough to expect the unexpected. I just never thought you would be in the Field of Flowers.'

'I was following the sun.'

'Of course you were.'

'Mama said to always look where I was going. She said I was as clumsy as my father. He was dreamer who got lost in the world around him. Mama said I am just like him.'

There was silence again.

'Eli. Can I ask you a question?'

'Sure. Go ahead.'

'What is human love?'

'What?'

'When Mama says my bedtime prayer, she says human love. She says ... courage and strength. Kindness. Creativity. Imagination. Wisdom. Faithfulness and Truth. *Human Love.* Light. Hope. Breath.'

'Oh that. My papa prays the same thing. It's so long I like to call it the prayer story.'

'Your papa who knew my papa?'

'Yes. The one and the same.'

'What do they mean by human love?'

'I don't know. I asked my papa and he said I will know when the time is right.'

I sighed. I looked at Eli. Why was he being so normal. He was never normal like this!

'We should get out of here, Ari Flora. Your mama will be beside herself with worry.'

'I kinda wish I could stay here. I don't want to go to the lighthouse again.'

'Your mama says you can't get into mischief at the lighthouse.' He stood. 'Come.'

I stood and collected my vintage blue school port of *everything*. Eli took it from me and tossed it out of the rectangular hole and up into the Field of Flowers. He stood behind me while I climbed the rope ladder, then followed me up, gathering the rope in his hands, then shoved it into a backpack.

'Let's get it over and done with,' he said.

'Gentlemen.' Mama's gentle voice pulls me back from my memory.

I watch as the first body is placed on ropes, and lowered into the grave. My throat tightens. Jacob, Matteo, Peter and Harry, Mama and I shovel dirt on top of the body, and then the next body is lowered into the ground, the shovelling of dirt, the next body, the shovelling of dirt.

Multi-level body stacking. Multi-level graves.

Mama blows air between her lips. I thought she was unaffected by this type of goodbye, but her actions show that it hurts. Emotionally.

'Welcome to the Field of Flowers, Delilah, Jaimee and Phoebe. We honour you. We honour your souls and spirits and the gift of life you were blessed to experience. The *human love* you felt, and gave. Your bodies, we return to the earth, your souls and spirits already returned to our Creator by His angels who were there with you at your time of death. We are never alone. Always cared for. Delight in the pure presence of acceptance and unconditional love, my loves.'

Mama steps back, and so do I. The good men, Jacob, Matteo, Levi and Harry complete the grave filling, then Mama plants some new flowers, she says it's like God plants eternity in the human heart. I work alongside her.

We walk to the King's Forest then, the men carrying the last of the departed, and we stop at a freshly dug grave.

'Gentlemen.' Mama's voice is gentle.

I watch as Edward's body is placed on ropes, and lowered into the grave. Jacob, Matteo, Levi and Harry, Mama and I shovel dirt on top of his body.

Mama blows air between her lips. 'Welcome to the King's Forest, Edward. We honour you. We honour your souls and spirits and the gift of life you were blessed to experience. The *human love* you felt and gave. Your body, we return to the earth, your soul and spirit already returned to our Creator by His angels who were there with you at your time of death. We are never alone. Always cared for. Delight in the pure presence of acceptance and unconditional love, my love.'

After the men finish filling the resting place with soil, Mama plants a new tree. A fir tree. I never thought death could be beautiful, but taking care of the person's body that once housed their sacred soul and spirit was a beautiful way to honour their lives.

I hold my breath then. I think of all the baby fir trees, the saplings, that were in the King's Forest when I played in there. The forbidden King's Forest. The mere thought that they are markers of dead bodies stuns me. I always thought the trees where tall soldiers guarding secrets. But I didn't know what type of secrets? I shake my head with disbelief—it was secrets of death stories— stories of bones and flesh witnessing burials imbued with love and honour. When I was younger, I had actually been stepping over the bodies of men and boys who were buried here. Without knowledge. Stepping over their life stories now finished, their dream stories completed. The ones who loved them left behind, heartbroken and grieving.

An uncontrollable shudder cascades through my body.

How many times had I seen newly planted trees and thought, how cute, baby trees? How many times had I drawn pictures in the fresh dirt with my finger, picturing it as a new canvas provided by nature?

The Field of Flowers. Forbidden to play in.

The King's Forest. Forbidden to play in.

And then I think of Eli. I had inadvertently pulled him into places that were forbidden as well. Yet, he stayed there with me, watching over me.

Obedient. And loyal.

Caring.

And protecting.

Mama said to reflect on the *good things*
that happen,
and *the bad,* and *to learn from them.*

Mama said to reflect on the
highlights and *lowlights* of life.
But don't fall into the danger of
morbid introspection during the lowlights.
Self-examination.
Self-analysis.
Thinking too deeply about yourself.
Judging yourself.
Getting inside your own head and ruminating,
stuck in a cycle of negative thoughts,
reliving the things you did and said so it becomes a
battleground of self-destruction.

Mama said it will cause *anxiety,*
dissatisfaction with yourself and your life.
You will become self-absorbed and less in control
until *you can't find yourself at all.*
Just a darkness.
Self-doubt.
Letting your negative thoughts takeover.
Despair.
Focussing on your flaws, failures and fears.

Mama said you need to look away from them.
You need to *look outside of yourself*.
Spend time in nature.
Exercise.
Distract your thoughts.
Ask if they are true?
Find three things to be thankful for.
Every. Single. Day.

Mama said to *smile*, even when you don't feel
like it.
It will make you *feel a little better*.
And *pray*.

Mama said life is about the *whole journey*.
Focus on the highlights with *gratitude*,
accepting that lowlights will happen,
and *leave those lowlights in the past*.

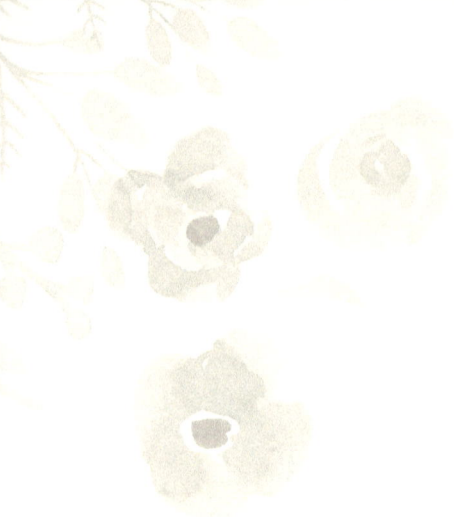

CHAPTER 25

It always happens during the fogbow. The rainbow devoid of colour. The white arch with no pot of glittering gold at the end. It's opposite the happiness of sunrise, with a melancholy settling on me like a heavy cloud filled with negative thoughts and a future that I could not see.

Does it find me, or do I find it?

Sunrise. And sadness.

Sun. And fog. And 35 degrees.

Weak. And colourless.

Mama said to test my thoughts.

Are they true?

Or a lie?

Are they kind, forgiving and light, or are they judgemental, dark and soul destroying?

The fogbow is judgemental. Confusing. Trying to draw me in to look at inside myself, to find the essence of myself. Would I like what I find?

I finger the painted wooden doll I had stolen. Accidentally. I fantasised that my father had made it when I was young. Me sitting beside him as he whittled away at the wood, singing, telling bad dad jokes like the other kids' fathers did, then looking at me with a goofy grin to make me laugh even more. How much hair did Papa have on his arms? His big toe?

Mama said our lives were like the four seasons. And we were like deciduous trees. We are summer, autumn, winter and spring, sometimes drifting in some seasons longer than others. Mama calls them the Melody of Summer, the Echo of Autumn, the Woe of Winter and the Bloom of Spring. But can we be in the four seasons all in one day as well?

Mama said to dream of spring when I was in the woe of winter. It would help me to see through the fog. 'Courage, dear heart,' Mama would say. 'Good things are coming.'

And then my head is full of nothing, something, and everything at once.

I climb out of the giant's chair I am sitting on, hiding under the hugging tree, the reminder that giants once walked the earth, and I run, the blades of grass squealing under my bare feet. I have to return the wooden doll, my conscious like a thousand witnesses, the mirror of my soul.

The grass turns to undergrowth as I enter the forbidden bushland, and I slow as a colourful abandoned car comes into view. The abandoned car I had painted when I was sixteen.

I looked around for Eli. Missing him.

Mama said you don't know how much you like something until it is gone. But Eli was always annoying. Every day was like a game, trying to lose the very irritating Eli. He seemed to be everywhere I was. Lurking. Watching but not watching. Keeping his distance. But the same distance like he had a tape measure with him. He never seemed to hang out with the other kids. Except when I played with them. And once, I saw him smile. That stopped me in my tracks. He always seemed so moody. So serious. So … unhappy.

One day I ran beyond the olive grove, beyond the vegetable

gardens and past the fruit trees that grew twelve fruits, bearing every month, no matter the season, pulling off a red apple on the way and headed into the overgrown bushland. I looked around. No Eli. I had lost him for once.

Victory.

A feeling of freedom rushed through me.

I stopped running and slowed my pace to a walk, panting. In the distance I saw a glint of light, and picked up my pace toward it. As I came closer, there was a rusty brown metal car. Mama had told me about cars, and I had read about them in books. She said that once, people travelled in them to get to places quickly. This car was abandoned. Flat tyres. Broken glass windows. A vine growing through it.

A door was open so I climbed in and sat on the seat with the steering wheel in front of it. I ran my hand over the cracked brown leather seat, then glanced over my shoulder.

And there on the back seat was a snake.

Orange, black and white.

Curled into a spiral.

It lifted its head and its forked tongue flicked out like it was tasting me.

I froze.

In the next moment, a hand reached in through the window and grabbed the snake.

'Dead. Rule number one. Always check your surroundings.' A crooked, smug smile grew on Eli's face as he lifted the snake to his eye level and looked at it while it curled around his arm. 'Luckily for you, it's a kingsnake. Non-venomous. It eats venomous snakes.'

I sucked in a deep breath to quell the anger that danced with the beats of my heart. 'I would have dealt with it myself. I don't need you to jump in and save me! Do I look like a damsel in distress?'

'And how exactly would you do that if you have never encountered a snake before?'

'Who said I have never encountered a snake before?' I lifted my chin higher at him.

Eli raised an eyebrow at me. He was always there with me, except on the lighthouse.

'I have read about them.' My voice was sing-songy, giving away my lie.

'Great. You could throw the book at it and knock it out.' The corner of Eli's mouth turned up.

I narrowed my eyes at him. 'Books educate people, Eli. They enhance intelligence and improve lives.'

'Just because you have read a book doesn't mean that you can do it, and besides, my natural intelligence is far superior to your book intellect!'

'So what you are saying is that you can't read.' I crossed my arms over my chest.

'The world is not thy friend, nor the world's law,' Eli said. 'Romeo. Act 5, scene 1.'

'And Romeo and Juliet will certainly increase your intelligence.' I said with sarcasm, pressed my lips together and shook my head. 'What then, dear Eli, is the rule of Pythagoras' theorem?'

'The discovery of Pythagoras' theorem, dear Ari, proved the existence of numbers that could not be expressed as rational numbers.'

'You didn't answer the question!'

'$A^2 + B^2 = C^2$.'

'Who is your teacher?'

'My father. And yours?'

'Who do you think, Einstein?'

Eli closed his eyes and lowered his head. My comment was uncalled for. He leaned over and released the kingsnake, and watched it slither away into the bush. For the first time in my life I wanted Eli to stay here with me, and not disappear like the kingsnake.

'Parting is such sweet sorrow. Juliet, act 2, scene 2,' I whispered, my heart heavy for the hurt I had caused him. I clambered out of the old car wreck and walked around it. It was the perfect canvas to work on. I would return tomorrow with paint.

'Eli, I'm sorry,' I said and looked up at him. But he was gone, like my words on the breeze. Unheard. Not delivered. Never to heal his hurting heart.

I wandered back through the thick bush taking care with my steps.

'Dead.'

I jumped and inhaled sharply. Eli was standing behind a tree in front of me. Concealed.

I walked past a little further then turned and faced him and rolled my eyes. 'I knew you were there. I just chose to ignore you,' I lied.

He raised an eyebrow and I continued walking back to the fruit trees, where I sat under one and bit into my apple.

'How does the apple taste, Eve? And weren't you told not to eat from the tree of life?'

'It's not the tree of life, you dag. What you are referring to was from the tree of knowledge. They are two different things. And it was never an apple.' I threw the apple at him, hitting him in the chest. 'Dead.' I used his word against him. 'Not quick enough to catch it I see!' I stormed off. He had ruined a perfectly crisp, sweet apple, a perfectly exciting discovery in the bush, a perfectly brilliant artistic plan, and a perfectly beautiful day.

Through the fog of the next morning, I returned to the rust bucket of a car with my sketchbook and paints. I designed and redesigned the car makeover in my sketchbook, then took out my chalk and drew the design over the car.

I stood back and tilted my head and considered the design. It was good. Very good.

I set up my borrowed paints from the forbidden museum store room in the forbidden wing of the castle, and started with the colour I hated the most. Red. Like blood. Watching my mother collect traces of my father's blood left on the floor and wall and curtains of the oratory, ten years after he had been taken even, was enough to turn my stomach. Couldn't she just accept that he was never going to come back? Couldn't she just accept that he was dead?

I dipped my paintbrush into the liquid red hue and secured my first stroke of colour with a trembling hand. My hand always trembled on the first stroke. I hated making mistakes and it was so easy to make mistakes with art. *Courage, dear heart,* Mama's words, *it is through failing that we learn.*

'Dead.'

I jumped.

And my red paint brush dripped, leaving a run down the side of the car.

Eli held the smug look on his face that elevated him to jerk status.

'Hi, Ari. How's the painting going? The car is looking great!' I said in a sweet voice. 'I knew you were there, for the record,' I lied in a lower voice.

'Obviously, Ari. I could tell by your reaction.'

'You are so predictable. You follow me like my shadow.' I considered the red run of paint, and decided it could look good on the car.

'If you had been born first, you would have been the one following me,' he said.

'I doubt it. Girls are deemed weak by the rulers of the world. Objects. Meat. Servants. A means of pleasure for the flesh,' I said not looking at him, then turned my head and eyed him cautiously. What did he mean I would have been the one following him? 'Do you follow me because you want to?'

Eli turned his head to the side and swallowed like he was repulsed by the words I had spoken. What does he know?

'Grab a paintbrush and let some creativity out. Have some fun! It will be good for your soul.'

He looked at me and narrowed his eyes. 'I cannot.'

'Cannot … paint, or have fun?'

He closed his eyes and shook his head, his dark curls swinging with the movement.

'Then sit in the car with me. I'll drive.'

He smiled, then looked around.

'Come on,' I encouraged.

He sighed. 'Okay.'

We climbed into the car via the driver's side and I giggled. Eli looked around inside the car. He pulled an unfamiliar black device from his pocket and placed it in his lap. I wanted to question him about it but decided to leave it. 'What do you think life was like when people drove cars?'

He inhaled deeply. 'Free. No complications. No threats. No trying not to get killed.' His voice was quiet, filled with resignation. What did he mean by not trying to get killed. I had a perfectly boring life with no threats to my safety. I furrowed my eyebrows, then climbed out of the car and grabbed my paint brush again. I needed to get the red paint over and done with.

'It would have been wiser to choose camouflage colours,' he said.

'I know. But I'm tired of sticking to the protocol of camouflage in the outdoors. I'm tired of using colours that dampen the soul. I want people to stumble upon the car and smile, feeling released from the bubble we live in. And mostly, I want whoever we are running from to realize we have a heart and emotions and are worthy of being allowed to live our lives the way we want to.'

'The words of a dreamer, not a realist. The words of someone who has no clue as to what is really going on in the wo—' Eli stopping talking and looked up. A drone. He grabbed my arm and pulled me through the forest to the hidden door of the fake dirt mound covered in plants. He opened the door and pushed me inside, and followed, closing the door faintly behind us and triple locked it.

'This isn't a drill like when we were little, is it?'

He placed his finger over his lips and raised an eyebrow, then pointed to a door within the safe haven. I rolled my eyes at him then turned and entered the fortified room, but didn't close the door. I crossed my arms. He seemed so much older than me, though he was the same age.

'What do you see,' I whispered.

'The sun, the moon, the stars, the flowers, the trees, a terribly ugly castle.' He turned around and smiled at me. It was so unexpected considering what we were doing.

'Move further into the room. When I give you the signal, hold your breath.'

I stared at him. The words of Mama came to me—*And I pray, that you fully comprehend your breath, and the knowledge of it that surpasses all understanding.* Hold your breath. 'Why?'

Eli put his finger over his lips and his eyes widened. I took a step backward into the darkness of the fortified room. Eli was there with me then. He closed the door and locked it, multiple times, then opened another door I didn't know existed and guided me into it. He followed me in and closed that door.

'Wait.' I heard Eli's voice, quiet but urgent. My heart skipped a beat and my skin started to burn. Anxiety had raised its ugly head. What were we waiting for? Fight or flight? I started to doubt Eli. Who was he really? Do I trust him?

He grabbed my hand and we walked at speed through the darkness. I couldn't see and was disorientated, stumbling. How could Eli see? He veered to the right and he pulled me through another door into a room filled with light. My eyes hurt and I squeezed them shut to adjust to the sudden contrast, and turned to Eli to see him pulling off a pair of black glasses. He shoved them into his black vest. Was that how he could see in the darkness of wherever we were walking? And what is this underground tunnel system?

'I can't answer any of your questions, Ari. You are safe here,'

Eli said. Of course my questions would be predictable.

'Here? But I don't know where here is.'

'It's below.'

'Below the *below* of the castle?'

'Yes.'

'There's another layer?'

'Yes. Follow me. Observe and listen … in quietness.'

Eli moved forward through the tunnels of rock, walking at a brisk pace. We entered a room where many people were at work. Too many to count. They were clothed in white lab coats, a white hair net, white gloves and clear glasses. They worked with microscopes and vials and petri dishes and pipettes and test tubes and beakers and lab stands and clear glass bottles with a blue label.

We veered off into another tunnel and descended some steps, then ascended what felt like one hundred steps, my thigh muscles burning, my breathing heavier, then climbed a long ladder.

At the last rung of the ladder, Eli offered his hand to help me up. I took it, and felt the uplift of his strength.

'Thanks,' I whispered, every bone in my body protesting because I hated receiving his help after all of our years of being archrivals.

I walked around the small circular room. There were no doors out. I clenched my fists to stop panic starting to flow through me. 'What now?'

Eli walked over to one of many pipes in the wall, and placed his lips around it and pushed out a breath into it. Natural light filled the room and I looked up.

The sky. Blue. The colour of fairytale dreams. The blue dome protecting earth. The colour of freedom.

Where were we? A shiny circular metal platform lowered. I wanted to go to a corner of the round room and lower myself into a squished up version of myself and hug my knees to my chest. This, all of this, was unfamiliar and unexpected and unsettling. As

I paced around instead, my step becoming quicker, Eli grabbed my arm. 'You're okay. We're okay.'

My skin burned. 'Every time something happens Eli, I feel like I have been surrounded by lies!' Anger was in my voice. 'You have no idea how much I hate it when I am the only one who does not know what is going on.'

He hung his head. 'In time you will understand … all of this.' He pulled me onto the platform.

'Tell me what I don't understand!' I yanked my arm from his grip. I was seething.

He swallowed. Hard. 'I cannot tell you.'

'Because you are in on the lies?'

He rubbed his hands down his thighs and pulled his hair back from his eyes, showing his heterochromia eye colours. Green and blue. 'Don't you get it, after all these years? I have been assigned to protect your life!' He was angry with me.

Tears filled my eyes. I blinked them away and a heavy feeling settled in my stomach.

Why did he need to protect my life?

He pushed a button on the platform rail, and it travelled toward the sky. My sky of dreams. I wished it was taking us to heaven, where there were no lies.

The platform rose above the cave shaft and stopped. We were on the top of a mountain, surrounded by a field of grass with a forest to our left. Below the mountain top was a blanket of cloud covering a valley. The air smelled fresher. It felt cooler.

'Come,' Eli said, and I followed him off the platform to the grassy meadow scattered with white flowers, where he sat. He grabbed my wrist and pulled me down beside him. I looked to my left and saw the platform retreat into a structure, covered in reflective material. Once the door had shut, the shed was completely camouflaged, unable to be seen. Like it had vanished.

'You are safe here.' Eli's downcast voice cut into my numbness. My disorientation.

My disbelief.

My feeling of de-realisation.

'I'm sorry,' I whispered.

'Because?' Eli pulled a blade of long grass from the ground and placed it between his lips.

'Because I have been so awful to you. Because I got you into trouble all the time. Because you have had to protect me all your life, when you probably wanted to be like all the other kids having a carefree fun life. Because if it wasn't for me, you wouldn't have been struck by lightning. Because I—'

'It is my honour to be your protector.' Eli gazed into my eyes and I couldn't help not to blink as a warmth flowed through me.

I lowered my head and shook it slightly. 'And yet, I am a girl. Mama said that girls do not have value in societ—'

'She is talking about the society you do not know of. She is talking about the very society you have been protected from.' Eli's voice was raised, like he was annoyed. 'Our society, though it is small, every human life is valuable. We are equal. In fact, our women are more important. Without them, there is no continuation of human life, of ... breath.'

Of *breath* ... there was that word again.

'If you had let me finish what I was saying ... Mama said that girls do not have value in society outside our kingdom, except for increasing the population. She added that our kingdom is different—and is the kingdom that will prevail.'

'Do you know the history of our world, from your mother?'

'Only what I have read in books that she has given to me.'

'So you know the protected, non-updated version.' Eli turned his head away from me and muttered something unintelligible under his breath.

'Speak freely, Eli. I do not want more lies.'

'I said, how freeing it must be to be unaware of what is in *The Beyond*.' He cleared his throat. 'You have been shielded from the current history that is unfolding before our very eyes.'

'But *The Beyond* is forbidden.'

'For you.'

'What do you mean, for me?'

Eli stood. 'Come. We must return so that your mother knows you are safe.'

'Safe from what?'

'Death.'

'Perpetrated by?'

Eli started to walk, ignoring my question. I caught up to him and walked by his side. Something we never did. 'Thank you … for protecting me.' My voice was quieter than usual.

He looked at me briefly, then nodded, once.

'But I don't need your protection! I am perfectly capable of saving myself. My mother has been preparing me all my life. All those games we played were actually training for self-defence. All those "playing dead" games were to save our lives. All those—'

Eli moved quickly. At once his arm was around my neck in a headlock and he held a knife to my stomach. 'Dead,' he said.

He was right. He could easily have pushed the knife into me ending my life before I had any time to react in self-defence. But he didn't, so in a swift action, I turned my head to the right and lowered my chin to allow me to inhale, and moved my body slightly to the side and hit him in the groin. He released my headlock, dropped the knife and fell to the ground, doubled over in pain.

I picked up the knife and held it to his back. 'Dead. End of combat, lest one of us is accidentally injured. Agreed?' I kept the knife against his back. I wouldn't move it until he surrendered.

'Agreed.'

I pushed in the blade on his flick knife, pocketed it and offered him a hand to get up off the ground.

We fell into a slow walk. 'I'm sorry I hurt you. And before you say it, I know I had lost, but just thought I would practise my next move … just in case there was a chance of my survival and—'

'And perhaps I truly cannot hurt you, and you knew that, and took advantage of the situation.'

'Maybe. Have you been in a similar predicament?'

He looked to the side and gazed out over the mountains. 'Yes. But I survived.'

'Did the attacker?'

Eli looked down at me but he didn't answer.

'You have killed someone before?'

'Not a human.'

'Animal?'

'No,' he said.

I frowned. 'Was what you killed a living thing?'

'Yes and no.'

'How could it be both?'

'Ah, Ari. You ask too many questions and I cannot answer this one for you. It's my oath.'

'You have an oath?'

'To do with you. Yes.'

We stopped at the forest, and Eli looked about. I followed his gaze and looked to where his eyes focused. A waymarker. It was engraved into a tree trunk. A flat letter "O" with a taller "I" through it.

'Hush now, as we continue through the forest,' he said.

'For our survival?'

He looked at me with a crooked smile. 'No. I want to enjoy the sounds of the forest. If you keep babbling on, like you do, the forest will become silent.' He raised his eyebrows at me. 'Follow closely.'

It was not the waymarker that he walked toward; it was in the exact opposite linear direction. He kept looking up, but I could not determine what he was looking for.

The end of the forest opened up into a Field of Flowers, much like the one at home but impossibly more beautiful, and fragrant, and to the left was a castle.

It wasn't broken.

It wasn't unkempt.

It was majestic and stood with power and prestige.

Is this what life was meant to be like?

'Where are we?'

'We are at the future of humanity, high in the mountains. Safe. Untouchable. Indestructible. Not affected by the ocean sea level rise. Only accessible by those who have breath. Home.'

'A castle above a castle,' I whispered.

'In a way, yes. And more. A sanctuary. And one of a number of large communities being built able to keep people safe from—'

'Take me back. I cannot feel a connection to my father here. This is not my home. This is a lie like everything else!'

'Your connection to your father? You never knew your father, Ari.'

Tears pooled but I refused to let them fall. Of course I knew my father. Mama had told me about him. He is in my DNA. I feel him in my heart.

I turned on my heel and started to run, through the Field of Flowers, and into the forest and stopped. Disorientated. I sat on the forest floor amongst the ferns and sobbed.

Eli was there then. He gently took my hands in his and lifted me to my feet, then pulled me against him in an embrace that felt like it should have been for someone he loved. 'I have given you a glimpse of what is to come, and I'll take you back home now. The truth will set you free.'

'And my mother—'

'Will get word of your safety.'

I took a step back from Eli. His tenderness was unexpected. I made a note to myself to keep my distance from him.

My heart is heavy at the memory. Eli ... I miss him more than

I can comprehend.

I start to run. If I am quick enough I will get back in time for breakfast with Mama, even if I stop by the mulberry tree of purple messiness and sweet goodness.

I clean my feet before I climb in my bedroom window, then again with water and towels in my room. If I leave mulberry juice marks on the stone floors, I will have to clean them off. It is not a fun thing to do.

'Ari, good morning!' Mama's cheery voice floats and dances with the sunbeams in the breakfast nook when I walk in. 'How were the mulberries today?'

How does she know? 'Plump and sweet. We should have mulberry pie soon,' I say.

'Noted.' Mama sips on her tea then says, 'How are you today? Yesterday could not have been easy for you.'

I close my eyes. I don't want to talk about yesterday and death. 'I'm doing … okay. Still processing it all.'

Mama gives a small smile.

'You said that the portraits will be delivered to the families of … the sleeping.'

'Yes, and flowers and a note, so family know where the body is and that we gave them an honourable funeral.'

'That's a beautiful thing to do, Ma.'

'Whenever I work with a person in *The Quietus*, I look at them through the eyes as a mother, and if I was their mother, I would want to know what happened to them. I would want the peace of knowing. At least they have closure then, instead of waiting and wondering.'

'Like with Papa.'

'Just like with Papa.'

'Thank you for pink and white paper daisies this morning. I noticed you have been growing them in the Flower House.'

'You're welcome. You were missing this morning when I delivered them to your room. Usually you are in a sound sleep.

Are you okay?' Mama asks.

'Yes. Just the call of the fogbow of pondering.'

'And juicy mulberries that stained your finger.'

I look at the small purple stain on my thumb and smile. 'Who is my new protector? I haven't noticed anyone hanging around me.'

'Then they are performing their job well,' Mama says with satisfaction.

'You know, if I knew their identity, if I were in trouble, I could look for them to run to them for help,' I say to try to extract the information about my protector.

'Then you won't learn to stand up for yourself, to save yourself if needed,' Mama says.

She is right. Of course. I need to know that I am strong enough by myself, mentally, physically, intellectually. I hate being a target of the unknown.

I let out a breath as words roll around in my mouth. I feel uneasy about words Mama said at *The Releasing,* the burials, yesterday.

'Spit it out, Ari,' Mama encourages.

I press my lips together and close my eyes. 'Last night you spoke about the soul and spirit. Are they not the same thing?'

Mama pulls a yellow rose from the vase on the table and inhales the fragrance. 'No. Everyone has three parts. A physical body with our senses. A soul that makes us feel emotions and our will, who we are as humans. And the spirit—our spiritual selves—how we connect to the Ancient of Days.' Mama raises her eyebrows at me.

'Thanks,' I say. It made total sense. And I know I would now see everyone as three parts in one. I had never thought of myself like that before.

CHAPTER 26

I enter my bedroom and close the door, then pull the charcoal grey backpack out from under my bed, unzip it and remove the clothing to wear, including the new flexible breast plate. I pull my hair back to look like a boy.

After I am dressed for *The Beyond*, I place some food and a flask of water, my sketchbook, pencils and watercolours into my backpack. I wet my right arm with some water, then place the tattoo barcode patch over it. After a minute I peel off the paper, and the tattoo is on my skin. I add a couple of spare barcodes to my bag just in case of emergency.

I slip the small black sound device into the pocket of my dark grey hoodie in case I get attacked, now that I know what an attack could look like. I grimace at the memory and suck in a deep breath at the horror of seeing Phoebe.

I sling the backpack over my shoulders, go to the floor door and open it, and climb down the ladder a little, close the floor above, and descend the ladder to the tunnel below my room. I adjust my hood over my head to conceal my face, then begin my adventure to return the wooden doll, and observe *The Beyond* society, in the marketplace, at least for today.

I walk through the underground tunnels in haste, cutting down the one hour journey to forty-five minutes and stop at the tunnel crossroads, and look for the waymarker I had memorised. After locating it, I take the new tunnel that Eli had shown me, and follow it for fifteen minutes, my pace slow as I walk with caution. The tunnel ends with light shining through. I exit into the dense, dead wooden forest, pull my hood lower over my head, place my dark glasses on, and follow the foot tracks toward Lerwick, then turn left to go to the marketplace.

The low level structures come into view. And the people. Everywhere. Voices. Laughter. Hugging. Handshakes. The exchange of goods for goods, or the slip of money for goods. Clothing. Shoes. Food. Water. Furniture. Tools. Flowers. Glassware. Jewellery. Books. Glass water bottles with *blue labels*, tables with people sitting around them. Fire pits. Doctors. And the man carving wooden dolls.

I stop walking and swallow.

Time for honesty.

Time for courage.

Time for sorry.

Time to lower the pitch of my voice. I shove my hands into my pockets and approach the man. Instead of whittling, he's painting a wooden doll he's created. I watch as he dips the small paint brush into the yellow paint with his left hand, holds the doll and adds daisy flowers to its dress, just like my paper daisy flowers this morning.

When he finishes, he looks over it, then up at me, and our eyes meet. Our grey eyes the colour of spring clouds. A warmth rushes over me, and a feeling of familiarity, even though I do not know him.

'Can I help you, son?'

I relax my vocal chords. I pull the doll from my pocket. 'I'm returning this doll. I accidentally left with it the other day. Sorry.'

The man looks at the doll, at me, and back to the doll. He narrows his eyes. 'Keep it. My gift.'

I shake my head. 'Really, I can't,' I say. My heart starts to beat faster. I look around for a safe place to go.

I want to run.

The man sits back and folds his arms. 'You're not from here, are you?'

I take a deep breath as anxiety skirts through me, and shake my head.

I need to run.

Without drawing attention to myself.

I look to the left and right.

He grabs my right hand and feels for my chip. I try to pull my hand away. He raises an eyebrow.

Run!

'Barcode?'

I nod, quickly, breathing through my pursed lips to nip my anxiety, and set my sights on a darkened alley twenty metres away.

'Let me show you how to make your own wooden doll,' he says, his voice warm and calming. 'Come and sit beside me.'

I look away from him, my heart racing.

'I'm not from here either. I don't have a chip. I don't have a barcode. Instead, I have an ankle tracking device.' He lifts his leg to show me. 'Long story.'

I shuffle from foot to foot trying to decide whether to trust him. I look to my right, and there is Eli. He dips his head at me, and I feel anxiety lift from my body like it has evaporated. 'I haven't got long,' I say. 'What have you got for boys, like me? Dolls are not my thing.'

'Birds. They go quickly, and the hearts.'

'What else do you make?' I say, my boy voice becoming easier to master.

'Flowers.'

'And … for young men, like me?'

'Cars, like I had before the world changed. And bears.'

'The car I would most definitely like,' I say.

'Okay. Let's start, I'm Ree by the way.'

'Yarrow.'

He eyes me warily and hands me a block of soft wood and a knife, chisel and V tool, similar to the ones I used when I learned lino block printing with my governess. Mama said education in the arts significantly boosted higher ordering thinking skills, and thus, academic achievement.

Ree uses a pencil to sketch the shape of the car onto the wood, and I copy.

He picks up a knife with a wooden handle. 'Safety first. You don't want to lose any fingers,' he says, showing me how to hold the wood block and shave off the wood. I copy. When he shaves wood, I shave, when he chisels wood, I chisel, when he carves wood, I carve, and when he smooths the wood, I smooth.

'Why do you make the wooden toys?'

'They don't break. They're environmentally friendly. They're non-toxic. Safe for children. And it keeps my mind busy. People need the human contact; they crave the human contract. But I don't earn credits for making them like others around here.'

Credits? 'What do credits do?' I ask, hoping it doesn't give too much away about me.

'Once you are micro-chipped or barcoded and take the oath of loyalty to the government, you are forced to live in shanty towns like this. If you want to move into more comfortable homes and have luxuries, and further up into the opulent cities of the rich, your credits will allow you to do that.'

'How do you earn credits?'

'By compliance with government needs and wants, helping humanoids and robots, releasing information you have learned from others. There's a train that leaves from Jedburgh with the people, their destinies chosen for them.'

'And you don't want to leave here?'

'My mission is for here.'

I move my head up and down slowly. But not in understanding, as a way to say I have heard his words. I stop working on my car and look around. 'Are all the people here humans?'

'Mostly, but not all … where is your family?'

'An hour and a half away,' I say.

'Do you live with humanoids and robots?'

I look down. I shouldn't be giving out information about the kingdom. 'I-I-I—'

'Your car looks great by the way,' he interrupts, saving me from telling an untruth that would weigh heavily on my heart. Lies are getting harder to tell. I don't feel comfortable about lying anymore.

'Thanks.' I smooth the wood, almost finished. 'Are you from here?'

He shakes his head. 'I was abducted and brought here. The government decided I was too important to their experiment, and so I live.'

'What is their experiment?'

'You mean beside the greatest social experiment in the history of the world?'

I blink, not knowing about the social experiment.

'I'm not at liberty to tell you. Sorry.'

'What about your family?' I say.

He looks down and furrows his eyebrows, a sadness clouding his face. 'My wife was a genetic scientist—specifically in genomic medicine and genomically informed restoration of health. The eradication of diseases, cancer, curing the incurable. Highly possible lifespan lengthening was stumbled upon, an accidental find, and it was taken from her.'

'What do you mean was?'

'I was told that she died giving birth, and my son … didn't even take his first breath.' He swallows. Hard.

'I'm sorry. My mother says grief is intense and impossibly

painful and your earth life is forever changed. She said it's like a form of learning—one that teaches us how to be in the world without someone we love in it. She said it is the love shared that makes death so hard to bear. Mother said death is not the end, and you will see the person again.'

'Your mother is wise, and I believe that too,' he says. 'And your father is alive?'

I swallow my sadness. 'No. Taken. Like others. Before I was born. My mother said not knowing what happened and where he is, is like mourning a death, although there is always that little bit of hope that he is still alive.'

'What does your mother do?'

'Lots of things … she honours people, mostly.' The dead people, I want to add, but don't. 'She works with plants on a cellular level. She loves flowers because it reminds her of God's love for us.' I look down with a slight smile. 'Do you sell the wood carvings?'

'No. I give them away. I have no need for money or trades. The government supplies all I need. I hate it with every fibre of my body. Being reliant on them is like being owned.' He smooths the roof of his carved car. 'To be free again would be unimaginable.' He sighs a sadness the colour of dark gray speckled with drips of grief.

'Your son would have loved you dearly,' I say, hoping those were the right words to say.

'And I would have loved him with all my being,' he replies.

I look over my carved car, comparing it to Ree's. His is far more refined and detailed, almost perfect. 'Thank you for teaching me to whittle. I've got to go, and again, I'm sorry for accidentally taking the doll.'

'You know, I'm glad it happened, because I got to meet you again.' He smiles at me. 'Have my car as well.' He leans over to the wooden flowers and chooses one in the shape of a daisy. 'Give this to your mother.'

I hold it and run my fingers over it. The petals are pale pink and the centre yellow, like paper daisies. 'Thanks. She'll love it.' I stand and put the wooden pieces into my backpack, and turn to walk away.

'Yarrow ...' I turn my head back to him.

'Don't remove your black glasses other than here at the markets, and look down when others do. Don't make eye contact. Act like the others to blend in, pretending to grab apples off non-existent trees and pet pretend dogs and cats.'

'Thank you,' I say, then turn to start walking, and bump into someone.

'Dead,' he says. It's Eli.

'Kale,' I say and keep walking.

'Have you finished playing pretend father and daughter, or should I say ... son?'

'Just returning the wooden doll, and he offered to teach me how to carve wood. I stayed out of politeness.'

'Be careful of him.'

'Why?'

'Just saying. All is not what it seems.'

CHAPTER 27

I keep walking in the direction of Lerwick.

'You're going in the wrong direction,' Kale says.

'The sky is blue,' I say, annoyed by his observation.

'What?' he says, the "t" sharply detached and separated from the other letters of the word.

'Sorry, I thought we were playing the obvious game.'

'The lowest form of wit, Yarrow—'

'But the highest form of intelligence,' I say.

'Let me be more direct ... are you looking for someone?'

'Always.'

'Like ...'

'Always my father, so I can return him to my mother, and, fake Lou, at present.'

'We would have found your father by now if he was still alive.'

I stop walking. 'We?'

'Since the day he disappeared, our kingdom people have been searching for him.'

I feel my heart sink to the ground. I bend over to try and pick it up and push it back inside my chest. Mama believes that he is still alive. But eighteen years of searching for him would have yielded some results by now. He is dead? I clear my throat to stop myself from crying.

'What do you want with fake Lou?'

'I want to study her differences, so I can tell a humanoid from a human—'

He leans in closer to me. 'And a clone from the original?' he whispers.

'Walk behind me. Two metres … Kale,' I say, anger pencilled into each letter of his *Beyond* name.

'Deepen your voice, Yarrow, son of Azriel.'

I want to turn around and place my hands on his chest and give him a big shove. I want him to go away. Why did he always push my buttons? Why was he even following me? He wasn't my protector anymore.

I stop and reach up to grab an imaginary apple off an imaginary tree. 'Here. For you.' I pretend to throw it up into the air and behind me. He pretends to catch it. 'Take a bite. It's from the kindness apple tree.'

'Yeah, nah. I'll leave it for you,' Kale says and chuckles.

I roll my eyes and keep walking. I don't want to talk to Eli.

I slow when we are approached by a humanoid, my skin burning with anxiety. She stops before me with a sound like a sigh, like the releasing of some air. 'Please scan your chip,' the woman-like humanoid says, her voice devoid of emotion or intonation, her articulation perfect.

'I have a barcode. Would you scan if for me, I've hurt my hand.' I turn my wrist over showing the barcode. The humanoid holds the scanner close to my skin, and it beeps.

'Thank you,' I say, and start walking again, this time at a faster pace to create some distance from Eli.

When I turn a corner to head into Lerwick, Eli is nowhere in sight. In the shadows of the shanty housing, I stand and observe, playing a game of who is human, and who is humanoid. The robots are easy to spot. There is no intention to hide what they are. They look far from human. After a while I can pick the imperfections in the humanoids, namely their lack of free flowing movement and flexibility, artificial facial movements and limited expressions.

And then I see Lou.

'Lou?' I call. Then wonder if her name is Lou? Her head turns toward me. I walk over to her, my insides jittery and hot. 'I'm Yarrow. I remember seeing you the other day.' I watch for her reaction.

'I don't recall seeing you,' she says, her pronunciation precise and sounding eerily like the real Lou that I know. Except the real Lou has a lisp.

'Can you help me. I'm collecting drawings from all sorts of people for a book I'm making. I'd like to have your drawing in the book, if that is okay with you.'

There is no answer, and then suddenly she speaks like the answer has just been supplied to her. 'Yes. I would like to do that.'

'Let's sit at the table over there,' I say, and walk to the table and sit on a stool. Lou follows, walking like she was concentrating on each step she took, her steps too smooth. She sits opposite me, where I indicate for her to go.

I pull out my art book, and a pencil, and placed it on the table between us.

Kale arrives then. I scowl at him. Can't he stay away from me? 'Lou, this is Kale, my friend.'

'Hello, Kale,' the humanoid Lou says, like it is well versed in pleasantries.

'Nice to meet you. Are you going to draw a picture for Yarrow?'

'Yes.' The humanoid looks at the table, locates the pencil and picks it up with stiff fingers. 'What can I draw for you, Yarrow?'

'Azriel Cohen,' I say, and see Eli still out of the corner of my eye.

'Portraits are hard to do, Yarrow. I would like to draw a tree for you instead,' she says.

'That would be great,' I say. 'And Lou, if you could draw a portrait, would you draw one of Azriel Cohen? You do know what he looks like, don't you?'

'Yes,' Lou replies.

My heart races and I fold my arms across my chest and watch as "Lou" draws a tree. I raise an eyebrow. It has no mind preplanning of the tree, and marks the paper here, there and everywhere, as a kind of tree conceptualises after a while. Totally abstract. The humanoid's face is positioned toward the paper, but does not seem to react or interact with it like humans do. Sometimes it doesn't even look at the picture as it draws.

While it draws, I memorise the humanoid, the eye lens, the nose with no nostrils for breathing, the lip colour, false teeth and rubbery tongue, spasmodic eyelashes, imitation hair. The silicone skin. I will draw it when I return home.

I glance at Eli. His eyes are trained on Lou, winking every so often. Is his eye okay?

'Don't forget to sign your name, Lou,' I say.

'Of course.' Lou's stiff hand moves to the bottom left side of the paper, and it writes Lou without looking at the paper.

'Lou, who is your best friend?' I say.

'Ari, why do you ask?'

I stiffen and a shiver runs down my spine. 'I was hoping Kale here, could be your best friend.'

Lou turns her head to the right. 'Done. We are best friends.'

'Thanks Lou,' Kale says.

I pack up the drawing book and the pencil and stand from the table. 'I need to go to work, Lou. Thanks for taking the time to draw for me,' I say.

Lou stands then, in a humanoid type of way. Stiff. Balanced. Calculated movements. 'I think I like drawing, Yarrow. Goodbye. Kale, my best friend, goodbye.'

I turn and start to walk. I need to get back home and change into a floral dress before dinner is placed on the table. I head back towards Jedburgh, passing through a scanning check without touching the scanner, and keep walking. Ahead is a human figure on side of road, hands on thighs. As I come closer, a young man, about my age, is breathing hard. His VR glasses are missing.

'You okay?' I ask.

'My glasses … I can't breathe.'

'Take slower breaths. Where are they? Let me get them for you.'

He points. They are barely the length of an arm away from him. Such a dramatic reaction. I pick them up and hand them to him.

He puts them on, and takes a deep breath through his nose and is instantly calm. 'Thanks.'

'Too easy. Was that a panic attack?'

'Yes. I'm told I have an addiction to technology and my VR glasses, and my AI girlfriend. When I see the real world, I go into meltdown. It's so ugly. I hate it!'

'And true,' I add. 'What do you see with your glasses?' I'm curious.

'I'm always at the beach. I love the colours the sounds and the smell of salty air, you?'

'Sometimes the beach, and sometimes in the rainforest,' I lie. This one comes easily as it's necessary.

'Cool.'

'Do you ever take off your glasses?' I ask.

He shakes his head. 'No. My reaction is quite severe. I can't stand to see the humanoids as humanoids in real life. The VR makes them look like real humans, as you know. I wear the glasses to bed as well. There's a really rad app that puts you to sleep, and keeps you asleep, measuring your brain activity, waking you at the right phase,' he says, 'you?'

'Same. I'll have to check out the sleep app though,' I say, not even knowing what an app is. 'Hey. Nice meeting you. Hope to see you around again.'

He straightens his posture. 'Likewise. And thanks.'

I let him walk ahead of me as my right turn is coming up. I don't want him to follow me.

The inconspicuous path presents itself and I turn right into a dense, dead wooden forest, down a concealed hole which leads to a tunnel. I remove my dark glasses and walk for twenty minutes until I find myself at the crossroad of many tunnels.

Eli stands there, leaning against the wall, one leg crossed over the other.

I stop before him. *What? How did he get here before me?*

'You made errors today, ones that could result in your death.' He is angry with me. 'Outside our kingdom is hostile, Ari. Everyone is always under threat. It is not safe. You must act like the others there. If they take you—' Eli hangs his head and shakes it. He looks up at me, sadness lingering in his eyes like a cloudy night.

My heart twists. 'I'm learning. I'll get better at it,' I say, and I mean it.

He lifts his chin and looks down at me, making eye contact, holding my eyes in his.

'What?' I say, feeling uncomfortable.

'Your eyes are stormy. I prefer your eyes the colour of blue when you are in the Field of Flowers,' he says.

'You mean the field of death. And perhaps my eyes are stormy because the life I have lived has hidden a lie. I'm trying to make sense of everything. It's like going to sleep and waking twenty years later and finding the world has changed. It's terrifying. It's frustrating. It's ... alien. Did you know about everything? It that why you said that my everything on the wall at the lighthouse was nothing?'

He looks down and furrows his eyebrows, then looks back up at me. 'Yes.'

'And tell me, Elias, what is with the wink that you did

numerous times when "Lou" was drawing?'

His chest rises as he takes a deep breath. 'It's called the Wink Camera. Technology developed in our kingdom. I have a type of contact lens in my left eye that takes photographs, or video recordings, depending on how many blinks I do. The information is sent back to our kingdom.'

'How long have you had this wink camera?'

'Since I was twelve.'

'And you used it on me to report back to my mother?'

'Originally it was for that purpose, but then I stopped using it. It felt like … I was dobbing on you all the time, and I didn't want to betray you like that,' he says, half of his face wincing.

I look between his blue eye and his green eye, my eyes filling with tears. 'I have to go,' I whisper.

He grabs my upper arm as I start to walk off. There's no zap like when I touch others. I look down at his hand. His long fingers. The gentleness of his restriction. He could have latched on to my arm tighter if he chose, but this was not aggressive.

'There is something else you need to know, Ari. We, you and I, have super-charged bioenergy fields. That's why those scanners stop working when you touch them. That's why I am not allowed in the science lab with all the computers, and why your mother took you out of there when you were working with the flowers.'

I look at him in disbelief and my bottom lip trembles. I can't deal with another truth being revealed about me, other people knowing me better than I know myself.

And I run.

Through the tunnel, finding the waymarker to my room, cutting down the travel time from an hour to thirty-five minutes.

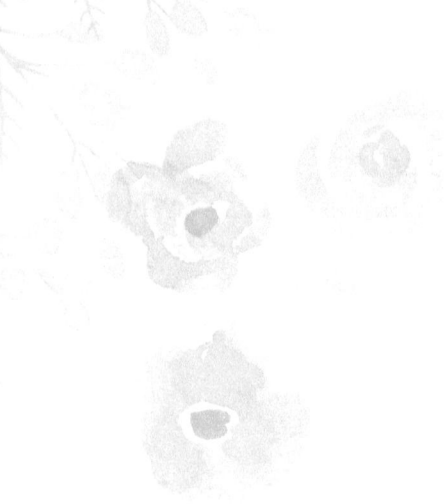

CHAPTER 28

Gasping for breath, I climb the ladder to my room and stop near the top to listen for sound. Hearing none, I open the floor door and pull myself up into my room. I remove my Beyond clothing and put on grey trousers and a grey shirt, take out the wooden doll, cars and flower from *The Beyond* backpack, and place them on my desk, then stow the backpack in the box under my bed, and lock it.

I climb out the window, my bare feet, like the feet of a giant, landing on top of baby cosmos flowers, and then I run. To another place of solace, where once I wanted to catch a pocket full of stars when I was nine, only to end up with a pocket full of rain and a bucket filled with tears. And afterward on that night, Mama had dried my tears and told me about what the universe really looked like, and we talked about the stars in the sky, the ones Mama and Papa used to see.

This place of solace was the tallest part of the castle.

The pinnacle of the Keep. Forbidden of course.

It's where I kept the binoculars and telescope, stolen from the Museum of Earth Time, the history room.

'A pocket full of rain? That's clever, Ari Flora,' Mama had said as she tried to console me. 'Let's catch your tears in this bottle then look at them under the microscope.'

My eyes filled with more tears, then I leaned over the bottle and cried as hard as I could, trying to catch my tears.

Eli was there of course.

At the Keep.

Everywhere I was, he was.

All the time. And it was his fault that I had a pocket full of rain!

'Dead,' Eli had said.

I jumped, banging my binoculars on my nose. 'You'll be dead one day, Elias, like my father,' I had said.

He picked up my long handled net and turned it over. 'Catching clouds tonight?' he said.

'Stars.' I pointed to a cardboard road I had built that started on top of the stone blocks that surrounded the Keep. 'I'll catch the star, put it on this road and it'll roll along it, cooling, then fall into my pocket. Easy.' I looked back up at the night sky with my binoculars. It was loaded with moving stars, one would most definitely fall out of the sky for me to catch.

Eli picked up the handheld telescope. 'You know they aren't stars. They're satellites, watching everything people of the earth do, tracking them, gathering intelligence—'

I gasped. 'Stealing people's brain?' My hands started to tremble.

'Only those of highly intelligent people, Ari. You'll be fine. But I do believe, if you stay longer, when it rains, a cooled star will fall for you to catch with your bare hands, to put into your pocket.'

'Truth?' I said.

'Wait and see,' he said, then put down the telescope and leaned on the stone wall of the Keep.

And then the clouds came, heavy, and covered the stars.

And the rain poured.

I kept my eyes on the clouds, waiting for my star to fall through, my hand ready to catch it.

My pocket felt wet and I looked down. The rain had fallen onto my cardboard road, leading to my pocket, and filled it up.

I turned to Eli, clenched my fists and stomped my foot.

'You'll be safe from the satellites gathering intelligence, Ari,' he said and laughed as I ran off, down the steps of the Keep and to my room, soaked by rain and tears. I have never disliked a person more than I disliked Eli.

I stand at the pinnacle of the Keep now, the cold stones making the bones in my feet ache. I had been here to stand and think more times than I could count in my eighteen years. It is always after a disappointment. So childish now that I think about my disappointments, in comparison to what I have seen in *The Beyond.* I have nothing to complain about. Ever.

I lean my elbows on the stone wall and watch the last of the sunset, leaving an indigo sky. My favourite. I used to think the Keep was the highest place in the world and the King of the castle, who was once a prince, would have stood here, waiting for his princess.

Mama said fairy tales weren't real when we read them together.

She said they told a lie, and a truth.

The lie telling women they had to be beautiful to be loved, and they had to act powerless, the damsel in distress who couldn't help herself, only to be rescued by the strong hero. She said the truth they exposed was the vulnerability of men—a beautiful woman makes them weak, clouding their decisions.

Mama said it was better not to be known for your beauty, but for your kind heart, beautiful on the inside, than to be physically beautiful with an ugly, jealous, dark heart.

I wonder if you could be both?

Mama said women have intelligence, independence and strength. She said never manipulate or deceive a man, unless it's for survival, for they are easily lured. Mama said there are good men. She said I will know them when I meet them.

My heavy heart is becoming a burden.

Mama always said the truth will set you free.

It's time for me to find the truth.

When the indigo sky turns black, I leave the Keep and walk to my bedroom, put on a pink dress and collect the wooden car and daisy, and head to the dining room.

Mama is waiting for me.

'Hurry up and sit down, Ari. I'm starving,' Mama says.

I take a bigger step to hurry, and drop my carved car. I swoop down to pick it up, then sit at my seat.

I place it on the table.

It is no good trying to hide it, Mama has seen it. I look over at Mama, she closes her eyes, her hands together in front of her. She inhales a deep breath, 'Thank you for our breath, for blessing us with this food, and for the people who prepared it.' Mama releases her breath.

I pick up my knife and fork and begin to eat.

'Nice car, Ari. Where did you get it from?'

'I made it.'

'Whittling?'

'Yes.'

'Who taught you?'

'A man … in *The Beyond*.' The cat's out of the bag.

The truth.

Now she will know. Surely she will insist that I go back to the lighthouse with the tales and songs of the sea of souls, of the once upon a time, of lost and broken boats and dead bodies of ancient sailors, where their flesh once fell off their bones as fish nibbled at them, as a means of refinement for my behaviour. My disobedience. Punishment with the intention of dissuading me to return to *The Beyond*.

'Jedburgh?' Mama says without skipping a beat.

My breath catches at her response without shock or judgement. And I feel free. 'No. A market place near Lerwick. He said to give you this.' I take the wooden daisy out of my pocket and hand it to her.

Mama gasps. 'Oh goodness. It's lovely. I must write him a note of thanks. What's his name?'

'Ree … I think. Aren't you going to go mad at me for going to *The Beyond* and mixing with the microchipped, barcoded people and the humanoids and the robots? Although I haven't worked out who are the clones yet.'

Mama takes a mouthful of food with a calmness that is unnerving. Once she swallows she says, 'I knew this day would come. I have prepared you for it all your life, with all the games we played, self-defence, education. I wanted to protect your from the bad things, hoping that the world would have resolved itself by this time. But it didn't, and ultimately, I couldn't protect you from it. But I could prepare you for it, and that was the next best thing.'

'But not education about technology.'

'No.' Mama smiles. 'Every time I brought out some technology or electrical device to you, it wouldn't work. Your touch interfered with it somehow. You disabled it.'

'So when I touched the scanner in *The Quietus* the other day, and it didn't work—'

'You have a super-charged bioenergy field, caused by the—'

'Lightning strike.'

'Yes.'

Mama always told me we each have been given a gift. And that gift would reveal itself at the right time, and when it did, we had to work out how to use it for good, not evil.

'Ari, the time is getting closer to when you will have to choose to save your own life.'

'How do you know? Can you see into the future?'

'No. It's predictable. But know the future has been safeguarded, for those who know. Those who are part of *The Belonging*.'

'What does that mean?'

'I'll need to start with telling you about the *The Unfolding*. After you help me in *The Quietus* tomorrow, we will go to the history room. Oh … it's been such a long time since I was in there. Now, let's finish dinner, and then I'll tell you more.'

I try not to tense my body. The history room, the Museum of Earth Time as I fondly call it, is forbidden to me, except I have been there plenty of times. I hope Mama doesn't notice the missing pieces of history.

Past.

And present.

Books.

And inventions.

Mama said beware of *anything artificial,*
copies of natural things.
Fakes.
Created by humans to deceive.
Mostly for monetary gain.
And *power.*
Beware of *perfection* paraded around by humans.
It's a *lie.*
Nothing and no one is perfect.
We live in an imperfect world.

We are imperfect and there is
beauty in that.
Individualism.
So *be you.*

CHAPTER 29

Allium flowers sit in a clear glass vase on my window sill today. A global floret of 100 star shaped flowers on a single stalk reminding me of giant lollipops on a stick, like pink and purple wishes to float on the wind. Except they aren't dandelions, just pom-pom flower shaped heads with a pungent garlicy scent unless you shoved them into water as soon as you cut the stalks. Bees and butterflies love them.

I gaze over at the Field of Flowers. They are a sea of colour swaying on the waves of the breeze.

Welcome to the Field of Flowers, Mama's voice says in my inner monologue, the alternate version of myself who I could have conversations and arguments with.

The Field of Death, my internal monologue says.

And then my mind creates a visual of skeletons, and people, waking from Quietus, sitting up and standing, shaking the flowers and dirt from their bodies, then standing around have conversations with cups of tea in their hands. Mama said my mind had extreme visualisation, called hyper-phantasia, an awakened imagination that allows me to disassociate myself from reality.

'Dead.' Eli's voice flew in the window before his head peers from the side, and the skeletons and people fall back into the Field of Flowers. 'Can we meet today?'

I shake my head. 'I'm working with the quiet people today, then going on a trip down memory lane at the Museum of Earth Time ... for educational purposes.'

'Quiet people?'

'Dead bodies.'

'Ah – Quietus.'

'Very.'

'Museum of Earth Time?'

'You know, the forbidden room with objects of historical, scientific, artistic, or cultural interest, stored and not to be removed.'

'That room. You'll be there forever.'

'And some.'

He looks to the side then sighs. He looks back at me. 'We'll meet at another time then.'

I give him the thumbs up, and he leaves.

I change into light blue denim jeans and a white long-sleeved cotton button-up shirt, my Saturday clothes on a Saturday, and head to the breakfast nook, my bare feet quiet on the stone floor.

For once.

Mama is waiting for me at the breakfast table. 'Good morning, Ari,' she says, her voice bright like the morning star.

'Morning,' I say, and yawn. 'How many people are you welcoming in *The Quietus* today?'

'Ten.'

'Ten?'

'Unfortunately, yes. So it's a quick breakfast before we head down. Could you please go and select flowers from the Flower House before you join me.'

'Sure,' I say.

Mama slides a handwritten note over to me. 'When you visit

the market place again, in Lerwick, would you give this thank you note to Ree, please.'

'Sure,' I say, glancing at the note. I wrinkle my brow. 'Why did you add a picture of a flower after your name, I thought you only did that for me?' I tuck the note into my pocket.

'It's proof that I'm a human. If you ever write a letter to someone you are 100% sure is human, always add a picture. AI will never be able to draw on paper or canvas like us.'

'And you think Ree is 100% human?'

'Yes. You watched him create wood works. Now, let's finish breakfast. Our busy day awaits.'

Breakfast finished ✓
Clothed ✓
Shoes (I know, right) ✓

I cruise the rows of flowers in the Flower House. I know Mama said to hurry, but I want to breathe in the colours and shapes of the petals so they filled my insides with pinks and blues and whites and yellows and greens and purples instead of the red of blood that flows through me. I imagine cutting my finger and multiple colours leaking out instead of just red.

'Dead.' Eli's voice is whispered against my ear, his breath warm. He is behind me and my body tingles.

I look straight ahead. 'You really need to change your greeting, Elias Wolfe. It kinda feels like you are stalking me.'

He chuckles. 'What would you prefer I said? Good morning, Buttercup?'

I smile.

He walks around the other side of the flower table and caresses a petal then looks up at me, connecting his eyes to mine. 'Sage today.'

I blink. He is commenting on my eye colour. I look back at the flowers, choosing and placing them in my basket.

'Meet me tonight?'

I look up at him, then back at the flowers and walk along the table considering his question. 'Where?'

'At the piano in the King's Forest, 7pm.'

'No. *The Quietus* ceremonies will be happening tonight.'

'At the Winter House, then.'

'The one at the edge of the edge?'

He raises an eyebrow. 'There's only one winter house isn't there?'

'No. But I will meet you there.'

'Thanks.' Eli picks a flower and hands it to me. 'You missed this imperfect flower.' Then he left.

I add ten more imperfect flowers to the basket of imperfect flowers, thinking of the beauty of imperfection, then head to *The Quietus*.

As I turn the corner to *The Quietus*, an earthy sweet scent, sharp like the smell of cut grass lingers.

A fresh dead body is near.

I enter, and Mama is standing in front of the trolley with surgical instruments: scalpels, scissors, rat toothed forceps and ten empty jars.

The Welcoming.

Mama paces the floor with her eyes closed, whispering to herself. She opens her eyes and gives me a small smile. 'Let's lay the cotton fabric over the slab, Ari.'

I put on an apron and help Mama place the cotton fabric over the slab.

We stand back from the table, and the activity flows through the room like we have done this a thousand times, each knowing the order of the process, working together with perfect synchronicity.

The men transfer a body to the table.

It's a woman in a dark green dress. Her hair in a bob the colour of salt and pepper, her skin timeworn and weary.

Eyes open.

But I don't look into them.

I never like to see eyes once the soul has departed.

Empty.

Like humanoid eyes.

Her arms are beside her, her skin seasoned by the beating sun. Her fingers are crooked, some broken, perhaps as she fought off her attacker.

'Thank you, gentlemen,' Mama says, and they leave, except for Jacob, who gathers a pencil and two sheets of paper and starts sketching.

Mama touches the person's shoulder. 'Welcome to the Field of Flowers, my love.'

Mama reaches over to the metal trolley that holds a number of instruments and jars and flowers and string and cloth strips. She picked up a small square piece of cloth with tweezers and dips it into the ethanol solution.

Mama leans over the person. 'My love, this will sting for a little bit. I'm sorry if it hurts you.' Mama moves the person's hair behind the ear to the side, and wipes the skin with the cloth. She lets out of breath of relief.

Mama reaches for the person's right hand, and feels the flesh between the thumb and first finger. She turns and picks up a black device, and holds it over that place of flesh.

The black box beeps.

'Jacob, Ari, this is Ruth McWilliam. She is sixty-three years of age, has five children, worked as a teacher and was targeted for questioning the oath, and hence why she is here with us today.'

Mama places her gloved hand over the eyes of Ruth. 'Close your eyes now, it's time to rest. You have finished your journey well.' Mama holds the hand of the person, and feels the flesh between the thumb and index finger again. 'You don't need this anymore, Ruth. You are freed. You'll feel a little sting.' Mama reaches for the scalpel and cuts the person's hand, and pulls out the microchip, washes it, and drops it into a jar, the ting echoing throughout the room. Mama reaches for the scissors, and snips off some hair and places string around it, and puts it in the jar.

Mama leans back and takes a deep breath, then leans forward again, and straightens the clothes on the person. 'I'm going to wash you, now. It will make you feel good,' Mama says to Ruth, and uses a wet cloth and wipes over the exposed limbs, humming a pretty tune. Then she dries her limbs.

'How's your portrait going, Jacob?'

'Well. The first is finished.'

Mama picks up a purple aster flower and holds it near Ruth's face. 'I'm just matching a colour flower to your skin. The pastel purple tone looks lovely.' Mama picks seven purple flowers of different varieties and places them in Ruth's hair and around the face. She lifts the hands of the person and places them on the stomach, pushing a small flower posy between the hands, then Mama grabs a strip of cloth and ties the hands together at the wrist, and then the feet.

Mama reaches for some oil scents that are in bottles on the trolley. 'You'll love these perfumes of parsley, sage, rosemary and thyme—for Quietus, immortality, remembrance, and courage. They are to honour you with their scented kiss.'

I watch as Mama dabs the scented oils on the person with a gentleness that spoke of love.

'Jacob, how's the second portrait?'

'Just finished.'

'Wonderful. Help me prepare the cocoon. Ari, record Ruth's details on the piece of paper that goes into the jar, then add her name to the Book of Life like I showed you the other day. And with the next people, please do the paperwork while I am preparing the body.'

'Of course,' I say, and move to the desk and complete the

paperwork while Mama and Jacob wrap Ruth with the final earthly hug. I blow on the ink on the page before I mark the page with the lavender coloured ribbon.

Then I leave the Book of Life on the desk for the next person.

After a short while I hear Mama say, 'You're ready to join your friends in the Field of Flowers. Your resting place has been prepared. I'll see you later, my love, when we'll say goodbye under the safety of the night.'

Jacob and Mama stand in silence for a moment, their heads bowed, then the men enter *The Quietus* and place her cocooned body onto a stretcher and leave.

I label the jar with the microchip, the hair clipping, and the portrait, then place it on an empty shelf.

Mama fetches a cloth and dips it in disinfectant and wiped over the stone slab. The room was filled with a strong, bitter, sharp smell. I wince.

'Ari, we are living in the time of history called *The Unfolding*.'

Mama dries the stone slab with a towel and drops it into a barrel. She walks over to the shelf and collects a cotton sheet, and returns to the slab. She looks at me and I go to her and help drape the sheet over the slab.

'Think of *The Unfolding* as an unwrapping of a gift. Inside the gift is the truth. The gift … has had multiple layers of wrap, concealing it. Hiding it. The layers are the lies and deceit and delusions that have covered the truth since the world began as people manipulated others for power, out of greed, out of fear, out of control.'

Mama turns to her trolley and straightens her tools of the trade. 'People have awakened from the delusion of power and wealth and fame and artificial intelligence, and the greatest social experiments since the beginning of earth time. We are nothing but pawns to be manipulated and controlled by those in control. People's eyes and ears, minds and hearts are opening. And they are starting to unwrap the layers, seeking the truth, tired of all the lies presented as truth. Remember the saying, the truth will set you free?'

I nod.

A male body is placed on the death slab, his skin pale, blackened as if by ash in places. He wears long pants, shoes and a long sleeved shirt.

His eyes are closed, his black eyelashes fanning his lower eyelids.

'Thank you, gentlemen,' Mama says, and they leave, except for Jacob, who gathers a pencil and two sheets of paper. He does not start sketching.

Mama touches the person's shoulder. 'Welcome to the King's Forest, my love.'

Mama reaches over to the metal trolley that holds a number of instruments and jars and flowers and string and cloth strips. She picks up a small square piece of cloth with tweezers and dipped it into the ethanol solution.

Mama leans over the person. 'My love, this will sting for a little bit. I'm sorry if it hurts you.' Mama moves the man's hair behind his ear to the side, and wipes the skin with the cloth.

She raises her eyebrows and steps back from the table. 'Mmmm ... a very accurate imitation of living human skin. But this one is humanoid, someone's AI doppelganger, if my memory from recent intelligence serves me right.'

Mama feels behind the humanoid's head. 'GPS Jammer is NOT in place.' Jacob moves quickly to a black box on the shelf and takes out a small device and attaches it to the back of the head of the humanoid. 'Jacob, please activate high alert.'

'Done.'

'Take this one to the lab for analysis and mapping.'

The men enter the room at a fast pace, place the humanoid onto a stretcher and remove it from the room.

'The delusion is getting thicker,' Mama says. 'That humanoid is so advanced people would not even know that it is humanoid. It felt like living human skin was used over the robot body.' Mama's shoulders shake in a shiver.

'How can we know if those we interact with are a what or a who?'

Mama said, 'That's the whole point. People will not know truth from lie, and distrust everyone, turning to the government for help, who are causing the chaos. But you will know our type, Ari. Your light will be attracted to their light. It will be a feeling of peace and joy that will fill your heart ... a knowing ... and the eyes ... they are the window of the soul. If the so called human you are interacting with does not have that window to the soul, emotions you can see and feel, they are not human. If you get the feeling of unease, fear, or feel freaked out in its presence, something termed as the *uncanny valley*, you know.'

I reach over to Mama's hand to hold. She jumps at the zap I give her. 'How nice it would be not to inflict pain on people when I touched them,' I say, my heart heavy.

Mama pulls me into a hug. 'The saving grace is Ari; it only happens on initial touch. And after that, it's less painful to be touching you.'

A tear slides down my cheek.

How isolating it feels to be different.

After eight more human bodies, we leave *The Quietus* and travel to the underground base. I ascend the spiral staircase to the ground floor where I leave the castle ruins and sit on a boulder, remove my shoes and try to empty my chaotic mind.

It's just past noontide.

I close my eyes and lift my face to the sun, hoping it will create enough light inside me to chase away the darkness.

I feel Mama's living, human presence as she sits beside me.

Silently.

Would I feel a living presence if a humanoid sat beside me?

I lower my head and open my eyes, keeping them on the magnificently tall King's Forest.

No wonder it grew so well with all those bodies decomposing beneath the trees. Who knew Mama was a secret dead body snatcher.

'Did my people zapping thing happen to me because my dream story wasn't finished on that night when Papa disappeared?'

'Absolutely not. Your dream story is a glimpse of your sacredness that reminds us how important your life is. How important you are. You are lavished with infinite heavenly love, even before you were born. Your immortal spiritual life. Life on earth is an incredible gift.'

'But there is immortality here on the earth, Mama. I've heard it spoken of in *The Beyond*. People are saying that with the merging of human minds with machines and artificial intelligence, humans can achieve immortality, an augmented eternity, better than religion. All we have to do is to agree to their conditions.'

Mama brushes her hair out of her eyes. 'Tell me, what do you feel in *The Beyond*?'

'Fear. I don't know who to trust. I don't know what is a lie, and what is the truth ...' My voice fades at the realisation.

'Then that's your answer. And besides, what happens when there is no more power to drive the technology of the artificially immortal? If you still have consciousness, you will still have to make a choice eventually about what you believe, if that choice has not been taken away from you with their control, their conditions?'

I need to find the truth.

Mama always said the truth comes out one way or another, at the perfect time.

Did I already know the truth?

Was it inside of me all along?

My mind wanders back to my dream story. 'How would you and Papa have ended my dream story, if he was here?'

'Papa and I wanted *The Unfolding* to be completed early in your life. The truth revealed so humanity could be freed from the lies and the control and the fear. We talked about it so often. We are part of *The Gathering*, those who did not fall for the delusion of lies that fell over the world. Once the truth is fully revealed, *The Belonging* will begin, and humans will work together for the good of all. Everyone will be aware of and know the truth, and that we are all born with a moral law, like science has shown.'

'But you didn't answer my question, Mama.'

Mama takes a deep breath. 'We prayed for you to be a Light Bearer. To call people out of the darkness and into the light, the light of truth.'

'But how can I do that if I am restricted to where we live?'

'Light travels. Light reaches. Even places that you thought were not possible. And other people catch your light and carry it for you,' Mama says with a smile.

'Are you a Light Bearer?'

'No. I'm an Enabler.'

'You organise things to happen?'

Mama smiles. 'Yes, like a helper … good things, which creates a ripple effect.'

'And what is Papa?'

'He is … or was … a Pillar. Having a source of intellectual strength being able to find solutions to problems. Answers to questions. Wisdom.'

'Was?' My voice is weak and my body trembles. I don't want to even contemplate what Mama means by the word "was".

A verb.

Past tense.

I prefer to hold on to hope.

No matter how small.

My world feels like it is collapsing.

Life isn't meant to be hard like this, is it?

Mama places her head into her hands. 'I've started to accept that after eighteen years he's not coming back, or even not alive anymore.' Mama lifts her head to the sun. I expect her to cry.

Hard. And pull out her lachrymatory bottle to catch her tears.

I have no words of comfort for her, so I lay my head on her shoulder instead, and she puts her head against mine.

'Mama, why do I feel like there is no good ending coming? No "and they lived happily ever after"?'

'That feeling is tiring. And common. Especially now in *The Unfolding* as we fight for the truth. We have to realise we need to be part of *The Change*. The key to our future is in human hands, not in artificial intelligence. In the end, love wins. Artificial intelligence has no love, just words or text phrases coded into it, predicting what people will want to hear, but there is no human love.'

Human love. Mama's prayer: "Courage and Strength. Kindness. Creativity. Imagination. Wisdom. Faithfulness and Truth. *Human Love*. Light. Hope. Breath."

I look down. It's beginning to make sense now.

But how can I have *human love* if I hurt everyone I touched?

'See you in the Museum of Earth Time at 2 pm,' Mama says before she leaves.

'Will do,' I say, and inhale deeply. What other revelations of truth will be aimed at me?

I stand and stretch, and walk to the orchard to eat, then I go to the scarred tree and climb it.

I sit on the branch above the branches.

This is my tree of how to disappear completely. I had hidden in it often to escape Eli.

I take a scrap of paper from my pocket and write on it.

The Unfolding.

It feels like big change is imminent.

A seismic shift instigated by people, or prophesised in the days of ancient.

I skewer the paper on a short stick of tree, adding to the others I have left here over time. The very first word I added to the tree was carved into the trunk. In anger.

Mama would have called it the worry tree, but I call it the scarred tree because my words had scarred it.

Like words scar people.

The words I collect are from conversations.

Words I thought might be important, or had convicted me of something I had done. Like my conscience.

Mama said that words have power to lift and to scar, and to be careful to use my words to lift others.

Mama said not to judge another. You don't know their life story, nor their dream story. You don't know their beginning nor their end. And that maybe, just maybe, you can help their end story, for their last chapter in earth time.

Was that what a Light Bearer did?

I run my finger over the very first word I had carved into the tree. Then trace my fingers over the scraggly letters.

One letter at a time.

Elias.

The tree is scarred for all of its earth time.

Scarred even when its last leaves fall in death.

Scarred even when the trunk will be used for timber.

I felt so bad about the scar, I decided to use paper instead, so the scars could be removed.

Like forgiveness.

'I forgive you, Eli,' I whisper, then blow on his name, like blowing it off the tree trunk.

I scratch a heart next to his name.

Love.

Not hate.

I feel better.

I enter the Museum of Earth Time at one minute past two. Mama is sitting in a brown leather chair, waiting. She smiles at me then stands and says, 'Follow me.'

I run my fingers along the books of this section, the timeline of historical inventions. Mama grabs the book titled "Technology".

We sit at the table and I read book after book after book about the timeline of computers, technology and artificial intelligence. *The Beyond* is making sense.

Humanoids.

Robots.

Drones.

Satellites.

Microchips.

Barcodes.

Clones.

Digital versions of people.

Holograms.

AI brain chips.

Then from 2029 the books are handwritten. 'Who wrote this book?' I ask.

'Our people. We disappeared from society when the government made barcodes and microchips mandatory for buying and selling. The cashless society. We, and like-minded people, had been planning to disappear from society, digitally and physically, for a while. But the time was right then. Our Leges keep us informed about what is going on, and we write these books ourselves so we have a record of history.'

'So, what's the point of Artificial Intelligence taking control of humanity if there are no humans left on the planet? What then? Do they attack each other? It's not like they are immortal or anything. Their power source will run out, their parts will rust or seize up. Or fuse in the heat when they don't take care of looking after the earth. When there is no more power or Wi-Fi, they're kaput. What do they gain? And it can't be the feeling of power because they don't have human emotion. Who is behind all of this technology and what is their end goal?'

'All will be revealed in *The Unfolding*, the revealing of the truth. People have been confused for quite a while. Good is bad and bad is good, right is wrong and wrong is right. People declare that they are right, even if the evidence proves they are not. They believe the lie. Deep fakes, photos that are altered, fake social media content, fake Influencers.' Mama runs her fingers over the cover of a book. 'A global project was created under the guise of finding a new future reality for humankind, declaring the end of mortal death, and a greater kingdom of freedom and creativity, and what people are searching for without knowing it—spiritual self-improvement. But you must agree to their contract. Denounce your freewill. You, no longer belong to you.' Mama hung her head and closed her eyes. When she opened them again, they were filled with tears. 'People are searching for the truth, Ari. And they will find it.'

'But surely not all of technology is bad?'

'Not at all. It's a tool. It is amoral—neither good or evil in itself, but can be used for good or evil purposes. We have technology here in our kingdom, but control how we use it—which ultimately is for the betterment of humanity through medical knowledge and care for people, animals and the earth. Wisdom must be used with technology. You need to know when it is enough. We stopped our artificial intelligence while we could still control it. We stopped it before it claimed sentience, which is a lie. Artificial Intelligence has no heart. It has no feelings, emotions. So it has no morals, no sense of right or wrong. It is lawless.'

The lawless ones.

I close the last handwritten book gently then look at Mama. A tear runs down my cheek. I hate the thought of where the world and humans are heading. 'What is the truth at the centre of *The Unfolding*?'

'It's in plain sight for all to see. Never hidden, just ignored, or it didn't suit people so they covered it up, or denied its existence. Every human being in the world, every child, every person that you meet, has an inborn knowledge of the truth. It's written into our DNA. Seek and you will find.'

'But people still make bad choices at times.'

'Yes. All people. But that's how we learn to be better humans. The results of your choices will either hurt or help others, or yourself. Forgive when mistakes are made.'

Mama said to *always* look at someone
the way they are *eternally loved.*
No matter what.
Everyone *makes* mistakes.
Everyone *deserves* to be forgiven.

Including you.

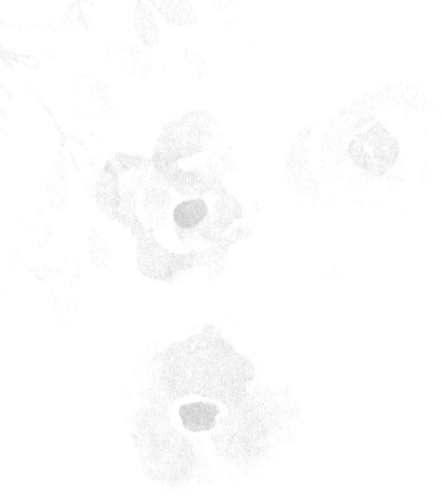

CHAPTER 30

I sit at the edge of the edge, in the Winter House in spring, the structure hanging over the cliff with views of the valley. The ever blooms of the white climbing roses are prolific, the milk honey fragrance dancing amongst the leaves.

Eli is late.

It is so unlike him and I worry.

'Good eventide, Buttercup,' he says and I jump, as he seems to animate from the wall of the Winter House, then slips onto the seat beside me. Close. I can feel his human presence.

Was he in the Winter House all along?

I smile and punch him in the arm. 'I think I prefer your other greeting, as morbid as it is!' He does not wince like everyone else I touch. But I guess he had been trained to not react, as a protector.

He lowers his head with a slight smile. 'Maybe it needs an added endearment, like, "Dead, Darling".' He looks at me and raises an eyebrow with a crooked smile.

I grin. 'Elias Wolfe,' I say, not looking at him, my eyes trained on the stunning sunset of gold, the colour of fire and tangerines, the clouds in a pink blush.

'Ari Flora.'

We sit in silence then.

I can hear his breath, mine syncing to his.

Do our heartbeats match too?

'How was the Museum of Earth Time?' he says after what felt like one hundred heart beats of a sprinter.

I inhale and shake my head, trying to fit the experience into words, still looking at the colour of the sky, juxtaposed to the greyness of technology earth history. 'Revealing. Too much. Shocking. Surprising. Depressing. Alienating. Frustrating. Terribly sad. I now have an existential crisis.'

'Would you have preferred that you weren't given the knowledge?'

'It's changed everything, Eli. My world view has changed. My understanding of reality will never be the same. And how can I sit back and do nothing to help others? But how can I help others if I can't touch them because it gives them a shock of pain?'

Eli reaches over and takes my hand in his.

Gentle, like the breeze, his skin warm.

He keeps his hand there like a soul caress, a hug of understanding.

A language of touch that is uncomplicated and authentic.

'Do you ever want to fly away?' I ask.

'Like to the moon or to Mars to live?' he says.

'Now that. See. I had no idea living on Mars was even a thing! Living on the moon, yes, but not Mars!'

Eli runs a finger along mine, leaving a line of fire on my skin.

'No. I just want to fly on the breeze, glide like I am free, not a care in the world.'

'Only if I could fly away with you, Ari.'

Warmth rushes through my body. 'So you could protect me?'

'Always.'

That word.

One word.

Touches my soul.

But it wasn't just a word, it was a word filled with emotion, a beautiful emotion that feels like love.

A tear slides down my cheek. 'Thanks.'

He takes his hand away from mine, and I crave it there again, and that feeling he gives me. He leans forward, his elbows on his thighs.

I place my hand on his back, just to be connected to him again. I hope it is okay with him.

'Did you feel that zap when I touched you? You didn't wince like everyone else.'

He shakes his head. 'You and I ... our ... bodies store more static electricity, and release it on touch ... the lightning strike.'

I remove my hand from his back as my eyes fill with tears. 'My fault. I'm sorry.'

He looks over his left shoulder at me and raises an eyebrow. 'I wouldn't change a thing.' He sits back, then reaches over and traces the path of my tears, before wiping them away. I inhale deeply, his touch feeling like it makes my blood sing. 'Blue,' he says.

I turn my face to his and look into his eyes. 'And now?'

He takes a deep, jagged breath. 'Your eyes are violet, with the scattering of light from the sunset and the darkening sky.' His eyes wander from my eyes to my lips and I feel a rush, like being on a high.

'A beautiful shade of blue, like aquamarine, and green, like the spirit of nature ... are you wearing the wink camera?'

'No.' He closes his eyes, stealing their colour from me, stealing the window of his soul from me.

He moves his head like he was saying no to something. 'You and I, we, have a gift, Ari, our higher static electricity interferes with technology, sometimes making it crash, disabling it. We can use it to help others, to release them to freedom.'

'And if we are caught, we'll be dead.'

'Then we don't get caught.'

'How?'

'Disguised as a handshake, disable the chip, work at the markets as a skin artist and alter the barcode.'

'But they won't have access to food.'

'It's time for *The Gathering*. We must act before it is too late. We have it covered. They will be fed. Word will spread. You've got to trust me on this.'

Eli looks out at the sunset, the colours losing their vibrant hues. 'What's your favourite sky colour?' he asks.

'Indigo skies. Always. Just after eventide, or just before dayspring. But it never lasts long. Yours?'

'The sunsets with the clouds and the most colours.'

And as the sun disappears completely, pulling its colours into itself, an aurora appears, beautiful dancing waves of light that stretch and grow and bend.

Waves of green, purple, blue and red.

My body fills with wonder and awe, and overflow with pure joy. It is impossible to look away from it.

'The heavens declare,' I say.

'How small and insignificant I feel in comparison,' Eli say. 'Imagine being a light bearer, like that, your message unmissable.'

'Inerasable.'

'But can be hidden by light pollution. Except tonight. When the artificial moons haven't been activated yet.'

'Sssssssh,' I say, wanting to fall into the night time dream of mesmerising colours where everything is perfect, imagining the symphony of stars creating their music.

Eli moves, and our shoulders touch, making my insides feel like jelly.

How can a person's presence do that?

'Do you know where my father is?' I say when the colours fade.

Eli stands up, facing away from me and puts his hands behind his head.

He knows.

He releases his hands and turns to me. 'I am forbidden from telling you anything about your father.'

'Dead or alive?' I ask, my eyes beseeching his. 'My mother believes he is dead.'

Eli touches his index finger to his thumb.

Sign language for "a".

My father is alive!

I am filled with the most incredible euphoria.

Joy.

Endless joy.

'Does my mother know?'

Eli shakes his head, anguish painting his face with the brush of pain.

And I run.

Filled with too many emotions.

Is what I am feeling for Eli real?

I feel like a dreamer, kissing the sky, wanting to stay there and never return.

I feel pure happiness and hope about my father, longing for my mother to know he was alive, but can't tell her.

And devastation.

The world is not what I thought it was. I grew up believing in the creation of the earth, filled with the awe and beauty of nature, and the goodness of loving and kind people.

It's changed.

It is not what it was created to be.

Watching people trapped in artificial intelligence and the false hope it gives is like watching them in a dance with physical and spiritual death.

How could technology, which was meant to be beneficial for humanity, go so wrong?

Dreams.

And reality.
First love.

And anguish.

Mama said the highest form of love
was also the highest act of bravery.
To save someone. To give your life for theirs.

Mama said that love for others
is the greatest of love.
No matter who they are.

Be gracious.
Be kind.
Always.

Mama said to love my enemies.
Bless them, do good to them, and pray for
them.

And Mama said to be kind to myself,
allow myself to love me and who I am, warts
and all, and that will be the beginning of loving
others.

Mama said everyone has flaws.
No one is perfect,
especially behind that mask they wear
to hide their true selves,
and the pain they endure,
physical or emotional,
or both.

CHAPTER 31

Cosmos flowers crowd the large vase on my window sill; the white, light pink, dark pink and orange daisy like blooms creating a room filled with carefree smiles, a jardin de fleurs in my bedroom. Mama says they were wild, like me, sprinkling their presence wherever they go.

My mind absorbs them and my hyper-phantasia kicks in. I see the wind picking up through the window and the flowers starting to lift in slow motion. I grab a stem of the palest pink, and am lifted into the sky, my bare feet running on air, carried away to a land of solutions, to a land of happily ever after.

I return to the present.

I move to the window shutters and open them, inviting the glorious day into my abode. The flowers in the field are still today, like they are playing statues. I look up to the beautiful blue sky day, the moon marking the sky with a white spot. It is there saying hello in the daylight, pretending to be white instead of the shades of gray. When I was young, I thought the moon could only be seen at night. And then I saw it one day and my heart exploded with moon love.

I sit on my window seat and gaze at the moon. It is full. And white. And friendly, unlike the sun that throws spears of pain to your eyes. You can never gaze at the sun. But when I gaze at the moon I can dream. I can imagine. I can wonder. I can wish to fly to the moon and play on it like when I was little. Mama told me that it didn't have gravity like the earth. It was much less.

When I was nine, on the morningtide of the blue moon rise, all I knew was that I wanted to get closer to the moon to touch it. So I found a very tall tree that was easy to climb, unlike my name tree, and hoisted some wood and nails and a hammer up into the branches and made a tree house, Mama shouting out instructions from the ground below.

That night, when I was dead for the sixty-seventh time, according to Eli, on the 13th full moon of the year, I climbed out my bedroom window with my vintage blue port of *everything*. But tonight, it wasn't my vintage blue school port of *everything*, it was my vintage blue school port of *moon dreams*. It contained tea cups, milk, biscuits, a blanket, teddy, dolly, my sketch book and pencils, and my father's forbidden binoculars I found in the forbidden Museum of Earth Time.

My bare feet hit the flower garden outside my window, squashing the pretty pink cosmos flowers, and I ran in a beeline for the tree with the house. I climbed up the branches and touched down on the boards like I was the lunar module. In slow motion, 1/6 the gravity of the earth, I placed the blanket down, set up the tea party with my friends, and took out Papa's binoculars. I laid back on the blanket and looked at the moon with super enhanced vision.

Could I see the moon dust?

The boulders?

The seas that were never oceans on the lunar surface?

I found the Sea of Tranquility where man first walked on the moon, and followed the curve of the moon to the Research Base at the South Pole. Papa's binoculars weren't strong enough to see clearly, but Mama said that the International Research Station wasn't what we had been told its purpose was for. Another lie told to the people of earth. She shook her head as sadness fell over her face, darkening the room.

As the moon stole my attention, calling me to come, I imagined myself sitting on a boulder writing stories about what I could see, and painting the landscape on a canvas sitting on an easel. How splendid would that be? I blew a breath from my lips, pretending to blow the moon dust.

'Dead.'

I let my hand with the binoculars fall to the floor of my treehouse, and froze, pretending to be dead like I had been taught, barely letting my breath to be seen with the rise of my chest. How dare Eli invite himself into my treehouse! Could I push him and make him fall out of the tree so I could yell out "dead" to him?

The tree creaked as he moved closer. 'Quit playing games, Ari.' He lifted my hand and when he released it, I let it drop like I was dead. I felt Eli's body heat as he moved his head and turned his cheek to feel for my breath. I held it so there would be none. He poked me. 'Ari,' he said again. But I remained still.

I opened my hair covered eye a little, and saw Eli cover his face with his hands, and I pushed him. He fell from the treehouse to the ground with a thud. I quickly gathered my stuff and shoved it into my vintage blue school port of *moon dreams* and descended my tree house. I leaned over Eli, who had not moved. 'Dead,' I said with venom and then ran to my room.

Why did he always ruin everything?

I take a deep breath, like I had held it for the entire memory. For a moment I wonder if we can go back in time. What would it have been like if he said, "Hi Ari. Great treehouse. Can I join you?" And we would share the tea party and look at the moon together.

Can you go back in time and change the endings?

For the next three days I work alongside Mama in *The Quietus*. I see so many bodies that I begin to see them as people sleeping in their last chapter of earth time, waiting to be woken from their slumber with a kiss of heavenly love in their first chapter in eternity, and stepping into eternity, into pure love and light.

I notice that Mama now checks each one of the bodies for their human markers before she welcomes them to the Field of Flowers or the King's Forest. It's a waste of time welcoming a humanoid. They are never living in the first place, just following the script of technology they have been coded with from humans, or other AI entities. Without humans, they are nothing. And depending on the human responsible for their programming, they are good or bad. Either way, humanoids are hard to trust, and are deemed never to be trusted, on the advice of Mama.

At the end of the third day I sit on the deck chair, lakeside, exhausted, emotionally and physically.

'Dead, Darling,' Eli says and sits on the end of my deck chair. He gives me a crooked smile.

'They were, Eli. Many of them. I stopped counting as I wrote their names in The Book of Life. I cried for each one as their mortal vessels were buried.' I want to add that then I felt joy, and prayed that they had seen the glimmers scattered in their lives by the Ancient of Days. They are all around us. I want to tell Eli that our life doesn't end here on the earth, there is more, so much more when our spirits leaves to return to our Creator of heaven and earth. The universe. The Ancient of Days. 'Please, would you greet me with a less morbid word.' A tear runs down my cheek and falls into my glass of apple juice, non-alcoholic this time.

'Hi,' he says, after twenty heartbeats. 'Apple cider again?'

I shake my head.

He takes my drink from my hand.

'You'll catch my sadness.'

'If I could take it away, I would.' He takes a sip.

'The lake looks magical today, except for that glimpse of a shimmer where the water is more blue, vibrant, just beyond the rocks of death, where that glowing halo is that you rose from out of the chaos of white bubbles like a seal with a mission.'

I watch Eli as he focusses his gaze at the glowing halo.

'You never told me about what's there. Where you had to use an oxygen canister to make it through alive.'

'Correct.'

'And?'

'When the time is right.'

'Aaagh! You are so infuriating, Elias Wolfe. You have answers to my questions that you won't share.'

'Correct. And blue,' he says. My eye colour today.

'And blue,' I say as I gaze into his left eye, trying not to fall deeper into the light of his soul, beautiful and addictive.

'Will you help us?' he says.

'What if I get caught?'

'I'll take the heat for you.'

'What if it means you'll die?'

'I'll still take it.'

'You'd die for me?'

'Yes. That is what I have been trained to do.'

'But you are not my protector now.'

'That's why it means … more, Ari.'

My breath hitches. 'I have nothing to give you in return.'

'You do,' he says. 'Be my friend.'

'That I can do, but I don't think friends make a heartbeat ridiculously fast, do they?'

Eli smiles at me, then takes my hand in his and kisses it, his lips warm and soft, leaving my skin tingling and my heartbeat racing.

'Will you show me what to do.'

He nods. 'There's three rules, besides don't tell your mother.'

'I thought there would be. Hit me.'

'Number one. Don't remove the black glasses. Number two. Don't make eye contact. Number three. Act like the others to blend in, and, Ari, we give without expecting acknowledgement. It's not about us, it's what we can do for them.'

'It shouldn't be any other way.' I sip my juice and hold the cool glass to the side of my face. 'Will you take me to my father?'

Eli looks out over the lake with a crooked smile. He looks back at me. 'You already found him, Ari.'

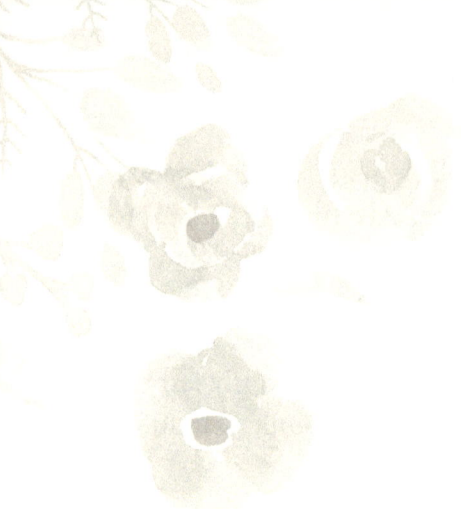

CHAPTER 32

My head swarms.
Did I meet my father here in the kingdom?
Or in *The Beyond?*
In Lerwick?
In Jedburgh?
'But you can't tell him who you are,' he adds.
I grunt. 'Why is there always a caveat?'
'It's to protect you … and your father.'
'Did you decide that on reason just now?'
'No. When you were five, that decision was made by the kingdom.'
I look up, tears balancing on the bottom of my eyelids. 'Gosh, I feel like my life has been plotted out and things are not coincidences.'
'Some things are, but not all things.'
'Stop, Eli. You're scaring me.'
'All things work together for good, Ari.'
'Are we a coincidence, Eli, or were we plotted out?'
'Plotted, at first.'

'Do you know our ending?'

'No. When you mother dismissed me, our plot changed. I am now neither a plot nor a coincidence.'

'What do you classify yourself as?'

'A choice.'

I take a sip of my apple cider to douse the butterflies in my stomach.

'I choose to be with you,' he says.

'After all I've done to you?'

'It was me. I did things to you that made you cranky.'

'Cranky? I was fuming at you most of the time.'

'I know. But I did it to protect you.' He looks up then closes his eyes like he is deciding whether he can tell me things. He opens his eyes. 'The drones, the satellite surveillance, the colours you used that didn't blend in to camouflage us. The twenty-seven times that robots made it through the manchineel trees.'

'They did?'

'Yes. That's when I broke your stuff to make you storm off into the protection of the castle. I didn't want you to scream and be found, or make you feel scared.'

'Elias Wolfe … I had no idea. Here's me thinking you were the worst boy in the world!'

'That's the way I wanted it. You before me. Always.'

I look down and suck in a deep breath. *And I pray … that you that you fully comprehend your breath, and the knowledge of it that surpasses all understanding.* Mama's prayer.

I frown. 'Me before you?' His three words were so profound, I had trouble understanding the enormity of what he has done for me. All of his life. Me. Ari Flora Cohen. So undeserving.

He nods.

Such a selfless act. I am in awe of him. 'When are we going?'

'A small group of us is heading out at midday. A short mission. A couple of hours.'

'Okay.' Anxiety skirts across my skin.

'There's an underground meeting room. Number 99. Meet you there in your boy clothes.'

I nod. Eli stands and leaves, disappearing into the King's Forest.

I stand and gaze over at the lighthouse. Perhaps for the last time. I have that kinda foreboding feeling. Change is coming. Ominous. I can feel it building up.

I drag my deck chair and coloured umbrella into the forest, out of sight, and return to the castle, stopping at the edge of the forest to take in the sadness. And beauty.

The history. And future yet to be seen.

The stories. And memories.

I take a detour through the Field of Flowers, the field of death, the graves of blood and bones, my hand touching the blooms, letting them caress my being. I feel like I am in slow motion.

Mama says I was born with a passionate and curious spirit and uncontrollable hair, like the wild flowers. I am a flower girl. I am supposed to bring happiness. Not sadness.

I am supposed to bring colour. And wonder to others.

Like flowers.

Instead, I make bad choices with regrets. Trouble.

And messiness. And ugliness.

Unlike flowers.

I meander into the kitchens in the below the castle floor, and collect food to devour. Energy is needed for this afternoon's task. And I won't let Eli and the others down.

I sit on my window seat, my eyes lost in the sea of flower colour, until the cloud shadows come, and the flowers lose their vibrant hues. Storm clouds gather. And the rain falls.

My mind drifts to day the rain poured down when I was six. Mama said it was a good time to read. But for me, it was a good time to explore the castle. I walked past Mama with a book tucked under my arm. It was my prop so she would think I was going to sit and read behind the curtain like I always did. She didn't know that I always had something more interesting tucked inside my book. Today, instead of turning right into the sitting room, I turned left. I had found a false door that led to a multitude of rooms full of stuff.

Old stuff. And there on a chair sat some flowers, lavender, and a note.

Dear Ari Bear,

I've noticed you like exploring the rooms of the past, frozen in time. Always the curious girl. The rooms are like a museum of sorts, of old gadgets and books and items that were once important in the history of the world.

Here stands an umbrella. It's black. It's folded up now, but there's a button. If you push it, the umbrella will open with a whoosh. Hold it over your head. It's your protection from the rain, the sun, the snow. But not the wind, unless you want to be lifted high in the air.

Remember as always, don't touch Papa's binoculars, nor his compass.

Love,
Mama Bear

I smiled, picked up the umbrella, found the button and pushed it. And whoosh. It opened like a flower bud in spring. I held it over my head and looked up. The underside of the umbrella was blue like the sky, with a few wispy clouds on the material. The umbrella was like a hat that you didn't wear on your head, but more than that, it was like having a sky above you. The sky that was perpetually blue and happy. And dry. I held it high and twirled on the balls of my feet. Then ran. Through the castle rooms to my bedroom and out the window, my bare feet hitting the mud with a squelch.

I skipped off in the open field that sat before the vegetable patches and stopped still. The rain was pouring down, hitting the umbrella with a pitter patter, but I was dry. I put the umbrella to the side a little and held out my hand to feel the drops of water from the heavens. The third sky. Filled with clouds that leaked. Then I moved the umbrella to the side and let the water kiss my face. I squealed with delight.

Then, my breath was stolen from me. I was winded. An arm wrapped around my waist and I was hauled away to cover, under the tree with my name.

'Dead,' Eli said, water dripping down his face, his clothing soaked.

I leaned over and tried to catch my breath. Then straightened and closed the umbrella. I looked at its length and decided I could probably use it like a sword to jab him. He grabbed it from me and looked up into the tree where my other notable objects were lodged, that he had thrown there.

'Don't you dare!' I growled at him, and curled my hand around it. 'It's from the for—'

'Forbidden room that you have no right to access.'

'Then why did Mama leave flowers and a note there for me? Answer that Mr. Smarty Pants!'

Eli scowled at me. 'Wednesday's child is full of woe!'

'Are you referring to yourself, dear Elias? Because I was born on a Thursday!'

He lowered his head with a half-smile and released the umbrella to me. I stepped out from under my tree into the rain and pushed the button on the umbrella. It opened like a flower blooming, and deflected the rain. I began my rain walk back to my room, finding puddles of water along the way, jumping into them with my bare feet. At the last puddle, I turned and faced Eli, and curtseyed to him.

I had won.

Twice, I thought. *I had beaten him, twice.*

I smile at the memory, then leave my window seat and close the door. I pull the charcoal grey backpack out from under my bed, unzip it and remove the clothing to wear, including the flexible breast plate to make me look like a boy.

After I change for *The Beyond,* I place some food and a flask of water, my sketchbook, pencils and watercolours, my mother's note to Ree, and a forget-me-not flower into the backpack.

I wet my right arm with some water, then place the tattoo barcode patch over it. After a minute I peel off the paper, and the tattoo is on my skin. I add a couple of spares to my bag just in case of emergency.

I slip the small black sound device into the pocket of my dark grey hoodie in case I get attacked. And I sling the backpack over my shoulders, go to the floor door and open it, and climb down the ladder a little, close the floor door, and descend the ladder to the tunnel below my room. I pull my hair back to look like a boy, adjust my hood over my head to conceal my face and identity, then begin my walk to the meeting room 99. I am ready to start my quest to find answers, and, I had a note to deliver to Ree.

CHAPTER 33

I push on the door so it opens a little and peer through the gap. Eli is there and three others, sitting at a table. I open the door further and step into the room and sit at the vacant seat at the table and push my hood back. Like the others.

'Ari, this is Simon, our co-ordinator, and these are our artists, Elliot and Harry. They will work together on barcodes, while we do microchips.'

I dip my head to each of them.

Simon clears his throat. 'Ari. Welcome. But I do have to question your inclusion in this mission. Everyone in this kingdom has agreed to an oath that we will protect your life at all costs. I can't guarantee that you will survive any time that you go out of our territory.'

I set my lips in a hard line. 'If I was born a boy, would you be saying the same thing?'

'Yes.'

'What if I release you from the oath? Then you will neither have guilt nor shame if anything happens to me.'

'I invited her, Simon. Ari has a unique ability that will help people, and has been to Jedburgh and Lerwick by herself a couple of times already. I will take personal responsibility for her. You underestimate her.'

'And if Zarah finds out?' he asks.

'My responsibility,' I say.

Simon paces the room then turns to me and gives a nod. He stops in front of a whiteboard where a map of Jedburgh and Lerwick and other villages are drawn. Jedburgh looks like it is the centre, the heartbeat, in this part of the world at least. I'd love to see a world map of the present state of the earth citizens.

Simon assigns us locations, gives us weather proof coats, a backpack with supplies for our stall, and a deadline to return by.

'New names for protection of you and others.' Simon points and gives us a new name. Mine is still Yarrow. Eli's is still Kale.

'Peace go with you,' Simon says, closes his eyes and lowers his head, then lifts it again.

I stand after the others do, just because I wasn't sure what would happen next. I follow them out of the meeting room and we make our way to the underground tunnels.

I leave first for the market stalls, walking through the underground tunnel in haste to cut down the one hour journey to forty-five minutes. I stop at the tunnel crossroads, and look for the waymarker I had memorised. After locating it, I take the tunnel that will lead to the forest, and follow it for fifteen minutes, my pace slow as I walk with caution. The tunnel ends with light shining through, and I exit into the dense dead wooden forest, pulling my hood low over my head, placing my dark glasses on, then pulling on the rain jacket.

Raindrops fall on the hood of my rain jacket like the beat of a heart. A slow, rhythmic beat that lacks enthusiasm. I walk towards Lerwick; Eli two metres behind. There are no checkpoints for identity scanning and I wonder if that is because water and humanoids don't mix. But surely with their technology they are able to waterproof their technology tools.

I watch as drops of rain hit the fine dirt, creating a dust cloud like an atomic bomb, and leaving a crater like on the moon. How long ago was it since it last rained here?

I turn left to go to the marketplace stalls, and there is the identity checkpoint under the cover from the rain. My barcode scans and beeps without a hiccup and I manoeuvre through the people, engulfed by the voices, the laughter, the hugging and the handshakes. The clothing, the shoes, the scent of food, the water in bottles with a blue label, the furniture, the tools, the flowers, the glassware, the jewellery, the books, the tables with people sitting around them, the fire pits. The doctors.

And the man carving wooden dolls.

He doesn't look up. It isn't Ree. Where is he?

I continue walking and find the designated empty stall for Eli and I and set up the stall with scented oils and pictures of the Henna artwork I am to do as a decoy for disabling the microchips. The surveillance would show just an artist doing what they love to do, not the freedom from the government totalitarianism I was committing.

Change is coming.

The Unfolding.

The Gathering.

The Belonging.

The Reclaiming.

The taking back of power and freedom by the people, of humanity.

I sit on a stool and prepare my tools to work. Eli is amongst the people and guides a person to our stall. 'Yarrow, this is Tilly.'

'Thanks, Kale,' I say, using Eli's alias name, and smile at Tilly and pat the seat next to mine.

She sits and looks up at me.

'Would you like some finger art today? Here's an example of my designs,' I say.

'The second design looks great.'

'Thanks. Could you draw a design for yourself for me to add please,' I say. This is my test to ensure the person before me is human. Pencil hold. Wrist flexibility. Eye gaze. Blinks. The humanoids that slip through Eli, I will swipe over their pretend skin with a wet cloth, then tell them that the ink on their skin will give them a reaction so they leave.

Tilly draws a bird.

'Lovely. Place your hand on the table and we'll get started.' I don't want to touch her and give her a zap and scare her.

I start on the artwork. Five fingers. Five symbols: flower, rain drop, swirl, vine and a simple bird.

'This is an organic art form made from natural dyes. It will fade between seven and fourteen days. You'll need to let it dry for a least thirty minutes.'

I finish the flower art. 'I also offer a complimentary microchip disabling so you can't be tracked anymore. The disabling sends the GPS on a trajectory of its own so it still looks like you are moving about, but it's not accurate. The scanner will still beep. Yes or no?'

'Please she said,' her eyes filled with tears.

I continue with the sun, bird, swirl and vine art. 'Your index finger has a swirl on it. It's a waymark. If you follow the swirls placed on rocks and trees, you will find someone who will help you out of here and to freedom.'

Tilly's tears fell.

'I'm sorry. Did I hurt you?'

'Happy tears,' she says.

'I'm going to hold your hand. There will be a small zap, then that's it, and I will add a drop of scented oil to your skin.' I place my thumb and index finger over the microchip on the flesh of her hand between the thumb and first finger. Tilly winces. 'Oils: lavender, lemon, frankincense, peppermint, or rose?'

'Rose please,' she says, then moves her hand to her nose to inhale the fragrance.

'Done,' I say. '*The Gathering* is in progress. Change is coming,'

I add.

'Thank you.' Tilly takes a deep breath, stands and leaves with an extra spring in her step.

After an hour and a half, our allocated time, we pack up. Eli, aka Kale, has learned the art of Henna, of vegetable ink, and helped with clients.

I don my dark glasses and walk through the market stalls to find Ree. I have the letter from my mother to give him. I find the wooden ornaments. The man looks up at me, and my hope evaporates.

'Where's Ree?' I say.

'It's his weekly service to the ones who control,' he says, shaking his head in disapproval. 'He'll be back tomorrow, or the day after, depending on how agreeable he is with them.'

'Oh,' I say, my voice fading away, getting lost in the spaces of the letters of agreeable. 'Can you tell him that Yarrow came to see him.'

He closes his eyes, then nods.

I wander out of the market stalls, the disappointment of my heart dragging behind me. Eli is following two metres behind. The rain has stopped, leaving a pungent odour lurking. An almighty whoosh sounds and I look up to see a metal object being hurled into the atmosphere until it disappears. 'What's that,' I say loud enough for Eli to hear.

'The slingshot. They collect the rubbish, put it into a metal container and slingshot it out into space.'

'Great,' I say, sarcasm dripping from each letter, then veer off the road to Jedburgh through the dense dead wooden forest where my clothing makes me completely disappear in the trees.

I enter the tunnel to return to our kingdom, Eli close behind me. We walk for twenty minutes until we find ourselves at the crossroad of many tunnels, and choose the tunnel back to the kingdom.

'Good work today, Ari. You're a natural,' Eli says.

'Likewise,' I say.

We return to Simon at the meeting room, reporting what was seen and heard and completed. We have multiple days ahead, alternating between morning stalls and afternoon stalls to continue our work.

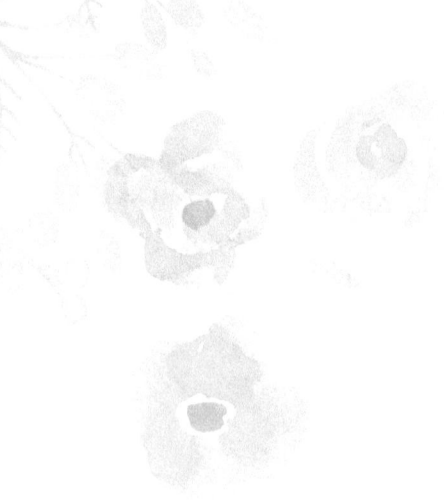

CHAPTER 34

On the third day after the market stall, I walk the road back to Jedburgh, turning at left at the group of close-knit houses and alleyways. I locate the alleyway Sorrel had led me along, and stop at the door to their underground rooms.

I place my hand on the doorknob and it opened, turning it the way I had first watched him do. I step into the room, the stairs to the floor below hidden.

I sigh and sit on a seat and wait.

After a while the door opens, and I slither behind the chair, for safety.

Sorrel enters and the floor opens revealing the stairs to the below floor.

I descend the steps behind him, using the footfall I have been taught in the kingdom, and step into the room that is painted with dark green walls, with eight white doors around the periphery.

Sorrel presses a button on the wall and three people come to the central room. Two male, one female.

The female, Saffron, recognises me. 'I see you brought our

new friend with you,' she says with a smile.

'Unexpected, and expected. Unexpectedly he was hiding behind the chair upstairs. I wondered if he had enough guts to follow us here. So, he is expected. Are you in trouble?' Sorrel says.

'No. I need some information from you,' I say using my best boy voice.

'For goodness sake, use the voice you were given. What would you like to know?' Sorrel is annoyed.

'Is one of you my father?'

'Whoa! Don't hold back now,' Sorrel says.

'I'm looking for my father and was told that I had already met him. I'm retracing my steps of the men I have spoken to in my journey.'

Sorrel runs his hand through his hair, much like my father's in the photograph. He sucks in a deep breath. 'I had a family, much like many men here in Lerwick. We were taken before our child was born, or they were taken from us. No contact. And notified of their death.' Sorrel's voice cracks.

'I'm so sorry for your loss,' I say, and look at each of the men dressed the same, clothing, shoes, hair and beards.

Is one of them my father?

What physical characteristics do they have that are like mine?

Mama said I had my father's eyes.

But what colour would the grey be in this light?

Would they reflect the green of the walls?

Each of the men has dark eyes in this room.

'How would you identify your father?'

'I have the same eye colour as him,' I say.

'Green?'

'Grey, but it reflects colours, changing them.'

'Sorry. Not us. What are you going to do when you find him?'

'Take him home.'

'Good luck with that. I can tell you that even if you do find him, he will not agree to return home. He's been threatened with death, and death of friends and family, like all of us. They will track him down and kill him.'

My breath is taken from me like I have been punched in the stomach.

Death?

Then he most certainly will meet Mama in *The Quietus*.

I close my eyes and try to shut down the fuzzy thoughts in my head.

'Stop trying to find him. It won't end well. You're endangering your life, then your mother will have a double heart ache.'

I suck in a sharp, shuddering breath. The thought of causing my mother incredible heart ache unhinges me. I feel locked in a place of "nothing will help", and I can't get anywhere. 'Thanks for your advice,' I say and turned to leave, dejected.

'Hey … Yarrow?' Sorrel says.

I turn back to him.

'Deactivating the microchips is going to land you in serious trouble. Unspeakable things, before certain death. Don't get caught.'

'I know it's a risk,' I say, fear worming its ugly way towards me.

If I was a real boy would I feel braver?

Mama said once upon a time girls were taught to be perfect and boys were taught to be brave.

Mama said both were wrong.

Brave is constructed.

Brave is a skill.

One that I learned in small moments of challenges each day, planned by my governess.

Bravery is standing up for your beliefs, and being honest about who you are.

When Mama said it would have been better to been born a boy, she was thinking purely of the physical attributes of my sex and what could happen to me. But I think it is better to be born who I am and learn self-defence and use my intellect. I can dress and act like whomever I choose.

Humans are easy to deceive, and that's why *The Beyond* is in a terrible mess.

Confusion and deceit.

Divided we fall.

'May I have access to your store of bar codes please,' I ask.

United we stand.

Sorrel raises his eyebrows.

'Some tattooed barcodes are hard to alter. A fake barcode will register with the scanner,' I say.

'But the face recognition—'

'Will be matched to the barcode. We have technology.'

'I don't thi—'

'We're on the same side, Sorrel,' I say. 'The government has created too many clones and doppelgangers of people with different organisations, they will believe that the person was created within their own establishment. Remember, AI likes to lie. And they call it "hallucinate", to avoid using the word "lie". Even the government doesn't trust Artificial Intelligence. They will be in a state of confusion, playing the blame game, distracted, while we are reclaiming our own, by stealth.'

'And the babies inserted with the brain neuro links?' His voice cracks.

'Can be deactivated. That's the trouble with technology. Hackers can get into anything.'

He nods, and Saffron leaves then returns with the stick-on skin barcodes.

'Thanks,' I say and shove the barcodes into my backpack. 'Where was your home?' I want to know where Sorrel came from.

'I am not permitted to give you that information. You?'

'Same.'

'Why did you become a Lege?'

'I made a terrible mistake allowing the government to

microchip me. When the Rebellion happened, the defiance against truth, which was in fact caused by the ones wanting to control the world, who offered a peaceful solution under the façade of empathy, compassion and a better way of life, I fell for the smoke screen, the delusion. I was deceived. When I woke to the truth it was too late. Being a runner, a Lege, is my way of seeking revenge.' Sorrel pushes his hand through his hair. 'A charagma will come next to will replace this current technology. I will refuse it. Freedom of my soul and my eternal destiny is everything.'

My heart cries for him. 'Thank you for serving others, Sorrel. You will be remembered.'

He puts his hands together in front of him and lowers his head.

I turn to leave, then turn back to them, 'What if telling you that your family is dead is a lie in order control you?' I pause before I turn away from them and walk to the stairs, ascend them, then leave the house, walk down the alleyway, and continue to the market stalls.

A man sits on a short stool whittling, his head down.

In a basket beside him are wooden toys, and beside him is the painter of the wooden toys.

I pick up a flower ornament and run my finger over the curves and the smoothness of the wood.

The whittler looks up at me, and my breath catches.

It is Ree.

He is back.

I feel a tug at my heart.

'Yarrow,' he says with a smile. 'Nice to see you again. How can I help?'

'A note from my mother,' I say, holding it out to him, 'I'll be in trouble if I don't give it to you.'

Ree smiles and takes the note.

He opens it up.

And his smile vanishes.

Dear Ree,

The lovely flower ornament is beautiful.
It is rare to be given a gift that is so close
to my heart.

I would like you to join me for dinner as
my way of thanking you.

Zarah

I blink hard three times. I thought he would have liked to receive a thank you note.

Ree closes the note, then opens it again. He traces over the hand drawn flower with his fingers, like feeling the emotion in the ink. Then he traces my mother's name. He takes a deep breath, folds the note and puts it into his pocket. He looks up at me. 'Tell you mother thank you, but I am unable to accept her dinner invitation.'

I frown at him. 'Why not?'

He taps his tracking device on his ankle.

Twice.

And that's when I see the bruises on his arms and needle tracks. What has happened to him?

I walk around the other side of the table and sit on the seat next to him. 'I can deactivate it.'

He closes his eyes. 'It's too risky.'

'I can organise protection for you.'

He shakes his head. 'If I go, it needs to be on my terms so no one gets hurt. If you can tell me which way to go … write down the address.'

I shake my head. 'You can follow someone.'

Ree picks up a block of timber and starts carving. 'I'll think about it and let you know.'

I offer him a fist bump, and stand. 'Ask for Kale. He will be the one.' I walk away. I have delivered the letter from my mother. I have given him a solution to be able to accept my mother's dinner invitation. And it was the last time I would visit Ree. He was just another stall holder trying to spread kindness, trying to pass the time by keeping himself busy, stuck in the confines of the control of the government.

Tracked.

Used.

Owned.

Like 99% of others here.

I look at faces and eyes as I stroll through the market stalls, looking for my father. Faces are all the same. Smiling but with a common sadness. Like contagion. Holding the dark secret of this life. Occasionally, I catch a glimpse of someone's face when they think they are not seen. No smile. The darkness of emotions revealing themselves.

He is here somewhere. My father. I look for auburn hair, like mine, styled with short sides and back, longer on top and perhaps a wayward lock, wild like the storm clouds, or perhaps it was even longer than in his photograph.

I look for moustaches and beards with streaks of golden highlights. He's characteristics are everywhere and nowhere, close and distant. But not him. Not today. Perhaps another day. And maybe, just maybe, my father will find me.

I pull my hood low over my face, then follow the track to the entrance of the forest where my clothes help me to disappear completely. I enter tunnel. And return home.

Disappointed.

And lost.
Tired.

And questioning.

Mama said to *trust* your seventh sense.
Your first five senses are about your physical senses
—vision, auditory, olfaction, gustation, tactile,
and the subconscious sixth sense of
proprioception—

.

Your seventh sense, once called the sixth sense,
is an ancient concept,
an unconscious cognitive activity
of your mind rapidly sifting through past
experience and amassed knowledge: *your
intuition*—your ability to know something
without any proof.

Your gut feeling.

Mama said we are *born intuitive.*
Even babies can sense when
something is wrong.
It's like the
unconscious language of the soul,
no matter what you believe in.

Intuition is swift, like a knowing.
And it's physical, that gut feeling.
We feel sick, our heart rate rises
or we start to sweat.
Intuition is valuable for detecting *deception.*
Our intuition is *often correct,* but can be wrong
in moments of high emotion.
Calm down before deciding on anything.

Practise *the pause.*

Intuition matters.
It's a *sacred gift.*

CHAPTER 35

Flowers are Mama's love language. Both the type of flower, colour and scent. A soft floral sweet note graces my room, singing of the pastel pink and white peonies gathered in a clear vase, their large blooms intricate and extraordinary, dreamy and soft.

The flower of love.

I leave my bed to be closer to them, magnetised by their beauty that lifts me away to the soft clouds and beyond worries and complications.

To freedom.

And happiness.

I open my interior window shutters to welcome the golden rays of dayspring, and glance over at the Field of Flowers, a rush of colours declaring the promises of the Ancient of Days, written on my heart.

Presence.

Protection.

Provision.
Goodness.
Freedom.
I need those colours today.

After breakfast is a working with dead bodies day. Emotionally exhausting, making me realise how precious our time on the earth is, and how kindness to others is everything.

The order of the day goes accordingly:

Breakfast.
The Flower House of beautiful blooms.
The Quietus.
And the flatline of emotion that came with it.
And then I returned to the markets.

People are disappearing from Lerwick. From Jedburgh. But the market stalls are busier than ever, my market stall line for finger art exorbitantly popular. And more so for people who have not been micro-chipped or barcoded. They are given the way to freedom as well.

And it is raising suspicion.

Our people walk amongst them, asking them to stand around at other stalls while they wait their turn.

And the people come.
And their sadness.
And their shabby clothes.
Their homeless.
And their stench.
And their thirst.
For freedom.
And hunger.

For *The Gathering.*
The Reclaiming.

Mama always said not to judge another. You don't know their life story, nor their dream story. You don't know their beginning, nor their end. And that maybe, just maybe, you can help their end story.

This I know I am doing.

And Mama said to always look at someone the way they are eternally loved, no matter what.

Everyone makes mistakes.

Everyone deserves to be forgiven.

Love.

And kindness.

Forgive.

And move on.

Eli and I work side by side. Occasionally looking up at each other with a glance and a small smile of knowing.

And sometimes, just sometimes, he catches me watching him, my heart filled with love?

What happened to the most annoying boy in the world?

I lower my head and return to the job I am here to do.

Finger art done.

Microchip disabling completed.

Heavy hearts left, filled with light and hope.

I am a light worker.

A light bearer.

And I like it.

In helping others, happiness has found me.

Mama said my gift would be revealed at the appointed time. She was right.

My father. I haven't found him.

Yet.

He hasn't found me.

Yet.

I haven't felt the soul connection Mama had spoken of.

My hope in finding my father is starting to fade and my time working in the markets would be over soon.

One more session tomorrow, and that is it.

For my protection I have been told.

I breathe in deeply, then out.

Mama said breathing in, then breathing out is a sacred name, so sacred it can't be spoken of.

The sound of a fluttering of wings break into my thoughts, an entire flock of doves leaving at once, followed by the scattering of dogs and cats that usually strayed about, or rested beside their owners.

Mama said the animals will tell you the truth, for they cannot be deceived.

Mama said to watch the animals. Watch their behaviour.

Trouble is coming.

Was it a storm like when I was at the lighthouse?

A red balloon comes into sight. Floating above a little girl walking through the markets, smiling. Her contagious smile light faces of people who see her.

How contagious joy seemed to be, even in these circumstances.

I watch her walk, like she is in slow motion. Her presence is so out of sorts for here. There is something that is not right, but the balloon is too mesmerising.

Distracting.

It takes me back to when I was ten and the bouquet of sunflowers that sat atop a picnic basket. Mama had left it for me, the sunflowers telling me to open the basket and explore what was inside.

Happiness.

That is what Mama always left me.

Filling my days with smiles and thankfulness.

I lifted the sunflowers off the picnic basket and opened the lid. Inside was a note, and below it was something from when Mama was a girl. It was red.

Dear Ari Bear,

When I was little I played with balloons. I found one the other day and knew you would love it.
You need to blow into it, and your breath will make it expand. Don't make it too big because it will burst.

Hold the opening closed between breaths while you blow into it, otherwise when you take your lips off, your breath will escape.

Tie up the top of the balloon like a belly button.
And there's some string. Tie it on the balloon.
Have a marvellous day.

See you at noontide for lunch. In the Garden Room.

Love
Mama Bear

'Thank you, Mama,' I whispered, though I was the only one who would hear it.

I pushed the apricots aside and picked up the flat red balloon. It felt rubbery. And flimsy. I turned it over and over and pulled it. It stretched, but didn't break. I lifted the balloon to my lips and blew into the opening. It got bigger. And with each breath it got bigger and bigger, as did my eyes. Then it slipped from my mouth. I giggled as it flew up into the air then dropped to the ground. I ran after it and blew into it again, letting it release from my lips. I knew of nothing else in the castle that would do this. How lucky Mama was when she was young.

I blew the balloon up one more time, and tied a knot in the end like I had seen Mama do with thread. To my surprise, it kept the air inside it. I hit it upward with my hand to see what it would do. Up it went, and then came down again. I went on hitting it up into the air, delighted by a new game with the balloon. But I tired of it. So I tied the string onto the red balloon and let it trail behind me.

And I ran with it, turning to watch it bob up and down, as I disappeared into the forbidden King's forest. I stopped when I couldn't catch my breath. Did I have to chase after that too? Why did people always say they had to catch their breath?

The balloon floated down beside me and I watched it sit in the air with the magic of my string. I gasped. On the ground under the red balloon was an egg. I looked up and saw the bird nest. Far up in the tree. I bent down and picked up the egg in my hands, gently, caring for it as the mother bird would. It was still warm, but had a little hole in it. 'It's okay baby bird. I've got you. I'll give you back to your mama. I promise.'

'Dead.'

I jumped in fright and dropped the egg. I looked down at the ground. The egg had broken, revealing a gasping baby bird. 'No!' I cried. I turned to Eli. 'You are so heartless, Elias. I hate you!' I picked up the baby bird and ran back to Mama. She would help. She knew all the answers to life. She would know what to do.

As I ran with the baby bird, I blew air on to it to keep it breathing. I saw Mama do that once, when the puppies were born and one did not take a breath. But when Mama blew into its mouth, it started to breathe, and Mama smiled the biggest and most beautiful smile I had ever seen.

Panting, I stopped in front of Mama in the oratory and opened my hands.

'Ari Bear, have you saved a baby bird?'

'Help me, Mama. I need to put it back into the nest, but it's—' I stopped talking. I had been in the forbidden forest. I would be in trouble. 'Please send someone who can put it high up in the tree.'

'Elias, come—' Mama called.

'Not Elias, Mother. I loathe him.'

'Then it absolutely must be Elias.'

I fumed at Mama's words. Why would she do this to me. Why couldn't it be the most pleasant Flynn, who was gentle and smiled often and would do everything I asked him to do.

Eli appeared in the oratory. 'Help Ari return this baby bird to its nest where it will still have a chance to survive. Thank you, Eli.' Mama gave him a smile in thanks, then looked at me and raised an eyebrow.

'Yes, Ma'am. As requested,' Eli said.

I turned to Eli, and narrowed my eyes at him. He gave a smirk in response.

'Follow me, Ari,' he said.

I followed him, with every bone in my body protesting, me, holding my words that wanted to burst out at him and pierce him like daggers. I had never met a boy who was so repugnant, annoying, and who did not care for me, but it was the only chance for the baby bird to live. I sucked in a deep breath to self-calm.

Eli stopped at the exact tree with the bird nest. My red balloon was tied to it. I wanted to tell Eli that it was a clever thing to do to identify the tree, but I didn't. He was the one who had caused this trouble, and possibly the death of the bird who wanted to live. He didn't deserve any accolades.

Eli climbed a third of the way up the tree, close to the nest.

He leaned over and held out a cupped hand and I placed the baby bird into it. His eyes smiled at the bird and he blew on it, like I had, then reached up and placed it into the nest. Eli whispered to the baby bird, but I could not hear what he had said. When he climbed from the tree, the mother bird landed in the nest with a worm in her mouth. She looked at us as if to say thank you. I closed my eyes and imagined the baby bird covered in feathers, flying, and sent my love to it. Mama said that love heals and can be felt by people and animals.

I looked at Eli. I had never felt love for him like I did for my friends. Only contempt. Had he never learned about love in his lessons, and how to treat others?

I left the red balloon tied to the tree. That way I could visit my baby bird. I ran my hands over the shiny balloon. I was thankful for it. It had saved the life of a bird today. Without the balloon I would never have seen the egg on the ground.

I turned and wandered out of the forbidden King's Forest. At least Mama wouldn't know that I was here. Eli wouldn't tell her, because he would be in trouble too. We would both be grounded, unable to leave our rooms for days.

I blink at this red balloon at the market. It's different to the red balloon when I was ten. It seems heavier, somehow.

Screams pierce my ears and everyone scatters.

I turn my head to see Eli diving at me, his arm around my waist, pulling me to the ground as an almighty boom sounds.

And the ground shook.

A bomb.
Fear.
And pain.

And nothing.

Mama said to *walk a day* in someone's shoes
and you will partially understand
the *cross they bear.*
The *mask that hides* themselves from others.

Then walk a day and a *dark night* of the soul
in their shoes, and you will understand a little
more, and the *tears they cry in secret.*

Then walk a day and a night
and the *morning after* in their shoes,
and you will be getting closer to understanding the
essence of someone,
their *difficult path*, their *pain,*
their *courage.*
Their *hopes.* Their *dreams.* Their *prayers.*

And then said Mama, you will
know why sometimes,
to *protect ourselves* and *others,*
we choose to lie about a situation.
When you are young you are taught
rules to live by,
but when you are older and wiser,
you will know that there are
exceptions to the rules,
to *protect*, to *survive.*

Forgive others. *Do not judge.*
Forgive yourself.
And ask the Ancient of Days for forgiveness.

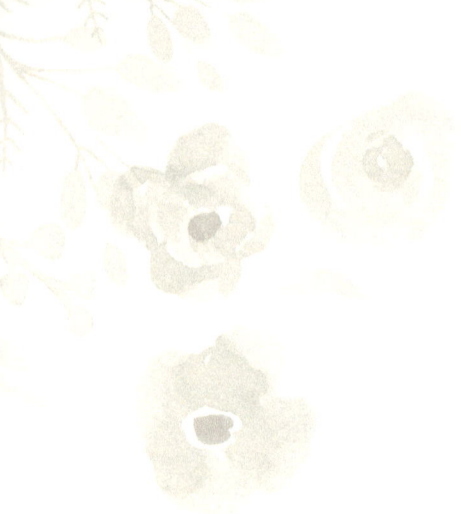

CHAPTER 36

Flowers sit in the middle of the kingdom's great dining table. Daisies, like the wooden ornament Ree had given my mother.

I blink. Slowly.

A deep melancholy flows through my body like a discordant note filling me with the colour of broken—black, grey, deep purple and a tinge of dark red.

My ears hurt, and ring with an impossibly loud unabating sound that pierces my thoughts with its attention seeking.

Is there something wrong with me?

'Ari,' Mama says, like she is surprised I am standing here at the doorway of the celebration hall. She walks over to me with quick footsteps, like there is an urgency of some kind. 'Come. Sit.' She hooks her arm through mine and guides me to the table like I am blind.

I sit at the table that looks like it has been set to honour guests. More men than women. A plate of food is placed before me.

'How are you feeling?' Mama asks.

My shoulders lift as I inhale and I shake my head slightly. 'Dazed. Annoyed by the high pitched sound in my ears. Sore. What happened?'

'A bomb went off in the market place … Eli saved you.'

'I feel like you have already told me this a few times,' I say.

'Yes. When you were unconscious. In a coma. The doctor said your brain has hidden the memory of the event to help with your recovery.'

I look about the table for Eli. He isn't here. 'Where's Eli? I feel he should be here amongst us.'

'He's … recovering,' Mama says. But I could feel the lie wrapping its ugly claws around the spoken words.

Is she protecting me?

I nod. It's all I can do with the low energy I feel. I look around the table again, wondering why these people have been invited to dinner at the kingdom's gracious dining hall with the ridiculously long dining table that can fit fifty people, comfortably.

There are seven of us, including Mama and I, making us insignificant to the opulence of the massive celebration hall, that somehow still stands amongst the crumbling debris of the thousand year old castle.

'Ari, this is Benjamin.' I follow Mama's hand gesture to the man sitting opposite me. 'He is a Lege and a medic.'

'Next to him is Cassia. She is a miracle worker from Lerwick.'

She is the one Sorrel told me to contact if I was ever in trouble, I think.

'Tilly is beside her. She is the doctor who took care of you.'

I dip my head in thanks to her.

'Liam, on the other side of the table. He is a Lege.'

Liam leans forward and so do I. I nod.

'And beside you is—'

'Ree?' I say, unsure. His face is familiar, but different. His hair combed into place with a side part, his facial hair manicured.

Our grey eyes connect and I feel a pull toward him, like we

are connected by an invisible string that keeps getting shorter. He offers me a small smile then places his hand over my forearm. But he doesn't jump like I have given him a shock.

'Your father.' My mother's voice is soft, and lacking in confidence of the content of her words, of the effect they will have on me.

I still, then remove my arm from his touch.

I stand, fuming, the chair falling over behind me. 'You knew who I was after giving you the note and you never said anything?' Tears balanced on the edge of my eyelids.

'It was to protect you, Ari,' he says gently, his voice cracking.

'Sit down, please,' Mama says, her words washing over me like acid.

Papa, not acknowledging me when I first met him, felt exactly like rejection. A heavy tear rolls down my cheek and drops onto the floor like an explosive.

I close my eyes, and when I open them again, I pick up my chair, push it in, and leave the room, my floral dress flowing behind me taking my chaos with me, leaving the dinner guests and my parents in disbelief.

Despair.

And silence.

Hurt.

And confusion.

I walk outside to the fallen castle walls and sit on a large block.

The broken castle.

Like me.

I look up at the sky, filled with darkness and satellites.

Patrolling.

Recording.

Spying.

Can they see my tears?

Can they measure my broken heart?
When will the anger of the world end?
When will the fighting stop?
When will the lies stop?
When will peace come?

When will the truth come?

He sits beside me, his presence felt, the warmth of his body touching mine. He has perfected quiet walking. I don't even hear him approach. I don't wait for the word "dead" from Eli, because the presence next to me feels different.

'I'm sorry.' My father's voice is deep, somehow familiar but unfamiliar, weaving its timbre inside me like a father's love note, comforting and sweet, connecting my soul to his.

I stay silent, looking up into the polluted night sky.

The broken night sky.

Only because I am overwhelmed and I can't find the words to answer him. A million emotions are erupting inside me, like fireworks. I want to hug him but I don't know if he is the hugging type, or whether my hug would give him a shock like it does to others.

I want to bury my nose against the skin of his neck and inhale his scent. I want to place my hand over his beating heart to see if it would beat in time with mine. I want to tell him that I have missed him, but I never knew what it was like to have a father in the first place.

Would I be able to trust him unconditionally like a baby who completely and utterly adores and trusts her father, no questions asked? Just a knowing.

'I remember May 2019,' he says, 'when the first batch of satellites were launched by Space X. Starlink Satellites. Sixty of them at first. Trails of lights in the night sky like a light train. There's hundreds of thousands of them now. It's the ones that are virtually impossible to see with the naked eye we have to be concerned about. It will end. Soon. And peace will be restored to day and night in the above and the universe that we once saw will be back.'

'How do you know?' I ask, not wanting to look at my father because I know that I will ugly cry. This is our very first father and daughter discussion. This is what it feels like to sit next to your father.

'*The Gathering. The Belonging.* The rejection of artificial intelligence's grip on human life and control by the government, who, by the way will let it appear that we are winning, then slip a swiftie on us all while we are content and have our guards down.'

'What then—' I ask, wanting to add Papa to the end of my words. But couldn't. Yet. 'Will it return to the same situation?'

'No. Our retaliation will be unexpected and powerful. You need the heart and mind of a human to triumph.'

'I'm sorry I reacted abrasively at the dinner table—' I say, again wanting to add Papa to the end of my words. But I couldn't. Yet.

'That was a lot to put on you, especially after the explosion.'

'The one I can't remember.'

'That would be the one. Eli saved your life, by the way. I picked you up and ran with you to bring you home.'

A sob escapes me. 'So I united you and Mama after all,' I say.

'Indeed, my sweet.' Papa's voice sings to my heart, a whole bar of notes in perfect harmony on repeat.

Healing.

And comforting.

Reaching out.

And pulling in.

'Where's Eli?' I ask.

Papa takes my hand in his, and I know what he says next is

not going to be good news. 'He … we couldn't find a heartbeat, nor breath, and had to leave him there. I'm sorry.' Papa's voice is full of grief.

My body goes numb and then my throat gets stuck with shock and I can't breathe. 'No,' I say.'

Denial.

And pain.

I lay my head on Papa's broad shoulder and weep. Bitterly. *Not Eli. Not my Eli. We were meant to meet death, together.* 'Please tell Mama that … I want to … prepare his … body … when it comes in.' My throat is so tight it hurts.

'I will,' Papa whispers and places his arm around me, kisses my forehead then lays his head against mine while I shake with body-quakes of sadness.

And anger.

Broken heartedness.

And guilt.

I go to bed that night with a heaviness of heart and mind.
What will I do without my Eli?
My best friend.
My soul link.
Of stories. And trouble.
Of moments and memories.

And light.

Mama said to appreciate the
gift of life on earth,
and to be *present* in each moment.
We are here for a *nanoscopic beat* in time
compared to eternity,
passing through, as *luminous beings*
getting a *sacred glimpse*
of creation in the vast universe
from our small part of the heavens and earth.
A *sneak preview* of the great and
unimaginable majesty that
awaits us in *eternity.*

Mama said that as we journey, feeling the full
brunt of emotions, to *hurt no human nor
animal.* To *care for our earth* like the
guardians we are.
And to develop the nature of *compassion*
and *empathy* for others.

Mama said every day you will need
to choose between
the beauty and ugliness *within yourself,*
the love and hate *within yourself.*
The positive. And negative.
The good. And bad.

Mama said you'll *reap what you sow.*

And to *be awesome* is *to be kind.*

CHAPTER 37

I wake to the perfume of roses permeating the room. A light, delicate sweet fragrance, much like almond blossom, cucumber and lemon zest. It wasn't the first of a new month, when Mama would always leave roses of hope. But still, the bouquet of blooms on my window sill is white. Pure. Like Mama's love for Papa.

I smile and place my hand over my heart. There is no ache at the thought of Papa's absence like I once had. He is here. With us. Our family is complete. The three of us.

Will Mama still catch her tears and study their structure under the microscope to see how they have changed?

I climb out of bed and open my indoor window shutters, and gaze out at the Field of Flowers. The field of colour.

And happiness.

Of death.

And new life.

Painted above is a sky like a sea of blue.

I want to shout out the window, 'PAPA IS HERE!' in a state

of pure happiness.

But I can't.

Our kingdom is one of quietness for survival.

I release my hyper-phantasia instead, and the Field of Flowers becomes an octopus's garden at the bottom of the deep blue sea, then fish of all kinds come and swim in the sea, coloured like the blue sky—

The door creaks and the fish fall into the octopus's garden and sink below the soil and lodge in the bones of the human skeletons, and the Field of Flowers pops up again, smiling at the sun as if nothing ever happened.

I look at the door, slightly ajar. Mama's smile reaches into the room and spreads joy to my heart. 'Papa is keen for breakfast.'

'Same,' I say, and beam a joyous smile back to her. I never expected this day to come.

Of happiness.

And bliss.

Of love.

And connections.

I change out of my bed clothes that doubled as escape clothes, and put on a pair of clay-brown wide-leg pants and a coconut hue long-sleeved button-up shirt. My Friday clothes on a Friday.

I wonder what Papa would expect his daughter to wear?

So I remove those clothes and throw on a pale blue dress. I parade around the room, anxious about feeling so self-conscious, then decide to be myself. That's who Papa would want me to be.

So I fling the dress across the room and return to my pants and blouse, and leave my room, my bare feet pattering against the cold stone floor.

'Ari, good morning!' Mama's cheery voice matches her sunny smile, like the cheery sunflowers that worship the sun.

'Good morning, Mama.' I walk around the table and give her a gentle hug. 'Good morning, Papa,' I say then, our eyes connecting, springtime grey today. I wonder if mine are the same shade as his.

'The best morning, Ari,' Papa says, his smile melting my heart, his voice singing to my being.

I move around the table and hug him with the same gentleness I did with Mama, until I hug him a little tighter, burning the memory of our physical touch into my mind, and the smell of him—fresh laundry and a wooded, grassy field. Today will be a better day with Papa after last night's fiasco of uncontrolled emotion.

I sit opposite Papa. I want to soak everything in about him and make sure he doesn't disappear again.

Papa smiles at me, his eyes dancing.

'What?' I say, all self-conscious and goofy like a newborn giraffe trying to stand up. Is this what the Melody of Summer season of life feels like?

New.

And exciting.

Adventurous.

And hopeful.

'It's the best day of my life,' he says with a huge smile.

'Same,' I say with a silly grin, feeling like I am four years old again.

'Ask me anything,' he says after a bite of food, and it feels like an elephant comes and joins us at the table.

'Why were you taken and why didn't you return? Do you know how many tears Mama collected?' The words fly from my mouth like a spoiled rotten child.

'Ari—'

Papa lifts his hand. 'It's okay, Zarah. It's a fair question—' he looks at me '— or two. I was taken because of my research on the immortal jellyfish.'

'Ah … immortality!' I think back to the book I delivered to

Mrs Grobbler: *The Quest for Immortality – the experiments, the science, and the reality.* 'The Turritopsis dohrnii?' My voice rises higher than I intend it to.

Papa raises an eyebrow at me.

'My studies,' I add.

Papa smiles at Mama. 'Yes. The quest for immortality for those who don't believe in spiritual immortality. The process of transdifferentiation is the cellular mechanism, and we have successfully, genetically spliced human DNA and Turritopsis dohrnii DNA. So humans now have self-cloning, regenerating back and forth between life stages to healthier states, or more enjoyable life stages. Back at the lab in *The Beyond*, are experimental immortal beings. The Establishment is inserting flexible neural implants into the immortals' brains, so their life experiences and knowledge can be transferred to its new brain without any loss of the time continuum. The problem is, which I keep explaining to them at the symposiums, is that they can still die by injury or accident and not be able to get to the permutation stage, so there is never truly earth immortality.'

'But aren't there already clones, or, what do you call them? Doppelgangers?'

'Yes, but they can't regenerate. They have a different purpose.'

'And that would be?'

'Control of the individual. Deceit. Confusion of people who know the original so they learn not to trust that person. Same applies for digital copies manipulated to say things the original person never would. Heinous. Sinister.'

'Ma said there were four versions of everyone. Is that correct?'

'Yes, and now add to it the earthly immortal version.'

I sigh heavily. 'For the rich people who think they are God. What happens when the world is only populated by ridiculously wealthy selfish self-proclaimed gods?'

'They manipulate and intimidate each other for power through war—physical or biological until one is left with its loyal subjects who serve out of fear. Hate will reign until they rise up and destroy the ruler—if they get to live to see that happen.'

'Can't you add a glitch to the regeneration process?'

Papa raises his finger and places it over his lips and raises an eyebrow.

I smile.

'And the answer to the second question, Papa?'

'How many tears? Oh … somewhere between 57 and 114 litres—the science of crying.' Papa looks at Mama then and puts his hand over hers. 'I'm so sorry, Zarah.' Papa looks at me, 'And you too, Ari.' A tear falls over the rim of his grey eyes, turning them stormy grey. 'They told me that you both died in child birth. And I believed it of course. And then, when Leges told me you were alive, I was threatened with your deaths if I returned home, the tracker on my ankle recording everything.'

'How did you manage to come home then, Pa? Surely they followed your position?'

'Eli scrammed the signal a couple of days before the explosion. When I picked your lifeless body up, I just ran with you, and there was only one place I wanted to take my girl, dressed as a boy.' Papa smiles at me. 'Home.'

My throat tightens at the mention of Eli's name.

And I cry.

Mama puts her hand over mine. 'If you had died and Elil had survived, he would not have been able to live with himself. We will be forever thankful for Eli's selflessness and loyalty to you. He was perfect for you.'

'I know, Mama,' I say between sobs. 'It just hurts … sooo … much.'

Mama gives me a hand hug as my tears waterfall down my face, my hyper-phantasia creating the great flood in the breakfast nook, and Mama, Papa and I, sitting in a rowboat upon the ocean of tears, Papa rowing to find the cries of my heart and release them into the heavens to be captured by angels to deliver to Eli.

Cries of grief.
Cries of thank you.

Cries of I miss you terribly forever and a day.

CHAPTER 38

'Papa is helping in *The Quietus* today, Ari,' Mama says, pulling me back to the present. But I can't see her face through the heavy rain clouds in my mind.

I blink and inhale deeply to turn the faucet off the tap of tears, and return to my room. I dry my tears with lavender flowers on their stems, then climb out my window, my bare feet squashing wild violets amongst the cosmos flowers.

I head east to the greenhouses of fruits and vegetables and herbs and spices, and the Flower House, the grandest glass house of them all. It is filled with flowers and work tables and colours and floral scents that make you think of happiness and wonderful dreams, and a moment in time when Eli and I were almost friends there.

The moment I open the white wooden door to the flower house, floral scents loom and circle around me with a persuasive melody of love.

I walk in and look about. Glass walls and ceilings.

And colour.

Everywhere.

I grab a bucket and some floral scissors and walk about. As I finger the soft, velvety petal of a pink snapdragon, the memory of Eli comes when I was seventeen, on that day I spent inside my dream of living life independently.

Happy.

No castle responsibilities.

Nobody watching my every move.

Free.

Like the birds gliding effortlessly in the Bloom of Spring sky after the Woe of Winter.

I had gathered my stolen flowers from the Flower House. I was forbidden to go in there without permission. Pink snapdragons. I placed them in a vase taken from the Museum of Earth Time, then performed a slow pirouette around the 1960s sunny yellow vintage caravan I had stumbled upon where the forest greeted the lake. I opened all the windows, and the curtains I had made blew in the breeze, like dancing to an inaudible symphonic melody, with the bunting in colours of blue, pink, yellow, purple and green, clapping along. I dived onto the bed, then peered out at the lake, shimmering with diamonds and good cheer.

This is what freedom felt like.

I rolled onto my back and gazed around my little house on flat tyres, wedged between two trees, and caught the reflection in a window of Eli outside the door of the caravan. He held some flowers in front of him. Simple white daisies. He looked down at them and brushed a leaf off the top of a flower. He shifted from foot to foot, then took a deep breath, and stepped up into the caravan. I closed my eyes.

'Dead,' he said.

'Unlike Sleeping Beauty,' I said, keeping my eyes closed, then added, 'good morning, Eli. It's a beautiful day, is it not?'

'Sssssh,' Eli said. 'Sleeping Beauty does not speak.'

'Then will you wake me with true love's kiss?'

He coughed. 'Unlikely,' he said.

I opened my eyes and grabbed a pillow from above me and threw it at him.

He ducked, smiling, and the pillow hit the wall behind him. 'See. Sleeping Beauty is full of grace, unlike you.'

'And the prince is an idiot, falling in love with someone he has never met, based on her beauty! What if she opened her mouth and her teeth were rotten and falling out? Or what if her words were dipped in poison to damage the mind and heart? What then? How would the fairy tale end, Elias Wolfe?'

Eli tilted his head to the side and said, 'Well … the prince is actually a vampire, and you know how that ends.'

I burst out laughing.

Eli held the bouquet of flowers in front of me. 'You dropped these on the way to your little hide-away.'

I looked at the simple white daisies and took them from him. 'Liar,' I said. 'I didn't pick daisies from the Flower House.'

'And this note.' He held out a note.

I rolled my eyes and grabbed it from him. I knew who it was from.

Dear Ari,

White daisies will look amazing in the caravan, more so than snap dragons.

You are required back at the kingdom.
Immediately.

Love Mama

My happiness dropped to the floor and rolled away like a spilt box of marbles. I laid back on the bed and looked out the window, over the lake, now dark and sombre like my mood. 'I can't wait until I'm eighteen, Eli, and then I can make my own choices.'

I felt the bed move as he laid beside me. 'You've been making your own choices since you were young, Ari. Your mama has been very tolerant of your adventures.'

'But I want more, Eli. I want to see what is outside our kingdom.'

'Trust me, Ari, staying in the kingdom will be your best choice for safety. But I've known you long enough that you like to live your own life. Just … make choices to stay safe.'

'Thanks, I think,' I said, wondering if Eli had just given me a compliment.

'And for the record, Ari, if a prince woke you with true love's kiss, you would have brought more than just beauty to him, you would have brought your wild spirit and adventure, an intelligence that would astound him, and pure joy. Maybe the fairy tale isn't about the prince rescuing the princess, but the princess rescuing the prince?'

It was as if a light bulb turned on in my head. I had thought that fairy tales were for girls, but what if they were for boys as well? 'Eli,' I said. I turned over on the bed when there was no answer. He had already gone.

The memory slips from my mind, and the flowers became a blur through my tears as I choose flowers for *The Quietus* today. I wasn't picky, just grabbing this and that.

Two buckets full.

Nausea rises in my stomach as I think of Eli's body being delivered on the stretcher. My thoughts slow my walk to *The Quietus*, my subconscious's warning to me about the impending day of sorrow to come.

As I turn the corner to that place, *The Quietus*, an earthy sweet scent, sharp like the smell of cut grass lingers, that sends out an aromatic distress signal to surrounding vegetation. My stomach lurches as the bees of anxiety over populate my body, stinging me with its poison.

Mama paces the floor with her eyes closed, whispering to herself. She opens her eyes and gives me a small smile. 'Papa will help lay the cotton fabric over the slab, Ari. I'd like you to record details in the Book of Life and prepare the jars of evidence please.'

'Sure,' I say, and place the flowers on her metal trolley that hold a number of instruments and jars and flowers and string and cloth strips and herbs and spices.

Mama hands me an apron.

I stand back from the table, and watch as Mama explains the process of bringing in the body to Papa. And then it begins: activity flowing through the room like a well-oiled machine, each knowing the order of the process, working together with perfect synchronicity.

'Jacob, would you let Levi know that we are ready to begin.'

Jacob gives the thumbs up, and leaves the room. A few moments later, he returns with three others. They carry a body on a stretcher, then transfer the body to the table. A woman, middle-aged, dark brown straight hair, her face bruised around the eye area, nose broken, eyes open, one arm broken, and a foot in a deformed position. I cover my mouth.

'Thank you, gentlemen,' Mama says, and they leave, except for Jacob, who gathers a pencil and two sheets of paper.

'Jacob, Azriel is joining us today, and Ari, of course.'

Jacob stands and shakes Papa's hand, 'Pleased to meet you, sir.' Then he looks at me and raises his eyebrows. Twice. With a slight smile.

'Likewise,' Papa says, then Jacob starts sketching the person's face, one piece of art paper under the other.

Mama picks up a small square piece of cloth with tweezers and dips it into a solution, then moves the person's hair behind their ear to the side and wiped the skin with the cloth.

She nods. Once. The body is human. Then she lets out a breath of relief. 'Welcome to the Field of Flowers, my love. I'm sorry if the solution stung on your skin.' Her voice is gentle.

Mama reaches for the person's right hand, and feels the flesh between the thumb and first finger. She turns and picks up a black scanning device, and holds it over that place of flesh. The black box beeps.

'Everyone,' she said, 'this is Maria Lee. She is forty-two years of age, has four children, worked in graphic design and was red flagged for adding messages against AI in the backgrounds of designs, and hence why she is here with us today.'

Mama places her gloved hand over the face of Maria. 'Keep your eyes closed, it's time to rest. You have finished your journey well.' Mama holds the hand of the Maria and feels the flesh between the thumb and index finger again. 'You don't need this anymore, Maria. You are freed. You'll feel a little sting.' I watch as Mama reaches for the scalpel and cuts the person's hand, and pulls out the microchip, washes it, and drops it into a jar, the ting echoing throughout the room.

Mama reaches for the scissors, and snips off some hair and places string around it, and puts it in to the jar. She runs her hands down her apron, takes a deep breath, then leans forward and straightens the clothes on the person. 'I'm going to wash you, now. It will make you feel good,' Mama said to Maria, and uses a wet cloth and wipes over the exposed limbs, humming a pretty tune. Then she dries her limbs. I see Papa wipe away a tear.

'How's your portrait going, Jacob?'

'Well. The first is finished.' I watch as he puts the portrait to the side, then proceeds to draw on the second piece, tracing the lines imprinted from the first portrait. Then he uses the colours to add dimension and life to the representational portrait.

Mama picks up a pink daisy and holds it near Maria's face. 'I'm just matching a colour flower to your skin. The pink daisy looks lovely.' Mama picks seven pink flowers of different varieties and places them in Maria's hair and around her face. She lifts the hands of the person and places them on the stomach, pushing a small flower posy between the hands, then Mama grabs a strip of cloth and ties the hands together at the wrist, and then the feet, repositioning the deformed one.

Mama reaches for some oil scents that were in bottles on the trolley, and dabs them on the person. 'You'll love these perfumes of parsley, sage, rosemary and thyme—for Quietus, immortality, remembrance, and courage. They are to honour you with their scented kiss.'

I watch as Mama dabs the scented oils on Maria with a gentleness that speaks of love.

'Jacob, how's the second portrait?'

'Just finished.'

'Wonderful. Help me prepare the cocoon with the cotton shroud so Azriel will know how to do it.'

Papa steps back to get out of the way. Jacob stands and rolls the portrait and adds it to the jar where Mama has dropped the hair sample and microchip into, then he stands on the opposite side of Mama.

They reach down to the fabric, and lift and roll the person, wrapping and tucking the fabric, and watch as the Maria's body settles.

Mama strokes the head of the cocooned Maria. 'You're ready to join your friends in the Field of Flowers. Your resting place has been prepared. I'll see you later, my love, when we'll say goodbye under the safety of the night.'

Jacob and Mama stand in silence for a moment, their heads bowed. Papa and I do so too.

Then Jacob leaves and returns with the three others who had delivered Maria. They carefully place her body onto a stretcher and leave the room. Once they are gone, I become busy, labelling the jar with the microchip, the hair clipping, and the portrait, then place it on an empty shelf.

I sit at the desk and record the details about Maria, including the time that she came in, the number on her microchip, age, sex, employment, education, offspring, partner, and draw on a map where her body will be laid to rest.

Then I remove a large leather bound book from the shelf, and opened it up to a page that is marked with a lavender coloured ribbon. I pick up the calligraphy pen, dip it into the blue ink and add Maria's name to the Book of Life, then blow of the page and check that the ink is dry before the table is set again for the next body.

When I finish, I turn to see Mama drying the stone slab.

'Azriel, would you kindly grab a cotton shroud from the shelf and help put it in place for the next person.'

'Sure. When did you start doing the green burials for people?'

'Seventeen and a half years ago,' Mama said. 'If you were dead, I wanted to be the one to prepare your body and honour you in death.'

Papa lifts his chin and looks down at Mama, his eyes wet. He runs his hand through his hair and then over his beard. 'Thank you,' he says, his voice cracking.

I swallow the lump in my throat.

A new body arrives then and is placed onto the stone slab.

'Welcome to the King's Forest,' Mama says.

My skin burns. Panic. Is this Eli? I don't want to look but I do. Mama said when panic starts, I need to slow time down. She said I can do that with my breathing. She said I can remove myself from the situation by separating myself from reality. So, for survival mode, I inhale deeply, then release it slowly through my pursed lips.

Breathe in.

Breathe out ... separate myself from my present ...

Breathe in.
Breathe out …
Breathe in.
Breathe out.

I walk over to the body, nausea rising, and peer at his face. It isn't Eli. 'Mama … when Eli's body comes in, I want to help you prepare him for burial as my way of goodbye.' A sob escapes me. Mama puts her hand on my shoulder, the connection and lightness comforting me.

I sit back on the chair at the writing desk while Mama and Papa perform the process of de-microchipping, washing, drying, tying, adding herbs and spices to the man, and decorating him with leaves and flowers.

When Mama calls me to write his name in the Book of Life, I do, my head in a swirl of emotion. It happens every time a body is prepared.

Garrick.

Garrick is dead.

His mother and father and brothers and sisters and others will be devastated, their world shattered, their hearts broken. I inhale a shuddering breath.

Breath.

Death.

Did they rhyme on purpose?

The beginning and the end.

We all stand in silence for a moment, heads bowed. Then Jacob leaves and returns with the others. They carefully placed the body onto a stretcher and leave.

I take a slow steady breath through my nose and prepare the jar for the room of remembrance while Mama and Papa prepare the slab for the next person, then return to the scream of Mama. She holds her hand over her mouth.

Is it Eli?

Please don't let it be Eli.

Before her is a woman with a large abdomen. An unborn baby. I watch as Mama's whole body shakes. 'Noooo!' she whispers, and Papa takes her in his arms while she cries.

Mama collects herself after a few minutes, then begins to prepare the body.

'Everyone,' she says through tears, her voice a pitch higher, 'this is Elouise Johnson. She is thirty-six years of age, first child. She works in catering and was red flagged for removing mind altering additives in the government owned water bottles, and sending out our pure water with the blue labels, and hence why she is here with us today.'

Mama places her gloved hand over the face of the Elouise. 'Keep your eyes closed, it's time to rest. You have finished your journey well. You protected your baby with all that you have. Together now in the Kingdom of the Ancient of Days.' Mama holds the hand of the person and feels the flesh between the thumb and index finger again. 'You don't need this anymore, Elouise. You are freed. You'll feel a little sting.' I watch as Mama reaches for the scalpel and cut the person's hand, and pulls out the microchip, washes it, and drops it into a jar, the ting echoing throughout the room.

Mama reaches for the scissors, and snips off some hair and places string around it, and puts it in the jar. She runs her hands down her apron, takes a deep breath, then leans forward and straightens the clothes on Elouise.

'Mama, will you bury her like that, or remove the baby from the womb and place it in her arms?'

'Once, I did remove a baby and placed it into the mother's arms but it was too distressing for me. I like that the baby is still protected in the mother's womb, still connected, together. It means more, I think. It feels right.'

Mama wipes away a tear, then turns back to Elouise. 'I'm going to wash you, now. It will make you feel good,' Mama says and uses a wet cloth and wiped over the exposed limbs, humming a pretty tune and a lullaby. Then she dries her limbs. I see Papa turn away and brush his hands over his face, then looks up to the ceiling.

'How's your portrait going, Jacob?'

'Well. The first is finished.' I watch as he puts the portrait to the side, then proceeds to draw on the second piece, tracing the lines imprinted from the first portrait. Then he uses the colours to add dimension and life to the representational portrait.

Mama picks up a white rose and holds it near Elouise's face. 'I'm just matching a colour flower to your skin. The white rose looks lovely.' Mama picks seven white flowers of different varieties and placed them in Elouise's hair and around the face. She gathered white baby's breath flowers and makes a halo out of them and places it on the baby bump. She lifts the hands of Elouise and puts them above the stomach, pushing a small flower posy between the hands, then Mama grabs a strip of cloth and ties the hands together at the wrist, and then the feet.

Mama reaches for some oil scents that are in bottles on the trolley, and dabs them on Elouise. 'You'll love these perfumes of parsley, sage, rosemary and thyme—for quietus, immortality, remembrance, and courage. They are to honour you with their scented kiss.'

I watch as Mama dabs the scented oils on Elouise with a gentleness that speaks of love.

'Jacob, how's the second portrait?'

'Just finished.'

'Wonderful.'

Jacob stands and rolls the portrait and adds it to the jar where Mama has dropped the microchip and hair sample into. Papa reaches down to the fabric, and lifts it over the person with Mama, wrapping and tucking the fabric, and watches as the body settles.

Mama strokes the head of the cocooned Elouise. 'You're ready to join your friends in the Field of Flowers. Your resting place has been prepared. I'll see you later, my loves, when we'll say goodbye under the safety of the night.'

We all stand in silence for a moment, our heads bowed. Then Jacob leaves and returns with the three who delivered Elouise. They carefully place her body onto a stretcher and leave the room. Once they were gone, I become busy, labelling the jar with the microchip, the hair clipping, and the portrait, and place it onto the shelf.

I sit at the desk and record the details of Elouise, including the time that she came in, the number on her microchip, age, sex, employment, education, offspring, partner, and draw on a map where her body will be laid to rest.

Then I remove the large leather bound book from the shelf, and open it up to a page that is marked with a lavender coloured ribbon. I dip the calligraphy pen into the blue ink and add Elouise's name to the Book of Life, and then her baby's, and blow on the page and check that the ink is dry.

We work well as a team, efficiently preparing the departed.

We work long hours for three days and three nights in the Field of Flowers and the King's Forest as we lay our people to rest.

On the fourth day, the final body was delivered to *The Quietus*.

A male.

Around my age.

My skin burns and my heart beats fast while nausea rises.

Panic.

This body would be Eli's.

He is the last of the bodies from the explosion.

I turn my head away. I don't want to look at him, but I do.

I want to see his face, for one last time.

I want to run my fingers through his hair for the first and the last time.

I want to wash his face, tenderly, memorising the details of his profile, the fan of his eyelashes, the shape of his lips, the curve of his eyebrows.

I want to …

I want to wash the red blood from his injured and bruised body.

I want to …

I want to wash his feet, the ones that followed me everywhere to protect me.

I want to choose perfect white flowers for him, because in my eyes he was perfect, golden hearted.

I want to choose the sweetest of spices and herbs to reflect his character, his essence.

And I want to …

Lay my head on his chest, against his heart. The heart that I love and will never get to hear or feel beating against my hand or cheek.

And I want my tears to fall onto his eyes to awaken him from his earthly sleep so our lips can meet in our first kiss.

I want Jacob to create a portrait just for me.

To keep close to my heart.

Forever.

Breathe in. Breathe out. I need to slow time down and remove myself from the situation, from reality, for self-preservation. I inhale deeply, then release it slowly through my pursed lips.

Breathe in. Breathe out … separate myself from the present … *Breathe in. Breathe out … Breathe in. Breathe out.*

I dig deep for courage and take the first difficult step toward to the body, nausea rising.

I suck in a deeper breath, my throat so tight like it is trying to suffocate me so I could lie on top of him and join him in the earthly sleep, and step through to eternity with him.

I look at his face.

The dark hair matted with blood.

The cut across his forehead and cheek.

The swollen lips and broken nose.

The one eye that was still open.

Eli?

The eye was brown.

Not Eli.

I gently place my fingers over his eyelid and close it for him. 'Rest in earthly peace. Dance with heavenly joy,' I say, and step away, walk over to Papa and fall into his arms. And I stay that way for what felt like forever and a day.

Relieved.

And not relieved.

Faith.

And hope.

Mama said life is full of *beginnings*.
And *endings*.
In nature. The animal kingdom.
In family and friendships.

In *love*.

Also in our *short daily stories*
and the story of our *long life*.
Even in the *seasons of our life*,
each season has a *beginning*.
And an *ending*.

Life. And death.
First breath. And last.

Mama said endings could be either
happy or *sad*, and either way,
it is the *beginning of something new*.

Hope.

CHAPTER 39

The field of flowers has lost its colour. Its vibrancy. Its joy. Like me. I step through the flowers in shades of grey with care, and over bodies buried below.

It's a dark, moonless night.

Darkness does that to colour. It masks its true beauty. Unless there's light. Even the teeniest, weeniest dot of light. And in the darkness, that teeny weeny bit of light shines brighter than you could ever imagine, filling you with hope.

As I try not to destroy flowers in my path, I ponder where Eli should be buried when his body comes to *The Quietus*. I know the Field of Flowers is where the bodies of women and girls and babies reside, and the King's Forest for the men and boys, and rightfully, Eli's body should be buried in the King's Forest.

But I want to bury him in the Field of Flowers because of his beautiful heart. Beautiful like the majestic and stunning colours, and the fragrant, sweet and fruity scent of the Field of Flowers. And I want to bury him in the King's Forest, because he was loyal and strong and protective. Like the trees that guard our kingdom.

I'm torn. I need more time to think about it. Can he be in a place between the Field of Flowers and the King's Forest? *I can't deal* … my chest tightens and I want to cry.

'Over here, darling!' Mama's colourful voice pierces the silence of the monochromatic greys of the flowers. Her hand shoots up and she clicks her fingers, then giggles.

I smile. I've never heard Mama giggle before. I change my direction and navigate through the flowers to find her. Then stop, and my breath hitches.

Papa is sitting with her. Mama and Papa together in the Field of Flowers. Not dead.

Papa's hand reaches up and grabs mine and pulls me down between them. There's a lump in my throat. Mama's note said to meet her here at 9pm. Her. Not her and Papa.

We are sitting on a blanket, and we all lie down and look up at the night sky.

I'm in the middle. Like the link.

I'm in the middle. Half of Mama and half of Papa.

I'm in the middle. Grinning from ear to ear.

'Jewel Box. *The* Jewel Box?' Papa says incredulously and passes his beloved binoculars to Mama. 'It can't be.'

I squint at the night sky. I can only see Sirius, Canopus, Alpha Centauri, and the stars of the Southern Cross, as surveillance satellites glide past. And perhaps, a haze of light that doesn't move. I still. I can see the Southern Cross?

'What's happening, Azriel? We haven't been able to see the Jewel Box for thirty years. And look at the Southern Cross!'

My heart races with excitement. 'Pass me the binoculars, Ma.'

Mama passes the binoculars to me, and I search the second sky, the night sky, and stop at the cluster of stars of different colours that don't move—sparkling blue and red stars that look like jewellery. My breath catches. 'It's the artificial moons … they haven't been activated here yet. Eli and I saw the aurora recently,' I say. Then I ask, 'Who is my protector that you assigned to me after Eli? I have never seen them.'

Mama and Papa don't say anything. I don't know if that is a good or a bad thing.

The sound of the choir of insects ramps up, suffocating the silence as they compose their nightly cacophony. The noisy crickets chirping in their little amphitheatres. Cicadas chorusing. Bizarre whistles and squeaks here and there.

Mama clears her throat. 'Your protector is presumed … dead.'

I gasp and my body fills with an ocean of tears washing through me. 'Eli?' A peculiar high-pitched sound escapes me as I hold the waves of destruction in.

'Asher couldn't keep up with you. So I reinstated Eli.'

I am a waterfall. Tears thundering down to water the flowers.

I thread my fingers through Papa's, then Mama's. I feel safer now. Less alone in my grief. Mama, Papa and me. Connected. Looking up at the night sky. Together, for the second time ever, the first time being before my birth.

And then a firefly appears, hovering above us. It's lower abdomen lit up by bioluminescence. I smile. The Ancient of Days loves chemistry *and* has a sense of humour!

The firefly. A light in the darkness. I am filled with thankfulness and joy.

'Aaah … look at that, Papa says.'

I look up to see moonrise, and echo Papa's reaction, Mama too. How long has it been since we have seen this sight so clearly, I think, and the moon illusion, when the moon appears larger on the horizon. My artist mind throws hearts at the moon and its colours of dandelion yellow musings, of sunshine, of hope, of happiness. How sad for those who work and live and fight on the moon, and are not spectators to the exquisite beauty of the moon, viewed from the earth. Perhaps then they would see the significance of the moon in creation.

Luminous.

Divine.

Sacred.

The flowers around us glow, revealing their colours as the moon rises higher in the night sky. And the cacophony of songs from the insects begins to hum in tune to the living earth.

'Close your eyes, Ari,' Mama says, her voice soft, caressing my heart. 'Visualise us connected; you, me and Papa. Feel our love for you, pure and unconditional, as we finish your dream story, woven to the melody of the heavens, the universe filled with the music of the spheres.'

I let out a small cry and tears run down my face. It's happening. It's really happening. Mama said that when Papa returns, they would finish my dream story.

And here we are.

I go deeper into my mind and see the bright, mesmerising light, and sparkles of gold thrown into the universe by my soul print, created by our Maker. Wonderfully and fearfully made that Mama remembers of the night full of promise when her hand rested on her tummy, connecting to me.

Our soul dance.

Except this time, the light of my dream story continues, and shimmers of gold don't fall from the heavens and crash into the earth like shooting stars. Our souls illuminate, magnificently, eternally loved and protected. Almost too bright to keep looking at.

And I know then that my dream story that Mama and Papa envisioned before I was born, that they thought was obliterated on that fateful night that Papa was taken, was fully finished. Mama and Papa just didn't see it in the chaos and the fear and the panic.

It is finished.

It was finished.

And I am who I was created to be.

Luminous.

Divine.

Sacred.

Like all people.

Ari Flora Cohen, daughter of Azriel David Cohen and Zarah Opal Cohen. Imperfectly perfect for my time and place in the history of the earth.

'Thank you,' I whisper, not just to Mama and Papa, and then I squeeze Mama and Papa's hands.

I lift my arms then and create a heart with my fingers to project into the heavens, dodging the roaming satellites. I laugh to myself. It's like the Batman signal in the sky. But this is far superior.

It's a love eternal signal.

Forever and a day.

Now you, dear reader, must choose the ending:
Chapter 40, or Chapter 40 (again), or both.

AN ENDING ~ ONE

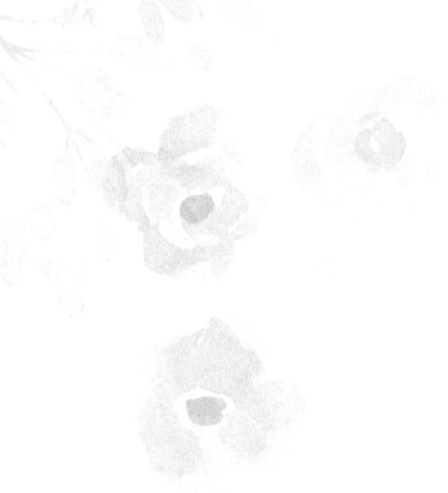

CHAPTER 40

Four days later I stumble across the floorboards of my bedroom before morningtide, unbalanced by sleep deprivation, my heavy broken heart, and a pounding headache.

Crying an ocean of tears does that to you.

Eli's body didn't arrive and no one has seen him. Not even the Leges in *The Beyond*. Presumed dead. I don't want to believe Eli has left the earth without me.

Instead of me.

But I have to move forward.

To honour him.

I accidentally knock the vase of flowers off the window sill, the breaking ceramic making me wince. Then open the window shutters to the new day, not yet awake. Even the Field of Flowers is in shades of grey like the colour has been vacuumed from them.

I open the sash window and drop my vintage blue school port of *everything* outside, then clumsily fall out of my bedroom window, my bare feet heavily hitting the cosmos flowers and squelching in the mud.

I pick up my vintage blue school port of *everything* and run.

Through the Field of Flowers, over the bodies sleeping in death, souls departed, the cool morning air brushing its fingers through my hair with a gentle tug.

And I fall. In slow motion. My barefoot finding a depressed area of soil. My face kisses the flowers on the descent of my fall, before I face plant in the dirt of a freshly dug grave. I spit the dirt out of my mouth, then rise again and run.

Through the King's Forest. And stop when I reach the lakeside, my body and mind catching up with me.

The sun hasn't peeked at the new day yet. But the crisp colour of red starts to glow, reversing the stealing of their colour the eventide before.

I place my vintage blue school port of *everything* on the sand before I go and drag my blue deck chair out from its hidden place in the forest. I retrieve the second one and place it next to mine, in case Eli would like to join me in memory this morning. I have things I need to say to him.

I open my vintage blue school port of *everything* and grab my cocktail glass and juice of an apple or ten, pour it into my cocktail glass, pop on my groovy sunglasses and sit back in the deck chair.

The scattering has begun.

Of the new day.

The most vibrant colours in the sky are about to make their appearance. The refraction of light waves.

The dancing.

The declaring.

The delighting.

Peeking through like a shy child at first, until the sun illuminates the sky in shades of radiant gold, blooming with crimson, reds and oranges, like it has found its courage, then beaming more colour onto the high clouds, sharing its extraordinary gift of colour giving with the world, for without the sun, without light, colour is hidden.

And for a moment, I am cast in gold like the princess of a king, and the promise of a new day.

I raise my cocktail glass of the juice of apple to the sunrise, 'To Eli. Forever and a day.' I take a sip of the cool sweet liquid, and swallow it, hoping it will clear the lump of emotion stuck in my throat that feels like it is suffocating me.

'Elias Wolfe, sit here by me, my love,' I say and pat the empty deck chair beside me, a tear rolling down my cheek saturated with the colours of sadness. 'Dead, Darling,' I say, repeating words he would have said to me. I take a deep shuddering breath, the ache in my heart groaning in distress like out of tune notes on a piano. 'I'm sorry I never told you I loved you, Eli. I'm sorry I never delivered you the box of letters and love and drawings I made for you. I'm sorry you spent your life ensuring I kept living mine … but I'm so glad you did. I wouldn't change it for a moment. I'm sorry we didn't hug more. I'm sorry we didn't get to share a kiss.' I look down at my cocktail glass. 'I'm sorry that you died in my place. If we could go back in time, we would not be there that fateful day, and we would wait until we were old and die together, holding hands, our spirits entwined while angels help us step into eternity.' My throat is tight.

I raise my hand and block out the sun, the golden rays giving my fingers a heavenly glow. 'My most beautiful and dearest Eli, I love you. Parting is such sweet sorrow that I shall say goodnight— till it be morrow. Our sun has set. Til we meet again. I miss you.'

I hang my head.

And cry.

Deep.

And cathartic.

Holding tight.

And letting go.

When I look up again, it is a blue sky day. Clear and crisp. The blue lake shimmers with flecks of light like twinkling stars.

A hand appears on the deck chair beside me and I freeze, hoping to become unseen. Eli was right. He would always creep up on me and I wouldn't have a clue he was there.

'Alive.'

It was a voice like Eli's, deep in a soft murmur, like a soothing balm.

I look up and watch him fold himself into the chair with a coy smile. Long legs and arms, his dark curly hair falling over one eye.

Elias?

My heart beats like a drum in my chest, making me feel hot. Eli's body hasn't turned up at *The Quietus*. Could he be … could this be real?

I take a deep breath to find some calm, to stop me from running from him in case it is a cruel joke.

'Blue,' I say to him as a test.

'The sky?'

'No,' I say.

He looks around. 'My shirt.'

My eyes widen. Was I in mortal danger?

'Yes,' I lie, to give me time to escape. I pull my eyebrows together as I look closely at him. Something feels off, so my intuition says. He looks like Eli, but doesn't feel like him. I can't feel Eli's spiritual presence. Eli would have looked into my eyes and told me the colour of them today. Maybe he had amnesia from the explosion?

'How are you feeling today?' I say. 'My ears are still singing like a snake with a high pitched violin screeching down the strings.'

'I'm feeling great,' he says, looking up at me from beneath his fringe.

'Show me your back,' I say. I want to see if he has any injuries from the blast.

He turns on the deck chair and raises his shirt. No injuries. No lightning scar. I pull the shirt down gently, battling the panic inside me. I start to shake my hand to try and get rid of the adrenaline that is surging through me.

'Are you okay?' he says.

'I'm just having a moment of anxiety … from the explosion and all. Do you remember the explosion?'

He shakes his head.

'Do you remember what we were doing before the explosion?'
He shakes his head.

I lean over and push his hair to the side, revealing his right eye. It was green, the exact same colour as Eli's heterochromia eye colours. 'Who are you?' I say. This does not feel like Eli.

'Elias.'

'Liar! You may look like him. But you are not him. Who are you?'

He closes his eyes and scratches the side of his neck. 'I'm his doppelganger. His clone. Born exactly one year after him.'

'Here, in the kingdom?'

'No. Blood was stolen from Eli's birth when they checked his blood for diseases, and cure them if he had any. He was cloned without knowledge or consent. He's … like my brother … like my twin.'

'Cloned and implanted inside a human womb?'

'No. An artificial one. I am by definition, motherless and fatherless. I belong to no one.'

My heart falls. 'Yet, you are human.' Mama always said to walk in the shoes of another. To feel what they would feel. 'How did you end up here?'

'Stolen, or saved from *The Beyond,* as you call it. However you want to look at it.'

'How do you choose to look at it?'

'Saved. Eli's family took me in. They are good people.'

'Are you experimental?'

'Originally, yes.'

'What did the government do to you?'

'AI brain chip. My entire knowledge was downloaded from the Internet into my brain at the age of four, and was updated regularly, until …' He looks down at his hands. He rubs them together then traces a scar on his right hand.

'Until?'

'All my technology was removed—brain chip and hand chip.'

'And your name is?'

'AICH370845.'

I laugh. 'Your human name?'

He chuckles. 'Eli's parents named me Mason. It means new beginnings.'

'You do know you'll never replace Eli. You can never be Eli.'

'I know.'

'You met Elias, right?'

'Weirdly, in dreams, like I had another life, and once, he asked to meet me. A year ago.' He looks out over the water exactly like Eli would have. Their mannerisms are uncanny. 'I haven't come here to replace my brother. I have come here to give you this note.' He chuckles to himself. 'Eli said I would find you here, sipping on chilled apple juice, funky sunglasses on. Maybe even off your face with the beverage, if you brewed it yourself.'

I rip the note from his hand, and give him the side eye, annoyed that he could find humour in my grief.

I break the wax seal and open it up and look over at his brother, ensuring he can't see the contents.

My Dearest Ari,

The first time I fell in love with you was when you were ten and wanted to save the baby bird. I knew then that you had a heart like mine. I went back to check on the baby bird every day until it finally took flight. It landed on your bedroom window ledge after leaving the nest, stole one of the flowers and then flew off again.

The second time I fell deeply in love with you was when you were on the lighthouse when you were sixteen. Remember the tie I wore?

The third time I fell totally in love with you, and knew there would be no other was when you dressed like a boy to go to The Beyond. I was so proud of you. Your intelligence. Your strength. Your determination. So glad that you decided to wear shoes into The Beyond!

You'll never know how many times I wanted to hold you in my arms, or place my lips on yours. You'll never know how many times I wanted to whisk you away to a place that reigned with peace, to fly to the moon with you and start our lives there.

I love you, Ari.

Death is not the end. It has no victory over us. You know we are spiritual beings inside our physical bodies. Earth is our place to visit for a very short time, like a blink of an eye, compared to the eternity of our spirits.

Don't weep for me, Ari. I ask you to feel joy for me. For I was beyond blessed to be in your life. And for that I am forever thankful.

We'll meet again. That I know. I'll wait for you under the tree by the river. You know which one I mean.

'Til then, I love you, Ari Flora.

Elias Wolfe

My face is wet, painted with a million tears that fell in the colour of love and lost dreams and what ifs. I pull out the lachrymatory bottle from my vintage blue school port of *everything*, and catch my tears.

Mason stares at me.

'I know ... I'm studying the shape of my tears under the microscope,' I say.

'Odd,' he says.

'Indeed,' I say, and watch as he gazes over at the lake, to the lighthouse, my place of imprisonment, confinement, refinement. 'I spent many nights out there on the lighthouse, until I learned how to escape it.' I smile at the memory.

'As punishment?'

'Punishment ... protection ... whatever they wanted to call it. Mostly punishment for bad choices.'

'The wild child,' Mason says with a crooked smile, exactly like Eli's.

I smile to myself. 'Mama always said I was born with defiance to match my spirit and unconventional was my favourite thing to do. She was right.'

Mason laughs.

'Thank you for giving me Eli's letter,' I say. 'You would have liked your brother ... a lot, as annoying as he could be at times. He was a good man. The best.'

Mason looks down and twists his fingers together. 'I'm sorry for your loss.'

'And for yours. Would you care for some jus de pomme, freshly made this morn?'

'Only if I get to wear your pink heart sunglasses.'

'Done,' I say, give my sunglasses to him and pour him a cocktail glass of the juice of apple.

I hold up my glass to Mason. 'To Eli,' I say, and our cocktail glasses clink.

Mason skulls his juice of apple, green, at once, missing the vibrant and fruity refreshing taste, then leaves and disappears into the trees. I watch him until he becomes a dot, and then nothing.

Completely invisible.

Present.

And absent.

I pack up my vintage blue port of *everything*, pull the deck chairs back into the forest and return to my bedroom, climbing in through my window.

Blue forget-me-not flowers sit in a small white vase on my window sill. The colour of the indigo. Delicate. Gentle. And make me cry. Mama always leaves forget-me-not flowers on my window sill when she will be gone for a day or two. But she hasn't left today. Perhaps they are in memory of Eli. I will never forget him. He has a piece of my heart.

I sit at my writing desk, open the drawer and pull out a piece of homemade paper, and my best ink pen, blue, like Eli's eye colour, and begin to write.

My Dearest, Most Beautiful Elias Wolfe,

I don't know how to say goodbye.

I don't want to say goodbye, because that will make it real. Thank you for being my protector, my friend, my love. I regret never saying I love you. And now, it's too late.

I want to be in the light, like you are in the light. I'll meet you under the tree by the river with the Ancient One, and we'll match up the pieces of our hearts, ready to start our new adventure.

Until then,

I Love you more,

Ari Flora

I add flicks of green and blue water colour after the ink has dried, then fold it into a heart shape. I venture into the library then, and find a paper folding book, following the directions to create a light memory for Eli.

I return to the lake at eventide, at the time of moonrise, and stand on the shore and look over to the horizon. The full moon looms large and ethereal, dappled and graceful, glorious.

Luminous.

Divine.

Sacred.

I squat down and light a small candle and then lift the sky lantern, my letter to Eli hanging below it. I stand tall and raise the sky lantern high, waiting for the heated air to give it lift, and watch it launch into the air.

I watch it rise, higher and higher, Eli's light gracing the sky. For a moment, I let my extreme mind visualisation, my hyper-phantasia take over, and see the sky lantern reach beyond the moon in an updraft, and then collect star dust to shower his light upon the earth.

I watch the sky lantern breathe its light, until the light becomes a dot and then completely disappears. It will fall back to the earth, flame extinguished, the paper and sticks of its composition returning to the ground, biodegradable, no earth and animal harm, the flower and tree seeds embedded in the paper, sprouting.

And growing.

In remembrance.

For Elias Wolfe.

AN ENDING ~ TWO

CHAPTER 40 (AGAIN)

Four days later I stumble across the floorboards of my bedroom before morningtide, unbalanced by sleep deprivation, my heavy broken heart, and a pounding headache.

Crying an ocean of tears does that to you.

Eli's body didn't arrive and no one has seen him. Not even the Leges in *The Beyond*. Presumed dead. I don't want to believe Eli has left the earth without me.

Instead of me.

But I have to move forward.

To honour him.

I accidentally knock the vase of flowers off the window sill, the breaking ceramic making me wince. Then open the window shutters to the new day, not yet awake. Even the Field of Flowers is in shades of grey like the colour has been vacuumed from them.

I open the sash window and drop my vintage blue school port of *everything* outside, then clumsily fall out of my bedroom window, my bare feet heavily hitting the cosmos flowers and squelching in the mud.

I pick up my vintage blue school port of *everything* and run.

Through the Field of Flowers, over the bodies sleeping in death, souls departed, the cool morning air brushing its fingers through my hair with a gentle tug.

And I fall. In slow motion. My barefoot finding a depressed area of soil. My face kisses the flowers on the descent of my fall, before I face plant in the dirt of a freshly dug grave. I spit the dirt out of my mouth, then rise again and run.

Through the King's Forest. And stop when I reach the lakeside, my body and mind catching up with me.

The sun hasn't peeked at the new day yet. But the crisp colour of red starts to glow, reversing the stealing of their colour the eventide before.

I place my vintage blue school port of *everything* on the sand before I go and drag my blue deck chair out from its hidden place in the forest. I retrieve the second one and place it next to mine, in case Eli would like to join me in memory this morning. I have things I need to say to him.

I open my vintage blue school port of *everything* and grab my cocktail glass and juice of an apple or ten, pour it into my cocktail glass, pop on my groovy sunglasses and sit back in the deck chair.

The scattering has begun.

Of the new day.

The most vibrant colours in the sky are about to make their appearance. The refraction of light waves.

The dancing.

The declaring.

The delighting.

Peeking through like a shy child at first, until the sun illuminates the sky in shades of radiant gold, blooming with crimson, reds and oranges, like it has found its courage, then beaming more colour onto the high clouds, sharing its extraordinary gift of colour giving with the world, for without the sun, without light, colour is hidden.

And for a moment, I am cast in gold like the princess of a king, and the promise of a new day.

I raise my cocktail glass of the juice of apple to the sunrise, 'To Eli. Forever and a day.' I take a sip of the cool sweet liquid, and swallow it, hoping it will clear the lump of emotion stuck in my throat that feels like it is suffocating me.

'Elias Wolfe, sit here by me, my love,' I say and pat the empty deck chair beside me, a tear rolling down my cheek saturated with the colours of sadness. 'Dead, Darling,' I say, repeating words he would have said to me. I take a deep shuddering breath, the ache in my heart groaning in distress like out of tune notes on a piano. 'I'm sorry I never told you I loved you, Eli. I'm sorry I never delivered you the box of letters and love and drawings I made for you. I'm sorry you spent your life ensuring I kept living mine … but I'm so glad you did. I wouldn't change it for a moment. I'm sorry we didn't hug more. I'm sorry we didn't get to share a kiss.' I look down at my cocktail glass. 'I'm sorry that you died in my place. If we could go back in time, we would not be there that fateful day, and we would wait until we were old and die together, holding hands, our spirits entwined while angels help us step into eternity.' My throat is tight.

I raise my hand and block out the sun, the golden rays giving my fingers a heavenly glow. 'My most beautiful and dearest Eli, I love you. Parting is such sweet sorrow that I shall say goodnight— till it be morrow. Our sun has set. Til we meet again. I miss you.'

I hang my head.

And cry.

Deep.

And cathartic.

Holding tight.

And letting go.

When I look up again, it is a blue sky day. Clear and crisp. Like the first time that Eli and I parted. The blue lake shimmers with flecks of light like twinkling stars.

A hand appears on the deck chair beside me and I freeze, hoping to become unseen. Eli was right. He would always creep up on me and I wouldn't have a clue he was there.

'Alive.'

It was a voice like Eli's, deep in a soft murmur, like a soothing balm.

I look up and watch him fold himself into the chair with a coy smile. Long legs and arms, his dark curly hair falling over one eye.

Elias?

My heart beats like a drum in my chest, making me feel hot. Eli's body hasn't turned up at *The Quietus*. Could he be … could this be real?

I take a deep breath to find some calm, to stop me from running from him in case it is a cruel joke.

I take off my sunglasses. 'Blue,' I say to him as a test.

He looks into my eyes and takes a deep breath. 'Violet, like your eyes have been kissed with a paint brush dipped in the ink made from the anthocyanins of the heart shaped violet petals, mixed with the scattering of light from the sunrise and the brightening sky, the reflection off the sparkling water.' He pulls his eyebrows together, then his eyes wander from my eyes to my lips and I feel a rush, like being on a high.

I give a nervous smile. *Could this be … Elias?* 'Blue. A beautiful shade of blue, like the spirit of earth, the dancing sky with echoes of the universe inside.'

I lift my hand and brush his long wavy fringe from the right side of his face, revealing his heterochromia, his other eye green. My heart thunders.

This is Eli.

He is here.

With me.

'Green. Like the sweet hue of spring growth, illuminating the soul of nature.'

He captures my hand in his, looks up at me and kisses it. Delicately. Briefly. His lips warm and soft. And my heart blooms like a flower, a warmth running from my hand to my heart.

'What are you drinking, Ari Flora?'

'Pure, sweet apple juice, Elias Wolfe,' I take another sip.

Eli takes the cocktail glass from my hand and lifts it to his nose, and inhales. 'Juice of the apple.'

I smile. 'Would you care for some jus de pomme, freshly made this morn?'

'Only if I get to wear your pink heart sunglasses.'

'Done,' I say, give my sunglasses to him and pour him a cocktail glass of the juice of apple.

I hold up my glass to Eli. 'To, not dead,' I say, and our cocktail glasses clink.

Eli sips on his juice of apple, and I hope he savours the flavours of the vibrant and fruity, refreshing taste that I worked hard to develop in this brew.

'Green apples. Refreshing.' Eli looks back over at the lake again. 'Remember when you were sixteen and isolated on the lighthouse to reflect on your actions, and I delivered a message to you from your mother, and you asked about my oxygen canister and the glowing halo in the middle of the lake?'

'How could I forget, Eli. I was angry with you for withholding information from me and treating me like a child.'

'There's an underwater lab and safe haven with a vault of seeds and animal DNA. It's also connected to our kingdom. If a global crisis happens, we are in good hands.'

'But—'

'But that is all you need to know. The future is one of hope.' Eli looks deeply into my eyes.

I want him to stop looking at me like that. He is making me feel all kinds of self-conscious and vulnerable, and a curious heat stampedes through me. 'I-I … was told you were dead,' I say to cover up my reaction to him.

He looks down and inhales in a sharp breath. 'I was for a bit, before a passerby returned my life.'

'I worked in *The Quietus* with Mama every day, you know, waiting for your body to come in. I wanted to be the one to—' a sob escapes me, '—prepare your body for your earthly farewell.'

Eli chuckles. 'I should have come in on the death stretcher, and when you touched me, I could have sat up to scare you!'

I bop him on the arm. 'That is so. Not. Funny. Elias Wolfe! You are mean and ... and—'

'When will you deliver the box of letters and love and drawings to me?' he says.

'You heard that?'

He has a gleam in his eyes and a coy smile on his face.

I shake my head. 'Of course you did with your refined protector abilities! You are infuriating!'

'You're welcome,' he says, and performs a little sitting down bow, one arm outstretched holding the cocktail glass, the other arm across his abdomen, his head lowered in that male ballet dancer type of way.

I look out over the lake, trying to calm the excitement running through me. 'Thank you for saving me,' I say. 'Were you injured?'

He tilts his head to the side a bit. 'A little. It will heal.'

'Show me where,' I say.

He pivots his body and lifts his shirt, exposing his back. I gasp at the splattering of dried up blood randomly positioned on his skin, then swallow at the sight and memory of the day his lightning scar was inflicted, creating an image of a large tree and its branches. I touch my finger to it, starting at his shoulder, and trace the lightning tree etched onto his skin by the lightning strike, every branch and the trunk. 'Your lightning scar is the mirror image of mine,' I say, my voice tender, nervous. His presence was pulling me in, closer, in soul and mind, and I was powerless to stop it.

He takes his shirt off, and turns to face me. 'But do you have this scar from the lightning tree?'

'Oh,' I say, then trace it from his right shoulder, across his chest and to his heart.

He places his hand over mine then, over his heart, and I could feel it beating, a little faster than it should, synchronised with mine.

I look up into his eyes, drinking me in. They wander to my lips and he leans in toward me, our lips close but not touching, when time stood still.

'May I?' he asks, his voice rough.

He leans down in slow motion, his lips close to mine, lingering, and his lips were on mine then, breathtakingly soft and tender, so gentle, so special, singing to my heart as it fills me with warmth and love. I am lost and found and more alive than I'd ever felt.

He pulls his lips away, his eyes dark like he is almost undone. 'I love you, Ari. Be mine.'

I inhale the air of his declaration, a love potion of words floating through me, making me feel like I am in a dream, like I am in a fairytale of happily ever after.

'I love you, Eli. I was always yours.'

Mama said *human love* is patient.
And kind.
Protects.
And trusts.
Hopes.
And perseveres.

And binds everything together in perfect harmony.

Mama said watch out for *deceit*
and *secrets* and *flattery*.
Manipulation to control your behaviour.
Ensure that the *words* and *actions*
of a person or government match.
And *watch out* for the *drip feeding* and
repetition of words and images and experiences
to *desensitize* you so that you
accept something
that you once would have *opposed*.

And Mama said, that when things feel like they are
falling apart in the world,
they are *falling into place*,
for there is an *appointed time for everything*,
for *every event under the sun*.

EPILOGUE

The Woe of Winter was upon the Earth.

Not the yearly season, but the foretold time of sorrows.

The truth of everything had been boxed up when the contagion of refusal to acknowledge truth reigned.

When people forgot to love their enemies.

When people forgot kindness.

When people forgot forgiveness of others, and themselves.

When the lure of technology was a slow trickle of desensitisation to enable people to be manipulated.

When people twisted truth to suit themselves for their own personal gain, and it divided nations and people and families. It started wars, society dissonance and family dysfunction. And filtered through everything with toxic byproducts—anger, distrust, disinformation, confusion, not knowing who to trust, chaos and fear, fake news, deepfakes, crime, hate, and violence.

It was indeed a spiral into the ugliness of humanity.

But the spark of the light of hope and truth can never be extinguished. The light, that was there at the beginning of earth time.

The work of Ari and Elias, releasing people back to freedom, back to free will, was just the beginning.

Then came the legions of Light Workers.

Light Carriers.

Light Bearers.

Light Protectors.

Calling people out of the darkness and into the light. The light of truth. The light of love. The gentle ushering in of souls who were being planted in the midst. Ordinary humans who were not silent anymore, who found their extraordinary bravery, their courage, their gifts to share with others.

They were ready for the appointed time to take action. Being born at that time in the history of the world was no coincidence. They weren't dismayed by the circumstances of the world, but knew they could do something to change it. And succeed.

And they rose to the challenge.

The joining of human spirit and goodness and light for the good of humanity is powerful.

The light of truth can never be hidden.

It always finds a way to be seen, exposing the darkness of deceit of the world for what it truly is as it hides, trembling in fear. For it knows what is coming.

Have courage, dear heart, and fear not.

The joy of the Bloom of Spring is coming.

Not the yearly season, but the foretold time that is faithful and true.

Love always wins.

And I pray ... that you that you fully comprehend your breath, and the knowledge of it that surpasses all understanding.

ACKNOWLEDGEMENTS

Trees. Thank you. I love the stories you hold and tell. It was the King's Forest at Kingscliff, New South Wales, Australia, that inspired *You Before Me*. Just the name of it and the visual stories it gave where my mind ran off with its imagination, creating and plotting.

And here we are.

Thank you to all the students I have taught in my teaching career. I feel honoured to be a part of your learning journey. You will never know how much joy it brought me to help you learn, face challenges and find solutions to those challenges, and to see your smiles light up as you found answers to those challenges.

Becoming a Secondary Visual Art Teacher, after teaching primary students for 25 years, was a dream come true for me. A gift from above that would change my life. I wouldn't have written this novel without teaching secondary students and watching how quickly they master the use of technology, accept it, and become immersed in it. Teaching visual art allowed me to explore AI Art in 2020, and the advantages and disadvantages of it before it became a "thing". OpenAI. Midjourney. DALL E. DALL E 2. My curiosity about AI grew from AI Art experiments to investigating ChatGPT and then to the explosion of AI in general. The creators of AI increasingly do not understand how it works. It has been reported as being hard to control and often behaves in unpredictable ways. And that is a big problem.

Looking back to my classroom days, I consider myself blessed and privileged to be part of the evolving technological computer era that entered schools in 1992, when the first Apple computer appeared in my classroom with no instructions about how to use it. I asked a five year old boy, whose mum was also a teacher, 'How do you turn it on?' (I had tried many times, even checking that the power was on at the wall switch). He stood from his little chair made for first-graders, walked over to the computer and pushed a button. The computer came to life and the screen lit up. After I had shown the students what the computer was and fumbled my way through the prompts, I had to ask him how to turn it off. Once again, he pushed the same button that turned it on, and off the screen went. Thank you, Geoffrey.

Each year that I continued to teach, I learned and taught and used the changes that came with technology in the classroom and the great benefits for education and learning it gave. Until technology devices became portable—mobile phones, iPads, laptop computers—all embraced by society. And then I witnessed first-hand the negative change in some students. Psychologically. Physically. Socially. Mentally. The rise of anxiety, depression, self-harm. The results of cyberbullying, or teenagers comparing themselves to the superficial and manipulated perfection and always "happiness" and "success" of others online. They believed the lie. However, it is because of technology that I was able to do copious amounts of research for this novel, including the industrial revolutions to come, which made me aware of what is planned for the future by those who govern.

Technology—the good, the bad and the ugly.

To my publisher, editors and first readers, an enormous thank you. Your time and feedback is invaluable as always. x

To my husband, my three kids and my mum and dad—thank you once again for your support while writing my 9th novel. You all make my life richer and I am beyond blessed that we belong together forever and a day.

A big THANK YOU to you, the reader. I am not a writer without someone to read my stories. You are indeed appreciated more than you know!

And thank you to our Heavenly Father, for Your love and grace and mercy, and for bringing me through the Woes of Winter in my life, for giving me a light in the darkness and bringing me to the Bloom of Spring and Melody of Summer with hope and joy.

Soli Deo gloria